THE GUILT OF THE PENITENT

Published by Apsley Press

ISBN: 978-1-0369-1262-8

Cover design: @coverbookdesigns

For Elaine

Contents

Glossary

Abroad – a medieval expression meaning '*beyond one's home*'

Apostolic Blessing – blessing given with the authority of the Pope

Araby – a general medieval term for the Arab world

Arbalest – a small hand-held crossbow

Ave Maria – Hail Mary – a common prayer to the mother of Jesus

Banieres – The major Craft Guild in medieval Tournai

Bardiche – a large, cleaver-like axe mounted on a pole

Baselard – a heavy, short, tapered dagger

Baxter – a female baker

Benedictine – monks who followed the Rule of St. Benedict

Book of Hours – a small, hand-drawn and written prayer book for personal use

Braes – trousers

Caput Lupinium – a 'wolf's head,' an outlawed felon

Cazzo – a common Italian swear word

Chancery – the medieval department responsible for the production of royal documents

Charles of Anjou – youngest son of King Louis VII of France

Cloister - a covered walkway in an abbey or monastery

Coif - a close-fitting cap, covering the top, back and sides of the head.

Compline – the last Church service of the day, around 9 p.m.

Convent – a religious house. In the medieval period, the term applied to both male and female houses.

Coney – a rabbit

Cordwainer – a shoemaker

Cotehardie/cote – a long-sleeved outer garment worn by both men and women

Cowdstream - a small brook that ran through Westminster

Crespine - medieval hair net

Cresset – a metal container, set on a pole for burning oil, tar or pitch

Curia Regis – the King's Court

Curfew bell - rang to signal that all were to be in their homes by the hour of darkness.

Deep in cups – drunk

Deodand – a payment to the Crown based on the value of whatever had caused a death

Destrier – a war horse

Dominican Beads – prayer beads that inspired rosary beads

Dortoir –communal bedchamber

Dues in adjutorium – first verse of the Vesper prayers (O God come to my assistance)

Dwale – medieval herbal anaesthetic made with belladonna (Deadly Nightshade)

Epicier – a trader in spices

Episcopal – relating to a Bishop, Archbishop or Cardinal

Fanchercherstrate – Fenchurch Street, London

Feast Day of the Holy Body & Blood – Corpus Christi, Thursday following Trinity Sunday

Feast Day of the Annunciation – March 25th

Fleming – a person from Flanders

Florentines – gold coin of the city of Florence (florin)

Franciscans – an order of monks founded by St Francis of Assisi

Galero - broad-brimmed hat with tasselled strings, worn by senior clergy

Gelou – dull yellow dye colour

German Sea – medieval name for the North Sea

Gorget – a fashionable band that wrapped around the neck

Hand of Glory – the dried and pickled hand of a hanged man

Household Knights – royal bodyguard

Hue & Cry – the process where bystanders were summoned to apprehend a criminal

Hutch – a wooden chest

Il Sonno del Lazio – a sleeping draught used by the monks of the Abbey of St Martin in Montecassino

Imperial Vicar of Tuscany – a noble governing Tuscany for the Holy Roman Emperor

In his cups – drunk

Jakes – toilet

Jerkin – a shaped, close-fitting outer garment

Jordan – urinal pot

Journeyman – a qualified tradesman employed by someone else

Kermes – vibrant red dye made from crushed beetles

King's Justice in Eyre – Eyre means 'circuit'. Judges moved within their area, administering justice

Knight's Fee – a payment by a knight to the King based on the amount of land held

Kyrie Eleison - Start of a Latin prayer – 'Lord have mercy'

Lambertazzi – one of the ruling families of medieval Bologna

Lauds – the dawn hour service

Lazar – a medieval name given to someone afflicted by leprosy

Legate – a senior clergyman; the personal representative of the Pope

Liegeman – a vassal who owes allegiance and service to a lord

Livery Company – trade organisations in the city of London

Magna Vico – the Great Street, the main thoroughfare through St Albans

Man-at-Arms – a trained, volunteers soldier, below the rank of Knight

Mantle - loose-fitting outer garment

Marcher Wars – medieval skirmishes on the English-Welsh borders

Maslin bread – a loaf, half-wheat, half-rye though could contain other grains.

Matins - pre-dawn Church service

Mea Culpa – Latin exclamation of remorse 'through my fault.'

Michaelmas – The Feast of St Michael & All Angels, 29th September

Middle Sea – Mediterranean

Moor – a medieval name for people from the Middle East and North Africa

Nave – the central area of a church where the congregation meets

Nones – the ninth hour after sunrise, about 3 p.m.

Nuncio - a messenger on horseback

Obedientary – the holder of a position of responsibility in a nunnery or monastery

Obeisance – a bow of acknowledgement

Oblate – a child given to the Church at a young age

Outremer – the land beyond the sea; the medieval name for the Holy Land

Palfrey – a riding horse suitable for long-distance travel

Papal Indulgence – a document granting remission for sins committed. In the medieval Church, every sin must be purified on earth or after death in Purgatory

Papal Magistratus – a council of senior clergy sitting as a court

Paternoster – the Lord's Prayer in Latin

Passant Guardant – lion walking right to left (*passing guard)*

Peascod – a tiny pasty shaped as a pea-pod filled with spiced apple or dried fruits with bone-marrow

Penitent – from the Latin *'paenitere'*, to repent

Penury – extreme poverty

Pontiff – the Pope

Prie Dieu – a prayer desk

Prime – the first hour of daylight

Prioress – the Head of a convent of nuns, ranking lower than an Abbess

Quarrel – the bolt of a crossbow

Reeve – the local official responsible for oversight of a manor or village

Refectory – the eating room of a religious house

Riffler – a common thief

Right of Gallows, Pillory and Tumbril – an ancient custom giving a Lord the privilege of inflicting capital punishment on those within his domain

Rondel – long-bladed dagger that tapered to a point

Royal writ – a written order issued in the King's name

Sacrist - a senior monk responsible for the monastic Church and its contents

Saint Edward – King Edward the Confessor, died 1066

Salipath – following the route of present-day Fishpool Street in St Albans

Sanctus bell – a bell rung to summon monks or nuns to mass

Seneschal – the principal administrator within a monastery

Sext – the sixth hour of the day, i.e. noon

Scrip – medieval satchel

Serjeant at Law – a man of law

Shambles – an open-air slaughterhouse and meat market

Shift – an undergarment

Shrine of the Martyr – the tomb of St Alban

Signum Crucis – the Christian sign of the cross

Skinners' Company – one of the Livery Companies of London, trading in skins and furs

Smithfield – London's main meat market

Sopwellstrete – present-day Sopwell Lane, St. Albans

Sosthenion – an ancient town located in present-day Turkey

Spice Road – trade route from the east, extending as far as China

Super visum corporis – an inquest held in the presence of the dead body

Stew – row of properties housing prostitutes

Stiletto – long, thin, needle-type dagger

Supplicant – one who asks God to grant something to them

Tanner – maker of leather

Te Deum Laudamus – 'God, we praise you' – a Latin hymn

Tenth Commandment – Thou shalt not covet

Terce – the third hour after the dawn- 9 a.m.

Terce bell – a monastic bell rung to summon the monks to service
Tonman ditch – the town boundary of medieval St Albans
Tournois - French silver coin of high purity
Venetian grossi – silver coins minted in Venice, 98% pure
Verderer - an official who looks after the royal forest
Vespers – the service of evening prayer, around 6 p.m.
Vill – a small village
Watlingstrete – Roman Watling Street running from London to the north-west
Wicket gate – a small, narrow door in a wall, usually for pedestrian access
Wimple – a head covering draped over the head and around the neck and chin
Wolf's Head – an outlaw

The Guilt of the Penitent

A St Albans Medieval Mystery Book Two

by M.A. Long

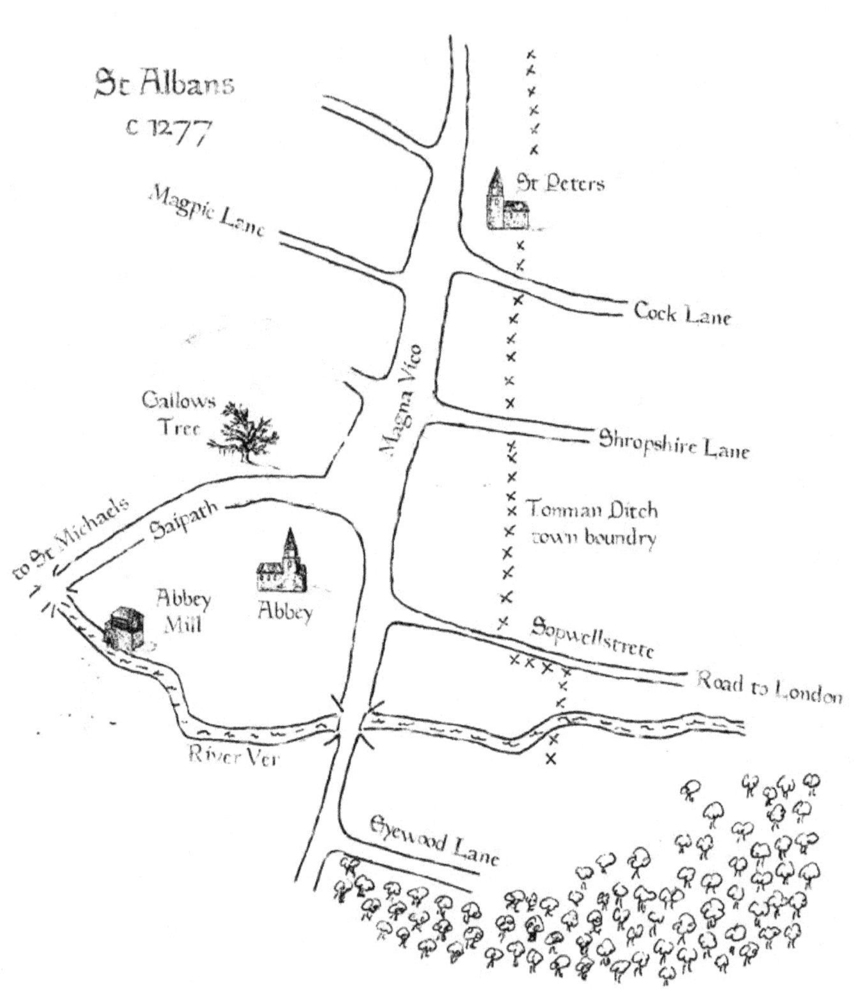

St Albans
c 1277
Magpie Lane
St Peters
Cock Lane
Magna Vico
Shropshire Lane
Gallows Tree
Tonman Ditch
town boundry
to St Michaels
Saipath
Abbey Mill
Abbey
Sopwellstrete
Road to London
River Ver
Eyewood Lane

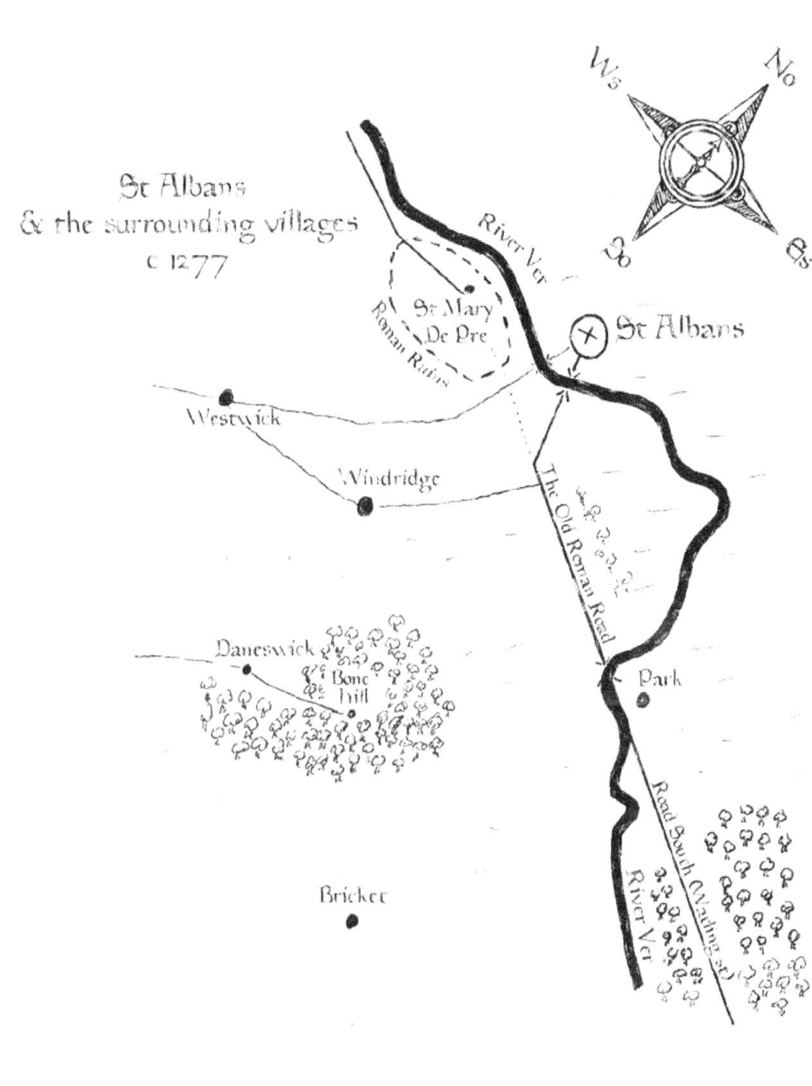

St Albans
& the surrounding villages
c 1277
No
Ws
Os
So
River Ver
St Mary De Pre
Roman Ruins
St Albans
Westwick
Windridge
The Old Roman Road
Daneswick
Bone Hill
Park
Bricket
Road South (Watling St)
River Ver

Ж

Prologue

The Church of St. Mary Magdalene, Windridge, Hertfordshire May 1277.

THE UNSEASONAL HEAT of the spring day had given way to low rumblings of thunder and the surety of a heavy storm. Crooked fingers of lightning danced in the dark southern sky, illuminating the tiny hamlet of Windridge and the ancient church at its centre. The rain came soon enough, crashing down in an intense fury. A chill night wind found the cracks in the walls of the Church of St. Mary Magdalene, causing the few lit tallow candles to flicker uncontrollably. Shadows danced up the walls, animating the painted frescos in a hallowed glow. But, the tops of the round arches were shrouded in darkness. The scratching and scurrying of mice interrupted the stillness of the night. The church was empty at this late hour, save for a single sinner kneeling before the holy altar. He was oblivious to the acrid stink of the solitary candle burning beside him.

His lips moved quickly, mouthing the *'De Profundis,'* the 129th Psalm.

"Out of the depths I have cried to Thee O Lord! Lord, hear my voice. Let Thine ears be attentive to the voice of my supplication." With each line, a whip cracked, biting deep into the boney, hairy back of the parish priest of St Mary's but drawing no cries of pain.

Another bolt of lightning crashed close above the church. The deep peel of thunder that followed shook the old building. The kneeling sinner appeared oblivious to the storm.

"Bless, O my God, the repose I am about to take, that, renewing my strength, I may be better enabled to serve Thee. Lord, hear my prayer."

Dark red wheals on his back broke into rivulets of blood that flowed down onto Sire Roger's unwashed habit, pulled to his waist, exposing his back.

"Oh, My Lord. *Mea Culpa. Mea Culpa.* I have sinned before you." The whip cracked again, its knotted ends biting deep into flesh. Tears of anguish welled in Sire Roger Wake's eyes. He had failed his flock; he was guilty of more than one mortal sin and had broken the Tenth Commandment. If God would forgive him, it was a thousand years in Purgatory where his soul would be painfully stripped of its wrongdoing, purged by fire and ice. The light from a single candle flickered and caught the golden cross on the altar before him, where the eyes of the crucified Jesus stared reproachfully down at him.

"Oh dear Lord, help me." He wailed a penitent cry to his maker, dropping the whip and falling prone to the cold stone floor, sobbing uncontrollably.

"O God, who willest not the death of a *sinner*, protect me this night and keep evil far from me." Sire Roger whimpered his intercession, unaware that death had slipped into his cold, dank church through a chapel side door as he uttered his lament.

The priest closed his eyes and recalled his transgressions against God and how easily he had succumbed to carnal temptation. What he had done was reprehensible, but the flesh was weak; he was weak. *The flesh; Oh! Their flesh.* He had known it was wrong. He knew it could damn his soul for all eternity, yet he had surrendered to desire. Even amid his supplication before God, the remembrance of the young bodies aroused him.

He had sought repentance and confessed his sins to a fellow priest. He had embarked on the three stages of the penitent: repentance; disclosure; intending to make reparation. He would admit all to the Town authorities. He would have to leave St. Mary Magdelene, his home for more than twelve summers, but he needed to go far away where no one knew Sire Roger Wake.

He rose to his knees and clenched his hands in prayer. "Merciful Lord, grant me repentance," he wailed. "Satan has lured me from the path of righteousness and I am a sinner." His sobbing intonation echoed around the church. He was sure that when the time came for him to meet his maker, a merciful God would forgive him.

That time came all too quickly for Sire Roger as death stalked St. Mary's. The praying priest didn't hear the muffled sound of leather on the stone floor of the Nave nor the gentle creak of a longbow drawn. He had just enough time to register the rush of an arrow before he slumped forward onto the altar steps, a shaft embedded deep in his bloodied, hairy back. Life ebbed slowly from his bleeding body, with his soul keeping an appointment in the fires of Hell.

Ж

Chapter One

The inn, 't Geschildert Huys' Antwerp, April 1277.

TUCKED AWAY IN THE shadowy corner of a small square off the Grote Markt, Antwerp's central market and downwind of the River Schelde, 't Geschildert Huys' was not a place you stumbled on by accident. It was the favoured inn of Antwerp's Butchers, rough, strong men who worked hard, drank even harder and eyed strangers with a simmering resentment that rarely boiled over into violence... but could.

't Geschildert Huys' was an L-shaped building over two floors, that wrapped around the two sides of the corner plot, a maze of internal nooks and crannies. It was a perfect place for the disreputable of the town to conduct business in secret. Its walls were upright planks of elm darkened by years of soot, sweat, smoke and a layer of fatty grime from a spit above the open hearth. A haunch of indeterminate meat, possibly horse, rotated slowly on the spit, turned by a young boy of no more than six years. Roughly hewn tables and benches lay tight together around the perimeter. A tallow candle spat a dull yellow flame on each one, its noxious fumes heavy with the rank stench of rancid beef fat. The air clung thick with the greasy haze, a reminder of the squalid comforts that 't Geschildert Huys' afforded its rough clientele.

It was late afternoon when Goyvaert de Tongeren entered, but 't Geschildert Huys' was already full of patrons, many deep in their cups, even at such an early hour. Goyvaert's arrival did not silence the low hum of conversation, for he was a frequent visitor and was here to meet with his business partner. Nonetheless, from the deeper recesses of the inn, eyes followed him as he made his way to a bench far from the hearth. Goyvaert did not make eye contact with the shadowed patrons, knowing many were thieves and cutpurses. Others would fear such men, but Goyvaert was a former man-at-arms in the army of the Duke of Brabant and had survived many skirmishes, fights and tavern scrapes. He was a Fleming and a Fleming was cautious. He had made many enemies over the years, so just to be sure, he employed two men as bodyguards. They came to 't Geschildert Huys' ahead of Goyvaert, sitting at separate tables, nursing jugs of ale, eyes peeled for threats.

At the rear of the inn was a row of large oak barrels, each with a wood spigot to dispense the frothy, brown liquid so in demand from the customers. In front stood the innkeeper, a big man, barking orders at the young boys, bringing the ale to the patrons and collecting the empty clay jugs. In the dark recesses, butchers, their day's work done, occupied the benches and tables dotted around the interior. Some supped contentedly at the ale, others played a shuffle game with coins, yet more laughed and joked about wives and women. Arguments broke out and sometimes, the candlelight reflected the glint of a blade. On such occasions, the bull-like innkeeper belied his appearance by swiftly intervening, swinging a thick wooden staff to make the men see sense.

There were always the whores' seeking customers, their faces grotesquely painted, and the front of their shift exposed so that all knew their profession. Today was no exception. Three moved between the tables, seeking to engage potential clients in conversation and requesting they be bought a jug of ale. One, a small-framed, dark-haired woman of twenty or so summers, scanned the room, looking for any heads that may look up at her as a sign of interest. She fixed her eyes on Goyvaert and inwardly recoiled. She had gone with him a few weeks before and suffered at his hand. Her cuts and bruises had only just healed; the trauma to her mind had not.

Clais von Emden shuddered as she now saw him looking back at her. He smirked in recognition, his lips curling upwards, revealing a row of brown teeth. She looked away, desperate to find a customer so she would not have to go with him again. Turning her back, she slipped onto a bench opposite two man-boys, butcher's apprentices, she judged. In the low candlelight, their faces showed nervousness. She gave them a false smile and reached to both, taking one hand in hers. She sensed Goyvaert standing behind her and caught his distinctive aroma, not of sweat and grime but a deep, earthy scent of patchouli. Clais shuddered once more, waiting, apprehensive about what would happen.

And then his scent was gone. She risked a half glance to one side and saw Goyvaert flirting with one of the younger whores, Isold de Hanenzuiger. They stood a dozen paces from where she sat and Clais sighed in relief. Isold was working her charms on Goyvaert, running her tongue over her lips, fingers suggestively brushing his braes. Goyvaert, for his part, was enjoying her attentions. However, Clais felt for the young girl, who could be no more than fifteen summers, fearing what Goyvaert would do to her once he had taken his pleasure.

Clais expected him to take Isold upstairs to one of the small cubicles, separated from each other by only a shabby curtain, but he did not. Instead, he led Isold back to his table and with a simple hand gesture, called for another jug of ale. Isold slid onto the bench beside him and continued her all-too-obvious efforts to make him employ her services.

Clais moved from her bench to the far side of the trestle table, sliding between the two man-boys, who nervously introduced themselves as Moresis and Pachier. The two already had too many ales and would be easy marks for Clais. They each handed her one denier and began to fumble. From the bench, Clais had a good view of where Goyvaert and Isold were seated. However, the flickering dull yellow light from the candle made details impossible to discern and the shadows made it difficult to see faces.

While Moresis and Pachier's breath quickened, Clais watched another man confidently approach Goyvaert's table. Immediately, two men leapt to their feet to intercept the newcomer. Goyvaert held up a hand to indicate it was all right and the newcomer slid onto the bench facing Goyvaert, who chose to push Isold away, tossing a few coins onto the table.

Sensing she had suddenly been deprived of a far higher payment, Isold wasn't about to leave quietly. She might only have been just fifteen summers, but the girl knew an uncommon number of swearwords and unpleasantries. Goyvaert's men grabbed her arms and dragged her away, still screaming profanities and cursing him with the damnation of ages.

On either side of her, the man-boys panted and moaned. Still, Clais was focused on Goyvaert and the newcomer, now engaged in an animated conversation. However, there was too much noise in the inn to hear any words. The newcomer was not the sort that usually frequented 't Geschildert Huys.' Beneath a cloak of kermes red, he had a fine, wide blue tunic reaching to his calf with a mantle and hood trimmed in a rouge that matched his stockings. All eyes in the dark recesses of the inn slid across him, some imagining the opportunity for robbery he presented. Such ideas would be quickly dispelled when they saw that he had bodyguards, three tall hulks of men wearing leather jerkins, swords by their sides and each exuding menace.

The three bodyguards positioned themselves close to the table where the newcomer and Goyvaert sat, but not too near that they became privy to the discussion. Opposite, the two man-boys with Clais slumped contentedly beside her, breathing hard, their exertions over. Clais was paying them only cursory attention, for her interest was fixed on the newcomer. Finding out who he was and that he was meeting Goyvaert would interest people she knew, and they would pay her good coin for such information. Had Clais von Emden known the newcomer's identity and the reputation that went before him, she would have thought twice.

The Church preached that although all people were sinners, everyone had good within them. The two men who sat, sharing a table and a jug of watery ale at 't Geschildert Huys', were God's exception to that rule. This newcomer and Goyvaert de Tongeren, were men devoid of compassion. They were soulmates in Hell, heartless and cold-blooded, schooled in the art of death on the battlefield. Goyvaert trusted few people in life, but he trusted the man sitting opposite. They were business partners. The Fleming managed the movement of orphan and foundling children from the port at Sluys up the River Schelde toward Tournai and Ghent or overland to Namur and then onwards into the lands of the Emperor of the Romans. The man opposite ran the English end of the operation.

The newcomer lifted his clay jug and took a long draught. He regarded his friend, whose hard, flinty eyes that gave nothing away. He gave a nod toward the bodyguards.

"Expecting trouble?"

Goyvaert laughed. "I always expect trouble, my friend."

"Who have you upset now?"

"The Banieres in Tournai are trying to muscle in on our operation." The newcomer could hear the annoyance in his tone.

"The Banieres?"

"The craft guilds of the town. Their leaders have demanded payment for each shipment we move through their town."

The newcomer shrugged; such payments were commonplace and often, it was simpler to pay rather than have authorities snooping around.

"Would it not be easier if we paid them to prevent unwelcome investigation?"

"Mayhaps, but they want half of the profits." Goyvaert gave an evil grin. "I am going to send the leaders of the Banieres a message to make them think otherwise."

He didn't need to ask what sort of message Goyvaert planned. Messages from Goyvaert were always direct, violent and brutal. He knew that soon, some of the Banieres in Tournai would suffer fatal accidents and that those who remained would then choose to modify their demands.

The newcomer leaned in close to his associate. "Now, my friend," he whispered, "what is it you needed me to hear in person?"

Goyvaert's face tensed as he sought the right words. "We have had word from Tuscany. A particular request for a maid of a certain type and look."

"Indeed?" His eyes quizzical.

"This is from the Household of the Imperial Vicar of Tuscany."

The newcomer's eyes widened, and his lips pursed; the Vicar of Tuscany, son of a French King and uncle to the new King of France, Philippe III. The Vicar of Tuscany was the much-hated Charles of Anjou.

"Do they not have maids in Provence and the lands of the foothills?" he asked.

"They seek a maid with long fair hair, of a certain build and around ten summers in years." Goyvaert paused. "And she cannot be base-born and must be well-bred."

His companion chuckled. "They will have to pay a pretty penny for such a maid." He leaned even further across the table. "Such a demand risks compromising our whole operation." He spoke in hushed tones. "No one misses an orphan of the streets or a foundling, but one high-born will be readily noticed and more than the constable will investigate. That presents a danger to us. We will have to proceed with the utmost caution."

Goyvaert fixed him with a searching look. "They are prepared to pay us five hundred Venetian grossi."

There was a sharp intake of breath. Five hundred Venetian grossi was a colossal sum, as much as the whole operation earned in a year.

Goyvaert looked at his friend on the other side of the table and could see that he was thinking about how to affect such a plan. Others in the inn were also watching. Two younger whores saw an opportunity; a man dressed in fine clothing, a man of means who might pay well for some company. Across from Goyaert's table, Clais, now free of the two man-boys, watched with amusement as the two young women preened their hair, pushed out their bosom and ran a finger over their front teeth. They approached the newcomer from behind, shuffling through the matted rushes on the floor. The younger of the two, a maid of perhaps seventeen summers, her chemise wide open at the front, laid a delicate, stroking hand on the hair of Goyaert's companion while her friend brushed herself suggestively against him.

His speed of movement startled Clais. In one sweeping movement, he leapt up, threw both maids to the ground and stood over them, his blade glinting in the yellow candlelight. From the dark recess of other tables came bellows of laughter and catcalls as the newcomer's bodyguards found the whole situation highly amusing. And in an instant, recognising that no threat existed, the mood of Goyaert's companion changed.

He reached down with both hands and gently pulled the two shocked young whores to their feet. He brushed them down with the back of his hand, lingering a little too long in places and then, bowing before them, invited both to sit down beside him. With the flick of his fingers, he summoned the innkeeper and ordered jugs of ale for his two guests.

Across the inn, Clais wondered how this man would treat the young whores; not as severely as Goyaert, she hoped. But she had learned something in the flurry of events, information, that people she knew would pay her good coin to know. One of his bodyguards had called him 'Giovanni.'

Ж

____

Chapter Two

The Royal Chancery, Westminster, May 1277.

THOMAS DE IBSTONE, SENIOR CLERK at the Chancery, sat up from his sloped writing desk and stretched his shoulders to ease the dull ache in his back. Many hours huddled over his desk, quill in hand, scribing documents, had taken its toll. Outside, an unexpected rain shower brought welcome relief to Londoners from the oppressive heat of the past few days.

Many summers past his fortieth year, de Ibstone had been a scrivener in the Royal Chancery since the reign of old King Henry. In the early years, he was proud of his place of work, boasting to his drinking friends how he served the King and rubbed shoulders with nobility. But the passage of time and the absence of advancement had soured him. The years had taken their toll and he had become embittered, resenting his work and the people he worked for. But the pragmatism of a wage outweighed his principles, so each day, as the sun rose, Thomas de Ibstone could be found in his tiny booth, scribing, transcribing and copying reports.

Raindrops spattered rhythmically on the roof tiles above his head in his third-floor cubby. Seniority meant de Ibstone was mostly left to his own devices. His work would be supervised and checked for accuracy if he was newly appointed. Only rarely did anyone review de Ibstone's copying. Reports from various Intelligencers came to his desk and he transcribed copies onto parchment for the Rolls. Elsewhere in the building, these were sewn onto the end of the Roll, making a continuous record for the year.

Thomas de Ibstone placed his quill in the small clay holder beside his inkhorn and sprinkled fine sand across the document he had just completed. He turned his head to listen for the sound of approaching footsteps and his eyes flitted one way and then the other, checking that he was alone. Reaching into his scrip, he lifted out a small object wrapped in linen. Alert to any sound that someone may be approaching, he placed the parcel on his writing slope before carefully unwrapping the linen covering.

Thomas looked upon a beautifully crafted Book of Hours written in Latin. It was no larger than his hand, with a cover of red calf leather tooled with gold inlay. He carefully opened it and lovingly turned its pages. Whoever had produced it was a master of their craft. The capitals at the beginning of the Psalms, the Canonical Hours and Prayers showed beautiful decoration. The Calendar of Saints Days, too, was wonderfully illustrated, with a verdant green vine running through it. It was a devotional book that would grace the household of any wealthy lady. Perhaps not a woman of the noble class, for she would have picturesque full-page Biblical scenes and a cover of purple. But this Book of Hours would serve its purpose. Thomas went to the final page of the Book of Hours and then counted ten pages back. He smiled to himself; Prayers for the Dead, an appropriate section, he mused.

Before him, on his desk was a short, metal knife, square at one end and honed razor sharp. He took the knife and brought the sharpened end to the open page. Counting down ten lines, he began to scrape carefully at the ink, gradually effacing the words. His movements were deft but precise until he had removed a whole line of text. From the drawer of his writing slope, he took a polished stone the size of a small egg and began to rub the stone over the area he had just removed.

Satisfied that the cleared line was flat, he lifted his goose feather, dipped it into the inkhorn, wiped the end and began to write. He penned only the first letter, placing the quill back in its pot, sprinkling a pinch of fine sand and waiting to see how the ink dried. It dried a slightly different shade from the ink above and below, but he was sure that only a careful examination of the Book of Hours would reveal that. He lifted his goose feather and dipped it into his inkhorn. With precise lettering that mimicked the existing text, he completed the sentence.

*"Vulpe. Quartus domus in Sopwellstrete oppido
Albani martyris, ante portas et viam Londinium."*

"The Fox. The fourth house on Sopwellstrete, town of the martyr Alban, before the gates and the road to London."
Thomas de Ibstone did not know the meaning of the message he scribed on the page. He had been well-paid to change the text. Two winters ago, he had been drinking in the Peauterpotte Inn in Cheapside, close by his lodgings. It had been a cold night with frost lying hard on the ground, but the inn had a roaring fire to keep the patrons warm. Having consumed too much of the inn's fine ale, he had fallen into conversation with a stranger, new to the city, although thinking back now, he mused whether it had been chance after all. The stranger, who he knew as Godfrey, had offered him money to show him a document affixed with the Chancery Seal. Thomas had drunk too many ales and Godfrey doubted Thomas could ever produce such a seal: he accused Thomas of boasting. His pride pricked, Thomas had sneaked a document out of the Chancery to show Godfrey and once he had done so, Godfrey le Keu had his man.

Over the following months, Godfrey gave Thomas the occasional purse, heavy with coin, in return for information. Thomas' work as a scribe involved copying documents containing sensitive and secret knowledge. He knew that he shouldn't be passing on such details and when he thought about it, none of what he told Godfrey could be of direct use to him. Godfrey had to be passing on such information to someone else. But Thomas didn't know who. The cash he received was welcome, albeit that most ended in the hands of local innkeepers.

Thomas had wanted to stop, but Godfrey turned, threatening him with a blade and a chilling, '*cooperate, or be found gutted in the Thames*.' Godfrey had given him an instruction. He was to find any references to the identity of a King's Man called *'le Reynard.'* It was a term Thomas had come across before, with guarded references and an occasional cypher transcript. He had no idea who this *'le Reynard'* was. But that was what Geoffrey, or at least the man who paid him, now wanted, the identity of *'le Reynard,'* and where they might be found. Thomas de Ibstone feared the consequences of failing his new paymaster. He had contemplated flight, but knew that he could be tracked down.

It had been chance that had given him the lead they sought. He had been tasked with copying a routine expense reimbursement of a Man-of-Law working for the Queen, Simon Lowys and was detailing the mundane expenses of a royal servant; 5d to the Ostler, John Ballard; 3d to a Blacksmith; 2d to a cordwainer; 4d to a Mistress Heacham for food; 3d for lodgings in Banbury; 1d to an unnamed informant, 1s 4d repayment to *'le Reynard'*. There it was before him. This Man-of-Law for the Queen had given *'le Reynard'* 1s 4d in coin. What had a Queen's Man-of-Law to do with a Royal Intelligencer? This Simon Lowys knows who le Reynard is, though de Ibstone. Over the following days, with as much circumspection as possible, he tried to find out about Simon Lowys.

What he discovered surprised him. He believed Lowys to be a lawyer, but it turned out that he was also in the employ of John of Berwick, which made him a King's Intelligencer. De Ibstone knew he was treading dangerously. John of Berwick was not a man to be crossed, so he proceeded with the utmost caution.

His scrutiny of past expenses revealed that Lowys had sought reimbursement for a Mistress Matilda Heacham on several occasions. And a single line on a copied document, almost a year old, revealed a Mistress Heacham of Sopwellstrete in St Albans. Further discreet enquiries revealed the location of Mistress Heacham's property and it was this he scribed into the Book of Hours before him.

Thomas de Ibstone did not know who the recipient of the Book of Hours would be. He was to pass it to Godfrey in the Peauterpotte Inn this very evening. He had one final act of scribing before he was finished. He had inserted the faux line but needed to tell the recipient where to find it.

He opened the Book of Hours to its first page, where a colourful image of the Virgin and child was surrounded on the page by a decorative border of coloured vines and coloured flowers in blue, red, green and gold. He picked up his goose quill, dipped it carefully into the inkhorn, drew it back on the edge to remove excess ink and scribed a small *'X'* at the bottom of the page. To him, it stood out as ugly against the book's beauty, but it would tell the recipient to look ten pages from the end and seek the tenth line down. Anyone casually examining the Book of Hours would likely not see its significance. Thomas de Ibstone did his best not to think about the consequences of his actions. He was worldly enough to know that by identifying those who knew *'le Reynard'*, he was likely imperilling their lives and that of the King's Agent. But Thomas Ibstone knew he was already far too deep in the misdeeds to extricate himself.

Ж

———————

Chapter Three

The Market Place, St Albans, May 1277.

WITH A HEAVY GRUNT, the young boy heaved the final four ox hides from the cart onto the pile already on the wooden trestle in front of his master's stall in the Leather Shambles beside the Bullring. The dull chimes of the Abbey bell for Matins had rung hours before. The boy stretched, his young bones aching from the heavy lifting. He closed his eyes and took in the hustle and bustle of the early morning marketplace. A cacophony of animal noises melded together, but he could make out the braying of donkeys, the whinnying of horses and the barking of dogs. Cartwheels rumbled rhythmically along sections of uneven stone cobbles, accompanied by the clip-clop of many hooves. Traders were bellowing instructions to their apprentices. Pie sellers alerted all to the quality of their wares.

The boy's name was Alward, but the others always called him *'boy'*. He was the junior of all the employees of Peter the Cordwainer, not yet enjoined and under the authority of the Master's two apprentices and journeyman. An orphan, he was perhaps nine summers old; he didn't truly know. A sharp slap across the back of his head broke his daydreaming. The other apprentices had bullied him from the first hour of his arrival at the Leatherworks in Northchurch a year earlier.

"Boy!" Walter, the taller of the two apprentices, fixed Alward with an evil stare. "You are on watch. When you see the Master return, you call out right away." He reached out and grabbed Alward's cote, pulling him close.

"You understand that, runt? Right away, or there'll be trouble." Walter pulled Alward onto his toes, leaning into him.

Alward flinched and nodded his head. Walter released his grip, pushing Alward towards the front of the stall. Alward knew how this went. Walter and Will Stamford, the other apprentice, would stay beside the cart at the back of the booth and sleep. It had happened many times before. On one occasion, Alward hadn't woken them in time and that night, when the household was abed, he received a beating for his error that had broken his jaw.

So it was, in the hour before Terce, that Alward, the boy, stood watch in the Leather Shambles of St Albans Market. He knew, as did Walter and Will that their Master was breaking his fast with Mistress de Brun at the Wheatsheaf Inn along the Magna Vico. He would likely not return until well after the Terce bell had rung. Alward gazed along the broad expanse of the great street and its unfolding market. The Leather Shambles lay at its centre, with Cordwainers Row where he now stood, beyond towards the Vintry and the Waxhouse gate to the Abbey. Above, towards the Church of St Peter, lay the Fish Shambles and, at a distance, the Butcher Quarter, Bothelingstock. The teeming rain of the previous day had abated and as Alward looked skywards, he hoped for a day without getting wet. Mindful of the threat from the two apprentices, he kept his eyes towards Hay Row, east of the Leather Shambles, looking out for Master Peter's returning from the Wheatsheaf, ready to alert Walter and Will as soon as he saw him.

Alward didn't see the young girl approach him. When he looked back towards the cart, suddenly, she was there. She didn't speak, staring at him like she had never seen a boy before. He found her stare unnerving. It was the deep green of her eyes, akin to lilies in a pond, which captivated him. The girl was smaller than him and perhaps younger. Fair curls framed her soft, round face, but looking at her clothes made him realise she was no beggar. She was not clothed in rags, but a fine cloth cote, such as the daughter of a merchant might wear.

And still, she stared at him, her head tilted down, her green eyes boring in on him.

"What do you want? Who are you?" he gabbled his words. The girl's presence was unsettling, though he didn't know why.

Her demeanour was that of a little girl lost, but looking beyond her, he couldn't see a man who might be her father.

"Are you lost?" The girl did not speak and Alward wondered if she might be a stranger, perhaps the daughter of a foreign merchant.

With her eyes firmly fixed on him, she raised an arm, took hold of his sleeve and gently tugged.

"Come." Her voice was soft but assertive. She's English, thought Alward.

"Come? Where?" he asked.

But she said no more, continuing to tug at his sleeve, pulling him away from the market.

Alward gazed behind him toward the cordwainer's stall and back to the girl and at that moment, he decided he would go with her.

Ж

Chapter Four

The Market Place, St Albans, May 1277.

PETER THE CORDWAINER wore fine, tooled leather boots, as was expected for a merchant of his trade. He had desired such boots since he left his native York to become an apprentice in Berkhamsted years before. These he made in his shop on Berkhamstede's Leather Shambles, using the finest Cordovan kid skin, not a year since. Thus, he regretted what he now had to do. The fashionable goat skin tip of his right boot made contact with his apprentice Will's stomach, curled up asleep beneath the booth.

"What the…!" The apprentice leapt to his feet, ready to grapple with his assailant until he saw the red-faced fury of his Master. Peter the Cordwainer lashed out, with his hands this time, cuffing his apprentice around the head.

From the other side of the booth, Walter, the senior apprentice, stirred, woken by the din. His Master's boot caught him full in the face, causing him to scream with pain, blood streaming from his nose and staining his teeth red.

As he stood, Peter grabbed Walter's cote, blood spotting onto his hand.

"Where is the boy?" he screamed.

Walter screwed his face, looking across at Will for reassurance. Peter was a bull of a man, four fingers beyond six feet with broad shoulders and tree trunks for forearms. He was someone not to be crossed.

"He was there," said Will nervously, pointing to the edge of the booth, "when you went to the inn to break your fast.

Peter the Cordwainer glared at his apprentice. "Well, he's not fooking-well there now, is he." The Master's ire made his native north Yorkshire accent more pronounced. "Where's he gone?" Another slap accompanied the question, this time aimed at Walter.

"Don't know," the two replied, almost in unison.

He grabbed the senior apprentice and pushed him towards the Magna Vico.

"Find him. Bring him back and I will tan his fooking hide."

A large shovel of a hand grabbed Will's matted brown hair and spun him around, pushing him towards the abbey.

The Master pulled the young apprentice's face so close he looked into the angry mouth and its brown teeth. The smell of stale ale made Will gag.

"I paid good coin for that little runt. You go that way," gesturing west towards the Vintry, "and fooking find him, or it'll be your hide I tan."

Will was roughly pushed to the ground and scrambled away to find the boy, vowing he would give him a good beating before the Master did for the trouble he had caused.

The dull peal of the Abbey bells rang for Prime and Peter the Cordwainer seethed. Worse, having despatched his apprentices to find the boy, he was alone at the stall and had to deal with the customers, rich and poor.

His mood wasn't helped by the appearance of an unkempt old man who had appeared and was busy handling the belts and boots on display. One look at him told Peter the Cordwainer that there was nothing here that such a man could afford.

"I seeks boots Meister,"

"Christ's fookin bones! You can't afford any of it, old man. Move on now, or I'll make you."

The old man tilted his head, his grey eyes fixed lazily on the Cordwainer.

"What makes you so sure I don't have the coin for what you have here?"

Peter regarded the dishevelled man in front of him. His woollen cote was faded and patched, the threadbare coif, drawn loose over his head from the morning chill, covering most of his matted, thinning grey hair. An ancient scar broke his greasy grey beard on one side of his cheek. A peasant thought Peter and a poor one at that.

"Just fook off, old man. I have real patrons to tend to."

The old man looked to both sides and broke into a toothless smile.

"I sees only one patron, Meister and I have coin enough to buy all of this." He gestured his dirty mitt at the range of boots, belts, scrips, purses and garters arrayed in front of him.

His other, equally dirty hand went inside his cote and pulled out a small cloth purse. He fiddled with its drawstring and pulled out a coin.

Behind the counter, Peter the Cordwainer's eyes widened. He sucked in a breath as he stared at the shiny golden coin framed against the grime of the old man's hand, all thoughts of the orphan boy gone from his head.

Ж

____

Chapter Five

*The Benedictine Convent of St Mary de Pré on Watling Street
Hertfordshire, May 1277*

ETRICE D' AULAY FELT the warmth of the late May sun on
her face, giving her a glow she had rarely experienced in the
two years that she had been at St Mary's. She was one of
nine women who lived at the Benedictine convent of St Mary de Pré,
a Lazar House, for all were lepers, shunned by the town.

The heart of St Mary's was the cloister, which ran around an
open space, and to which were attached the Church, the Refectory,
the kitchens and a small library. St Mary de Pré had little need of
accommodation for pilgrims; being a Lazar House, convent visitors
were few. On rare occasions, nuns from other convents, travelling
along the Roman road, would rest at St Mary's for a few days.
Indeed, just the day before, a visiting Abbess from Spain arrived,
breaking her journey south to Dover and a high-born lady and her
daughter had come but a day since, to visit Sister Agnes.

Betrice took shade against the cemetery's southern wall,
intended for the nuns and lay sisters but too frequently used for
Betrice's fellow lepers. Her thoughts were interrupted by the ringing

of metal on stone close by. She looked up and saw a solitary workman on the roof of the Church.

High above her, Robert atte Fletville, a journeyman Mason, stood with the heat of the late spring sun beating down onto his broad-muscled back. Rivulets of sweat trickled between his shoulder blades. The wooden scaffolding he stood on clung to the south-eastern transept of the church tower like ancient ivy. There was no relief from the noon-day sun from his vantage point atop the temporary framework. The freshly cut stonework reflected back on him and his eyes narrowed against the brightness. For respite, he turned away and gazed down towards the Cloister and the Roman road beyond, where just a few insect-like people were about their business.

St Mary's was a poor house despite its links to the Benedictine Abbey of St Alban, just two miles away. Such was its state of penury that twenty years before, Pope Alexander IV had granted a Papal Indulgence of forty days' remission of sins to anyone contributing funds to repair its crumbling buildings. That work was still ongoing, but the Lazar Priory of St Mary de Pré remained poor.

Robert atte Fletville was one of just three masons St Mary's could afford. He stared down towards the Cloisters, where a solitary figure appeared to be regarding him. Robert had been reluctant to accept work at a Lazar House; such was his fear of leprosy. On many occasions, he had heard stories of those who lived at St Mary's being greatly afflicted by the disease. But times were hard for Robert; coin and work were in short supply. Thus, he found himself working stone in a place he feared on this blazing hot day. His fellow mason, James of Redbourn, had sought to allay his fears by telling him that because lepers were enduring purgatory on earth, they would go directly to heaven when they died. They were, therefore, he said, closer to God than other people. But Robert remained wary.

His position high at the apex of the church roof gave him a panoramic view of the ancient Watling Street and the surrounding countryside. He watched, puzzled, as two travellers on horseback left the Abbey from the town gate, pulling a pack mule behind them. Struggling to guide their mounts, they turned north onto the old Roman road, moving with undue haste. That struck Robert as odd, as well as the fact that they travelled without guards, and it was strange for them to be on the road at this hot hour. He squinted to see the travellers better and sweat ran into his eyes. Wiping it away with his forearm, he could make out that the two were nuns. The events puzzled him. The law demanded that the gates be permanently closed, and no one was allowed out of the convent without the permission of the Prioress. On the rare occasion that one of the nuns left to venture into the outside world, it was to go into the town for supplies. The inmates of the Lazar House were never allowed to leave its precinct. The western wall that faced onto the old Roman road had large open gaps to allow them to beg from passing travellers. The puzzlement remained, but there was work to be done, so Robert began fettling the shaped ragstone to make it fit the vacant space on the tower above the altar.

Below him, Betrice d'Aulay watched him at work, fascinated by his skill with stone. At length, she returned to the cloisters and found the Lazar House was in uproar. Her eight fellow inmates were seated in animated discussion. A low moan came from Esmie, a rambling woman who the others tolerated, believing she was touched by the Holy Spirit.

"They taked her," cried Esmie. "They Comed upon her an taked her."

"No Esmie. She upped and left with Sister Mercy. She told no one, she left, no one took her." It was Marjorie, one of the older residents who spoke.

"I saw her go," Amice said proudly, scratching at her neck. "They skulked out before the Sext bell and weren't at service." Amice was one of the newer residents and revelled in gossip.

Betrice made no sense of what was being said. "Who has gone? What are you talking about?"

"It's the Prioress and Sister Mercy," the obedientiary Amice announced to anyone listening.

"They've gone."

Ж

Chapter Six

The Boar Inn, Fancherstrate City of London, May 1277.

DEEP IN THE SHADOWED RECESSES of the Boar Inn, slumped on a rough, wooden bench, a man, hood pulled up tight over his head, stared at a half-full clay ale jug. Like many of the inn's customers, he had that 'far-away' look. The Boar Inn, a stone's throw from the Tower, was a popular establishment and there were others sat in shadows nursing the dark, bitter ale in front of them. But the man was oblivious to the few customers at this late afternoon hour. His choice of bench was not random. From where he sat, the man could see customers enter the inn and make an initial judgement about their character.

At length, an outwardly well-dressed man of the merchant class entered, looked around and sidled onto the bench beside him. Closer examination of his cote and hose would have shown it to be highly fashionable in the last years of old King Henry, third of that name. Like those elsewhere in the Boar Inn, their brief conversation over two fresh jugs of ale was hushed. A handful of coins slid across the rough wooden table towards the newcomer, who swept them up in a single motion and dropped them into his purse before departing as quickly as he entered.

Seeing the man leave, the innkeeper's wife shuffled across the rushes to his bench.

"Another jug of ale, good sire?" she inquired, setting a fresh jug in front of him before he could reply.

He held up a hand to wave her away.

"Nay, Mistress, I am done."

She moved closer to him. "Just one jug, sir, you will feel better for it." She leaned in close. He looked up at a face that had once been pretty but now showed the lines of time.

"I don't just serve ale, sir," she said suggestively, laying a hand on his.

"Nay Mistress," the man shook his head. His hand went to the purse at his belt and he tossed a few coins onto the rough oak table and stood. The Innkeeper's wife gave an obsequious bow, scooping up the money as the man headed for the door.

"Mayhaps next time. Now do you come back good sire and bring your friends. Tell them of our fine offering."

Ignoring her words, he lifted the latch on the heavy oak door and stepped outside. The darkness of the Ragged Staff gave way to a bustling street in late afternoon London sunshine.

Simon Lowys blinked, accustoming his eyes from the heavy gloom of the inn as he stepped into the brightness of the busy city street. The sun was at its strongest and copper, tin and pewter objects glinted on the market stalls lining the streets.

Costermongers offered their wares, calling out to every passing stranger. "Best peascods, hot sheep's feet, many-a-pie." Even in the heat, ragged young children raced around following passers-by, begging for coin and looking out for opportunities to snaffle fruit or a loaf from unsuspecting stallholders. He could make out the unmistakable ring of hammer on an anvil and nearby, blacksmiths plied their trade. At least the heat made it easier to pick his way through the piles of refuse, faeces and detritus that covered the street, now baked hard and needing only a shower of rain to become the river of foul-smelling excrement that was its normal state.

Simon was very aware of the looks that regarded him from the shadowed recesses as he walked up Fanchercherstrate towards the royal fortress of the Tower of London. Cutpurses and rifflers preyed on the unwary, even in the daytime. But attuned as he was to threats to his body and purse, his thoughts were far away, as they had been when he was in the Boar Inn.

The Tower of King William lay ahead of him, its Caen stone gleaming in the sun. As Simon veered off Fanchercherstrate into Marthe Lane, he saw her, an apparition that stirred long-buried memories.

For an instant, he believed it was Amy, his departed wife. Amy, whose dark brown hair cascaded, untamed in the days before their wedding vows bound them. The maid had the same sparkling eyes. Simon halted in disbelief, yet the maid swept past him, oblivious to his gaping stare.

The resemblance was uncanny: the same height, the same graceful form. Amy, his wife, had passed away two years before, giving birth to their stillborn son. This maid was the same height and her shift suggested a shapely body, just like his late wife. And then she was gone. He wondered if she was related. Amy was the daughter of a Guildsman of the prosperous Skinners' Company from Walbrook in the city and she had a younger sister, but she had died from the pestilence, before Simon knew Amy.

Seeing the maid and her resemblance to his dead wife brought memories flooding back. He had known Amy for five years, but they had only been married for three. Indeed, he had only just started paying court to her when he went to Outremer with the King and Queen. He married her upon his return.

And then, just before Michaelmas, two years since, he lost her. His grief threatened to drown him in its depths. His work as a man-of-law and Royal Nuncio was a lifeline, a distraction from the pain, but he never forgot her and his love for her never diminished. Simon believed he could not love again but now found his thoughts of affection flitting between Amy and the enigmatic Isabella la Rus.

Twice in the past year, Isabella had saved his life. He had confronted her in the Wheatsheaf Inn, believing she was a member of the deadly coven of witches, the Daughters of the Shadows. Little did he know then that she was the King's Intelligencer, a figure known only as 'le Reynard.'

Together, they rescued the King's daughter and destroyed the coven. Simon was intrigued and enthralled by Isabella, but she remained aloof. He had gone to the Wheatsheaf Inn to find her the previous August only to find that Isabella had impersonated the owner, Mistress de Brun, as part of her cover to get close to the coven. It was symptomatic of his dealings with Isabella. He did not truly know her or who she indeed was. He had not seen her for nearly a year, but now, she, like Amy, was never out of his thoughts. Simon had moments like this when the darkness of loneliness swept over him. He contemplated remarrying, but his thoughts lay with only one living woman.

Marthe Lane was its usual, busy self with the noise of a London morning. Traders' cries of '*Make way now*' competed with each other. There was the cacophony of whinnies and neighs of carthorses and pack animals. The less fortunate beasts, destined for the slaughterman's knife, snorted and bellowed as they were driven on their final journey towards Smithfield. The backdrop to the hustle and bustle was the smell, a heady, pungent blend of animal dung, human excrement and the river. It was the familiar aroma for the Royal Nuncio and man-of-law and somehow, it lifted his gloom.

Ж

____

Chapter Seven

Tothillstrete, close to Westminster gate, May 1277.

IN THE DEEP RECESSES of his slumbering mind, Simon Lowys became aware of a thumping sound nearby, but he ignored it and rolled over in his cot. But the sound wouldn't be ignored. *Bang! Bang! Bang!* A reluctant Royal Nuncio rolled out of bed, wincing at the coldness of the floor rushes beneath his feet, even though the summer approached. He moved lazily to the small window overlooking the alley and pushed open the wooden shutter. A blast of chilled late spring air blew in and assaulted his face, waking him and he peered out onto the darkened street.

"Master Lowys...... Master Lowys." The voice of a young lad called to him from the pre-dawn gloom below, but he could not make out anyone standing there.

"Show yourself," shouted Simon and the shape of a gangly youth appeared from beneath the eaves, illuminated by the dull flicker from a candle lantern.

"What is your business at this hour?" Simon paused. "And God's teeth, what hour is it?"

"It is well beyond Lauds, Master Lowys and Sire John does demand your presence at the Chancery."

"Tis not yet dawn," groaned Simon. As the King's Intelligencer, John of Berwick commanded and others responded. Does the man not sleep? Simon thought to himself.

"And who you are?" he shouted into the gloom as an afterthought.

"I am Robert, Master Lowys, Robert de Berdesfold; I was brought to the Chancery to work for Sire John but a few days since. My father is also named Robert de Berdesfold, after his own father and my father and Sire John fought alongside each other in the Marcher Lands many years past. I hail from a small …"

"God's legs, man, stop your gabble. I have no need of your life tale." Simon gave a deep yawn.

"I will be down presently. Wait there."

Simon didn't rush. He poured cold water into a bowl and splashed some across his face, rubbing his eyes to remove the traces of sleep. Running a wet hand through his long hair, he tied it back in a Q knot. His battered cote and hose lay on the coffer at the end of his bed, which he sat on to pull on his fine Cordovan leather boots.

He picked his way slowly down the steps into the lower chamber and with no time to break his fast, he lifted the latch on the solid oak door and stepped out into the chilled air of an early London morning.

"Master Lowys," Robert de Berdesfold bowed deeply. To Simon, it appeared like moving shadows, the darkness of the pre-dawn barely illuminated by de Berdesfold's lantern.

"Get up, man. You have no need to make obeisance to me."

"Yes, Master Lowys… Sir... Of course….."

Simon grabbed at a shoulder, pulling de Berdesfold towards him. The dull candle flame revealed not a grown man but a startled, unbearded youth of perhaps fifteen years.

"God's teeth, man, what are you wearing?" Robert de Berdesfold stood before him dressed in a bright serge cote and a cloak dyed with the deepest kermes, the height of fashion at the King's Court.

de Berdesfold stammered a response. "This is....it...I always," but his words went unfinished as Simon pushed the youth ahead of him. "You lead the way. Hold that lantern high as you go." A command, not a request. Robert de Berdesfold did as Lowys instructed and held the lantern up above his head, throwing long shadows onto the lane ahead. Behind them, the first grey smudges of the new dawn danced on the eastern horizon.

Simon's modest lodgings in an alley off Tothillstrete, beyond the Western gate of the monastic precinct, lay minutes from the Chancery inside the Royal Palace at Westminster.

He had lived there for three years, the home he had shared with his wife and would have shared with their stillborn son. In the two years since her death, he had not moved. The house held precious memories for him.

As his mind dwelled in the mists of time, they turned to head toward the river, walking past the small parade of workshops adjacent to his rooms. The area around Tothillstrete was a mixed community of merchants and traders. A Baxter, the widow Hegarth, was already hard at work, her ovens roaring even at this early hour. The adjacent cobblers and the warehouse of Belenge, the Brabant epicier, were in darkness, as was the home of John of Geddington, the barber-surgeon, still abed no doubt, thought Simon.

The only other people abroad at this hour were the occasional prostitute on her way home and sensing an opportunity. Ahead of them lay the bleakness of the Almoner's fields, the disappearing thin crescent moon behind them, throwing little light to help them on their way. They crossed the sturdy wooden bridge over the Black Ditch and to one side loomed the walls of the Benedictine monastery, enveloped in darkness. This was a much-travelled route for the Royal Nuncio and he kept the Cowdstream between them and the fast-disappearing brightness of the moon, knowing that if he did so, he was heading east.

It wasn't long before the imposing walls of the Royal Palace loomed before them. A pair of cresset torches flaming in their metal sconces illuminated the imposing wooden gates. Three young, armed guards watched their approach suspiciously.

"*Hauh!*" A guttural command came from an unseen guard to one side, the Palace guards still used the old Norman word for '*halt*'.

"Approach slow and state your business," came an instruction from the darkness as two of his fellows circled behind Simon and de Berdesfold in case of trouble.

Simon stepped forward ahead of de Berdesfold, allowing the dim lantern to throw shadowed light onto his face. "I am Simon Lowys, Royal Nuncio to Her Grace the Queen and I have business with My Lord, John of Berwick."

The Guard Serjeant stepped out of the shadows, standing directly in front to appraise the Royal Nuncio.

"You are early risen, Master Lowys. God give you good day."

"And you, Nate," replied Simon, recognising the guard serjeant from when both men were on crusade to Outremer seven years before.

"Still keeping them on their toes, I see,"

"Aye," Nate Brynkhill grinned, stepped back from the light and gestured his arm.

"I thought it was the King's colours coming down from Charing when I saw the red and bright gelou," said the serjeant, gesturing at de Berdesfold, prompting a ripple of laughter from Simon.

"Master Lowys and his," the serjeant looked de Berdesfold up and down, shaking his head, " and his…. companion may pass." He paused and added, "Well done, lads."

Simon Lowys and de Berdesfold passed through the side gate into the Palace complex of Westminster. A Royal Place had been first built on this site in the reign of old King Edward, the last Saxon monarch after whom the present King was named. Following the conquest, King William made Westminster his base in London. It lay directly beside the Thames and was two miles hence from the city and its squalor, disease and unpleasantness. But despite the freshness of the early morning, the low tide wafted the rancid aroma of the river smells towards them.

Years earlier, before she became Queen, when Simon was first appointed a Nuncio to Her Grace, it had taken him many months to navigate the labyrinth of corridors and chambers within the palace complex. The heavily polished oak panelling along every corridor made each one appear much like every other.

Once inside the palace, Simon and de Berdesfold walked briskly along the narrow, gloomy, labyrinthine corridors towards the Chancery. There were few clerks about at this early hour and apart from cursory greetings to guards, Simon spoke to no one.

On the upper corridors, local cleaning women were sweeping the wooden floors. Floor rushes were not used in the palace corridors; they were cleaned daily. Simon knew most of the women and greeted them with a welcoming, 'God give you good day, Mistress.' The cawing call of early-morning roosters echoed from without as Simon entered a suite of rooms that faced onto the river. He instructed de Berdesfold to wait there for him before he rapped loudly on a heavy oak door and was bade entry.

It had gone the hour of Prime, yet John of Berwick, Steward of the Queen's Household and Chief Intelligencer for King Edward, was busy at his oak writing slope. He moved a goose quill across a parchment with stuttering strokes. Berwick did not lift his eyes when Simon Lowys entered the chamber, gesturing with his left hand to sit on a bench on one side of the chamber.

"I will be with you presently, Lowys." The reedy tones of the Chief Intelligencer resonated beyond the chamber into the empty corridors. With a few more 'harrumphs' and deep sighs, John of Berwick concluded his business with the parchment, sprinkled fine sand onto the ink and a few seconds later tapped the document on the side of his table to allow the sand to drop to the floor. With no more thought, Berwick tossed the parchment roll to one side and raised his head to stare at Simon Lowys.

" You have concluded that business in the city, I trust?" It wasn't a question.

"Indeed, my Lord. We know where the King's goods finally ended up, and the new Sheriff, Henry Frowke, has arrested all those involved. They will appear before the Justice of Eyre at the next Sessions."

John of Berwick pondered on the response. "Good! Good!" Lowys knew this amounted to praise from the King's Intelligencer.

"And the business in Winchester? How fares that investigation?"

Two weeks before, Berwick had summoned Simon and dispatched him to Winchester to investigate the murders of Licoricia, a prominent Jewish woman of business in the town and her Christian maid. Licoricia was one of the wealthiest women in all England and a money lender to both the King and the senior nobles of the realm. Her business dealings extended over southern and southwestern England; that she should be murdered in what appeared a bungled robbery was highly suspicious. A poor saddler who had fled the city was named as the murder suspect by the local jury, but Simon found there was no evidence other than malicious gossip against him. Simon's investigations led him to three prominent members of the Mercers Guild, but they closed ranks and he could not find conclusive proof to bring a charge.

"The case remains open, My Lord. There is talk of a stolen holy icon, though I know not what it might be. There are suspects, but no proof offered."

"Baah. Berwick gave a snort of dissatisfaction. "Bad business! Bad business, indeed. His Grace will not be happy."

John of Berwick was not a man you failed. He had his people across the realm and served as a conduit of information to King Edward as his Chief Intelligencer.

"Now, Master Lowys." Berwick's mood changed from melancholic to business. "Have you heard Holy Mass this day?"

"Nay, My Lord," replied a shame-faced Simon, wondering whether daily attendance at Mass was expected of him.

"My Lady, the Queen is hearing Mass as we speak. She rises early these days to hear the first service after Prime."

Simon tried not to show puzzlement; why was Berwick telling him this? Did he expect a reply?

"We are to join her once the Mass is finished." And with surprising agility for a man of his advanced age, John of Berwick leapt up from his writing table and quickly moved towards the door.

"Come along, man; we cannot keep Her Grace waiting."

Simon Lowys had worked as a Nuncio for Queen Eleanor for almost ten years, but he still was apprehensive on the occasions he had to meet with her.

Ж

____

Chapter Eight

St Stephen's Chapel, Palace of Westminster, May 1277.

FINE STRANDS OF LATE dawn light pierced the coloured glass of the high windows of the partly built St Stephen's Chapel. Set deep in the Royal Palace, overlooking the river, the mellow tones of Sire Walter de Winterburn echoed around its sparsely filled interior. The chapel was more than a century old and served the King and Queen's personal devotion.

The early light framed a solitary woman kneeling on an ornately carved prie-dieu before the altar. She was deep in prayer, making her Latin responses to Sire Walter's intonations. Painted images of the Apostles and the story of Nebuchadnezzar from the Book of Daniel decorated the chapel walls.

"*Ite, missa est,*" boomed Sire Walter, "Go, it is done."

"*Deo Gratias,*" the woman responded in a whispered but assertive tone.

The Mass had ended, and Sire Walter reposed to his Sacristy, yet the kneeling woman remained deep in her devotions. Behind her, three of her Ladies knelt at a larger, shared prie-dieu, apparently in prayer but awaiting her first movement. The wooden latch on the door behind them lifted with a loud thud. The two men slipped into the small chapel and without words, they took their place at the back.

Simon Lowys inhaled the musty, incense and beeswax smell he had always associated with churches. The aroma always took his mind back to the small Church of San Silvestro in Viterbo seven years before when he had witnessed the slaying of his lord, Henry of Almain. He stepped back tight against the limewashed wall as the lady left her prie-dieu and walked towards where he stood with John of Berwick. Her three Ladies-in-Waiting followed demurely behind her, keeping half a dozen paces back.

She did not acknowledge the King's Intelligencer and her Nuncio beyond a cursory inclination of her head. The solid wooden door opened before her and a royal guard no doubt watched through a discreet viewing hole, doing his job. Her Grace, Queen Eleanor of Castile, swept out of St Stephen's Chapel into an antechamber.

"My Lord John, thank you for attending me." The Queen addressed her Steward in courtly French. He bowed low before her. Simon loitered behind him as protocol demanded.

"And you, Master Lowys." She half-turned to regard the Royal Nuncio. "God give you good day." Simon made his obeisance with a deep, formal bow.

"Come," she gestured towards a corner of the chamber where a solid oak bench lay against one wall. Queen Eleanor sat, Berwick and Lowys stood in front of her and her Ladies-in-Waiting took their positions on the far side of the room.

"*Maître Lowys sait-il pourquoi il est ici ?* Does Master Lowys know why he is here" She addressed the question to Berwick.

"Nay, Your Grace. He is unaware."

She shifted on the bench and half-turned to face her Nuncio. "Master Lowys, I fear we are in need of your services once more."

Queen Eleanor's eyes widened, and her lips tensed. "Master Lowys, do you know Lady Hawise de Belame? "

Lowys thought and nodded. "She is one of the Ladies who attends upon you, My Lady."

"*Oui*! She has been with me these eight years. She has a sister, a widow, the Lady Matilda de Lascy. Her husband, Lord Gilbert, was killed in a skirmish in the Welsh Marches some years since."

Simon didn't know of that but wondered what relevance this had to him.

"Master Lowys. But two days ago, Lady Matilda and her young daughter visited the Convent of St Mary de Pré. It lies but a few miles beyond the Shrine of the Martyr, St Alban and her late husband's sister took the veil there." She paused to draw in a breath. "Tis a Lazar House," she said, making the Signum Crucis.

Queen Eleanor paused, her fingers rubbing Dominican beads while Simon took this in. Queen Eleanor fixed him with a look of urgency.

"Lady Matilda's daughter, the Lady Jeanne, went missing whilst there."

"Missing?" Simon knew protocol and knew he should not be speaking in the presence of the Queen unless asked a question, but he spoke, nonetheless.

"Yes, Master Lowys, missing. She simply disappeared from the Convent. Lady Matilda was conversing with her relation in the cloister and the Lady Jeanne was in the garden when she was last seen."

Now Simon could see and understand what was being asked of him.

"You suspect one of the inhabitants of the Lazer House?"

"Nay. Nay! I think not! But I do need you to locate the Lady Jeanne, Master Lowys," implored the Queen. "As a matter of urgency. I trust you greatly after what you did for His grace and I, last year."

Memories of rescuing the Queen's daughter Elenora came back to him, visions he had spent months trying to forget. A bloodied Maud Blount lying dead at his feet, a crossbow quarrel embedded in her chest and images of the beguiling Isabella la Rus, who had saved his life.

"Master Lowys, I am trusting you to find the Lady Jeanne. My Lord Berwick will make the necessary arrangements for you to speak with Lady Matilda. She is beside herself with sorrow."

"Of course, your Grace. Do we afear for the life of Lady Matilda's daughter?"

The muscles around the Queen's eyes tightened.

"You have the right of it, Master Lowys. She may have got herself lost, but that surely is unlikely in a walled community. She has been taken, though why, we know not."

"Your Grace." The reedy tone of John of Berwick interrupted. "Master Lowys is already heading north to a manor, Windridge, south of St Albans, to investigate the death of a priest."

"A man of God is dead?" inquired the Queen. "If Master Lowys is being sent, Master Berwick, do you believe it suspicious?"

"Aye, Your Grace. He was slain in his own Church and Master Lowys here goes north soon. Now, he will investigate the death of the maid as his priority: only when she is found will he go to Windridge if your Grace agrees.

Queen Eleanor turned to her nuncio. "Will you need help in this, Master Lowys?"

Simon went to respond, but John of Berwick laid a hand on his arm.

"I have help already close by, should it be needed, Your Grace."

The Queen nodded. "Of course, I would expect nothing less, Master Berwick."

Both men took this as their signal to leave. They made a low and respectful obeisance and backed out of the chamber.

Once in the outer solar, Berwick stopped.

"The priest's death was to be your priority, but this search on behalf of Her Grace needs must take precedence."

He gave Lowys a quizzical look. "You know of the priest's death?"

"Aye, my Lord."

"The County Sheriff, Lawrence de Scaccario, has been struck down with the pestilence. The under-sheriff position is vacant, but I believe the local Reeve may be able to assist you."

"Aye, my Lord, I thank you, but who is the help you spoke of?" inquired Simon.

Berwick cleared his throat. "Ah, yes! St Alban's is but a short day's ride from the Chancery would require real assistance."

Simon did not like the sound of this and felt something was coming his way, something he wouldn't like.

"de Berdesfold. I want you to take de Berdesfold with you and show him the way to do things."

It took a moment to realise who Berwick was referring to; the youth who had awoken him that morning.

"God's teeth! de Berdesfold? He is but a callow youth. How can he assist with my investigation?"

"Come now, Lowys, you were a youth once. He is young but keen."

"And never stops his blather."

"That's as may be, but his father and I fought alongside each other in the Marcher Wars. I must tell you, Lowys, de Beresford's father is well-regarded by His Grace the King."

Simon knew when he was beaten, further protest would get him nowhere; young de Berdesfold would go north with him.

Ж

____

Chapter Nine

St Peter's Church, St Albans, May 1277.

IT WAS THE FEAST DAY of the Holy Body and Blood, a special day for the Church. Even though it was daytime, the arches of St Peter's rose into darkness. The aroma of damp, incense and beeswax permeated the interior. Before the altar, a solitary figure knelt on the small, simple prie-dieu. A folded cloth had been left thoughtfully on the knee bench to bring some relief from the hardness of the oak. Head bowed in reverence; she was just another pilgrim making her devotion. Her lips moved in silent intercession. She bent low to slip a hand underneath while praying. Her fingers felt a small rectangular object wrapped in cloth. Deftly pulling it out, she slipped it into an inside pocket in her sleeveless cote. She sensed movement. From the corner of her eye, she saw a priest approaching.

"*Je me confesse à Dieu,*" she began to chant aloud. "*Je me confesse à Dieu.*"

Seeing before him a woman ready to confess her sins to God, the priest's mood buoyed and he headed to the Confessional on the far side of the chapel. He had come from the Sacristy when he saw her. She was unknown to him; her green cotehardie with its scalloped decoration told him she was no peasant. Moreover, how she intoned, "*Je me confesse à Dieu,*" with a precise accent, indicated she was not English. As he walked to the Confessional, he confirmed this; her face had the olive hue of one born in the lands of the Middle Sea.

Sire Thomas found hearing a woman's confession reaffirming. They were inherently feeble, prone to lust and sin and in need of his spiritual guidance.

"I will be with you presently, my child," he said in his best French. She continued her chants. "*Je suis ici pour me repentir.*" But repentance was the last thing on her mind. From the corner of her eye, she watched him cross the church and waited until the priest was out of sight by the Confessional before rising and swiftly making for the door. When the priest finally realised that the women had left, it simply reinforced his view that they were the weaker vessel, incapable of acknowledging their sins.

The woman did not consult the Book of Hours until she had returned to the house in Chingesberiestrete. It was a modest property in St Michael's, rented on a long-term basis and usually occupied by a widow who had been well-paid to vacate the house and visit relatives. A stranger appearing in their midst might spark suspicion, so a story was told of her being a prosperous French relative of the widow's husband, who had travelled to Hertfordshire to pay devotion at the shrine of the Martyr and others.

Once inside, she removed her white wimple and replaced it with a fashionable coif and crespinette to hold her long, lustrous dark hair. She lit four tall beeswax candles and laid them in a semi-circle on a table, placing the linen parcel in front of her and carefully unfolding the cloth. The Book of Hours was beautiful. She opened it to the first page, an illuminated Virgin and Child, crafted by one with a true gift for such work. Her eye fell to the foot of the page and a single X . She laid the book on its cover and counted ten pages back. A decorative Capital, the letter 'M' began the 'The Liturgy of the Virgin' prayers to the mother of Jesus. Pressing down on both sides to flatten its pages, she ran a slim, olive fingers down it until she reached the tenth line.

Her practised eye told her it had been scribed by a different hand, but most would not have noticed.

"Vulpe. Quartus domus in Sopwellstrete oppido Albani martyris, ante portas et viam Londinium."

"The Fox.The fourth house on Sopwellstrete, the town of the martyr Alban, before the gates and the road to London."

She smiled. The spy in the Royal Chancery had done well. Of course, she couldn't be sure if this was where 'le Reynard' lived or was a base from which he operated, but it gave her somewhere to observe the comings and goings of The Fox.

Ж

____

Chapter Ten

Benedictine Convent of St Mary de Pré on Watling Street
Hertfordshire, May 1277.

SIX BLACK-CLAD BENEDICTINE sisters huddled close, crow-like, on the worn stone benches of St Mary de Pré's cloisters, their voices low, in hushed discussion. In ordinary times, those voices would be stilled, their heads bowed in reverence, listening to the missives of their Prioress, Hilda of Whitby, but Prioress Hilda had suddenly left without warning, as had her sub-prioress Sister Mercy, a day since. Six sisters remained, all of whom had dedicated their lives to the women of the Lazar House. But they were directionless in a situation they had never experienced.

All had been at St Mary's for varying years, although none of the six was a novice. Sister Agnes was the most senior, having more than twelve summers among the poor, blighted women.

"We must assume that Prioress Hilda and Sister Mercy will not return." A red-eyed Sister Agnes spoke with a certainty she didn't believe. Still, she knew because of her seniority, it fell to her to reassure the others.

"Someone among us needs must take charge and send word to Father Abbot at the Abbey."

Although St Mary de Pré lay just a few miles northwest of the Abbey of St Alban, as a Lazar House, the Abbot's obedientiaries rarely visited; indeed, Agnes thought it had been years since one had come to see them.

"It must be you," the youngest nun, Sister Otha, addressed Agnes. "You are the oldest and have the most years of all among us."

Agnes regarded the young nun. Otha was perhaps twenty summers old and had been placed at St Mary's by her family when she was a child. Her father, Baldwin de Lamoureux, with three older daughters, made Otha an oblate, a gift to the Church at the convent of St Ethelburga at Barking. But Otha had never truly taken to the cloistered life. She had been sent to St Mary's as a punishment for her disobedience in following the rules two years before.

Agnes shook her head. "I may have the years, Otha, but I do not possess the wisdom or the knowledge to act until a new Prioress is appointed." She spoke with true humility.

A softly spoken nun, the unassuming, fresh-faced Sister Joan, spoke up. "Sister Agnes has her own woes with her niece lost. We cannot burden her more."

There was a murmur of agreement among the others. All knew of the abduction of Agnes' niece from the grounds of their abbey but a few days before.

"Could we not ask the Iberian Abbess staying here to break her travel to Dover and give help to us?" It was Sister Cecilia, the cook, who spoke.

"Aye! Tis only for a short time," agreed Sister Joan enthusiastically.

"It is a good thought," nodded Agnes. "She could assist us for a short time if she would stay her journey but for a few more days."

There was a murmur of agreement at a possible resolution to their difficulty. It took but a little longer for the nuns to agree that Sister Agnes, as their senior, would approach Abbess Constanza that same morning before Terce and plead for her help.

The Abbess Constanza de San Andreas de Anroyo now occupied the guest rooms adjacent to the Prioress's chamber. Sister Joan brought the Abbess and her young servant, a pretty novice of about twenty summers, warm water to wash and diluted ale to drink upon arrival. In her few years at the Lazar House, these were the first guests Joan could remember who had chosen to stay. Some of the nuns received family on occasion, though this, too, was rare. That thought brought to mind Agnes' sister who, with her daughter, had visited her at St Mary's just a few days before, only for the young maid to go missing. Strange things are happening here, thought Joan. She had volunteered to go with Sister Agnes to see Abbess Constanza. In truth, she had to bring fresh rushes for the floor and empty the Jordan, giving a reason to speak with the Abbess.

Sister Agnes knocked lightly on the oak door of the chamber.

"Pray you enter." The reply in courtly French was soft but assured and the tone was that of someone used to being obeyed. The Abbess Constanza de San Andreas de Anroyo sat on the window seat of the guest chamber, using the muted light to study a parchment. Beside her, the young novice, quill in hand, was scribing a document.

Both nuns bowed their heads in obeisance. Joan frowned involuntarily, hoping the Abbess hadn't noticed. She had expected to find the Abbess Constanza and her novice knelt on the Pre Dieu, deep in prayerful devotion. That they were not but studying documents and scribing surprised her.

Sister Agnes came from a good family. She was a de Lascy whose ancestors came to England with Duke William and who held many manors on the Welsh borderlands. Agnes was fluent in Anglo-Norman French and noted that her courtly French was impeccable despite the Abbess being from Iberia, a convent northwest of Burgos. Joan gave the older nun a slight push in the back to prompt her to speak.

"My Lady A-A- Abbess," Agnes began, trying to find the words to make this request. "Our community has been plunged into turmoil; Our Lady Prioress and her sub-Prioress have left us, disappeared without word. On behalf of our community, I beseech you to help us"

The Abbess Constanza looked up from her parchment, frowned and reflected on what the older sister had said.

"You do say your Lady Prioress and her deputy have gone, and you know not where? When was this?"

Sister Joan gave a hurried summary of the events of the past few days as Abbess Constanza listened intently.

"Have you yet sent word to Father Abbot?"

"Nay, we have not," replied Sister Agnes.

"Pray you to tell why? He needs must know of this."

"There are other things, Mother Abbess." Sister Joan interjected. "Not days since, a young maid went missing from the orchard, the niece of Sister Agnes here."

"Disappeared? Your niece?"

"Aye. Just disappeared," replied Agnes.

Sister Joan shuffled on her feet, anxious to add to what Agnes had said. "And there was the dreadful death of Sire Roger, our confessor, but some weeks since," she added.

"Tis true," Agnes was nodding in agreement. "I afear that Satan walks through St Mary's. That is why I have not told Father Abbot and the reason why I implore you to intercede to help us."

Agnes's eyes filled with tears as she regarded the woman she hoped would be their saviour. Studying her closely for the first time, Agnes realised that the Abbess was barely the age of Sister Joan, very young to hold such a high position. That suggested she was of a high-born family with influence in the Church.

Although the Abbess hailed from far-off Iberia, Agnes noted that she didn't have the sun hue common to people from that region. Her small face was pale, with a perfect nose and sharp blue eyes that seemed to take in everything and everyone around her. A black Benedictine habit reached down to the ground, but it appeared tailored and showed off her slim figure. Her white coif, secured by a perfect veil, framed her face, but a lock of soft red hair had escaped across her pale cheek. A might uncommon, thought Agnes, as it was the practice in England for nuns to have their heads shaven so that they might be closer to God.

But the Abbess Constanza de San Andreas de Anroyo exuded authority and calm. She now stood, deep in thought, before the two sisters.

"How many sisters are present in the convent?"

"We are six," replied Agnes.

"And afflicted women?"

"They are just nine souls."

The Abbess rolled her lower lip over her teeth, deep in thought.

"I will stay my journey for a time to help you." Joan's face relaxed and she left out a visible breath at the Abbess' words.

"There is an obligation to inform Father Abbot, which must be done with haste. I shall do that for you." The Abbess turned to Agnes. "I wish you to convene the sisters in cloister and I shall address them. Afterwards, I shall speak with the lost souls."

Agnes and Joan thanked the Abbess profusely and left to convene their fellow sisters in cloister.

Agnes couldn't let go of a nagging thought as she departed the chamber. It entered her head when she first met the young, confident Abbess. And the lock of soft red hair that escaped from beneath the veiled coif. There was something, not alarming or concerning, but precisely what that was, she couldn't say.

Ж

Chapter Eleven

The Abbey of St Mary de Pré, Watling Street, close-by St Albans,
May 1277.

THE YOUNG MAID, the Lady Jeanne de Lascy, had been missing for nearly four days when Simon Lowys rode north on Watling Street toward the Abbey of St Mary de Pré. His thoughts turned to the lovely, warm summer morning, with the sun beating upon him from a cloudless sky. A thin trail of sweat trickled slowly down his forehead, stinging his eyes and dust from the King's Highway clung to his damp skin.

But Simon was not in a good mood. Ever since he had left Westminster, his ears had been assaulted by the non-stop questioning and comments from an enthusiastic Robert de Berdesfold. Their departure had been delayed by de Berdesfold having to change his clothes. Simon refused to let him wear the bright, garish garments of the court and found him a plain brown linen shift and cote, which the youth donned reluctantly. De Berdesfold sulked as far as the village of Charing and from there onwards, words tumbled from his mouth.

"Have you been on missions for Her Grace before, Master Lowys? What is the Queen like? Have you ever met His Grace the King?

How far before we reach the old Roman road? Have you been to St Albans before?" His questions went on and on.

Once on the Roman road, de Berdesfold appeared concerned about Wolf heads. "Have you ever been attacked, Master Lowys? Would that copse ahead be a likely ambush point for Wolf heads? How far to the next village? Should I draw my sword?"
Most of de Berdesfold's questions drew silence from the Royal Nuncio.
Simon snapped back at the youth where the old road crossed a broad ford at the village of Darnells.

"God's teeth, boy! Hold your words; you are hurting my ears." He immediately regretted saying it, but the youth was silent for a few miles until they entered the vill of Park, when his questions resumed as if no ill words had crossed between them.

They skirted the town of St Albans, travelling through St Michael's village, where Simon's thoughts returned to a night the previous year when he had faced death, only for his assailants to be slain by a mysterious saviour. Isabella la Rus saved his life that night, although he was unaware of it at the time. She would save his life again that summer as they battled the conspiracy against the King by a coven of witches, the Daughters of the Shadows. Isabella, the enigmatic King's agent known as '*le Reynard*', had occupied his thoughts for many nights since then. But she had disappeared from his life despite his trying to locate her.

Word was sent ahead to the Convent of St Mary de Pré to expect him. But, the Chancery had been careful not to indicate the purpose of his visit. News that a royal official would descend upon any religious house was rarely well received. At St Michael's Church, Simon halted to water the horses in the cool water of the ford on the River Ver.
Both man and youth splashed water over their faces to refresh themselves.

"Now, young Robert," Simon tried to be earnest. "When we reach the convent, it is important that all you do is listen and watch. Do you understand?"

"Aye, Master Lowys, but I mayhaps be able to help you in your…" Simon cut him short. "Listen and watch, no more! Later, when we are out of earshot, I shall give you a chance to ask me questions; one or two questions, but you must resist the temptation to speak and let me do my job."

The Royal Nuncio looked directly at the young man, inviting a reply.

"Aye, Master Lowys," he beamed with enthusiasm.

It was but a short journey of a few miles from St Michael's to St Mary's, and they arrived at the weather-worn gates shortly after the bells rang for Nones.

A loud shout came from within a small, run-down wooden gatehouse beside a wicket-gate.

"God give you good day, good sires." A small, wiry man of middle years stepped out of the cool, shadowed hut. The man gave a bow. "I am Jonnas, Keeper of the Gate." He said in a west-country drawl. "How can I help thee?"

Simon gave a small saddle bow. "I am Simon Lowys, Royal Nuncio to Her Grace the Queen."

Jonnas peered wide-eyed at Lowys as if his gaze could test the integrity of the Nuncio's word.

"I heard told that a King's Man was coming, but….." he tailed off.

"But, what?" Simon was intrigued.

"But we have had some problems these past days, Meister." He chewed on his lower lip as if keen to say something more. "What I cannot say, but the new Abbess will tell all. I shall get one of the obedientiaries to take thee there."

"New Abbess?" John of Berwick had told Simon that Prioress Hilda would be expecting him. Now, the gatekeeper Jonnas spoke of a new Abbess.

"You mean Prioress, do you not Jonnas?"

"Nay, Master Lowys. Our Prioress," he hesitated, "She is not here."

"But she was told to expect me."

"Aye, as maybes Meister, but tis a visiting Abbess in charge now, since ...."

He paused. "Nay. I should not say more. I will fetch Sister Agnes and she will tell all, if she can."

Jonnas atte Gate grabbed the bridle of both horses and led beasts and riders into the outer courtyard before closing the gate behind them.

Simon swung one leg across his saddle and deftly dismounted. Robert de Berdesfold tried the same manoeuvre but slid clumsily off his mount, landing in a heap on the cobbles. Jonnas tied the palfreys by the reins to a metal ring in the shaded outer wall.

"Do rub them down for me and give a feed of oats, good man," Simon patted his palfrey's neck and passed a coin to Jonnas, who gave a grateful bow.

"Thank thee, Master Lowys. I shall fetch Sister Agnes for you. If you do wait here, I will be but a short time." Jonnas turned and walked quickly towards a stone building in the far corner of the complex that had seen better days. He climbed a set of badly worn stone steps attached to the outside and slipped through a door.

"Wait here with the mounts," Simon instructed Robert. "Use your eyes and tell me later what you see."

"Tis a Lazar House, Master Lowys; will I not see Lazars and nuns?"

Simon fixed him with a hard stare. "Just tell me later all you see. Spare no detail, however small."

It was but a short while later that Jonnas reappeared, walking with head bowed behind a black-garbed nun of middle years, who strode briskly towards the new arrivals.

There were no pleasantries. Ignoring de Berdesfold, she looked Simon up and down. "You are the King's Man?" Her tone and pursed lips suggested she was not impressed.

"I am Sister Agnes, one of our obedientiaries. I shall take you to meet with our Pri...." She stopped mid-sentence. "Our Abbess. The Abbess Constanza."

"Your Abbess?" inquired Simon, puzzled by this development.
Sister Agnes appeared flustered. "She will explain all, Master Lowys. Do you please follow me?"

Leaving de Berdesfold with Jonnas atte Gate, Simon matched Sister Agnes's urgent pace towards the external stairs, ascending to the first floor. She opened two solid oak doors and they passed through into a long, poorly lit chamber, sparse with furniture but heavy with the aroma of wax and lavender. Sister Agnes bade Simon wait at a third door and knocked loudly before entering. In less time than it took to say a Paternoster, she returned.

"This is our solar, the receiving parlour of our Prioress. Abbess," she corrected herself. "You may enter."

"Your Prioress, but…..?" Simon began, but Sister Agnes was already through the door and not listening. As he followed, matching the nun's brisk pace, he pondered what she had just told him. St Mary's was a priory, a junior house to an abbey. An Abbess ran the latter, a Prioress, junior in status to an Abbess, headed a priory.

The Prioress's lofty solar was gloomy save for an open, tall west-facing window paned with a thin transparent horn that cast a waxy light into the chamber. Not glass then, thought Simon: a sure sign of a poor house. Oaken panels with a sheen of age lined the walls on three sides, with the window wall covered in a peeling limewash. A large, framed seat with its straw pallet lay on the far side and beside the window was a wide desk scattered with parchments, on which were ink and scribing implements. Two heavy oak chairs with soft, embroidered cushions lay on either side. Thin, fragrant beeswax candles threw dancing shadows across the wood-clad walls.

Sister Agnes departed without a word, closing the door firmly behind her with a loud click of the latch. Clearly, there was no need for the new Abbess to be chaperoned, thought Simon.
He remained close by the door, awaiting a formal introduction and unsure of the protocol when conversing with an Abbess.

She stood beside the large window, parchment in one hand, her back to Simon and appeared to be gazing out onto the open fields beyond the abbey walls. The Abbess Constanza, in her black Benedictine habit, was a slightly built woman. Turned away from him, Simon could not tell her age, but she was an Abbess, which spoke of years of experience and devotion. He coughed gently, seeking to draw her attention.

"God give you good day, Mother Abbess." He waited, hoping for a response, but none came.

Simon cleared his throat. "I apologise for the disturbance to your routine, Mother Abbess. I am Simon Lowys, Royal Nuncio to My Lady the Queen and I am here at her command. I needs must have words with you about important matters pertaining to this house." He paused, adding, "Not least perhaps about why I am meeting with you and not the Prioress Hilda, who was expecting me?"

Stood a dozen paces from him and still facing the window, her back to him, Abbess Constanza de San Andreas de Anroyo raised and tilted her head as if acknowledging his words, though her focus seemed to lay on a world beyond. A heavy silence reigned. Simon waited, unsure whether to repeat himself.

At length, she straightened, her black woollen habit rustling as she moved, swivelling slowly to face the Royal Nuncio. Deep blue, mesmerising eyes set firmly on him. He stood transfixed. Simon knew those eyes, that face, the pale pink skin and the lock of soft red hair which was forever spilling from the white coif under her veil. His mouth went dry.

The Abbess took soft steps towards him, her gaze never leaving his. A bright smile broke on her lips.

"Tis good to see you again, Master Lowys," said Isabella la Rus.

Ж

Chapter Twelve

Benedictine Convent of St Mary de Pré Watling Street, Hertfordshire, May 1277.

THE ABBESS CONSTANZA de San Andreas de Anroyo? You have taken the veil these months since I last saw you?"

She gave a melodic laugh. "Nay, I have not had that calling yet. I am pursuing Benuic, the assassin. Tis little wonder that he avoided detection these years since '*he*' is '*she*'. We now know Benuic is a woman."

Simon's eyes widened with surprise. "A woman, you say?"

"Aye. She fled the Abbey after the assassination attempt on the Queen failed and took ship to Boulogne using the alias of Abbess of San Andreas de Anroyo. I am seeking those who helped her by adopting the identity she did in the hope that I might flush out the traitors."

Simon could not disguise his confusion. "But how is it that you find yourself here at St Mary's acting as the Prioress?"

"Ah, tis a tale indeed. There was word that a man of the Church, who has supported the traitor de Montfort, had stayed here on the Feast of the Annunciation, as a guest of his cousin, the Prioress."

"And you were to question the Prioress?"

"Nay, to observe and discover what is afoot. But the Prioress and her deputy fled from here upon our arrival."

"Why would she do that?"

"Tis mighty strange indeed. But our arrival caused her great vexation, and she upped and left, afearing of the reason for our arrival. This convent is in much disarray and the sisters are fearful that Satan walks these walls."

Isabella wiped a hand across her white veil, pushing the lock of red hair back into place.

"On the business of Her Grace, the Queen." Simon briefly explained the disappearance of the maid, the Lady Jeanne, days before the death of Sire Roger and his despatch to St Albans.

"Sister Agnes told me of her niece and of the slaying of their priest. This is a place of great misfortune," suggested Isabella. "The maid does disappear; the Prioress flees upon my arrival and their confessor was slain in his own church some weeks since."

" Are these events separate misfortunes, or perchance they are linked in some way?" he asked.

A light knock at the door interrupted the conversation as a young nun wearing the white veil of a novice, her head low in obeisance, entered. As Simon turned to look, the young nun halted, wide-eyed in recognition.

"Why, Master Lowys," she exclaimed in surprised excitement. She rushed towards him, her face flushed, before recalling her current situation posing as a novice.

She wished to throw her arms around him in a greeting. But, composing herself, Alia Parys, '*Sister Mathilt*', bowed her head reverently. "Tis pleasing to see you, Master Lowys."

Simon Lowys grinned, as surprised as she. He had last seen Alia at the house of Mistress Heacham the previous summer. That was also the last occasion he had seen Isabella la Rus, when she was going by the name of Isabelle de Brun. He had sought her out at the inn she owned in St Albans only to discover not only was she not there, but the Wheatsheaf Inn, which he believed she had inherited from her late husband Thomas de Brun, was in the possession of the real Isabelle de Brun. That discovery had vexed him greatly and the passing months had done little to soften the blow. He still had no idea how she had pulled off the deception.

"I sought you out this August past at the Wheatsheaf in St Albans town." He hadn't intended to blurt it out, as it made him appear petulant. "And I met Mistress Isabelle de Brun."

His jaw tensed; his voice showed hurt.

"Fie Master Lowys." Isabella stepped back from him. Her expression composed and revealing little. "You know what work I do for His Grace the King."

"But your words were not true to me. I believed that you were Mistress de Brun and I went to find you."
"Master Lowys, do you look on me now and see a foreign Abbess? I have many roles and names in my work for His Grace. Do recall what I once told you: what you see with your eyes and what you know are not always the same."

The enigmatic reply was so typical of Isabella la Rus. The King's Intelligencer, known as le Reynard, operated in the shadows, her true identity known to just a few around the King. Simon owed his life to this woman, who had saved him from death on more than one occasion. Her small, pretty face, chiselled nose, thin, inviting lips and eyes the colour of a summer sky were truly alluring. Isabella las Rus was a woman who would always enchant men much as she had captivated Simon.
He had looked and failed to find her; now he was once more in the company of Isabella la Rus if indeed that was her name.
"Pray do say what brings you to St Mary's," Alia inquired. "Tis not a place I would expect to see a King's Man."
As briefly as he could, Simon explained the disappearance of the Lady Jeanne and the request from Queen Eleanor to come to St Albans to find her. Alia's eyes met Isabella's, each sharing the same thought.

"It seems that these are the days for disappearances," suggested Isabella, "but of all, the vanishing of a young maid is most troubling."

65

Ж

____

Chapter Thirteen

The Lazar House within the Convent of St Mary de Pré on Watling Street, May 1277.

ACROSS THE COURTYARD, Simon caught de Berdesfold's gaze. He inclined his head, indicating that the younger man should follow him. Glad of anything that wasn't attending to the horses, de Berdesfold walked purposefully towards his would-be mentor.

"Did you see anything amiss?" Simon's hushed tone could be heard by de Berdesfold alone.

"Nay, Master Lowys, twas all quiet. I saw but one nun and no Lazars."

"Naught else?" de Berdesfold shook his head.

"Did you look up?"

"Up, Master Lowys." de Berdesfold's forehead wrinkled in puzzlement.

"Aye, man. Look up and tell me what you see."

Robert de Berdesfold scanned the abbey buildings, his eyes squinting in the sun. Finally, he fixed on a lone man atop a scaffold, repairing the roof.

"I see a common labourer fixing tiles."

"And that tells you what?"

"That the roof leaks," suggested de Berdesfold nervously.

Simon harumphed. "I see a single mason repairing a roof badly in need of repair," suggested Simon. "One mason, which says that this is a poor community who cannot afford much-needed repairs."

"I now see Master Lowys," said de Berdesfold.

"Good. Now, I am going to speak with the women of the house. Do not be scared, for their affliction is not catching. But you must be observant. See if any avert their gaze or give any act that might say they lie."

One of the sisters, he knew not which one, had assembled all of the Lazar women in the cloister. The women sat close to one another; their ragged garments pulled tight to cover their disfigurement in front of this royal agent. One sister, Joan, sat with them for reassurance.

Simon briefly explained his purpose in being at St Mary's and asked if any of the women had seen the Lady Jeanne de Lascy.

Simon regarded the assembled women; some had their hoods drawn close across their faces, showing the redness of eye that characterised Lazars. Others, less embarrassed, allowed him to see their pock-marked, ulcerous faces. It became evident to Simon that one woman saw herself as their leader.

Brimlaf seemed to be the oldest among them. She did not seek to hide her disfigurement from Simon, although, at first, de Berdesfold recoiled from her, requiring Simon to elbow him in the ribs.

"Observe!" He hissed at de Berdesfold.

"Nay, Meister, I saw nothing and no one has spoken that they saw any maid." Brimlaf looked to her fellow inmates. "Did any see a maid these days past."

"In the orchard, was it?" A west-country drawl from another of the women lent heavily on the word.

Hooded heads shook. None had seen the Lady Jeanne; no one had witnessed her disappearance.

"Do any of you have reason to ever go to the orchard?" Simon inquired.

"Rarely, outside of the autumn harvest," Brimlaf replied.

Simon began to think that no purpose would be served by them remaining at St Mary's, so he made to leave.

"Etran…ger." It emerged as a guttural wail. All seated looked towards the edge of the group and the ragged figure of Esmie, her shawl pulled tight about her head.

"*Estranger*!" Simon picked up on her word.

"Strangers?" He addressed Esmie. "Did you see strangers?"

"Pay her no heed, Master Lowys," interjected Brimlaf. "She is touched, and her words do make no sense."

"What is her name?" Simon asked of Brimlaf.

"She is Esmie. But as I do say, she is not well in the head."

"Enfants. Gitanes. They taked her." Esmie's words came out as a wail. "Come up on her an' taked her."

Thoughts raced through Simon's mind. Had this woman seen the maid? Was she saying that the maid had been taken by strangers, children or gypsies?

"She has seen something," Simon suggested, but the others shook their heads.

"Nay, King's Man, pay her no heed. She knows not what she says."

"Esmie is possessed, Master Lowys. She lives in a world inside her head," opined Sister Joan. But Simon held on to the sliver of a chance that Esmie had witnessed the disappearance of the Lady Jeanne.

"What strangers Esmie? What children? Gypsies? Do you mean gypsy children? What did they look like?"

"*Jeunes etranger. Jeunes filles.*"

"Strangers? Young girls? Was she taken by young girls, Esmie? "

No answer was forthcoming from the hooded Esmie, just low guttural moans.

Sister Joan continued to urge Simon not to listen to Esmie's ramblings, but no one else had seen anything. Esmie alone appeared to have witnessed the abduction.

"Estranger. Estranger. Estranger." She kept repeating the word, locked in a world of her own that allowed no one else to enter.

Ж

____

Chapter Fourteen

The Abbesses chamber, Convent of St Mary de Pré on Watling Street, May 1277.

THERE WERE MORE ROLLED-UP documents on the large oak table in the Prioress' Parlour when Simon Lowys returned. Isabella la Rus and Alia were busy reading each before tossing them aside.

Alia picked up another rolled parchment and beneath it was a small scribed rectangular sheet with a broken green wax seal on one side.

"Mistress," she called out to Isabella and Simon watched as the King's Intelligencer glided across the room to her assistant.

Alia handed the small pale grey sheet to Isabella. "What is it, Mistress? Tis not a parchment."

Isabella scanned the document. "Nay, Alia," her voice held a note of excitement. "Not parchment; tis is what is called paper. I have heard word of it being made in Toscana, but tis might expensive."

"And the writing on it, Mistress, what tongue is that?"

"No tongue, Alia. Master Lowys, come, what do you make of this?" Simon was unaware that she had seen him enter. He took the paper and rubbed it gently between his thumb and forefinger.

"I have never seen the like of this." He studied the writing on the page. "It would appear to be a code, a simple one, perhaps?"

He returned the flimsy document to Isabella, who looked closely at the wording.

"See, tis but a simple cypher. Do you see how numbers can be substituted for letters based on their order in the alphabet?" Simon hadn't picked up on that, but he could see what she meant once she pointed it out.

"In words, the letters that are most oft found at the start of words are t, a, o, d and w. Do see here." She pointed out the short message contained no such letters.

"But do see here," she moved closer to Simon, and he drew in her exotic aroma of sandalwood. "This word of two letters, if it is a simple cypher; II is likely a B and V would be the letter E."

It took them little time to decipher the simple code. *Royal intelligencer privy to the secret. Be aware of a stranger.*

Simon was pleased with their efforts and, more so, for spending time so close to Isabella.

"Do see here, Master Lowys." She turned over the rectangle of paper and indicated the green wax seal. "This seal may provide a clue." The paper was the span of a hand and had been folded inwards from each corner, with the edges brought together in the middle and secured by the green-wax seal.

Isabella called Alia to come over and examine the paper. The three peered at the broken green wax.

Isabella pointed a slender finger. "This seal may tell us much. See here the imprint of a word, *gatio*."

"Tis no word at all," Alia said. "Does it have meaning for you, Master Lowys?"

The royal Nuncio shook his head. "Tis no word I know."

"You have the right of it, Alia," Isabella laid the paper flat on the table, "but I suspect a fragment of wax is missing. The word is not '*gatio*' but likely '*Legatio*,' a Papal Legate."

Simon shook his head. "Nay, I cannot believe a Papal Envoy could be involved."

"That is not what I am suggesting," Isabella's tone was brusque. "Whosoever sent this had access to a Legate's seal. Twas either stolen from or…"

"…was sent by one close to this Legate." Alia finished the sentence. "Though how did they know a Royal Intelligencer was to come here?" she asked.

Isabella drew in a breath, her lips tight. "You have the right of it Alia. Someone in the Chancery found out and alerted them."

A note of alarm sounded in Simon's voice. "If there is a spy in the Chancery, we must tell My Lord of Berwick that you are discovered."

"Nay, Master Lowys, not I. Do see this note." She lifted the paper and pointed at the translation she had scribed beneath the message. "It says, *Royal intelligencer privy to the secret.* That could mean you or me. But that it says, *Be aware of a stranger,* does show that the spy does not know the identity of the intelligencer, or they would have given a more direct warning."

"But the Lady Prioress fled upon your arrival."

"Aye, that she did. She took me as the stranger she had been warned of, but this message could equally apply to you, Master Lowys. See, the message says stranger, not strangers."

"So, you say one of us is found out."

"Aye, but that does not mean we cannot pursue the clues we possess."

"Mistress. This message," Alia interrupted. "See, it was done in haste, brief and rushed."

Alia showed the broken seal. "See how the seal has been affixed to the wax in haste. Tis to one side surely the sealing was rushed."

"You have the right of it, Alia. We must discover when it was delivered here and by whom?"

Isabella toyed with the green wax seal, tracing her fingers around its broken edge. As she did so, her lower lip curled across her front teeth, deep in thought.

"Green wax. Green wax." She was oblivious to the others around her, a thought forming in her mind.

"I know this seal. At least I have seen it before." She let out a slow breath. "But 'tis not good. For surtees, it is the green wax of a Papal Legate and there is but one of those in England, Bernardo Ravennate."

"A Papal Legate?" Simon expressed surprise. "How can it be? You know of him, this Ravennate?"

"I have heard word of his arrival at Court many months since, but I know not of him other than it was one of his senior deacons who had come to this place to meet with the Prioress. Twas his trail Alia and I were pursuing."

"Could this Papal Legate be behind the abduction of the Lady Jeanne?" asked Simon.

Isabella frowned and shook her head.

"Nay, tis most unlikely. What reason would there be?" She lightly bit her lower lip, her face a mask to her thoughts.

"We must discover more, " she paused, setting down the paper, "and discover how all are linked. We have the disappearance of the maid, the flight of the Abbess, the slaying of the priest, and this cypher message."

"Mayhaps they are not linked at all," suggested Simon.

Isabella regarded him with a long, fixed look. "Perhaps… Perhaps. But we must ensure that we pursue all to eliminate any connection."

Her eyes sparkled and Simon saw a familiar look. "Mayhaps, our inquiries are destined to cross paths once again, Master Lowys."

ж

Chapter Fifteen

The Refectory of the Benedictine Convent of St Mary de Pré, May 1277.

THE DAYS WERE STILL a month from midsummer and the light was still good in the hours after Vespers. Simon had requested to meet with Sister Agnes to discover what had happened when her sister visited, and Lady Jeanne had gone missing. They sat at opposite ends of the large table in the Prioresses chamber, with Isabella, the Abbess Constanza de San Andreas de Anroyo, seated between them.

The horn-covered window was thrown open, allowing the warm sun's rays to penetrate deep into the chamber, filling it with golden light. Simon couldn't help but regard Isabella sitting with her back to the window, giving her the appearance of a heavenly angel.

"Sister Agnes, I have been sent here at the command of My Lady, the Queen," Simon explained his reason for being at St Mary's.

"You needs must tell me all that happened the day your sister, the Lady Hawise, visited you."

In her persona as the Abbess Constanza, Isabella was there as a chaperone. She had discussed with Simon whether to reveal her identity to Agnes but decided, for the time being, to continue to play out the part of the Abbess.

"It was the Feast of St Urbanus, Sunday last. My brother's sister, Lady Matilda, had written to say she wished to visit. Twas a long time since I had seen my niece, Jeanne." Thin tears streaked down Sister Agnes' pale face as she spoke.

"Twas a joy to see my sister and niece. They came just after Nones and Jonnas, our gatekeeper, was expecting their arrival and showed them to the cloister. I came upon them and there was much rejoicing. Matilda and I spent the hours before Sext in discussion and then we three went to the chapel for the service."

"Forgive my intrusion," said Simon, "but what did you and the Lady Matilda discuss?"

Agnes shook her head. "Naught of great importance. The health of the family mostly."

"And the young maid, the Lady Jeanne. What was she about while you were in discussion?"

Agnes paused, reflecting. "She…. She, er, she was with us in the cloister, looking around. She was not interested in our talk. She is but young."

"She was with you when you went to the chapel for Nones?"

"Aye, she was. I was with my sisters below the altar and Matilda and Jeanne shared a prie-dieu at the front."

"You did not see her leave?" inquired Simon.

"Nay. We sang '*Dues in adjutorium,*' the '*Kyrie Eleison*' and a response. She left the chapel with her mother."

"And afterwards?"

"After Sext, there is some time when the sisters may reflect. Some choose to rest or reflect. I went with Matilda and Jeanne to the orchard. Tis pleasant there at this time. The fruits are beginning to set and there is a gentle shade from the heat of the sun."

"And the Lady Jeanne?"

"She was with us. The orchard is large and somewhat misshapen in the manner of the letter L. Matilda and I sat beneath a large medlar tree and Jeanne was wandering amongst the trees. We had sight of her and then…."

"Then?" Simon prompted her.

"Then she was beyond our sight. But we did not afear, for the orchard is walled."

"How high is the wall?"

"Tis a few inches beyond the height of a very tall man and made of flint stone," replied Agnes.

"And is there a gate from the orchard to the road?" It was the first occasion Isabella had spoken.

"Aye, there is a wicket gate that leads to a track down to the river, but tis always barred from the inside."

Isabella leaned in towards Agnes. "And was that wicket gate in view from where you sat?"

"Nay. Tis beyond where the orchard bends away from view."

"Did you see anyone in the orchard, or hear voices, mayhaps?"

"Nay, we saw no one and thought nothing of Jeanne being out of sight, for the orchard is enclosed. I heard no voices, just Jeanne singing to herself."

Agnes' eyes widened in recognition of a memory forgotten. "And her singing stopped. It stopped. And I thought I heard children's voices, though I gave it no heed."

Children's voices! Simon picked up on what Agnes had said.

"You do say you heard children's voices. Did you see any other children?"

"Nay, now I think on it, Matilda and I were reminiscing about the Lord Gilbert and in the background, Jeanne's singing stopped and another child, a different voice, spoke and then another."

"Was it a boy or a girl you heard?" asked Simon.

Agnes' brow frowned, deep in thought. "A girl's voice. Twas a girl's voice and more than one, I think."

"And when did you afear that the Lady Jeanne had gone missing?"

"Twas later, within that same hour, but we thought the orchard safe. We called for her and when we got no reply, we searched the orchard and then raised the alarm."

"Was the Hue and Cry raised?"

"Nay. This is a Lazar House and no one will come near. Our gatekeeper did a search and a few of the tenants joined him, but no sign of the maid was discovered."

"And the Lady Matilda?"

"She returned to Westminster the following morn, in great distress.

Ж

Chapter Sixteen

The Orchard, the Convent of St Mary de Pré, the beginning of June 1277.

ISABELLA SAT AT THE OAK DESK, her hand moving in deft, precise strokes between the parchment and inkhorn in front of her. As she drafted a communique for Abbot Roger de Norton at St Albans, Simon made his way to the cloisters and then through a gate that led out onto the orchard. Only his writ as a King's Man allowed him entry into what was a female domain.

He was surprised at how large the orchard was. Apple, pear, medlar, damson, quince and many other trees had shed their colourful spring blossom and thrown out fruits that promised a fine harvest later in the year. He could imagine the young maid finding great enjoyment playing under their branches. He had gone one hundred paces from the cloister gate when the orchard turned sharply towards the river. Those nearby the cloister gate could not see anyone here.

At length, he came upon the river gate, a small but solid oak wicket gate recessed into the tall wall, the combined height of a man and a child. Two iron hooks on either side were embedded into the masonry to accept a stout oak beam to keep out intruders, but the beam lay on the ground. Simon pulled at the gate and noiselessly, it swung open. Beyond, a lush water meadow ran gently down towards the River Ver. The grass was ankle-deep and a narrow, vague pathway heading down towards the river showed where feet had recently trampled the new growth.

Simon began to apply his thoughts to what had occurred. He imagined that this was where the Lady Jeanne left the Abbey. The beaten-down grass suggested that she was not alone, and the narrowness of the flattened grass path suggested children, not adults. They left by the wicket gate, but how did the intruders gain access to the orchard? He peered around. It was most unlikely they had come through the main entrance and past Jonnas atte Gate. Which meant, he thought, they had to have entered from the outside. He carefully examined the wall, heading along its exterior towards the cloister and then, discovering nothing that would explain how they entered, he went the other way, parallel to the river and the old Roman Highway. Simon found what he had been searching for where the wall turned to face the old town in the distance. The outer flint wall was in a state of disrepair and flints had fallen or been prised away from the weather-worn mortar, allowing footholds for an intruder to climb the high wall. It would have been simple for a child to scamper up and over open the wicket gate to allow accomplices inside.

What perplexed him was how they had known the Lady Jeanne was here? Had she and her mother been followed to the Abbey, or was it opportunistic? That was unlikely; a child in a convent was not to be expected. Was she seized for a reason? Who knew she would be here? Although she was taken by children, he thought it most unlikely that ones so young had planned this and moreover, what was their purpose?

He wondered if this was somehow a plot directed at Her Grace, the Queen, but quickly dismissed the idea. The Lady Matilda de Lascy was a sister of one of the Queen's Ladies, so, not someone directly connected to the Court. It made no sense to him. He looked down beyond the meadow to the River Ver. Had they taken her by boat? If so, that suggested grown men were involved, for children rowing a boat would be noticed. As he walked back through the orchard, Simon Lowys accepted that he had no explanation for the maid's disappearance and was completely at a loss regarding finding her.

Ж

Chapter Seventeen

The Abbesses Solar, the Convent of St Mary de Pré, June 1277.

IT SEEMS WE HAVE but one real clue." Isabella la Rus addressed her two companions.

"The involvement of children in Lady Jeanne's disappearance and the possible link of the Papal Legate in the absconding of the Prioress and her Obedientiary "

"Tis hard to believe that such a man of God could be somehow involved," suggested Alia.

Simon snorted derision. "I have crossed paths with such men of men of God. The Church has its share of rotten fruit."

Isabella turned to look at the royal nuncio, her face impassive but her deep blue eyes sparking. "The Holy Church is much challenged. Tis a difficult time."

"Why difficult? enquired Alia.

"Because the year past was a time of calamity for the Papacy," Isabella turned to Simon.

" I had heard that there were two Papal elections," replied Simon, wishing he had paid more attention to the gossip at the Chancery.

She laughed brightly. "Nay, not two but three elections this year past." She corrected him. "The Holy Father Gregory X died at the end of January, more than a year since and was succeeded by the Dominican Bishop of Ostia who took the name Innocent V, but he died after midsummer. Twas the Papal Legate in England ten years since who succeeded him, Ottobuono de Fieschi who became Adrian V."

"So, three Popes," said Alia.

"Nay, four Popes," Isabella corrected her. "Pope Adrian died of illness before being ordained as a priest and another conclave was held. They chose the Archbishop of Braga, who took the name John XXI."

Simon mentally chided himself for not knowing all of this. As a Royal Nuncio and servant of the Queen, he thought these were the things he should be aware of.

"But he has died, but weeks since, on the Feast of St Baudelius," added Isabella. "Twas tragic and he died somewhere well known to you, Master Lowys."

"Known to me?" enquired Simon.

"Aye! Twas in the Papal Palace at Viterbo. A roof in his chamber did collapse upon him and he succumbed to his injuries."

The mention of that damned hillside town brought back sad memories for the Royal Nuncio of another death six years before, a murder in a church he had witnessed and been unable to prevent.

"Viterbo is accursed," he suggested. "It holds no good memories for me." Alia noticed his mouth tensing in the sadness of thought.

"But we have yet another Pope?" asked Simon, keen to move on from the subject of the assassination of the lord Henry.

Isabella also read his face and the angst the memories stirred in him. "Nay," she said, "The Cardinals are yet in Viterbo and cannot agree, so there is no news on a successor. Yet there is a link. While the old Pope John lived, the Inquisitor Cardinal Orsini held power at the Papal Court."

"Orsini?" Recognition registered on Simon's face.

"Orsini! Orsini is in league with the snake Charles of Anjou and de Montfort. His hand was there in the slaying of my lord Henry of Almain in the Church at Viterbo these years past."

"Aye! Now his man is the new Papal Legate in England, Bernardo Ravennate."

"Do you say," the words came out slowly as Simon thought through the implications.

"And I am told Ravennate has a house nearby at Westwick given to him by the Abbot. It lies beyond the river close by the Roman road south."

Simon wondered how Isabella was so well informed, but he shook his head.

"We cannot be sure that all these things connect." He remained unconvinced.

"Nay, you have the right of it, Master Lowys, but consider what presents us." Isabella picked up the inkhorn from the desk and placed it on the open parchment.

"We have here the maid gone missing from the convent." Isabella lifted the paper message with the green wax seal.

"Here we have the coded message sent in haste to the Lady Prioress." She then placed the rustic clay lucerna lamp beside it. "And the disappearance of the Lady Prioress."

"We have, too, your presence here, Master Lowys and mine, a consequence of trailing the assassin Benuic. And the arrival of the Legate in the region."

"Aye," he said thoughtfully, "all our paths lead us here, to this Lazar House."

"And there is the death of that priest in his Church last year," added Alia. "Surely 'tis no coincidence, these things happening now, but they all appear separate. Can we be sure they connect?"

"The only way to be sure," said Simon ", is to visit this Papal Legate and discover what he knows.

Ж

—————

Chapter Eighteen

The Manor of Westwick, Hertfordshire, June 1277.

THERE WAS DANGER NEARBY, nothing that could be seen, but she sensed it. She froze, her reddish-brown coat blending seamlessly with the lush undergrowth of the woodland around her. Excited, predatory eyes gazed upon her. She picked up the scent of the hunters on a gentle breeze wafting through the verdant canopy above her. Her choice was to stand or run. She gave a sharp wheeze through the nose and never heard the hiss and the rush through the air of the arrow that took her life in the forest that morning.

"An excellent arrow, Giovanni." It was said with sincerity, although Bernardo Ravennate, the Papal Legate to the court of King Edward, first of that name, wished he was capable of such accuracy.

Beside him, his Steward, Giovanni di Bologna, was thinking the same, inwardly pleased at the clean kill of the young doe. Giovanni always hunted deer with small two-bladed arrowheads, always well sharpened, five fingers long and four fingers between the barbs. It reflected his attention to detail in all things, a trait that the Legate greatly appreciated.

"The next one will be yours, Your Grace," he said.

The huntsman and his apprentice were already at the corpse of the slain deer, his verderer tying the legs to a pole to carry it back to their cart at the far side of the woods.

Bernardo Ravennate enjoyed hunting. He loved the chase and the stalking of the beasts, but he just wished his maker had given him a better aim. The woodland and forests of England were the preserve of the King, but as the Papal representative in England, he had royal dispensation to hunt deer on six occasions during the year. Today was one such time.

His Steward, Giovanni, accompanied him everywhere, serving as a manservant, personal bodyguard and enforcer. Skilled with a hunting bow and an excellent swordsman, Giovanni was a battle-hardened veteran of the violent city-state wars of northern Italy.

As the huntsman and his boy walked past them with the doe trussed to a pole, Giovanni placed his hand on the animal and silently gave thanks to God for his aim. It was an illogical act for a man such as he, but Giovanni did not wish ever to miss, not for the sake of the beast but for his own pride. Bernardo had not brought his running dogs with him this morning, as the plan was to stalk a young deer. On other occasions, when he went hunting '*par force*,' the running hounds were used to tire a stag or boar. Once the beast was slow enough, Bernardo would finish it with his spear or sometimes a sword.

"That deer will feed us well for many weeks to come," suggested the Legate.

"Indeed," said Giovanni, "and I will have the kitchens age the haunches for the winter months."

Bernardo smiled his agreement. As much as he enjoyed hunting, he loved feasting and fine foods just as much. With the kill made, the Legate's enthusiasm for the day's hunt had waned and he instructed Giovanni to return to Westwick.

As he gave the instruction, Giovanni put a hand on the Legate's arm and pointed to a shallow mossy gully one hundred paces downwind, surrounded by mature beech trees. A pair of coneys frolicked on the bank, unaware of the hunting party regarding them as dinner on the morrow.

Giovanni whispered, "Your kill, Your Grace. Aim for the lower one, t'will be a clearer target." Bernardo Ravennate reached out his left hand and his huntsman handed over his bow and a single arrow. Very slowly, Bernardo notched the small, barbed arrow, raised his bow and took careful aim.

The arrow flew, straight and true, but it was as if the coneys sensed the danger that rushed toward them. Before Bernardo's arrow reached the gully, both coneys raced off and it struck deep into the earth.

They rode side by side, following the sunken track toward Pimlico. Bernardo's red, broad-brimmed galero was pulled low to keep the sun from his eyes. Giovanni's soldier's eyes never stopped moving, scanning the terrain ahead for danger.

"How goes our venture, Giovanni?" enquired the Legate.

"I understand the last shipment proved very profitable, says my man in Sluys. We have a profit of nearly one thousand tournois."

"Very pleasing," smiled the Legate, "And even more rewarding that we do God's work on behalf of the foundlings, providing them with a new life."

Giovanni wondered whether his Master was truly naive enough to believe this was about saving lost souls or whether it salved his conscience to think thus.

"Indeed, Your Grace, God's work."

It was Giovanni who had come up with the idea. London had many foundlings and orphans, and he convinced Bernardo that the children were being sent to the continent for a better life as indentured servants or groomed in religious houses for a future as lay brothers and sisters. He had told the Legate of wealthy merchants in Ghent, Bruges and elsewhere in Flanders who would pay a premium to bring such children into their households.

Giovanni knew, of course, that the truth was different. He doubted whether any of the transported children ever ended up as servants in the homes of the Flemish elite.

When Bernardo was appointed Legate a year earlier, Giovanni had been sent ahead to locate a suitable manor away from the cities and towns. He had seen Westwick and it suited the Legate's needs perfectly. It was close to St Albans and, but a day's journey from Westminster and London. When in London, Giovanni had been surprised at the number of orphans begging on the streets; it so reminded him of his childhood and an idea began to germinate in his mind. Who would miss orphans, waifs and foundlings? From his own childhood experience on the streets of Bologna, such children disappeared all the time, with no one to mourn them.

Taking the children from the streets of London proved ridiculously easy. He employed other children to lure them away with promises of coin or food. Then, having been subdued with dwale, his men brought them to a remote, ancient barn west of St Albans that was part of the manor of Westwick.

Giovanni had arranged a network from this holding place to move the children to Harwich and then by sea to Sluys, where his man, Goyvaert de Tongeren, a former mercenary who once stood beside him in battle, moved them onwards.

Giovanni had told the Legate of this charitable plan to give the waifs and orphans an opportunity in a new land. Bernardo wholeheartedly approved, quoting Matthew Chapter 18, *'Whoever welcomes one such child in my name welcomes me.'*

But Giovanni's plans had nothing to do with charity. Goyvaert de Tongeren was heartless and pitiless, perfect for fulfilling the European end of the operation. The law would call him a *'procurer.'* Far from finding work as indentured servants in the houses of wealthy merchants, the young maids among the children ended up in Paris, Avignon, Piza and even Outremer. Whoever had sufficient coin could purchase a child, provided they knew where to find Goyvaert. Giovanni rarely thought about it, but on the occasions he did, he imagined the young maids ended up in those cities' fetid taverns, stews and whorehouses.

He knew, too, from something Goyvaert had told him, that the young boys commanded a high price and had every possibility of being bought by a prominent member of city society and even senior clergy.

"God's work indeed, Your Grace," he opined as their horses trotted slowly towards Westwick. "God's work."

Ж

Chapter Nineteen

The old Roman Road west out of St Albans towards Westwick, June 1277.

SIMON LOWYS FOLLOWED the old Roman road west out of St Albans early the next morning as the Abbey Sanctus bell chimed to summon the brothers to prayer. His willing palfrey took him gently past the stark ancient ruins, thrown into relief by the rising sun, as he made steady time. After a short while, isolated, small wattle and daub cottages gave way to open countryside and the defined highway became a deeply rutted track. Thick, verdant hedgerows rose on either side and ancient trees leaned across so close that their branches entwined to form a canopy over his head, blocking out the morning sun and throwing his route into shadowed relief. Cooing wood pigeons gave an almost musical accompaniment to his journey, interrupted only by the raucous cawing of angry rooks. He was only too aware of the threat posed by wolf heads. A lone traveller on an isolated road, bordered by thick shrubs and trees, made a perfect opportunity for those who lived on the very edge of society.

Keen that his young mount didn't sense his anxiety, he slackened his grip on the reins as the palfrey picked its way, avoiding the larger ruts and water-filled holes. Judging by the gouges and unevenness, it was a frequently used route, but this morning he was alone, having passed no one in either direction since he picked up the ancient by-way. The light breeze funnelled dust along his path

The manor of Westwick was yet another possession within the purview of the Abbey of St Albans. It lay a mile from the highway, shielded by an ancient, dense birch wood. Simon urged his mount on as the road snaked its way through the expanse of silvery trees. It came as a surprise when the Manor House of Westwick opened before him. It was grander than he imagined he would find in such a remote spot. He pulled hard on the reins and leaned back in the saddle. His thought had been that as the Abbot held the manor, funds were unlikely to have been invested in it. Revenue was prioritised for the Abbey and its buildings. But as he took in Westwick Manor, he could see that it was far from run down. He judged that it had been recently renovated, which was understandable if it was to be used by a Papal representative. The thatch was recent, and the walls gleamed with fresh limewash. The foundations were of flint laid with lime mortar and the substantial oak beams that rose up to support the upper floor were infilled with wattle and daub. It was surprisingly big, and its windows had stone mullions infilled with glass. The house of someone who demanded luxury . The house sat on a gentle slope so that it was visible above its outer defensive wall. It had no moat, but the stone flint and ragstone wall was the height of one and a half men.

The roadway left the birch wood and crossed into open pasture as it led to the manor House gates. These were wide double gates made of strong timber, elm perhaps thought Simon. Obviously, the inhabitants of the manor house were not expecting trouble, for the gates were open, with just a single guard in a gaudy livery.

As Simon rode slowly through the gates, the man stepped forward to both intercept and hail him.

"I give you good day, Meister. May I ask your business?" The smiling guard had stepped in front of Simon, firmly grabbing the palfrey's bridle. A steely-eyed, elderly steward appeared and welcomed Simon with a flourish. He politely enquired of Simon's business and invited him to accompany him inside.

The steward alighted the stone steps with exceptional speed for a man of his age and swept toward the Solar. There, he threw open the large, double doors, indicating that Simon enter before leaving his presence.

The upper chamber faced east. A row of perhaps ten stone mullioned windows looked out onto pasture and open strips beyond. The windows stretched the full length of the room and framed in the nearest was the imposing presence of the Abbey Church, sat high on the horizon. All around him, there were signs of abundant living. No expense was spared on the oak panels that lined the walls. Heavy iron sconces at head height between each mullioned window held flickering golden pillars of beeswax candles, their flames dancing and illuminating the gloom. On the far wall was a wooden shelf groaning under the weight of a dozen heavy leather-bound volumes. At one end was a large carved oak throne raised slightly up from the rush-covered floor. Above it, glinting in the candlelight, hung a magnificent ornate golden crucifix.

Engrossed in his surroundings, Simon didn't hear the man enter at the far end of the chamber, only becoming aware of a heavy, savoury scent as a voice spoke.

"I welcome you to my house, Master Lowys." The words came in halting English and, to Simon's ears, sounded as if each came with an 'a' on the end. He turned to see a bird-like man bejewelled with rings, slight and slightly shorter than him, with the hue of someone from the southern provinces that bordered the Middle Sea.

Simon bent low and made his obeisance and half enquiringly said in English, "Your Excellency Bernardo Ravennate?"

The man regarded the royal nuncio before offering a bony right hand for Simon to kiss his episcopal ring. Simon knelt before him and brought his lips to the thick band of gold topped with a red gemstone, a ruby perhaps, he thought. But as his lips brushed the ring, his eyes were drawn to the Legate's middle finger next to it and the gold signet ring, with its recessed image, the symbol of his Papal authority and a thin trace of green wax in its cracks.

Bernardo Ravennate abandoned his attempt at English and slipped into courtly French, with which Simon was equally familiar.

"And how may I assist one of King Edward's men?" asked the Legate. His French was well accented, but it confirmed for Simon that Ravennate was a man of the South, for this was an accent he had heard when en route to Outremer some years before.

"Your Excellency, I am here at the command of My Lady, the Queen, to pay her respects to you as the Legate of the Holy Father and offer her commiserations for the sadness and loss of our beloved Pope John.

Ravennate bowed his head and made the Signum Crucis, muttering the '*Requiescat in Pace*' for the soul of the dead Pope.

"My Lady bade me to bring this invitation before you."

Simon handed over a parchment inviting the Legate to attend a ceremony with the Queen to bless the land inside London walls, recently granted to the Dominican Order for their new Friary.

"Ah! Our beloved Lady of the English," Ravennate paused. "Such a good servant of the Church. I am not one to believe the criticism of her by the Master of the Franciscans."

Now, why has he made such a jibe? Simon wondered. The Master of the Franciscans, John Pecham, was no friend to the Queen, claiming her property purchases from Jewish moneylenders were usury and unchristian. Simon chose to ignore the Legate's comments.

Ravennate had stepped back to flop onto his fur-cushioned Legate's throne. Even seated, his head was above the standing Simon's. The Legate's small, bejewelled hand reached for a small gold bell on a table beside the throne. A well-dressed servant appeared from the chamber's far corner as if walking through the wood-panelled wall. It took Simon a few moments to realise that the side panelling gave the appearance of meeting the far wall; in reality, that was an illusion. There was a small, man-sized gap through which servants could slip in and out of the Legate's chamber.

The servant approached the Legate and, without bowing, leaned in and whispered in his ear. Ravennate's eyes flicked towards his man.

"*Si, Giovanni.*" Further proof for Simon that Ravennate was a man of the South. Giovanni lightly touched the Legate's shoulder before withdrawing the way he came. Simon's face remained inscrutable as he noted the easy relationship between the Churchman and his servant. It had struck Simon as odd that the man, Giovanni, didn't have the appearance of a servant. His fine clothing was far superior to what a humble retainer might wear, although perhaps they did things differently where Ravennate came from. And Giovanni had a familiar ease with his master. He was taller than Simon and towered over the Legate. In Simon's experience at Court, servants and stewards had soft hands and a pale pallor from long days inside. Giovanni was well-muscled, and his leathered skin bore witness to many years in the sun. Simon had mixed with many such men en route to Outremer in 1270 and knew a warrior when he saw one. Not a knight, though, more likely, a man-at-arms.

Perhaps reading the Nuncio's mind, Ravennate said, "Giovanni, my manservant. Now, Master Lowys, be seated." He gestured towards a smaller chair beside his. "Pray, do tell me what role you perform for Her Grace, Queen Leonor? He used her Castilian name; again, Simon thought that Ravennate was a man of the Middle Sea.

"I am her nuncio and Serjeant-at-Law, Your Excellency."

"Indeed?" Ravennate's genial expression never altered. "And it must be most interesting work for you."

"Aye," Simon was aware he was being pumped for information but chose to enlighten the Legate, nonetheless.

"I was sent north to St Albans many months past to investigate a coven of witches whose activities threatened the…… stability of the Kingdom."

"Do you say?" Ravennate's eyebrows raised in surprise. "I am a believer in Exodus Chapter 22, Master Lowys; 'Thou shalt not suffer a witch to live.' You were successful?"

From the corner of his eye, Simon saw a figure emerge from the concealed entrance. It was not Giovanni but a young cherub of a boy of perhaps six or seven summers, dressed in a bright cote and hose and with a shock of fair curls on his head. He carried a silver salver, a cut Murano decanter filled with a plum-coloured liquid and two green glass drinking vessels.

"*Mettilo qui, caro ragazzo*." He spoke softly to the young cherub in a Sicilian tongue Simon had picked up on the journey to Outremer. The young boy set the salver down on a table on the far side of Ravennate as instructed and poured two generous helpings of the liquid into the glass vessels. He stood before Ravennate, bowed and handed the Legate the glass. He then repeated the act for Simon before quietly withdrawing.

Simon's face remained impassive. As Alia had pointed out, there had been several coincidences over the past few days and now, here at the Legate's retreat, was another. He was investigating the disappearance of young children and here in Bernardo Ravennate's employ was a young boy.

His mind raced as he began to sip at the sickly-sweet wine. It may be unrelated, but he had a nagging sense that it was not.

Ravennate broke the silence. "Do you return to the Court this day, Master Lowys?"

Simon turned towards the Legate. "Nay, Your Grace. I am at the Abbey for some days yet. I was sent to the Convent of St Mary de Pré to investigate the disappearance of a young maid known personally to My Lady the Queen." He wanted to see where that revelation might land.

Ravennate's mask did not slip, but Simon was sure his face momentarily tensed.

"A young maid has disappeared, you say." His calmness had returned. "From where?"

"The Lazar House, at St Mary's" replied Simon. "The maid was the niece of one of Queen Eleanor's Ladies of the Chamber and she went missing these days past."

"*Sacre Dieu*. That is terrible." His concern sounded genuine to the Royal Nuncio, but his eyes told a different story.

"Have you succeeded in finding her yet? You have clues? Do you know who did this thing?" The Legate's words tumbled out.

"Nay. But I am hopeful."

Despite Bernardo Ravennate's efforts to control his demeanour, Simon was sure that he seemed rattled. Was he involved somehow? Did Ravennate know something?

Ravennate placed glass onto the salver, gently rearranging the glass and the decanter with his palm, pushing it one way and then another. Simon was sure the Legate was flustered and seeking time to gather his thoughts. Finally, Ravennate fixed his gaze on Simon and shook his head.

"I am appalled by this news you bring me, Master Lowys; you must allow me to give you every assistance I can in this matter. My people know many hereabouts and can put the word out. It is but a terrible thing and I shall pray to our Blessed Lady that the maid is unharmed and returned to her family. You must ensure I am kept abreast of your investigation." Ravennate picked up a small gold bell from the table beside him and rang it twice.

His 'servant' reappeared. "Master Lowys, this is my Steward, Giovanni di Bologna. He is a man with many contacts. I cannot do without him. He will surely be of help to you."

The Legate half-tuned towards his Steward. "Giovanni, Master Lowys here is a Royal Nuncio to Queen Eleanor. He tells us that a maid has gone missing."

Simon watched as di Bologna's eyes widened in alarm.

"Do you say Excellency?" di Bologna's face had recovered and became a mask again.

He may hold the title of Steward, but now, being close to Ravennate confirmed Simon's suspicion that the man was a warrior. Nothing in his bearing showed subservience. This was someone who gave commands rather than receive them. Perhaps he was the Legate's personal bodyguard?

"Master Lowys," di Bologna's southern Mediterranean accent drew out the words. "Do tell me of this maid missing from St Mary de Pré. I have many *connessioni*," he struggled for the word in French. "Connections. Yes, connections; it may be that I can be of help."

Simon remained impassive. He had told the Legate that the maid had been abducted from St Mary's, but di Bologna wasn't present when he had said this. How did he know the abduction had been from St Mary's?

"Any help would be most welcome," replied Simon, feigning enthusiasm.

"Who is this maid? A man such as yourself would not normally concern himself with the disappearance of a child."

"The missing maid is the daughter of one of Her Grace, the Queen's Ladies," said Ravennate. Not quite accurate, Simon thought, but he didn't bother correcting him.

"Indeed. That is a terrible thing. Have you got far with your investigation?"

"I am making enquiries," said Simon, "but it appears that the Prioress of St Mary's has also gone missing."

Over di Bologna's shoulder, Simon noticed the Legate's face harden and a thin line on his brow began to pulse. That Prioress Hilda had also disappeared, was unknown to the Legate.

"Indeed. That is a mystery." Simon could see that di Bologna's eyes contradicted his words about Prioress Hilda.

"Master Lowys," the Legate stood from his dais, his spindly knees now level with Simon's face.

"You must keep us appraised of your progress." Recognising that his audience was at an end, Simon bowed before the Legate, a low bow of deference.

"Your Grace, I thank you for your kindness and will send word should I hear of any news."

The Legate nodded solemnly and, with a wave of his hand, gave the Royal Nuncio permission to leave. Simon backed away for three or four paces before turning towards the door. He observed that Giovanni was beside Ravennate in hushed, animated conversation. Even before he reached the oak door, it swung open and another young boy, older than the cherub, bowed as Simon walked past him.

Simon followed the youth into the gloomy antechamber and down a narrow stairway to the entrance. The boy's heavily accented French was impeccable; if he had to guess, he was native to France. They arrived at the large wooden doors to the manor house, already thrown wide open to receive him. Upon his arrival, the smiling guard Simon had encountered earlier, stood outside, below the steps, holding his palfrey's reins.

As he left Westwick behind him and followed the track towards the King's Highway, it occurred to him that Windridge was close to Westwick, separated by just a few miles. Simon wished he had questioned whether the Legate and his man had known Sire Roger. But that would have to wait. He gave a sigh. He was no closer to finding the Lady Jeanne or to solving the murder of the priest. He wondered how to convey this news to John of Berwick and could only hope that Isabella fared better in her investigation.

Ж

———————

Chapter Twenty

The Abbesses chamber, Convent of St Mary de Pré on Watling Street, June 1277.

THE KNOCK ON THE OAK DOOR was gentle, almost deferential. "Pray enter, Sister," commanded the Abbess Constanza de San Andreas de Anroyo. Sister Agnes, head bowed, entered, with a sealed, folded despatch in her hands. The Abbess was seated at the desk, with her novice beside her, both surrounded by documents Agnes did not recognise.

"Mother Abbess," Agnes bowed with humility before she handed over the parchment. "Tis addressed to you and was left with the gatekeeper this morn." Agnes offered the dispatch to Isabella before retiring.

Isabella examined the letter before deftly sliding her knife under the wax seal, removing it in one sweep. She unfolded the parchment and scanned its contents. She then picked up the wax seal from the desktop and studied it for clues to its author. It was blood-red and without an impression. Isabella held the parchment up to the horn-covered window, seeing if it contained any hidden message, but there appeared to be no secret words. She laid it on the desk, flattening it with her hand as she read it more closely. It was brief and written in French, though she thought its expression suggested the author was not French.

Beside her, Alia picked up on Isabella's concern.

"Mistress is aught wrong?"

Isabella ran her tongue over her thin lips. "Mayhaps. Tis a terse message from someone unknown." She began reading aloud.

'I know you are not who you claim to be. I will be at the gate beyond the orchard after the Nones bell. Be coming alone.'

That last phrase convinced Isabella that the author was not French.

"Someone knows who you are," suggested Alia with concern.

"Nay, I think not, at least not who I am, but it is someone who knows that I am not truly the Abbess de San Andreas de Anroyo."

Only a few people at the Chancery knew Isabella was using that alias, reinforcing her long-held thought that there was a spy close to John of Berwick. Isabella wondered what this person knew and who they might be.

"What will you do, Mistress? That instruction *'Be coming alone,'* suggests a trap,"

"Aye, it does." Isabella knew she had little option but to make the meeting, though Alia had other ideas.

"Mistress, you should not go."

"I afear I have little choice, Alia."

"You do, Mistress, I shall go in your stead."

"Nay, I could not allow that; it would be far too dangerous."

"There would be some danger, though not to you. If we went to the meeting place early, you could secrete yourself somewhere unseen and offer protection if a threat emerges."

"But you look far too young to be an Abbess."

"Aye," responded Alia, sensing her argument was on the verge of success, "but if I wear your habit and cover my wimple with a heavy veil that reveals only my eyes, who will know my age?"

Isabella said nothing, thinking through Alia's suggestion.

"What you say makes sense, but I am uneasy about exposing you to such risk."

"But, is this not a risk worth taking, Mistress?"

"I will dwell upon it." Isabella could see the sense in her assistant's argument and mused that if she allowed Alia to take the risk, then she would be close by with her hand-held arbalest within the folds of her habit as a precaution.

The heat of the early summer day was still intense as Alia Parys, dressed in her Abbess'

habit made her way through the orchard towards the walled gate. As Alia now knew from experience, the heavy woollen habit of the Benedictine nuns drew sweat away from her skin, keeping her dry. Isabella had already sent word to Sister Agnes that important business would mean she and Sister Mathilt would miss the Nones service. Agnes may be scandalised, but it mattered nought.

From her vantage point in a dell in the water meadow, thirty yards from the wicket gate, Isabella heard the solitary bell toll for Nones and, in the distance, saw a dark-clothed figure of a man emerge from the trees, moving stealthily to wait beside the wall. Alia approached the wicket gate leading down to the Ver on the far side and out of sight of the loitering man. The hem of her black tunic swished against the dry grass as she walked. A white coif framed her face, which, as she had said, was covered by a veil, so only her green eyes could be seen.

Alia stood beside the gate, still, her head tilted to listen. A crow cawed somewhere close by, but Alia was focused on a smell, an aromatic scent that emanated from the other side of the gate. Positioning herself to one side, she lifted the wooden bar, deliberately making noise to alert whoever stood on the other side. With a slight push, the wicket gate opened, and Alia stepped through it.

The meadow lay ahead, dropping gently down to the river. Alia didn't need to turn around to know someone was behind her. She sensed a presence, her hand moving to the small arbalest concealed in her tunic that Isabella had insisted she carry. She stood still. Alia was apprehensive even though she knew Isabella was ahead of her, hidden where an ancient stream once carved a path through the meadow.

"Turn around," instructed a man's voice.

"I have come as you asked," Alia replied a little nervously. "Who are you and what is it that you want with me?" she inquired in French, turning to face him.

She looked upon a tall, dark man, broad of shoulder with his hood pulled low to hide his features. The exposed flesh around his eyes and hands showed a man who had spent many years in the sun. He was no nobleman but not a serf either. Although he was wrapped in an old woollen cloak, his boots gave him away. They were of fine leather, not the best, but beyond the means of a peasant. They were not caked in mud, suggesting they were well cared for.

"I know that you are not the Abbess de San Andreas de Anroyo." His manner was direct, and his French accent was that of a foreigner. "You are not the Abbess, but you are the one who helped the assassin of the Queen to escape these months past."

Alia feigned alarm. "I know not of what you speak."

"*Si, Signora*. You know exactly of what I speak."

So, from the land of the Middle Sea, she thought. "What do you want of me?"

"My friends at the Court say of you that you helped the assassin Benuic escape the King's Men."

Alia wondered if she should deny the accusation, but this man knew fragments of the truth. Better to remain silent and discover how much he knew.

"Were that the truth, what do you want of me?"

"My friends wish you to get a message to Benuic. We require his services."

Alia chuckled. "You believe that I can contact someone like that?" She was happy to play along with the foreigner who did not know as much as he thought he did.

"*Si!* It was you who helped the assassin to escape and perhaps he is still here in England. He has a woman as his intermediary and that my lady Abbess, or whoever you are, is you. You can contact him and engage his services for us."

Alia was doing her best to stop her heart from racing. It was working. The foreigner before her knew she was not the Abbess Constanza but had no idea about the true identity of her mistress. He wanted the assassin, which implied an important target. She needed to discover more.

"If I could contact Benuic, what message do I deliver? And what coin do you offer?

"One hundred gold florin provided he kills without suspicion. It must appear an accident." Alia said nothing.

"You are to meet me in Magpie Lane in the town at Vespers, on the Feast of Saint Vitus." His instruction was terse.

"And what name am I to convey to him?"

"Tis a King's Man and it needs must be done soon." Alia tensed.

"Above all, it must appear an accident; none must suspect otherwise." She hoped he did not see her eyes widen under her veil at this, fearful of the name that would come next.

"His name is Simon Lowys."

Ж

Chapter Twenty-one

The Lazar House of St Mary de Pré, St Albans, June 1277.

ONCE THE FOREIGNER had identified Simon Lowys as the target, he cautiously backed away, turning to take the path back to the King's Highway through the meadow. Alia was sure that such a man did not walk here; he would likely have a horse and groom hidden in the trees. She headed back through the wicket gate and the orchard towards the Abbesses chamber once he was out of sight; all the time, her heart racing with anxiety.

Back inside the wood-panelled room, she sat at the table and began to think. Isabella made her way back from the dell to join her and listened intently as Alia recounted the conversation.

"Tis Master Lowys he seeks to kill," she said, fighting back the tears.

"Tell me of this man." Isabella, too, felt shocked at the revelation but needed to focus.

Alia recounted every detail she could recall of his appearance, demeanour and tone.

There was more than just the imminent danger to Simon Lowys. From her hiding place, Isabella had caught fragments of the conversation. She had heard enough to believe that the foreigner was

103

Italian, his accent suggesting the north of that country. He had information that was known to just a few around the King and Queen and his Chief Intelligencer, John of Berwick. And he had let slip that he had friends at the King's Court, people who were important enough to be privy to general information but not in the inner circle to know the specifics.

Isabella laid out the small parchment message Sister Agnes had brought her earlier. She took the paper message with the green wax sent to the Prioress and placed it beside the parchment.

The slope of the letters in the script was the same. They had been written by the same hand. Would that be the Italian, she wondered?

Isabella laid out another small sheet of parchment on the writing slope in front of her, picked up a quill and dipped it into an ink pot.

With smooth, sweeping strokes, she began to write in French.

Point. Someone around John of Berwick and His Grace has let slip details about our pursuit of the assassin Benuic. A spy located in the Chancery.

Point. It cannot be one within the immediate circle because the details are flawed, and they do not recognise Benuic and the Abbess Constanza as one and the same.

Point. This information has been passed to the Italian. Who is he? Who does he work for?

Point. The Italian is not part of the assassination plot against Her Grace, for he would know about Benuic if he were.

Point. What, then, is this Italian up to?

Point. Is he involved in the abduction of the maid? He knew about the meadow beyond the orchard, which Lowys believed was where the maid was taken. A coincidence?

Point. The Italian had said, 'My friends.' Who are they?

Point. If they want Lowys dead, they could hire local thugs to do the job. Why must it appear as an accident? What is afoot?

Point. If they wished Lowys dead, he must have stumbled on something and perhaps doesn't yet know it.

Point. Benuic would need to make contact with the Italian and his people if the pretence was to be kept up and the conspirators exposed.

Point. The letter alerting the Prioress and the message to Isabella from the Italian were written by the same hand.

Point. The Italian appears to have links to the Papal Legate. Is the Legate involved?

Isabella placed the quill beside the ink pot and picked up the sand shaker, sprinkling a fine dusting across the wet ink. She waited while the ink dried and only then picked up the parchment to reflect on her words. There was a week, possibly less, if the Italian realised who the Abbess Constanza was or wasn't. Isabella recognised that she had to warn Simon Lowys that his life was in danger.

Alia's meeting with the Italian confirmed something else for Isabella: the Abbess Constanza de San Andreas de Anroyo would have to disappear. When the Italian met with Alia, she had drawn a veil tight across her face so only her eyes were visible. Her slight build lay hidden beneath the heavy black habit of the Benedictine Order, so she was confident he would not recognise her if he saw Alia again. Fortunately, the Italian had not seen Isabella; she could use that to her advantage.

The Abbess Constanza had served her purpose and Isabella realised that she must now resume the persona of 'le Reynard', the King's Intelligencer. This meant leaving the Lazar House at St Mary de Pré.

"Alia! We must away from this place with all speed."

"I think there is little danger that this stranger may identify you, but we must take no chances."

"Aye, you have the right of it," suggested Alia. "He saw what he wanted to see: a woman dressed in a nun's habit and no threat to him. I do not believe he suspected who I am."

Isabella stood and swept up the documents in front of her. "Now, we must move with all haste."

Alia was dispatched to gather their possessions while Isabella penned another letter to the Abbot requesting that Sister Agnes be appointed Acting Prioress. Isabella knew she needed to act quickly but would not leave before speaking with Agnes.

It was some time before Sister Agnes arrived, Isabella had considered telling her the whole story but, once again, thought better of it. She did not know if any of the Lazar women or the other sisters were in league with the former Prioress and did not want her identity to be compromised.

"Pray sit, Sister," Isabella instructed as Agnes entered the solar.

Sister Agnes was wide-eyed in astonishment at the news she received. "You have recommended me to be the Acting Prioress?"

"Aye," said Isabella, "With immediate effect. For reasons I cannot divulge, I am leaving after Vespers. I will leave it to you to explain all and may God guide your hand, Sister."

Overwhelmed by the news, Agnes bowed her head in reverence. "Thank you, Mother Abbess."

After the hour of Vespers, Sister Agnes was joined at the gate by her young colleague, Edith. Isabella and Alia were already mounted on their bay jennets, the large ponies Isabella favoured for journeys.

"God give you a good a, safe journey, Mother Abbess," said Sister Agnes.

Isabella nodded and turned as Joanas swung the gate open, and Isabella and Alia walked their jennets onto the road south towards the town.

Sister Agnes stood with Edith and watched the two ride into the distance, the dust billowing behind them until it finally hid them from sight. Agnes thought of the young, assured Abbess and reflected that the Benedictines of the southern lands must do things differently to us here in England.

The two women rode south steadily, entering St Michael's village and following the track north towards St Albans. The imposing Abbey Church loomed above them on the hill where the martyr had been killed centuries before. They skirted the monastic complex and entered Sopwellstrete, the narrow lane that led to the town's southern gate and the road south to London. Their destination lay at its far end, the modest townhouse of Mistress Matilda Heacham. She was a respectable widow of the town who provided safe lodging and necessary supplies for royal agents passing through the abbey town. She accepted and forwarded messages, passed on instructions and offered good food and a comfortable bed to agents of the King. Her husband had been John of Berwick's man and when he contracted the pestilence and passed to God, Matilda continued his work. She possessed valuable connections across the town and inside the abbey but outwardly was merely one of many respectable widows of the town.

Isabella had thought about their appearance. Being dressed as two nuns was necessary when leaving St Mary's and would pass unnoticed as they travelled into the town. And even in Sopwellstrete, two sisters of God, heading towards the London gate may not arouse suspicion. But they had to stop to enter Mistress Heacham's house and why would two nuns be visiting there?

When Robert Heacham had purchased the house thirteen summers before, he had done so as an agent of the Crown. This property on Sopwellstrete lay beside the Tonman ditch, the high, banked boundary of the town. Narrow alleys off the street gave access to the gardens at the rear. Isabella and Alia walked their ponies along one such alley to Mistress Heacham's large kitchen garden and the small outbuilding that served as a stable and prevented unwanted eyes from seeing who came and went.

Isabella and Alia entered by the door to the kitchen garden.

Matilda Heacham's kitchen lay at the rear of the property, from which came the aroma of freshly baked bread. If Mistress Heacham was surprised at the arrival of two nuns in her kitchen, her face did not show it.

"Isabella, Alia, tis good to see you both. I see you both have had God's calling since we last met."

All three women laughed at this.

"Well, you both do know where the chamber is and you may change there. Eat first and then change your garments." Isabella and Alia each took a stool and pulled it to the table, where Matilda laid fresh bread, a fine soft cheese, butter and a weak ale in clay jugs before them.

They ate, but both Isabella and Alia knew they needed to find Simon Lowys and warn him that his life was in danger.

ж

Chapter Twenty-two

Bone Hill Wood, near the village of Daneswick, Hertfordshire, June 1277.

EELING THE WEIGHT of the leather purse in his hand, Otul Fitzkeen could not help but think that this was the easiest coin he had ever earned.

"Do you open it? I know you want to," said the younger man standing opposite him in heavily accented English.

Stood before the old woodcutter's barn deep inside Bone Hill Wood, both men showed the build and scars of those who had fought in battle.

Otul gave a toothless grin. His sun-reddened face wrinkled with pleasure as he pulled at the purse drawstrings to reveal a bundle of silver pennies.

"I have put more coin in there for the..." The younger man paused, seeking the word in English, "...inconvenience that is to come."

Otul didn't understand.

"Two men will come for a maid. Pay them no heed and give them whatever they need."

For more coin, Otul was happy to oblige.

"Are there difficulties?" inquired the other.

"Nay! They are mostly quiet," replied Otul, keen to show he was in control. "I have had to fetter one lad who keeps trying to escape."

"Escape?" The word stung the younger man and he eyed Otul suspiciously. "One escaped? How far did he get?" The mood between the men became icy cold.

"Nay, Nay, not far: not far at all." Otul was more positive than he felt. "My lad Engulf tracked the boy and brought him back."

The younger man studied Otul closely.

"Did this boy speak with anyone?"

"Nay. I think not. Engulf found him before he reached the village. But this lad is hot-blooded and doesn't fear."

Otul watched the veins on his companion's face harden.

"Has this boy tried to escape?"

Even with his years of experience as a man-at-arms fighting on the Welsh borders, something about this man intimidated Otul Fitzkeen.

"Aye, he has. Three. Three times, maybes, four," he replied, hoping his answer didn't antagonize the other man. "He did try to convince others to join him, but they are too meek."

Otul Fitzkeen had always been wary of strangers and this man, Giovanni - in private, Otul called him the Tuscan- had killing eyes. In his years fighting the Welsh, he had met similar men with the same look: men who lived for the thrill of killing, men who revelled in inflicting pain on others. Giovanni the Tuscan was such a man.

Giovanni di Bologna's mood had changed. He didn't like loose ends and a child who had made numerous attempts to escape was likely to become a loose end and a danger to his operation.

"This boy, where have you tied him?"

Otul raised his eyes and inclined his head, indicating the hay loft.

Giovanni pulled open the wicket door and entered the barn. Otul was unsure about whether or not to follow, but he chose to stay where he was.

He strained his ears to catch what the Tuscan said to the boy but heard nothing. At length, he caught the sound of feet descending the wooden loft ladder and Giovanni reappeared, a long, thin blade in his hand.

He wiped the blade clean on a clump of grass beside the barn door before resheathing it.

"Get rid of it!" he said tersely, pointing at the loft. "And make sure that none of them try to escape."

Otul nodded his understanding as he sought to hold his shock in check. Giovanni fixed him with a malevolent stare.

"We cannot have any of these children breaking free and leading others to this location. You understand that Otul?"

"Aye," replied Otul nervously. "Aye, I understand."

"Good," said Giovanni, smiling maliciously as he placed a hand on Otul's shoulder, "Because, my friend, you are not about to let me down, are you?"

The implied threat was not lost on Otul Fitzkeen.

Ж

Chapter Twenty-three

The village of Windridge, Hertfordshire, June 1277.

WINDRIDGE LAY FIVE MILES southwest of St Albans and was the same as so many villages Simon had been to all over England. As its name suggested, it lay atop a low hill, perhaps a few hundred feet tall, west-facing and surrounded by cultivated strips. Windridge was little more than a hamlet. There was but one dusty track through the village with drab wattle and daub cottages on either side. The track would eventually lead to the church, an ancient stone-built building, which suggested to Simon that Windridge had been more prosperous in times past. He stopped at the blacksmith's forge, a stone building set away from cottages, to prevent the spread of fire.

A tall, thick-set man with a long, grime-laden beard looked up from hammering a piece of iron into a crescent shape.

"God give you good day, Master Smith. I seek the house of the Reeve."

The smith regarded the mounted man with caution. A hamlet such as Windridge received few visitors and strangers were always unwelcome. So, Simon thought it best to introduce himself.

"I am Simon Lowys, Nuncio to Her Grace, the Queen and King's Man." If anything, that merely served to increase the Smith's unease.

"I am here to investigate the death of your priest," Simon added, which seemed to satisfy the Smith, and his demeanour changed.

"Your presence is welcome then, King's Man."

"I seek the Reeve, Master Smith."

The smith thrust the iron rod he was working deeper into the bright yellow flames and came across to Simon's horse.

He took the bridle and stroked the beast's nose. "You will find Henry de Bray in his cottage. Tis the last one." He inclined his head to suggest a row of neat homes further down the track toward the church.

"I am indebted to you, Master Smith." Simon raised a hand in thanks before moving off slowly in the direction of the Church of St Mary Magdalene.

Simon stopped at the house of Henry de Bray and tied his palfrey to a bush outside.

He rapped on the door and a pleasant-faced, older man answered.

"Henry de Bray? I am Simon Lowys, Nuncio to Her Grace, the Queen and King's Man."

"Aye. Here about the death of the priest, is it?"

"You have the right of it, Master de Bray." The Reeve invited Simon inside. His house was a two-storeyed cottage, more prominent than others nearby. Inside, the décor suggested the hand of a woman. The room that overlooked St Mary Magdalene was tidy, with objects neatly arranged. The rushes on the floor were fresh and sprinkled with rosemary. Beside the fire, a small-framed woman dressed in a grey gown was tending to a cauldron over open flames. She rose and made her obeisance to Simon with a deep curtsey.

"My wife, Johanna," announced the Reeve. "Master Lowys here is to investigate the death of Sire Roger further." Simon thought he caught a flicker of alarm on Johanna's face at the mention of the priest.

Johanna indicated a stool beside the fire and invited Simon to sit.

"Some ale, Master Lowys?" Without waiting for a reply, Johanna crossed to a barrel in the corner and ladled a serving into two clay jugs.

Simon sipped the frothy liquid and was pleasantly surprised. "A fine brew Mistress."

"Aye," interjected the Reeve. "My Johanna makes the finest ale in Windridge." Simon was not about to disagree.

"Master Reeve, tell me of the circumstances of the priest's death."

Henry de Bray took a deep breath. "Well, it was like this, you see. Twas the Feast of the two saints, Phillip and James. We had a terrible storm that night and no one was abroad. It happened in the night, but Sire Roger was not found until morn."

"Who found the body?" interjected Simon.

"Twas I that found him. I was up with the dawn and was intending to see what damage the storm had done. I left here and saw the door to the Church was open." Henry took a gulp of ale and wiped his sleeve across his mouth.

"That was most unusual for Sire Roger, who was in the habit of always locking the church door."

"So, what did you do?"

"I went into the Church, twas cold despite the warmth of the past days. The storm had broken the heat, you know. And I saw Sire Roger on the floor before the altar, his back bare and an arrow piercing him."

"Master Reeve, I think it would help if we went to the Church, and you showed me what you saw."

"Very well," announced Henry, casting a worried glance at Johanna. "Come now."

They left his house and walked across to St Mary Magdalene's.

"He was here, laid across the altar steps." Henry de Bray pointed at a spot beneath the holiest place in the church.

"He lay face down?"

"Aye," replied the Reeve, "with an arrow deep in his back." Henry de Bray placed a finger on his back to indicate where the arrow had struck. "There was much blood, Master Lowys. He had been self-mortifying. I found a whip, tight with leather knots beside him and he had laid his back open."

Simon thought that this may be highly significant. He knew that some men of God regularly self-flagellated as an act of penance, mortification of the flesh being good for the purging of sins. But why would a lowly parish priest wish to mortify his flesh? What sins had he committed that he should undertake such an act?

"I left the arrow where it was, for the inquest."

"Where might this arrow have been loosed from?" inquired Simon, who was already moving to the rear of the nave. He found that the door to the church offered a direct line of sight towards the altar. He beckoned the Reeve to join him. Both men looked toward the altar.

"You have the right of it. Twas from here, I think, Master Lowys," said de Bray.

"You did say that this door was open, when you first came that morning?"

"Aye. Twas what made me believe something was amiss."

"And what time did Sire Roger usually lock the Church?"

"Normally long after dusk, once the dark had set in," de Bray.

"But twas in May and the darkness comes later. Do we take it that the killer knew the Church would be open? If so, then surely he is local, and a local man might be seen in the twilight hours before the onset of night."

Henry de Bray was confused. "I don't follow."

"I am trying to establish a time of death. Darkness comes perhaps four hours before the dead of night at this time of the year," explained Simon. "If the church is locked up by the ninth hour, it is unlikely that it is a random killing by a stranger coming in the darkness."

Simon made his way back to the altar. "Which suggests that the murder took place between Vespers and the twilight. Which would mean that there would be enough daylight for someone to see the killer."

"Ahh!" The Reeve was pleased to be able to add details that Simon didn't know. "But that night, there was a terrible storm, great thunder and lightning. There would be few people abroad on such a night."

"Indeed. That changes things. A killer would know that. But the storm would mean that the murderer must keep their bowstring dry, and their bow and quiver concealed." Simon was articulating his thoughts aloud.

He turned to the Reeve. "Was there anything unusual about the arrow?"

"Nay, the fletching's were just plain goose feathers, nought remarkable. Made as any might."

"Why would the priest take a whip to his back?"

Henry de Bray shook his head. "Nay, I cannot say. He was liked hereabouts, men more than the womenfolk. Now you say, but there was one who had vexed words with him days before his death."

"And that was?" enquired Simon.

"It were Hild, the wife of Bortwyn, the labourer."

"And what was the cause of these cross words?"

"I know not why she had such words, but Bortwyn had grumbled about Sire Roger. Felt he had been cheated over digging a grave. He says he was promised one penny, but the priest had not paid him. But it was Bortwyn's problem. I can't see why his wife was speaking so to Sire Roger."

Mayhaps this was a murder over money, though Simon quickly dismissing the idea.

"Thank you Master Reeve. Where can I find the house of Bortwyn the labourer?"

Ж

Chapter Twenty-four

The village of Windridge, Hertfordshire, June 1277.

AS IN ANY VILLAGE, a labourer was the lowest in the social hierarchy. Without a skill, they traded their muscle for cash or kind. The cottage of Bortwyn lay on the boundary of the village. It was a humble affair, a mix of old tree branches, wattle, daub and flint. Layer upon layer of reeds covered the roof, fixed down by twisted willow tines. Simon knocked at the door and a thin, worn woman of perhaps his own age answered. She blinked in surprise at seeing a person of importance at her door.

Simon bowed and announced himself. The woman, who Simon took to be Hild, backed away in surprise and called out for her husband in a half-hushed shout.

Bortwyn appeared. "Hild," his tone was reproachful. "Invite the King's Man inside."

Once inside the small, gloomy room that was the extent of Bortwyn's home, Hild gestured to Simon to sit on a small three-legged stool beside the fire. Bortwyn joined him. Hild moved to the far side of the room and began slicing root vegetables for her pottage. Beside her was young girl of about ten summers, the only child Simon saw.

Simon judged Bortwyn to be older than his wife by ten years. His round, ruddy face suggested a kind man. His muscular frame and weathered visage spoke of years of hard work outside in the employ of others.

"Now, King's Man, how can I help you?"

"Bortwyn, I am in the village to investigate the death of Sire Roger, your priest."

From the corner of his eye, Simon caught movement beside Hild. The young maid grabbed at her mother's smock and moved to half-hide herself from the Nuncio. While listening to Bortwyn, Simon took in the maid. She was a slip of a girl with hollowed-out cheeks and deep, vacant eyes.

Bortwyn saw Simon's interest in the maid. "Pay no heed to young Marjorie, Master Lowys; she is a strange one, so she is. Always in tears, never leaves my wife's side these days."

"Indeed," said Simon. "It is my belief that you had a dispute with Sire Raymond." Simon saw how the young maid's face tightened as he said the priest's name, her eyes widening.

"Twas no dispute. The priest owed me a penny for digging the grave of John Rofot these weeks past. But he did not pay me." Bortwyn cast his eyes around his small home. "Every penny is important to us, Master Lowys."

"I can see that, Bortwyn." Simon had the sense that Bortwyn was genuine in what he said. "And the words your wife had with the priest, were these also about the money that was owed?"

"Words my wife had with the priest. Nay, Master Lowys, you have that wrong. My wife had no words with Sire Roger; is that not right, Hild?"

Hild had turned away, no longer looking at the men, her focus on an onion. "Tis true, King's Man."

"Mistress, I know that you did have cross words with Sire Roger just days before his death."

Bortwyn tilted his head in the direction of his wife. "You said not of this to me, woman."

"Nay, now I think on it, I reproached the priest for having words with Marjorie and telling her that she was wicked and sinful, as were all women. She is but a maid, so how could she know sin?"

"So, you thought to confront Sire Roger about his words?"

Hild's eyes blazed. Simon could see anger there. "Aye, I did. The priest had no right to speak so to my daughter, she being so young and all."

"And what had Marjorie done for Sire Roger to accuse her of being wicked?"

"Nothing," snapped Hild, "nothing at all." She reached out and pulled her daughter closer. "She is a good girl. She is not sinful."

Simon noticed the tears in the young maid's eyes and was sure he was missing something, but he could not put his finger on exactly what that could be.

"I meant no offence, Mistress. I merely seek to establish the facts of Sire Roger's death." Once again, Simon saw the young maid recoil at the mention of the priest's name. He turned to Bortwyn.

"Master Bortwyn, who else in Windridge could help me find out about the priest?"

Bortwyn thought for a time. "Have you asked Henry the Reeve? He knows much about what goes in the village."

"Aye, I have already spoken with him."

"Speak with Ardith." It was Hild, now back busy preparing vegetables. "She is the cunning woman and knows much of the gossip hereabouts. She will help you."

"I thank you, Mistress. Where shall I find this Ardith?" Bortwyn gave him directions and Simon bowed to make his leave. As the door closed, he left to the raised voices of husband and wife as an argument began between them.

Ardith's house was on the far side of Windridge. As he made his way there in the pleasant sunshine, he reflected on Hild and what she had told him. 'She will help you,' she told him as if she was aware that Ardith knew something about the priest. And then there was the way Hild had snapped when he asked about her daughter and the priest. And what was he to make about the behaviour of the young maid, Marjorie? In addition, Hild had not told her husband of the exchange of words with Sire Roger. Somehow, there was a connection, possibly not directly to the priest's death, but it nagged him because he couldn't see the link.

He found the cottage of Ardith, the cunning woman of Windridge, at the furthest reaches of the village, close to a stream. It sat at the end of a row of three wattle and daub dwellings, the other two run-down and seemingly unoccupied, for no light came from within. Four other villagers he had spoken to had also directed him to Ardith, saying if anyone knew about Sire Roger, it would be her as his housekeeper.

It was late afternoon and the weather, though still sunny, was tempered by a chilly easterly breeze. Simon rapped hard on the old oak door and, at length, it was opened by a willowy woman as tall as Simon. Her pale, thin face, heavy with a scowl, showed she was not happy to see him, and she made no obeisance to him.

"Mistress Ardith, God give you good day, I am...."

"I knows who you be. You be the King's Man come to Windridge to discover who killed the priest."

"Indeed, Mistress," word spread quickly in this community, he thought. "May I come inside?"

She lingered on her side of the doorway, pursing her lips as if thinking about her response, before turning and walking inside. Simon followed her in. Beeswax candles illuminated the cramped, single chamber, not the cheaper tallow variety. The interior smelled like an alchemist's workshop, with ripe, pungent aromas of camphor, rosemary and ambergris. Though small, the chamber was very neat; thin curtains in one corner were pulled wide, exposing a small pallet bed with an old fleece draped along its length. A small fire burned in the hearth and a cauldron hung over it, emanating a delicious smell from her pottage.

She pulled a three-legged stool close to the fire and, with a wordless gesture, invited Simon to sit, while she took the stool opposite.

"So, King's Man, what do you want of me?" Her tone was blunt and defensive.

"Mistress Ardith, as you rightly say, I am here to investigate the tragic death of Sire Roger."

"Tragic?" She spat out the word with loathing in her voice. "Tis no tragedy he is dead, King's Man."

"You see some fortune in his death, Mistress? Was not your priest a good man?"

"Hmmmf." She snorted. "He will not be looking on God's face this night, that be sure. The fires of Hell have surely consumed him."

"You have," he corrected himself, "*had* a low opinion of Sire Roger, even though you kept house for him?"

"I did not keep house for him," she corrected him sharply. "I came in two days in the week and prepared his pottage and cleaned the chamber, no more than that."

"So why the low regard for him and why are you so sure his soul has gone to Satan?"

"I knows it is without charity to speak ill of the dead, but I holds not charity in my heart for that man. I saw him and I knows his … ways." Ardith spat out the last words like a piece of rancid meat.

"Sire Roger was a man of God, Mistress. What '*ways*' do you speak of?"

"Man of God indeed," she sneered. "He came to our village but years since, young he was, as many summers as yourself when he died and preening and prinking, such as a priest should not do."

"So, you do tell me that Sire Roger was a vain priest. Is that reason enough to dislike him so?"

"I knows what I knows. There were some who liked him greatly, like the widow Weaver. Always bringing him food and fresh brewed ale, she was. Always finding a reason to visit Sire Roger.

Her own man was cold in the earth these three years past and she being of an age with the priest and the sort that smiles coyly and flutters her eyes, so men do always come running to her."

"And did he? Come running to her?"

Ardith gave a short chuckle. "Mayhaps he may have done if she be a maid twenty years younger. Tis all I am going to say."

Simon was shocked. Was Ardith saying what he thought she was saying? Sire Roger and maids, not yet full-grown. If true, it threw a new light on the priest's death. He needed to be sure.

"Mistress, are you telling me that Sire Roger was guilty of lustful thoughts?"

"Hah! This is not a confessional, King's Man, but twas not for just his thoughts that God will punish him." Ardith closed her eyes, remembering something that caused her face to tense.

"A wolf in the fold, that one," she said, eyes still shut. "A wolf in our fold. And twas not just our maids, he ministered to young orphans, I did hear. Always the pretty young ones he invited to help him clear up. It was not right, King's man, not right at all."

This threw new light on Sire Roger's death. If what the cunning woman said was true, then many men with young daughters in Windridge and its parish beyond, had reason to want the priest dead. And what of the Bishop of Lincoln, had he known about Sire Roger's 'ways' when he sent him to Windridge?

"And one more thing," Ardith continued, "He were right fond of strangers."

"You mean people not from around here?"

"Nay. I mean strangers from other lands. One day, I brought some lye for the washing and he was there with a stranger. They were speaking in a tongue I didn't know, but the stranger was giving harsh words to the priest."

"What did this stranger look like?"

"I could tell he was not English from his clothes. Full bright and coloured they were. But he was something else. He was big and the priest was scared of him. He was not the sort you would expect Sire Roger to know."

"I see," said Simon.

She shook her head. "Nay, King's Man! You do not. This stranger was having harsh words with our priest over a young maid who cowered in the corner."

"A maid?" Simon immediately thought of Marjorie, daughter of Bortwyn and Hild.

"Aye, A slip of a thing not more than ten summers."

"And you knew this maid?"

"Nay, I had never seen her before, but I had seen her sort with Sire Roger before."

"Indeed! Did this stranger see you?"

"Nay. I came from the kitchen garden and saw what was happening through the open door. I could not know the words of his foreign tongue, but I do know that this stranger was threatening the priest."

"And this maid you saw?"

"When the man had gone, I went to rescue the maid. Sire Roger didn't move. He watched me but didn't move. I took her and hugged her and took her to the widow of Walter the Swain. She is there still. She has spoke not a word and jumps at her own shadow." Ardith closed her eyes, remembering the event.

"Mistress," The word brought her back to the present. "Did you not tell of your suspicions about Sire Roger?"

"Bah," she spat back at him. "And who would I tell? Which man in this village would believe me or any woman? And does I go to the priest in the next village? And tells him what? He may be part of it."

"So, you told no one?" reproached Simon. If Ardith had not shared her suspicions, then that made her a suspect. What she had seen gave her a motive, though he wondered whether such a lean-framed woman had the strength to pull a long bow.

"Well, told no, not as such. But I did my best to hint to some mothers about sending their daughters when he told the children his tales from the Holy Book."

"Sire Roger told stories from the Bible to children?"

"Aye, each Sabbath after the sun had passed its height. At first, it seemed a good intention to tell them of the tales of Daniel, Noah and Joseph and the little-uns went along. But then…." She tailed off, leaving the rest unsaid.

Ardith rose from her stool to stir the pottage bubbling over the fames. She turned to regard the Nuncio.

"Do you have more questions? This pottage is ready and I have just enough for one."

Simon's status as a King's Man did not impress this woman. Accepting that he would get nothing more from Ardith, Simon rose and bowed low.

"Thank you, Mistress, I have no further questions for you at this point, although I may return."

"And if you do, I will have no other answers, King's Man."

Simon made a bow and walked to the door, with Ardith close behind. He paused, turned and asked the cunning woman one final question.

"Tell me, Mistress, was one of the village women you warned about Sire Roger, Hild, the wife of Bortwyn, the labourer?"

Ж

Chapter Twenty-five

The Backstreets of St Albans, June 1277

IN THE MINUTES BEFORE curfew, Richard Pilk staggered slowly along St Peterstrete, his throbbing head punishing him for an evening of supping ale in the Wheatsheaf. His belly was full, his eyes narrowed and his gait troubled. His lodgings lay beyond Magpie Lane, but getting there would take him quite some time, as progress was slow, needing to reach out to steady himself with almost every other step. A tightness in his groin told him that he urgently needed to relieve himself. Ahead was a side runnel that led down towards the town boundary, the Tonman Ditch. Off it was a myriad of dilapidated lodgings, somewhere he ordinarily wouldn't frequent. At this hour, there was little light from the crescent moon for him to see the sticky morass beneath his feet, which caused the alley to smell like the sewer it had become. His foot touched something hard, dumped against a timber building; Richard pulled down the top of his braes and, with a satisfying sigh, began to relieve himself against the wattle and daub wall. Only when the relief of emptying his bladder had passed did he think to look at the bundle. Perhaps it was lost; mayhaps it was something of value; mayhaps his luck was in this night.

He bent low and poked at the shape shrouded in the near-darkness, happy now that he had relieved himself on its far side. He prodded the pile, which appeared wrapped in a cloth of sorts. The part facing him was hard, but that nearest the wall was softer.

Mayhaps some cloth merchant had dropped some ells of cloth, he thought. Truly, his luck was in. Richard bent down to examine the pile by feel; his head began spinning as he struggled to focus on the cloth bundle. He gently pulled aside the cloth and his fingers revealed another layer. High above, the crescent moon had risen higher, throwing half-shadows into the narrow passageway. Whatever was inside the pile had been wrapped beneath this fabric. Frustrated, he felt for his small knife tucked into his belt. He looked both ways into the shadows to ensure he did not have company and began slicing at the cloth.

Bent low, he worked enthusiastically, his fingers tugging excitedly at the fabric as he sliced, only to recoil as the ghostly face of a child appeared, illuminated by the low moonlight. Slicing open the cloth had released the putrid, sickly odour of death. The many jugs of ale he had consumed that evening made a reappearance as he vomited at the sight.

Richard Pilk staggered backwards, trembling in horror. His breathing quickened as his shaking increased. He had seen death before when his mother had passed away, but that was serene and peaceful, nothing like the horror that now lay before him. He stood and made to leave the scene. He knew the law demanded that he raise the Hue and Cry, but to what purpose? This child was long dead.

"Dickon! Dickon Pilk! Is that you?" The voice came from further along the runnel towards St Peterstrete. He was cornered; he could not leave and forget what he had seen. He couldn't run as this voice knew him and when the body was rediscovered, he would be placed at the scene of the crime.

"Raise the Hue and Cry!" he shouted. "Raise the Hue and Cry. There is a body here."

The voice had taken a dozen paces closer and Pilk recognised a drinking companion, Thomas Ducket.

"Ducket, I was taking a piss and found a child dead."

Thomas Ducket, in the alley for the same reason as Pilk, staggered the few paces to his side, gazed down on the corpse, recoiled at the stench of death and emptied his stomach onto the already putrid ground beneath his feet.

Neither man could now return home. Ducket went for the Constable, John le Tailour, alerting anyone he saw on the streets to be on the lookout for a murderer. On his way back to the scene with the constable, Ducket imagined how, in the months to come, he would retell this story for the price of an ale to anyone prepared to listen.

The Curfew bell had long since rung when John le Tailour, his assistant and Thomas Ducket arrived back in the alley. Le Tailour's assistant, a callow youth of eighteen summers, held the lantern high as the constable examined the child's body.

He turned to Richard Pilk. "You found this child?"

"Aye, I was taking a piss and discovered it, as you see."

"Was it open like this?"

Pilk hesitated. "Err... Nay. I thought it was a bundle of cloth dropped by some merchant, so I opened it."

"Indeed." The constable eyed the still-drunk man suspiciously.

"Tis true," interjected Ducket." I come down here to piss and saw Dickon. And twas I that raised the Hue and Cry and did summon yourself."

John le Tailour cleared his throat and grunted an acknowledgement.

He turned to the youth holding the lantern, "Wait here; I will send men to fetch the body and bring it before the Coroner."

"Can we go now, John?" inquired Pilk.

"Aye, you may go, but both of you will need to present yourself before the coroner on the morrow."

Relieved that the ordeal was over, Pilk and Ducket headed toward the Magna Vico and their lodgings, where each anticipated a scolding from their woman.

The Town Constable waited behind. The dawn light highlighted the frown on his face. John le Tailour regarded the corpse of the child. It was a boy of no more than ten summers. He pushed his lower lip over his front teeth, a habit he had when troubled. Another child's body, he thought; the fifth in the past year, but the first to be found inside the town boundary. The Seneschal would not be happy. Brother Gilbert had done all he could to conceal news of the previous deaths, but this discovery inside the town would make it more difficult. Le Tailour was not looking forward to that conversation and had the uneasy feeling that Gilbert would somehow seek to lay the blame for events with him.

Ж

Chapter Twenty-six

The Palatium, the Benedictine Abbey of St Alban, June 1277

AH, MASTER LOWYS, God's blessing be upon you." Brother Gilbert, the weasel-faced Seneschal of the Abbey, stood to greet the King's Man whom he had last seen a year earlier at the inquest into the death of one of the Daughters of the Shadows. He gestured to a bench opposite and Simon sat down. They were seated in the Palatium, the royal hall of the abbey. The large chamber was dimly lit by burning sconces, and at its far end, a small fire burned in a hearth, for the abbey was wealthy enough to have a fashionable chimney installed to draw the smoke. All around, the walls were decorated with bright wall paintings showing stories from the Bible.

The Nuncio recalled his last contentious meeting, with Brother Gilbert pettily fining Simon for failing to raise the Hue and Cry. Now, Simon found himself summoned to the Seneschal's presence for an urgent matter, important enough for a messenger to intercept him on the King's Highway with a summons to attend the abbey with great dispatch.

Lowys regarded Brother Gilbert; the resentment of twelve months since still lingered. Simon thought the Seneschal had aged

130

in that time; his whisps of hair appeared greyer and his fleshy face showed more lines.

The Seneschal cleared his throat. "Master Lowys, you are, I believe, engaged in royal business at the Lazar House of St Mary's?"

"Aye, I am," was Simon's cautious reply.

"Good. Good. Father Abbot does tell me you have sought a high-born maid seized from the abbey some days ago."

Simon eyed him quizzically. "Father Abbot is well-informed."

"Indeed. He received a communication from a visiting Abbess, I know not her name, who told him of your presence and your task for Her Grace."

Now, it made sense for Simon. Isabella had said she would write to keep Abbot de Norton informed.

"And, Brother Gilbert, pray tell me how that concerns you. Do you have information that may assist me in my enquiry?"

The Seneschal's small, sunken eyes darted left and right. A thin sheen of sweat reflected on his large forehead.

"There is something, Master Lowys, something that may be relevant to you."

Simon leaned forward, his interest piqued.

"This is most delicate, but we have had reports of maids go missing from within our demesnes these months since. Not many, you understand and the occasional boy."

"Indeed! And how many of these have been found?"

"Ahh. We have found some, two to be precise." He paused, seeking the correct form of words. "But sadly, neither lived."

"Do you mean they were alive when you found them?"

"Nay! God had seen fit to take both."

"And what did your Inquest determine as to the cause of death and the deodand?"

Brother Gilbert shifted nervously on his bench. The Benedictine Abbey of St Albans enjoyed historic, privileged legal rights, including the liberty to conduct its own Coroner's court.

Brother Gilbert combined his office as Seneschal with that of Coroner and presided over the sessions.

"I, er, we, thought it prudent not to have…." He cleared his throat once more. "We believed the children to have run off, so I deemed no investigation necessary. Once the bodies were found, the remains were too long dead to merit investigation."

"Christ's wounds! What the…." Simon stopped his profanity just in time. "So, you are saying you convened no Coroner's Court for these bodies? No Hue and Cry raised? No investigation as to the cause of death?"

"Master Lowys, you must understand we did not wish to alarm the local villagers. These people believed the children had absconded. They still believe so."

"Brother Gilbert, as you do know, the law demands that upon discovery of a body, the Cry is raised and an inquest is conducted within sight of the body."

The Seneschal stiffened, bristling at Simon's words. "I full well know the law, Master Lowys, but, on this occasion, I chose otherwise, so as not to panic our tenants." His hand trembled. "And…. I did not wish the good name of our Holy Abbey to be connected so to such evil."

"Two children go missing and are found dead." Brother Gilbert raised a hand.

"The two I spoke of and another found in the town last evening after the Curfew Bell," he said sheepishly.

"So, three have gone missing in all and three are found dead?"

The Seneschal shuffled uncomfortably. "Tis more." He squeezed the words out, his tone hushed. "More maids and boys have been reported as having absconded. I thought nothing of it, for the young to run away from their manor is not unusual.

But now I afear someone has seized these children and possibly is killing them."

Simon's mind raced as he sought to make sense of what Brother Gilbert had said.

"How many children have gone missing?"

"Seven." His lips contorted before he admitted, "Mayhaps more."

"And the three found dead, were any reported as missing? And what gives you reason to believe that the children who you say '*absconded*' are connected to the deaths of the other three?"

Brother Gilbert hunched forward, his fingers tapping the table as cover for his shaking hands. "One," he replied in almost a whisper, "and it seems the boy discovered last night."

"You know his identity?"

"Aye, he was John, the youngest son of Ordred, a base-born labourer from the manor of Sandridge, half a day's ride north."

"And this, John, was reported as missing?"

"Nay, one of the Constable's men is from Sandridge and recognised the boy."

"And the others, were they reported as missing?"

Again, Brother Gilbert shuffled uncomfortably on his bench. "You needs must understand, Master Lowys, that for some of our tenants, having one fewer mouth to feed is a blessing. Not all the children were told to us, twas John le Tailour the Constable who found out by his investigation."

"Tell me, Brother, even though you failed to hold Inquests, did you at least establish the cause of death for these three children?"

"Aye. All three were stabbed through the heart with a thin blade. Death would have come mercifully quickly."

Ж

Chapter Twenty-seven

Bone Hill Wood, near the village of Daneswick, June 1277.

THEY CAME FOR HER DEEP into the night. Which night it was, she could not tell, other than there had been many such nights since her terror began. She huddled in one corner of the large, dark space. She thought she was in an outdoor building: gentle draughts blew in through gaps between thick timber laths and the smell was a mixture of sweet hay and pungent animal droppings. In the blackness, she sensed a door opening close by and became aware of two large shadows entering, dimly lit by a flickering flame from a candle lamp. By the low light two men approached the other children who sat, pushed tight against the timbers. A young girl sobbed as her hair was grabbed roughly and the low light brought close to her face.

"Nay!" The girl's sobs were intensified by her being thrown back to the ground. The two men moved among the bodies amid more cries and crying, followed by a low, gruff, "Not her, nay, nay."

As they approached Jeanne, she pressed back against the timbers behind her. As the lantern light neared, she sought to make herself as small as possible, but a large, rough hand grabbed her hair and jerked her head upwards.

She smelt him before he brought the lamp close to her cheek and leaned in. The rank odour of urine and ale overwhelmed her.

"Tis her!" said the gruff voice.

"For surtees?" asked his companion.

"Aye, I am sure. Look at her garments." He grabbed her by her arm and pulled her up. From behind her, a hemp sack was thrown over her head, the smell making her gag. One of the two pushed her back, forcing her to move. She stopped, but another hard shove moved her forward towards a door.

"Wait," barked the gruff voice.

"What for?"

"These clothes she wears," said the gruff one. "They will fetch a good price. Shame to let them walk out of here."

"We have to have her alive, Kenric," said the now-alarmed companion.

"Fie! Do not say my name. I am not about to kill the maid; just take her garments."

Kenric, manhandled the girl through the door. Through the loose hempen sack over her head, she saw him before her, silhouetted by the moonlight, a knife pointed at her throat, the candle lamp in the other.

"Look, she is about so tall." He held his arm up to just below his armpit. "Take this and find one of them inside who is the same size and bring her here."

Kenric's companion took the lamp and went back inside. After a short while, he returned with a sobbing young maid. Kenric pointed to the distraught girl.

"Take off your clothing and leave them on the ground." This command prompted a wail of anguish. Kenric slapped her hard across the face, causing further tears.

"Now. Do it now." The sobbing maid untied the string at her waist and pulled the ragged, sleeveless shift over her head, dropping it to the earth.

"The shoes, too!" She removed the rough wooden clogs and petulantly threw them onto the earth.

"Now back inside," commanded Kenric, with a rough shove in the girl's back.

He turned to the girl who had been their target, who stood defiantly before them in the moonlight.

"Now, my lady," he sneered, "very slowly, take off your garment and shoes and put those on.

With great reluctance, the Lady Jeanne de Lascy turned her back on the two men and did as instructed.

In her thirteen summers, the Lady Jeanne de Lascy had never been in a cart, but the rhythmic trundle of the wooden wheels, the clip-clop of hooves and the rough timber floor she now lay on told her that it was a cart, on which, she now lay. Her head remained covered with the sacking, her hands and feet were bound and the ragged peasant garment that had been forced upon her itched and smelt of animal dung.

She lay alone on the rough-hewn planks. From the conversation she overheard, the same two men were now driving her somewhere. The man with the gruff tone, Kenric, appeared to be in charge. She had called out, demanding to know what they were doing, but that merely earned her a hard slap across her sack-covered face. The sacking made it difficult to see anything. The moonlight allowed flittering shapes through, but Jeanne had no idea where they were going or what they intended to do with her. She thought of asking again, but that would earn her another slap, and they would hardly tell her.

She took little comfort that she was still alive; they may still plan to kill her and throw her body where it might never be discovered. She could not think of a single reason why she had been seized or, indeed, why the two had now singled her out and bundled her into the back of this cart. She wondered how long she had been travelling but could not tell.

"'Tis down here now," said Kenric and the cart lurched sideways, rolling the Lady Jeanne into its side.

"See the river ahead; stop before the ford," Kenric instructed his companion.

The lane they took was rutted and bumpy and Jeanne was thrown from side to side, striking her head on the side of the wooden frame.

"Whoa! Whoa!" the cart juddered to a stop and Jeanne felt the cart lurch as the two men jumped down. Rough hands grabbed at her and she was hauled down and dumped onto the ground. The horse - she was sure it was just the one - snorted and the cart began to move again until one of the men called it to halt.

The moonlit night was still, allowing Jeanne to hear the swoosh of a knife being unsheathed. She tensed, awaiting the sharpness of the blade and the pain that would follow. Her bound hands were pulled upwards and the blade sliced through the cord that held them. Jeanne's terror was not over as her head was gripped by one of the men and wrenched backwards.

The one called Kenric leaned into her and, as before his odour and rank-breath assaulted her senses even with the hemp-sack covering her face.

"Now, my maid, here we part company." A foot pushed her hard and she began to roll. When she came to a stop, Jeanne sat up and scrabbled to pull the sacking from her head. She blinked, looking around to see where she was. Moonlight danced along a slow-moving stream beside her. She had rolled down its gentle bank. She saw no one but heard the rumble of a cart moving off from atop the slope.

She tried to call out, but her mouth was dry. Reaching into the stream, she cupped a handful of the cool water and put it to her lips.

"Do not leave me," she screamed, panic in her voice, but the low rumble of the cartwheels and the rhythmic sound of hooves faded into the distant darkness. She was alone.

The Lady Jeanne de Lascy reached down to untie her bound feet. The knots were tight and it took her some time and much wriggling of her feet to free herself. She stood and the realisation came that she was lost. The scream of a vixen broke the stillness. She had no idea where she was; her breathing was fast and ragged. She was alone at night, frightened and in a place she did not know.

Ж

——————

Chapter Twenty-eight

The manor of Westwick, June 1277.

BERNARDO RAVENNATE KNELT at his prie-dieu deep in silent prayer. He was alone in the small chapel, mouthing the words, his prayer beads moving swiftly across his fingers as he completed his sixth Paternoster. On the altar wall above him loomed a large wooden crucifix, the eyes of the Christ staring down at the solitary figure of the Papal Legate. A heavy door opened with a loud creak, breaking the stillness of the chapel and a figure entered, making no noise as he glided across the cold stone floor.

Giovanni di Bologna approached his master, standing respectfully to the side of the keeling Legate until his devotion was complete.

At length, Ravennate stood, stretched out and rubbed his numb knees.

"The aches get more with each passing season, Giovanni."

"*Si,mio Signore.*" Giovanni stepped in close to his master. "*Signore*, we have received word that may prove fruitful."

"Indeed?" The Papal Legate turned to his manservant. "And what is this news?"

"I have word that one close to the Assassin of Arles is nearby."

139

"Benuic? Benuic is in England still? No, surely not!"

"Perhaps, *Signore*, but it is true one of his circle is close. My people tell me that the Abbess Constanza de San Andreas de Anroyo is at the Lazar House of St Mary's on the Roman road north. I had already sent word that we require the services of the assassin."

Ravennate's eyebrows raised. "That is the alias one of Benuic's people used, but the assassin would not linger in England for fear of being caught. Could it not be the true Abbess Constanza de San Andreas?"

"Nay, *Signore*. I asked for a description. The real Abbess is beyond sixty winters on God's earth. This Abbess Constanza at St Mary's is described as not a maid but not old, perhaps of thirty of God's years in age."

"You have seen her?"

"I have, Your Eminence."

"Indeed you say," replied the Legate. "And Benuic is still being hunted by the King's Men." His mind whirred with possibilities, but his henchman articulated the thought for him.

"The troublesome King's Man, Lowys. It would be a shame for him if he were to fall victim to Benuic while he pursues his investigations."

"Aaah! So it would, Giovanni." Ravennate gave a hearty chuckle.

"Lowys is asking too many questions and Benuic could eliminate the problem."

"But, would not killing Lowys bring more King's Men down upon us?" suggested the Legate.

"Nay, *Signore*," Giovanni responded. "Not upon us, but upon Benuic, who after all is a wanted assassin whose death would be much celebrated. And there would be no trail to here."

Ravennate paused, stroking his chin. "Go carefully, Giovanni; we do not wish the assassin's wrath to fall upon us."

Ж

———————

Chapter Twenty-nine

The village of Park on Watling Street, Hertfordshire, June 1277.

THE FIRST STRANDS OF blue-grey dawn flickered on the eastern horizon. The lady Jeanne de Lascy winced. The wooden clogs had chafed and bloodied her toes, for she had been walking for many hours. Her breath was short and a sheen of sweat lay on her brow. She was doing all she could not to panic, for she had no idea as to her whereabouts. She continued to wonder why the men had seized her and then abandoned her in the middle of nowhere. Jeanne's greatest fear had been that they would attack her and take her virtue; a sense of relief washed across her when she was released. As she walked, she had the sense to seek a roadway, which, she hoped, would surely lead her to safety.

Her only saving grace had been the crescent moon, which cast enough light to prevent her from thrashing around in the woods. At length, she scrabbled up a shallow rise and was relieved to discover a wide trackway. Her dilemma now was which way to go. The moon was high above her. Her tutor, the Dominican Simon of Newburgh, had tried to teach her the principles of astronomy, but now she wished she had paid more attention. Jeanne recollected that the moon sets in the west, which, if she was correct, meant she should walk east, for Westminster lay to the east. But how far away was it? As she began walking, she was struck by the thought that the men may have taken her north, which would mean all her calculations were in vain.

The first rays of sunlight cheered her considerably and she resolved to walk as quickly as she could, though the wooden clogs made progress difficult and painful. Her breathing was laboured as she fought back the panic of being lost. At least now, each step she took was to the cacophony of the dawn chorus of birds. Ahead, Jeanne spied a grey smudge on the horizon – smoke; where there was smoke, there would be houses and people.

It was a small hamlet of just a few run-down cottages. The lady Jeanne de Lascy had never been this close to poverty and peasant dwellings. A dog barked somewhere close as others answered its call. A guttural shout came from one of the houses, silencing one of the animals. The wooden door of a cottage swung open, its leather hinges groaning under the weight and a small, wiry man stepped out into the brightening light of the early morning. He went to the side of his property and, with a huge sigh of satisfaction, began to relieve himself against the decaying wattle and daub. Jeanne averted her eyes and waited until the man had finished before speaking.

"Gentil monsieur, pouvez-vous m'aider." She immediately saw he didn't understand, so she switched to faltering English. "Good sir, can you help me?"

Osbert the Smith turned, startled at the presence of a young stranger eyeing her suspiciously.

"What do you do here?" His tone was wary. Foreigners were unwelcome in any village and to find one at this hour was deeply suspicious.

"I beseech you, sir. I need your help. Pray tell me, where are we?

The man was confused. The maid before him spoke French, which meant she was '*lordly*' by birth, yet she stood before him in rags.

A thought ran through his head. How lucky the maid was to have come across him, not Sim the Ploughman. Sim may have eventually helped the maid but would have had his way with her first, despite her youth. Osbert realised that he couldn't help the maid, but Sire Henri, the local priest, could.

"Come. Come." He gestured to Jeanne to come with him and walked slowly towards the church.

Wary as she was, Jeanne understood that this peasant sought to help her, so she limped her way behind him, the rough wooden clogs still chafing and cutting her feet.

Osbert feared that Sire Henri would be abed at this hour, and he was relieved when his loud knocks at the presbytery door were answered quickly.

"Osbert, my son, what is amiss?" Sire Henri de Wolde showed no annoyance at being disturbed at this early hour.

Having brought the girl to the priest's house, Osbert hadn't thought what he should say.

"Tis a child! A stranger."

Sire Henri frowned, not comprehending what Osbert was saying until a young peasant maid stepped from behind the wiry peasant.

"*Je vous prie de m'aider, mon frere.*"

Despite her ragged appearance, Sire Henri reacted immediately, recognising the maid as no peasant child. "Come child, pray you enter," he replied in courtly French.

It wasn't long before Sire Henri's housekeeper had salved and bound Jeanne's feet and sat her in front of a roaring fire with a bowl of hearty pottage to build her strength.

When she told the priest who she was, Sire Henri recognised that he had to act quickly to send word that the Lady Jeanne was safe. But who to tell?

Henri knew the Abbot had lay nuncios who could reach Westminster in a morning's ride, so he decided that he would take the maid to the Abbey of the martyr.

Ж

———

Chapter Thirty

St Peter's Church, St Albans, June 1277.

THE COOL INTERIOR OF St Peter's Church came as a welcome relief from the heat of the day. Giovanni di Bologna was a soldier, a veteran of many campaigns with scars to show it, but even he found this English summer oppressive. He stepped from the light into the cool, gloomy interior of the church with its odour of sanctity, incense and beeswax. Giovanni strode towards the altar, eyes scanning from side to side, seeking any danger even in this House of God. He genuflected before the altar and made the Signum Crucis, not out of faith but of a desire to blend in. It was the middle hour after Sext and there were just two people inside St Peter's: a woman kneeling on the stone floor, deep in prayer and a wizened old man lighting a candle in offering.

A young boy had arrived at the Legate's manor house with a sealed parchment addressed to him. It contained a terse message in French, instructing him to be at St Peter's beside the northern entrance to St Albans, in the middle hour after Sext. He was to kneel before the altar and await instructions. He knew that the message came from Benuic, the assassin.

Below the altar was a stone step where three prie-dieus awaited sinners to kneel and recite their penitentiary prayers. Above Giovanni's head, the roof timbers of St Peter's groaned menacingly, twisting in protest at the heat of the day. Giovanni had been in many churches in his life, but not always for prayer. His childhood was on the streets of the poor quarter of Bologna, the son of a whore. He had stolen from his first church when he was but five or six summers old: the Chiesa del Santo Sepolcro. His thoughts went back years to that afternoon and old, half-blind, angry Padre Pietro. He had squeezed through an opening left by workmen and taken a candlestick. Having stolen it he hadn't known what to do next; the coin he received, far less than the precious object was worth, had set him on the path of criminality. That road had ended at the age of twelve when he was caught and, as punishment, sent to serve in the mercenary army of the Lambertazzi, a powerful family vying for power in Bologna and beyond. Giovanni had grown from a boy to a man, serving the Lambertazzi, first as a stableboy and then as a squire. He trained as a man-at-arms, learned the art of war and had the scars on his lean, muscled body to prove it. Yes, over the years, he had been in many churches, rarely in prayer, often in looting, and, he regretted, sometimes in rape and killing.

A twinge of pain shot through his shoulder and he twisted his arm to seek relief. He was wounded saving a Bishop's baggage train in a skirmish some seven years before, in a village whose name he never knew. A grateful Bishop Bernardo had employed him ever since. Now Giovanni served a Cardinal of the Church and Papal Legate and, he mused, the boy had come a long way from the filthy streets of Bologna.

"You are deep in prayer or confession of your many sins, Giovanni di Bologna." A female voice broke his thoughts. He had heard no one approach, but a woman stood behind him.

"There is no need to turn around; I am here to facilitate your request, Master di Bologna."

"I have made no request for a woman, Mistress. I know not of what you speak."

"Oh, but you did. You sought the help of my master, Benuic."

Despite the instruction, Giovanni turned in surprise at the mention of the assassin's name. Staring at the face of the woman brought him no further clarity.

"Mistress! Begone! I have no need for a high-bred whore"

Jasliena van Leuven winced. At being called a whore. "You summoned Benuic, Giovanni di Bologna and I am here to represent the assassin."

Giovanni stared wide-eyed at her, a scar on his cheek tightening and standing proud.

"Mistress, I have already spoken with Benuic's representative and given instruction as to the task."

Now it was Jasliena van Leuven who showed surprise.

"Which representative of Benuic?"

"At the Lazar House at St Mary de Pré. The woman who says she is the Abbess de San Andreas de Anroyo."

Jasliena's body tensed, concern flickered in her eyes. The Abbess de San Andreas de Anroyo had been the alias she had used a year since escaping England after the failed assassination attempt on the Queen.

"It was not the real Abbess, you say?"

"Nay, my people tell me the true Abbess is old and this woman was but beyond a maid's years and never old."

Giovanni felt a trail of sweat run down one of his cheeks towards his salt-and-pepper beard. He sensed the woman had been surprised at his answer. He took the opportunity to look fully upon her. She was not what he expected.

She was plain-dressed in a simple shift and cote with a wool cloak. None of her garments were of the finest quality, thus she could have been any woman about the town.

Anyone entering St Peter's and gazing at the two would have found the contrast striking. Giovanni's fine garments said he was no peasant. Beneath his cloak of kermes red, he had a fine, wide blue tunic reaching to his calf with a mantle and hood trimmed in a red that matched his stockings.

Jasliena knelt on the Prie-dieu next to Giovanni, facing the altar as if in prayer.

"*Cazzo!*" Jasliena spat the word out and Giovanni flinched. The only women he had heard use such a swear word were the street whores of Sienna.

"This is not good, Master di Bologna. Not good." Her tone was measured and serious. "You have been duped. I can tell you that whoever you spoke to has no contact with Benuic."

"But my people tell me that one who helped the assassin escape England last year went by the alias Abbess de San Andreas de Anroyo."

Giovanni looked closely at the woman. The face framed in the white wimple could even be described as pretty, with its flawless olive skin and sensual mouth.

"Was that you? If you are the contact for the assassin, you would need to flee England and a woman of the church provides good cover."

"You have the right of it, Master di Bologna, which is why we are faced with difficulty." Deep in thought, she steepled her fingers and rested her elbows on the Prie-dieu.

Giovanni was also thinking, concerned that his plan was falling apart.

"I cannot proceed now, tis too much risk now that someone else knows," he suggested.

Jasliena held up a hand. "Nay! All is not yet lost. You gave instruction to this woman. So you have given her the name for Benuic to target." It was a statement, not a question. Giovanni nodded.

"Tell me now what message to pass to the true Benuic?"

Briefly, Giovanni outlined the death contract he sought.

"And the death price you wish to pay?"

"One hundred gold Florentines."

She nodded her head in agreement. The actions and words of this woman made Giovanni realise he had made a grievous error. This woman was the true conduit to the assassin Benuic. Whoever he had spoken with in the meadow knew of his plan and thus was dangerous and had to be eliminated.

He began to speak, "Mistress," but she raised a hand to still him.

We have two strands to follow, Master di Bologna. The person you identified as the target; that must proceed, although we must assume that they have already been alerted. Secondly, there is this unknown woman."

Jasliena turned to look at Giovanni. "You do not know who she is, do you?"

"Nay. Nor can I really say what she looked like, for she wore a tight wimple and veil with her nun's habit."

Jasliena stared hard at the wooden cross above the altar, not in prayer but to focus her thoughts.

"Whosoever she is, she must have a link to King Edward's Chancery." Jasliena paused. "Who was Benuic to target?"

"Twas a King's Man, Simon Lowys."

"Indeed! Simon Lowys," She repeated the name slowly and her southern Mediterranean origins became apparent in the pronunciation.

"You know him?" enquired Giovanni.

"I know of him. He played a role a year since in foiling the plot against the Queen. More than that, his name was given as one who could identify an Intelligencer of the Crown, or indeed, be that agent." She brought a single slim finger to her mouth and stroked her lips.

"Why is this Lowys a target?"

"He arrived at St Mary de Pré asking questions and then turned up at my master's manor. I fear he draws too close to a truth I would prefer is kept hidden."

Jasliena knew Giovanni was the enforcer for the Legate, but what intrigued her was another mention of St Mary de Pré.

"Is it a coincidence that this King's Man arrives at St Mary's, a place where we have friends?"

"Twas an error. We took a child, but it turned out she was a daughter of one of the Queen's ladies, and Lowys came to find her."

"And did he?"

"I do not believe so, we freed her."

Silence reigned while Jasliena considered her next step. Only the intermittent movement of the roof timbers, still creaking in protest against the day's heat, broke the mood.

"Lowys must be silenced," insisted Giovanni.

"Nay. Not yet, at least. Lowys likely knows who this woman is. Lowys arrives at St Mary's, where this woman is masquerading as the Abbess. If Lowys is removed, we are no closer to knowing her identity." A knowing look came across Jasliena's face.

"Lowys will have to tell us who she is or at least confirm her identity."

"You know who this woman is?" asked Giovanni, surprised.

"I do not know for surtees, but I suspect I do know who it may be. I do not have a name, but it may be one they call in the Chancery, le Reynard."

"Le Reynard?" The name meant nothing to Giovanni. "And how do you plan to have Lowys give us the name of this 'le Reynard'?"

She smiled, showing oyster-white teeth. "Why, Master di Bologna, I plan to ask him," she replied. "When we know the identity, you may deal with her." Her steely eyes fixed on the Legate's man.

"And then we will have King Edward of England kill Simon Lowys for us."

Ж

———

Chapter Thirty-one

The Guesthouse of the Benedictine Abbey of St Albans,
Hertfordshire, June 1277.

THE LADY JEANNE DE LASCY screamed in frustration as she repeatedly tried to pull the bone comb through her bedraggled, fair hair. The knots would not shift and she threw the comb to the ground. In the past few hours, she had gone from despair to relief and now, thanks to the priest Sire Henri, she found herself in the Guesthouse of the Abbey at St Albans. More than anything, she wished to see her mother.

Tears of joy flowed when the peasant Osbert brought her to the church and Sire Henri de Wolde spoke to her in French. She understood some English words, but her first language was the French of the Royal Court. Although Sire Henri did not know her, he grasped her story and immediately acted to bring her here to the Abbey. Jeanne understood that a messenger had already been dispatched to Westminster to inform her mother and Her Grace, the Queen, of her safety.

They had arrived after Terce. The journey from the village of Park on Osbert's cart had been rough and bumpy in the back, but she did not care. She was free of her ordeal. The Infirmarian, Brother

Simon, had been summoned and he, in turn, had sent word to a widow of the town to act as chaperone to the Lady Jeanne.

She and the young maid who accompanied her, bathed and cleaned the cuts, salved her bruises and gave her fresh, simple linen clothing.

"Now my Lady," said Matilda Heacham, "can we fetch you ought else?"

"Nay, Mistress. I am in your debt for what you have done already."

Matilda Heacham cast a glance at her young accomplice, who stood beside Jeanne with a sharp knife poised.

"My Lady," said Alia Parys, " I am going to try to comb your locks and cut out any stubborn knots that refuse to budge."

Jeanne de Lascy signalled her agreement, sitting still while Alia dragged the bone comb through her fair hair.

"How do you fare now, my Lady," inquired Alia, unpicking another knot in Jeanne's hair.

"I am greatly relieved and just wishing to see my mother."

"And she will be here soon, I understand." As her body warmed, Jeanne's colour had returned to her face.

"My Lady," began Alia, "what do you remember? I am sorry to ask, but it may help catch the people who did this."

The Lady Jeanne de Lascy closed her eyes, better to recall the terror of the past few days.

"There were lots of other children. I was brought to a barn, I know not where. I counted nine other children; all wore peasant clothing." As Alia probed for details, Jeanne recalled the smell, the coldness of the nights and how some children would be taken, while others arrived.

"When I was set free, they came for me in the night. There were two of them, both men, not full grown. One threw a sack over my head, but I could see shapes through it. They made me remove my garments and shoes and gave me peasant clothing."

"Do you recall ought else?" inquired Alia.

"The two were mismatched. One tall and the other smaller but wider." Jeanne's eyes welled up and Alia took her hand.

"I afear I still hold the smell. The barn stank of animals and urine. It was dreadful."

"My Lady, it is good to cry; remembering will help find these thugs. Let me go back to when you were taken, at the Abbey of St Mary de Pré. What do you recall?"

Jeanne thought for a moment. "I do remember. My mother was in the cloister, conversing with my Aunt, Sister Agnes. It is a convent with little to amuse, so I decided to go for a walk in the orchard." She screwed her face as if better to recall.

"There is a gate from the cloister that leads onto the orchard. I went through it and found myself alone among the fruit trees. I know not how long I was there before a voice hailed me."

"A voice? Did you know the voice?"

"Nay. It was a child. And she was not alone; a young boy was with her."

"What did she say to hail you?"

Jeanne thought for a moment. "She told me they had seen a strange fish in the river, as big as a man and would I like to see it."

"They spoke to you in English, then?"

"Yes, but I understand some English. I converse with some of my mother's English servants."

"My Lady, what did they look like?"

"When I saw the young maid, I thought her perhaps the daughter of a merchant, for she was not dressed as a peasant. Her clothing was fine-made. The boy stood further back and he was not so well-attired but still not wearing base-born clothing."

"But you went with these children?"

"I confess, I was bored and a fish that size intrigued me."

Alia was pleased that Jeanne was opening up to her. Any information she provided could prove helpful in tracking down other lost children. But then, the Lady Jeanne's demeanour changed. She recoiled as if frightened on seeing Robert de Berdesfold enter the chamber, pushing her slight frame hard against the wall as if to hide. He no longer wore what Simon Lowys had procured for him but was dressed in his bright serge cote with his cloak, thrown rakishly over one shoulder, dyed a pale hue of red.

Alia raised an arm. "Fie Master de Berdesfold! Wait if you please." She looked at the Lady Jeanne and could see the fear in her face.

"What is it, my Lady? This man is a friend; he does not threaten us." Alia took Jeanne's hand and gave it a squeeze. "Do look upon his face, my Lady and you will see he is not here to harm you."

Jeanne peered out of the corner of her eyes at the standing figure before her, accepting what Alia had said.

"Do see, my Lady, this is Master de Berdesfold; he is one of King Edward's men." Robert de Berdesfold's chest puffed out on hearing Alia describe him thus. What she said was not strictly true, for he was not yet a King's Man; indeed, he was not yet a man, but it pleased him to hear Alia describe him so.

"My Lady, you have never met Master de Berdesfold here, so what made you recoil when he entered?"

She pointed at his cote. "His clothing. The man who came to the barn wore such garments and had the same cloak in kermes."

"Tell me of this man, " inquired Alia gently. "Take as long as you need."

Jeanne composed herself, closed her eyes to recall and relived her first evening locked with other children in the barn.

"I know not where this barn was, only that the smell of animals and burnt wood was heavy. I left the orchard with the girl and the boy followed. A gate led onto a meadow which ran down to the river. She led me down to the bank, where I could see a small wherry moored at the jetty. I asked her about the fish and next, I knew, a hand was thrust across my face and a rag was pushed over my mouth. The odour on the cloth was bitter and the next I knew, I awoke in a dark barn alongside other children."

"Did you have other words with this maid?"

"Nay. I did ask her again about this fish, but she said nothing more."

Alia had already gleaned much valuable information about the abduction, but she wondered why the Lady Jeanne alone had been released?

"And, my Lady, tell me again, what was it about Master de Berdesfold here that caused you angst?"

Jeanne fixed her gaze on the young King's Man. " Tis his clothing, twas, on the second day, I was imprisoned in the barn where a man came. He appeared to be giving instruction to the guards." She pointed again at de Berdesfold. "His clothing was the same. When Master de Berdesfold came into the chamber, but awhile ago, I thought him the same man."

Alia took this in. "So his clothing was a coloured serge cote and a cloak dyed scarlet."

"Aye." A spark of recollection flitted across Jeanne's face. "Aye, the open barn door threw sunlight inside and I could easily make out his garments. I see many wearing such garments, for tis what many wear at King Edward's Court."

That, Alia thought, was very significant. Did it mean that someone with links to the King's Court was behind the abduction?

Alia continued to probe Jeanne about her release, although she could offer no explanation. Nor could she be of help in pinpointing the location of the barn. At length, Alia thought it best for the Lady Jeanne to sleep before her mother arrived from Westminster. She accompanied Jeanne to the guest chamber reserved for visiting senior clergy and sat with her while she slept, not even stirring when a thunderstorm broke over the town.

By the time Jeanne awoke, her mother, the Lady Matilda de Lascy, arrived at the Abbey and mother and daughter were reunited. Alia took her leave and returned to Matilda Heacham's townhouse on Sopwellstrete, ready to pass on what the Lady Jeanne had told her to her Mistress and Master Lowys. She didn't know that in so doing, she was about to place both their lives in danger.

156

Ж

Chapter Thirty-two

The townhouse of Mistress Matilda Heacham, Sopwellstrete, St Albans, June 1277

THE ABBEY TOWN OF ST ALBANS awoke to the earthy, cut meadow smell that often followed a thunderstorm. The oppressive heat had broken in the night, unleashing a torrent of rain that had the beneficial effect of cleansing the stinking streets of the town. It also made for a lovely morn.

Two people sat around the wooden trestle brought out from the kitchen so they could break their fast in the pleasant morning air. Matilda Heacham had laid out a meal of barley porridge, freshly baked maslin loaves, butter and a soft cheese she had made the previous day.

Simon had stayed at the Abbey guesthouse the previous evening while Isabella lodged with Mistress Heacham. When Simon arrived at Sopwellstrete, the ringing of the Terce bell was more than an hour away. He entered through the rear. Matilda and Isabella were already seated, waiting for his arrival.

"Mistress," Simon was respectful in addressing the widow Heacham first, although his gaze fell on the younger woman in a sleeveless kirtle of wool, her face framed by a tight, white wimple.

An enthusiastic smile broke across his face as he greeted Isabella, though he was disappointed that she remained impassive.

"Master Lowys," she inclined her head slightly.

Simon knew yesterday that the Lady Jeanne de Lascy had been found and agreed that, if she was questioned by a woman closer to her own age, it might elicit more detail.

As the only man present, it fell to Simon to say the blessing.

"Benedic, Domine, nos et haec tua dona quae de tua largitate sumus sumpturi, per Christum Dominum nostrum. Amen." Bless us, O Lord and these Thy gifts which we are about to receive from Thy bounty, through Christ, Our Lord. Amen.

"Amen," all responded. And they began to break their fast.

The aroma of the recently baked bread permeated the air; beside the loaves, a shallow clay saucer held stewed apple with a hint of expensive cinnamon, which they would be sharing with the wasps that had also discovered it.

"This is excellent fare, as always, Mistress," said Simon, appreciating the effort Matilda Heacham had put into the meal.

When she had swallowed her bread, Isabella complimented Matilda on the cheese.

"Tis freshly made yesterday, though it does not keep many days. I skim off the cream and churn it into butter."

"I agree it is mighty fine," suggested Simon. "When I was with Her Grace at Oxford, she was presented with a local cheese with a band of spruce bark around the outside to keep it together. This cheese is just as good."

Matilda Heacham didn't blush at the compliment but was delighted that her companions loved her cooking.

Gradually, the food on the table reduced, the stewed apple melding well with the barley pottage.

The conversation flowed, but not, Simon noticed, from Isabella, who appeared unusually reticent.

At length, she spoke quietly to him. "Master Lowys, I needs must have words."

"Have I done aught wrong, Mistress?"

"Nay, Master Lowys, but you must know something." Isabella stood up from the table and, addressing Matilda, said, "I am going to take a walk around the garden, Master Lowys. Will you accompany me?"

Simon did not hesitate and the two set off down Matilda Heacham's long garden, walking between the summer onions and leeks.

They walked side by side, not looking at each other and Simon sensed a tenseness.

"While we were at St Mary's," she began, "a young child came to the gatehouse with a parchment for me." She exhaled slowly, seeking the correct words.

"The sender believed I was truly the assassin Benuic and wished to meet face-to-face to engage my services."

"Indeed?" Simon was intrigued. "Do you risk meeting with this person?"

"Aye, Alia and I have already done so." Simon stopped, shocked at her response.

"You and Alia both? Was that not dangerous?" His concern was heartfelt.

"I think the place he chose was significant, for it was beyond the orchard, close by where the maid was taken."

They continued their slow walk, picking their way along the now freshly washed path. "And who was this person you met?"

"Twas Alia who met him. I watched from close by."

Simon grabbed her arm. "Alia? God's teeth, you both take a terrible risk."

"Fie now! Calm yourself. She was safe. I did not know him, but by his build, he was a soldier, but likely a man-at-arms rather than a knight. Alia says that by the way he spoke, he was from the lands of the Middle Sea."

"And what did he seek?"

"He offered one hundred golden florins to kill a man in the manner of an accident."

"A lot of coin," said Simon. " An important person then, or one who has got too close to the truth of something. Have you already alerted the target?"

She stopped, turned towards Simon and tenderly laid a hand on his arm.

"'Tis you, Master Lowys."

"What is me," inquired a puzzled Simon.

"'Tis you who is marked for death."

Simon gave a wholesome laugh, not the reaction Isabella expected.

"So, again, someone wants me dead. 'Tis not the Daughters of the Shadows still?"

"Master Lowys, this is a serious matter. 'Tis you, the assassin Benuic is to target."

"If you recall, Mistress, I have found my life under threat quite often this year past. You surely do, for it was you who saved me often."

"Aye, it was. But I may not be there to do the same this time." Simon was being too calm, she thought.

"Did you not hear me? The assassin plans that you have an accident. It could occur anywhere and at any time."

"And I will be vigilant, Mistress; you have my word. But am I to shut myself away? To stop my investigation?"

" 'Tis likely your investigation into the disappearance of the maid that has marked you for death." Isabella's voice was raised, and it carried the length of the garden; Matilda gasped and was about to say something but decided not to.

"I would agree with you. The death of the priest appears a local matter," suggested Simon.

"Tell me about the priest and his village," asked Isabella, keen that Simon did not dwell on the threat to his life.

Isabella listened intently as Simon related the village gossip he had gleaned from Windridge. He told of how Bortwyn, the Labourer's daughter, had reacted to the priest's name: the allegations of Ardith, the cunning woman and a murdered priest, held in contempt by the women and who, according to village talk, lusted after young maids.

Isabella picked up on what Simon had said and was mightily surprised he had not made the connection. She immediately saw how the two strands he was investigating might converge—the disappearance of young children and a priest who had a fondness for young maids.

"Master Lowys, do you not see that these things have a link? You visited St Mary's to discover more about the missing maid. You went to Windridge to discover more about a murdered priest and you find that he has a reputation among the wives for molesting children." When Isabella said it thus, it was plainly obvious that the events connected.

"Add to this we have reports of young children, waifs and orphans, going missing from the streets of this town and there is surely every possibility that all are tied together in some way. Do you not agree?"

"So, I am targeted because I have been asking questions about the priest and the maid?"

"Mayhaps, but you may have got too close to something occurring without you knowing."

"And where does this stranger who summoned you at St Mary's fit into this?" he snapped. Simon immediately regretted the tone of his words. In truth, now that Isabella had clarified the connection between the disappearance of the maid, the other children and Sire Roger, he was annoyed at himself for not having seen it.

"You asked of this stranger who sought out the Abbess Constanza at St Mary's." She paused for a short time to order her thoughts.

"It tells us that this stranger knew the Abbess was at St Mary's. Furthermore, he knew that this was not the true Abbess Constanza and he believed the person he met had links to the assassin Benuic. That makes the threat real."

They had reached the end of the garden, where it backed onto the Tonman ditch. Matilda's broad beans were growing well on their timber poles, casting a long shadow over the couple as they turned to head back to the house.

This stranger would know by now that he did not speak with the true Benuic's agent, so we needs must proceed with caution."

"Certainly, I must." It was a vain attempt at humour from Simon.

"But there is more we can deduce," Isabella continued. "This man seeks the employment of the assassin to eliminate you, so he seeks distance from the event. We needs must ask why so?"

Overhanging fronds of rosemary brushed against Isabella's green surcoat, wafting the pungent aroma into the air as she stepped forward.

"I compared the letter with the Legate's seal, alerting the Prioress and the message I received from this Italian and both were written by the same hand. That tells me the Italian has links to the Papal Legate. We must again ask if the Legate Ravennate is himself involved?"

Simon stopped mid-walk, recalling his visit to Bernardo Ravennate's manor at Westwick.

"God's teeth! Ravennate has an Italian Steward, Giovanni di Bologna; I met him when I went to Westwick. He is taller than me and his skin has the hue of one who has spent many years abroad. I met many such men on crusade and I know a soldier when I see one."

"That could well be him. The man Alia met had his hood pulled low to hide his features, but from my hiding place, I, too, saw the hands of a man who had spent long years in the sun."

She stopped, reached into the folds of her garment, and pulled a narrow cord stringed with small dark stones of black amber from it.

"Take these Paternoster beads, tis blessed at the shrine of St Thomas the Martyr and may help keep you safe." Drawing close, she looped it over his neck.

Isabella placed a hand on his arm and looked up into his face. A thrill raced through Simon's body.

"Knowing now who it is who threatens you does not lessen the danger to you." She smiled tenderly at him, a look he had never seen before, a mixture of affection and concern. A look he would take with him over the coming weeks.

Ж

____

Chapter Thirty-three

The townhouse of Matilda Heacham, Sopwellstrete, St Albans, June 1277.

AN EXCITED ALIA PARYS returned to Sopwellstrete before the Abbey bells rang for Nones, entering the house from the garden. Robert de Berdesfold had gone on ahead of her. She called Isabella, Simon, Robert and Matilda to the kitchen, where all five sat at the table as Alia related all that Jeanne had told her.

When she described why the Lady Jeanne had recoiled when de Berdesfold came into the chamber, Simon and Isabella's eyes met, sharing the same thought.

"Di Bologna," said Simon, "It has to be him."

"Aye, tis likely, but there is no proof yet against him. Many dress so at court, even you, Master de Berdesfold."

"This di Bologna, why do we not just arrest him now?" inquired de Berdesfold, pleased to be privy to the discussion.

"Aye, he is likely the man we seek," suggested Simon.

Isabella gave him a firm stare. "Indeed, if he is, then he is also the man behind the plan to have you fall victim to an accident."

"And I will take very good care," he retorted.

Isabella turned toward de Berdesfold. "Giovanni di Bologna has the protection of the Papal Legate."

"But Ravennate, the Papal Legate, is answerable under the law, is he not?" asked Alia.

As the man of law, all eyes turned to Simon, who thought for a time. "Perhaps, in law, but to be weighed against that is his immunity as a Prince of the Church. If he is accountable anywhere, it would be to an ecclesiastical court, not I fear, to the King's courts."

There was dismay around the table at this answer.

"But di Bologna is not clergy," said de Berdesfold. "Surely he could be brought before the King's Eyre?"

"Again, I would hope so, but he too may hold protection based on his employ by the Legate."

"Nay," interjected de Berdesfold. "This cannot be. Tis wrong. He goes about unchecked by the law, as if he is a wolfshead."

Isabella intervened. "Such talk gets us nowhere. We are on the trail of this group of child abductors, and we have a lead to meet with di Bologna in the town."

"Nay, that would be too much of a risk; what if di Bologna made an attempt on your life?

"Fie, Master Lowys. A man such as di Bologna will not take such a risk. By keeping the meeting as arranged, we may glean more of what is afoot and you, Master Lowys, must keep to public places when you are about. Take no risks."

There was a murmur of agreement around the table. "Mistress Heacham, when Master Lowys goes about his business in the town, will you keep eyes upon him?"

"Aye, I will," she replied.

"And I must scribe my report for Her Grace, even though I had little to do with finding her. I just give thanks to God that she is found safe," said Simon.

Isabella la Rus looked up. What had Simon just said? A thought came to her.

"You have the right of it Master Lowys. That is the intriguing element in all of this. Why was the maid found safe? Why was she released? They took her, so why release her and none other?"

"She did not know why they let her go," replied Alia.

"Master Lowys, you went to the Legate's manor house. Did he know of the maid's disappearance?"

"Nay, twas I that told him and informed him who the missing maid was."

"Indeed."

"Aye and when I told him, I saw alarm on his face, though it quickly changed."

"And then, after your visit, the maid and she alone is released. That can be no coincidence."

Ж

Chapter Thirty-four

The Manor House at Windridge, Hertfordshire, June 1277.

As Your Eminence can see, the income between Lady Day and the Feast of St John far exceeds our expectations." Giovanni di Bologna pointed to a parchment laid out in front of his master, Bernardo Ravennate.

"Income from Christendom for our special business has trebled. Tolls have increased. Payments in kind are stable and though we have several of our tenants in arrears, they…" His explanation was interrupted by a loud knock on the door of the solar.

Giovanni looked to his master, who gave an imperceptible nod of approval, whereupon Giovanni barked a command to enter.

The Under-Steward of the Papal Legate's Household entered the solar with an unnecessary flourish, puffing out his chest and striding purposefully toward Ravennate, deliberately ignoring Giovanni. Following close behind the Under-Steward was a woman and, a young man who appeared to be her servant, carrying a small, bright casket.

The Under-Steward approached the far end of the chamber where Ravennate was seated.

167

He stopped three paces before the Legate, gave a deep bow and with a booming tone, announced, "Mistress Amice de Shethesere of London and St Albans."

The Under-Steward moved deftly to the side before withdrawing, allowing Amice de Shethesere to step forward. She fell to her knees before Ravennate as he offered his right hand for her to kiss his ruby-topped Papal Ring, the symbol of his office.

Amice bowed her head in reverence and laid her lips gently on the ruby, acknowledging the authority of Bernardo Ravennate as the representative of the Papacy in England.

"Arise my child," said Legate. Amice stood before him, eyes lowered in submission, awaiting a sign to speak.

A faint smile broke on Bernardo's lips. Despite his vow of celibacy, he appreciated beauty and the woman standing before him was very comely indeed. A message from the Worshipful Company of Grocers in London had come a week earlier, requesting a personal audience. The Grocers were second among London's Great Livery Companies, immensely powerful and highly influential; their request intrigued him.

Bernardo had tasked Giovanni with finding out the purpose of the audience and it transpired that the widow of one of the Company's most influential members sought the Legates's blessing for a trading delegation they were about to dispatch to Araby. That they would send a woman to make such a request suggested how highly regarded she was within the circle of the Grocers' Guild.

"Mistress, I welcome you to my house," Ravennate said with his melodic Tuscan accent. Waving an arm to one side, he continued, "This is my steward, Giovanni di Bologna."

Standing beside the Legate, Giovanni bowed from the neck as he took in the envoy. She made a slight deferential bow toward him and began to outline the reason behind her visit.

Her elegance struck him immediately; she was the sort of woman who became more alluring as she aged. He judged her to be far beyond thirty summers with large, grey-brown eyes framed in a small, pale face, surrounded by a white-laced gorget. She was small in stature and her expensive green gown emphasised a womanly body beneath.

"Your Eminence will know of the Worshipful Company of Grocers, their influence and the good works that they do." Giovanni heard the words and became aware he was staring at Amice.

"The Company is sending a trade delegation to deepest Araby. Your Eminence will know, of course, that the Moors control all the routes of access to the lands of spices. Our delegation is seeking to find a circuitous route that takes us there but avoiding those lands under Moorish control."

"Quite so," replied Ravennate. "There are riches indeed if you can find such a route. I do hear there are pepper trees built on perilous cliffs guarded by serpents and cinnamon that needs must be harvested from nests of fantastical birds."

Such a plan was impossible, but Giovanni's expression remained neutral, masking his scorn. He knew the Moors of old and knew that although the Grocer's Company might spend years seeking a route that took them around Araby, they would find no access to the Spice Road, for the Moors jealously controlled it.

"Truly, Your Eminence is well-informed," she replied. "Which may help us, for, on behalf of the Worshipful Company of Grocers, I am here to ask humbly for you to give your blessing to our endeavour." Amice beckoned her servant forward. Eyes lowered, the young man took three paces towards his Mistress and nervously offered her the golden coffer he carried.

Giovanni watched as Bernardo sat transfixed, his gaze firmly focused on the small, shimmering casket. The Worshipful Company of Grocers was seeking his blessing and Giovanni thought, in such circumstances, it was both prudent and expected to offer him a bribe, nay, a gift.

The casket was about eight inches in length and some six inches high. Whatever the contents, he thought, it must be valuable. Technically, such gifts were the possession of the Church, but this was a grey area and he knew that Bernardo often kept such '*donations*' for himself.

Giovanni was fascinated now by Amice's smooth, delicate fingers as she turned the casket to face the Legate, lifting the lid to display its contents.

Giovanni looked puzzled as he gazed inside the casket at the remains of an ancient spear lying on a bed of crimson silk.

His master, however, appeared far more interested.

"Before you is the Holy Lance of the Archangel Michael, Your Eminence," explained Amice. "It was found by a monk at Sosthenion, beyond Constantinople, where the Archangel Michael appeared to the Emperor Constantine."

Eyes wide, Bernardo reached forward to touch the Holy Lance, gently brushing his pudgy, ringed fingers across it.

When words came to the Legate, it was as if he spoke to himself.

"*Now war arose in heaven, Michael and his angels fighting against the dragon. And the great dragon was thrown down, that ancient serpent, who is called Satan, the deceiver of the world.*"

Being more worldly, Giovanni imagined that some foreign huckster in a dingy tavern in Constantinople or somewhere similar had sold the relic and its provenance to a gullible monk for a sound profit.

Nonetheless, Bernardo looked up at Amice, joy across his face. "From the Book of Revelations, Mistress. Truly, this is the Holy Lance of the Archangel?"

"It is Your Eminence." Inwardly, Giovanni scoffed as the pretty woman offered Bernardo the casket. He grabbed it with both hands, pulled it close, and embraced it like a new-born infant.

"As you likely know," she continued, "St Michael is the Patron Saint of the Worshipful Company of Grocers and it was authenticated for the Company by the Archbishop of Genoa."

"Jacobus? Jacobus di Voragine the Arcivescovo di Genova?" he babbled excitedly, slipping into his native Bolognese dialect. "I know Jacobus, the Archbishop. I know him well. It is he, you say, who has authenticated this holy relic?

"He has," replied Amice, "Twas he who examined it closely and declared it to be the Holy Lance the Archangel used to slay the Serpent."

She addressed the Legate in perfect, courtly French, which told Giovanni she was a woman of some breeding. She was a grocer's widow so perhaps had married beneath her status. Mayhaps that was why the Grocers Guild sent her as their representative.

"And the Worshipful Company of Grocers wish Your Eminence to have it with their thanks and humility," she concluded. And he will willingly accept, thought Giovanni.

He was impressed with this woman, Amice de Shethesere. She had the Papal Legate eating from her palm, as might a tame bird; beauty and ability, he mused. Then, while the Legate caressed the box containing the Holy Lance, Giovanni caught Amice looking at him. Her mesmerising grey- brown eyes drew him in. He was becoming intrigued by this grocer's widow. As if flustered by Giovanni's attention, she turned back to Bernardo.

"If.. if it pleases Your Eminence, we can discuss arrangements for the Benediction at a later time." Was that a flush of colour that now spread across her face, wondered Giovanni? Was she embarrassed at seeing him looking at her?

"Indeed," replied Bernardo, still gently stroking the Holy Relic. "Mayhaps make such arrangement with my steward Giovanni here."

Now, it was Giovanni di Bologna who felt the flush of excitement. He had reason to be with this widow, to spend time with her and although he hadn't imagined he would, he looked forward to seeing her again. He had not experienced such longing since he was in Bore, some years before, when he had fallen for Diana, the fair-haired wife of his Company Captain, who had reciprocated his love. But he had lost her to the pestilence and he vowed then to close his heart to the love of women. He had been with women, wives, whores and fumbles with maids, but none meant aught to him. Those same stirrings he had for Diana suddenly resurfaced as he looked upon Amice.

She was addressing the Legate, but her allure had so engrossed Giovanni that he had not heard.

"I thank Your Eminence for this audience and I look forward to making the arrangements for the Holy Benediction." Bernardo gave her his Apostolic Blessing and she genuflected before backing out of the chamber, as protocol demanded.

"Master," said Giovanni as he stepped down from the raised dais. He moved across the rushes to lightly take her arm, guiding Amice out of the chamber.

Once they were through the door, both stopped.

"I thank you, Master Steward," she flashed him a coy smile. Standing close beside her, Giovanni could drink in the freshness of her aroma of lavender and bergamot. The bergamot made him think again of Diana, for its sunny freshness had been favoured by her.

"*Giovanni, per favore,*" he blurted out. "I am Giovanni, Giovanni di Bologna."

"God give you good day, Giovanni di Bologna. I thank you for your aid." She turned and began to walk toward the end of the landing, where the florid Under-Steward waited. On impulse, Giovanni followed her. "Mistress." She turned, as Giovanni leaned in toward her, once more drinking in her fragrance. "Permit me to escort you to your carriage."

Amice scowled, turned and walked toward the Under Steward, Giovanni in close attendance.

"Do you return to London, Mistress?"

"Nay! I am to pay my devotion at the Shrine of the Martyr. I stay in my townhouse, which is convenient for my devotions before the shrine of the martyr."

"Indeed Mistress. You have a house in the town?"

Amice stopped, turning her head to look at him. "Master Steward, why do you ask me so?" Her manner had become defensive.

"Nay, Mistress de Shethre."

She cut across him. " de Shethesere. Mistress de Shethesere."

"Mistress de Shethesere. I meant no offence. As we are to meet to discuss the arrangements for the Benediction, I was merely making small talk."

"Gramercy, then," she again flashed him the coy smile, which lifted his spirits. "In that case, to respond to your question, I have a house beyond St Albans, but close beside the Abbey precinct, near to the river."

They reached the main door, where, standing ready in the courtyard beyond was Amice's carriage and mounted guard.

As she approached her carriage, Giovanni reached out a hand to stay her arm.

"Mistress, when shall we meet to consider the arrangements for His Eminence and the Benediction?"

Amice looked up at him; her gaze lingered, the twinkling of her eyes pulling him in with every heartbeat. She paused.

"Soon, Master di Bologna............ I shall send word."

Ж

———

Chapter Thirty-five

The Magna Vico, St Albans Market, June 1277.

IT APPEARED THAT EVERY MAN and woman of the town had come out to the market early this humid June morning. Women wandered purposefully between the stalls, inspecting, examining and running the back of their hands over tactile bolts of cloth. Most vendors used wooden carts or planks of wood to display their wares. Some had awnings or sides made of heavy fabric hanging from poles to create a kind of booth. Close by the Waxhouse Gate of the Abbey and allowing the din of chatter to wash over her, a woman walked briskly past the Vintry and Cornmarket, where traders barked prices to prospective buyers and headed up the Magna Vico, St Albans' triangular main street.

No one noticed her, basket in hand, wimple pulled tight; she was one of many such women about the town this day. Her route took her past the many wares for sale: bread, meat, cloth, pottery, fruit, salt, cheese, eggs, fish, exotic spices, baskets, rope, chicken, ducks and geese. If she went to the far end of the Magna Vico, she would find sheep, pigs and cattle awaiting slaughter and their meat offered for sale. At the Abbey end, the air was fresher, with the prevailing wind blowing those visceral smells away from the town.

As always, she was careful where she placed her feet. Although the early summer sun had baked the ground hard, many animal droppings still littered the roadway. She had reached the stalls of the fine leatherworkers - the cordwainers - when she caught her first sight of him. Amid all the townspeople and traders, he didn't stand out, nor were his clothes particularly fine or his appearance striking. But it was him for surtees: the King's Man, Simon Lowys.

She was tall for a woman, but this man stood a few fingers above 6 feet with long, flowing, fairish hair pulled tight into a Q knot. He was no youth, perhaps of thirty or more summers, but his garments, though worn, said he was not base born.

She stood, watching him as he examined a fine Cordovan leather belt, running his fingers along it, then holding it to his nose to sniff its aroma. He did not notice her and after a short time, he moved on. The woman wanted to be sure the King's Man was alone. Earlier, he had been with an older woman, his wife's mother perhaps rather than his mistress, but she had moved on toward the meat market further along the Magna Vico.

The woman continued her leisurely pace, all the time stalking an unwary Simon Lowys. He arrived at the furrier's stalls adjacent to the Bull Ring. The bright, sunny day encouraged a mood of optimism about the town. Some sought the shade, to avoid the intense rays, but the woman did not mind the sun, coming herself from the southern lands.

He stopped to examine the wares at a framed booth laden with exotic furs in black, grey, white, red and bluish-grey hues. The woman sensed an opportunity to pounce.

Looking away from the stall, as if distracted, she transferred her basket into her left arm and barged into the back of the King's Man. The basket went toppling, spilling its contents of vegetables onto the ground, as had been her intention. Simon Lowys was pushed forward onto the stall and spun around in annoyance.

"Oh! Pray, do forgive me. I meant no harm, good sir."

The planned tirade of words never came from Simon's mouth. He looked down on a comely woman with piercing eyes set in a strong, pleasing face. Her flawless olive skin told him that she was not English born.

"Tis no matter, Mistress," he replied, helping pick up the vegetables. When it was done and the vegetables returned to the basket, Simon sought to strike up a conversation.

"Do you hail from St Albans, Mistress?" He judged from her wimple that she looked of an age with him and that she was likely a widow.

"Nay, I am a visitor, a pilgrim at the shrine of the Martyr," she replied coyly.

"Well, Mistress Pilgrim, I bid you welcome." He made his obeisance. "I am Simon Lowys of Westminster."

"Simon Lowys," she spoke his name aloud in her southern intonation. The time Simon had spent on Crusade with the present King and Queen some years before had enabled him to identify southern accents. Hers was Iberian, of that he was sure.

"Mistress…?" He left the question hanging, but the woman did not give her name.

The back of her hand seductively stroked a soft red pelt laid out on the stall in front.

"You have good taste, Mistress." The stallholder, until now a spectator, sensed the opportunity of a sale. His accent was also foreign from the north of Europe, though his broken, reedy English was quite understandable.

"It is what we call a Baltic Squirrel, Mistress prized for its lush but short red coat. You will find it makes an exceptionally fine lining to garments of all kinds."

He picked a pelt up and handed it to her. "Do you see the coat is short but…." He struggled for the words. "It is rich. No, it is luxuriant."

Sensing that the woman was much taken with the pelt, he pounced. "Is it for yourself, Mistress? I can offer you the very best price."

The woman continued stroking the fur, smitten by feel and look. "What is the price?"

"Whatever he says is too much," said Simon, standing close behind her.

Upset at the intervention, the merchant desperately tried to regain the upper hand.

"Mistress, if I may…."

"Show her the Vair," suggested Simon to the bemused merchant.

"She would not appreciate such…" His words tailed off as his eyes met the nuncio's.

The merchant ducked low beneath his stall. After some scrabbling, he pulled out a roll of sewn pelts, laying it out with a flourish.

"Come, mistress," Simon guided the woman's hands towards the rolled-out pelts. He noticed her delicate fingers adorned with just gold rings.

"This is what is called a Vair. The Varium Opus."

The woman had to admit that it was beautiful and had all the soft, downiness of the Baltic red squirrel fur but sewn together with an equally soft white pelt. Brazenly, Simon lifted one of her graceful hands and laid her palm on the sewn pelts. As he did, he took in her pleasing fragrance of amber and sandalwood.

"Do feel the softness," said Simon, aware that he was both explaining and flirting.

She stroked her palm against both the red and white fur.

"Is it not truly magnificent? It makes a wonderful lining or trimming to cuffs or collars. It suits you, mistress," interjected the vendor, seeking to keep control of a potential sale.

"Aye, mayhaps?," she replied disparagingly.

"Such fur comes from the far north," Simon said, eager to demonstrate his knowledge, but she interrupted his flow.

"… And the most prized is the belly," she continued, "which becomes a delicate snowy white during winter. Tis the most desirable season by far for the fur trade. The pelts are always at their thickest and silkiest at that time. Do you see how the backs and the bellies are sown together in a chequered pattern, which gives it its name, Vair"

Simon chuckled. "You know much about the fur trade, Mistress."

"Aye! Tis a trade I know well."

"I must say, Mistress," interjected the merchant, still keen on a sale, "such a Vair never looked better on anyone."

"The furrier is right in his words," said Simon. "It does suit."

"Mayhaps, but I have no need of it. I am here as a pilgrim, not to indulge myself in worldly goods."

She pushed it away, but a firm hand covered hers, holding it on the downy pelts.

"I want you to have this as a gift and I would feel great sadness if you refuse."

Simon's melodic, softly spoken words were almost hypnotic, convincing her she should accept. He seemed so nice, so genuine and friendly.

"Nay sir, I thank thee, but no." She did not want him to believe that accepting the gift would allow him to pursue her virtue.

"Mistress, I offer you this gift in all sincerity. I seek nothing from you in return."

She pulled her hand from his and the pelt with surprising strength.

"Nay. I am away, Master Lowys."

"Mistress." He bowed low. "Mayhaps, we shall meet again," He turned and disappeared into the market crowd, heading toward the stables beyond the abbey.

She watched him depart, his worn woollen cloak swirling behind him, occasional flashes of sunlight glinting on the sheath of his baselard dagger, this King's Man.

"Yes," she said, "we shall meet again, Simon Lowys."

As he pushed through the thronged market along the Magna Vico towards Salipath and John Ballard's stables, Simon Lowys's thoughts dwelled on the woman he had just met. He had not known many women in his life; he had just a few years with his beloved wife, Amy, before she was taken in childbirth. But like Isabella la Rus, this one intrigued him, and he enjoyed flirting with her. He scolded himself for not pressing her for a name.

As thoughts swirled in his head, Simon knew he fell for women far too quickly. He sensed this woman was confident, alluring, and not easily swayed or impressed. Her beguiling foreign looks fascinated him, and he could still recall her exotic aroma and her piercing eyes. A thought struck him. What colour were those eyes? He hadn't taken in that detail when he looked at her face, and now he deeply regretted that.

Had Simon noticed, he would not have seen the expected soft, radiant look of a kindly, gentle widow but brown eyes that were steely-sharp, cold and emotionless; the eyes of a killer, the assassin Benuic, Jasliena van Leuven.

Ж

____

Chapter Thirty-six

The Gallows Tree beside the gatehouse of St Albans Abbey, June 1277.

AT THE FAR END OF THE Magna Vico lay the Benedictine Abbey of St Albans. Its daily chimes regulated not just the holy brothers but the day of the townspeople too. The Sext bell had just rung for the sixth hour, summoning the brothers to their prayers as Jasliena van Leuven walked towards the abbey gates, heading for the stables that lay beyond. She drew little attention, appearing as just another woman about her daily business. There were few people around as she passed the mighty, gnarled, ancient oak standing large outside the main gates and cast her eyes toward the lightly swaying, headless figure secured by iron bars. What was left of the traitor, Adam of Brazbourn, swung gently from side to side in the warm easterly breeze, the groaning, clanking iron chains twisting like a grotesque weathervane. The Abbot, Roger de Norton, had wanted this foul reminder of a dreadful day in the Abbey's history removed, but King Edward had insisted it remained as a warning to all.

Long, tendrils of dry flesh clung to Adam's bleached bones, where the iron had prevented the crows' beaks from reaching.

Elsewhere, thin lengths of dirty brown wool danced free in the breeze, all that remained of Adam's fine clothing. His once firm right hand was now a hideous group of pointed, gnarled sticks that had once been his fingers. His left hand was missing, stolen in darkness by a necromancer to make a Hand of Glory to summon Satan and his acolytes.

An unreadable smile broke across Jasliena's face as she thought of the dear, sweet boy and how devoted to her he had been. She had befriended him more than a year since to give her the cover to plan her attack on the Queen. Adam of Brazbourn had served his purpose; it had been he who was seized by King Edward's men and tried and executed for the assassination attempt. Yes. the youth had truly served his purpose and she gave him no further thought as she turned towards Chingesberiestrete and a meeting with one of the town's whores.

Ж

Chapter Thirty-seven

The Ragged Staff Inn on Salipath, St Albans, June 1277.

SITTING ON A ROUGH, wooden bench in the far corner of the Ragged Staff Inn, Simon Lowys pensively ran his middle finger around the rim of a half-full clay ale jug. His thoughts were far away from the inn, a stone's throw from the Shrine of the Martyr, where he now sat, nursing the dark, bitter ale in front of him. He was oblivious to the inn's other patrons at this early afternoon hour. He stared at the brew as if it could provide him with the answers he sought. Although he had dismissed the threat to his life in a light-hearted manner, the reasons why he was marked for death nagged at him.

Moreover, he was puzzled as to why the Lady Jeanne, alone, had been released. The thought continued to gnaw at him as a dog with a bone. His mood was dark, as dark as the room where he now sat. Few rays of the bright summer sunlight made their way this deep into the inn, emphasising the gloom.

Simon shared the inn with a few others, some deep in their cups despite the weakness of the ale. One was draped across a rough wooden table, eyes closed and deep in sleep, while his two colleagues held an animated conversation about the best way to get to the house of a comely widow both knew, who lived close by in New Lane.

The Ragged Staff was like many inns Simon had frequented over the past six months. Its dark recesses were perfect for illicit trade and the occasional fumble. The smell within was a meld of rancid meat, wood smoke, spilt ale, vomit and sweat. The floor rushes squelched with every footstep and desperately needed refreshing. A few young, sleep-deprived pot boys with dirty aprons rushed about, clearing tables and bringing clay pots brimming with frothy dark ale. Occasionally, a jug would fall to the floor and a few eyes would turn in the direction of the sound. This was the first occasion he had visited the inn, where he met an informant who provided him with some useful background information on the manor of Westwick. The Ragged Staff was not somewhere respectable men would normally frequent, but with his informant now gone, he thought an ale would help him clarify his thinking. When he had entered, even in the shadowed dreariness of the interior, he sensed figures hunching their shoulders, pulling hoods down and shrinking into corners and hushed whispers of '*King's Man.*'

Far away in his thoughts, Simon suddenly sensed the presence of someone beside him. His eyes lifted from his half-full jug to regard the Innkeeper, a fat, jovial man of forty summers, his beard showing the signs of a recently consumed meal.

He beamed with false delight. "Can I offer you some rabbit pie, Meister? Tis cooked fresh this morn and with coneys caught but a day since. And poached in the finest stock with sweet malmsey from Gascony."

Simon doubted any pie in this establishment had ever been freshly made, and likely the only thing truly poached were the coneys, so he politely declined the offer.

"Mayhaps more ale then? You must be thirsty. Tis all good here in the Ragged Staff."

The Innkeeper regarded his customer. He had noticed him when he first came in and took him for a merchant's assistant. His cote was of good quality but worn in places. He carried a leather scrip, which he kept close beside him while he drank. No, not a merchant the Innkeeper reassessed his judgement: an official perhaps, not a cleric for he did not have a tonsure, or a minor official, mayhaps? Another table hailed the Innkeeper, who snapped his fingers, summoning a pot boy to bring them ale.

Two young man-boys entered the inn and peered around as if looking for someone before sitting on a table on the far side from where Simon sat. They made an odd pair, Simon thought, one small and stout but who would grow to be a hulk of a man and the other rakishly thin, with nervous, darting eyes.

His thoughts returned to the Lady Jeanne. Why had she been seized? She must have been taken in error, which explains why they released her. If so, he thought, when they seized her from St Mary's, they did not know who she was, but her clothing would have told them she was high born, yet she was still seized. He was beginning to clarify things in his head. Had someone sought a high-born maid but released her when they discovered she had links to the Crown? But why and why no ransom? And how did they find out she had connections at Court? The Legate, it had to be him.

As this line of thought gradually took form in his head, he became aware of a shadow over him. Looking up, a woman stood before him.

"God give you good day, fine sire," she said with false shyness. She was no maid but a woman of less than thirty summers. She leant over him, her exposed bosom in his eyeline.

"I have not seen you here before." She gave him a toothy smile, teeth framed between her heavily rouged lips.

"A man like yourself would appreciate good company and there is no better company in this town than Anabil le Polter, as all would say."

Simon had no wish to go with one of the town whores; the only woman in his thoughts since the death of his Amy was the enigmatic and distant Isabella la Rus.

"Begone, woman. I have no desire to be in the company of a harlot," he snapped.

Anabil recoiled at the harshness of his response. "You wound me with your cruelty, Meister," she replied with feigned indignation.

Simon at once was regretful of his words.

"I am sorry, Mistress; I did not mean to cause distress."

She sighed heavily, letting her head drop as tears welled up in her eyes.

"I did not think such a fine man such as yourself could be so heartless," she said, seizing the opportunity to sit on the bench across from him.

She reached for a cloth, tucked discreetly under the sleeve of her shift and wiped her eyes.

"Mistress, again, I do so apologise for my tone. I did not mean harm by my words."

Her lips puckered. "Mayhaps then, you might buy me a jug of ale," she whimpered, "To truly show your sorrow," the tears having surprisingly dried up.

Simon knew that he should refuse, send her off and not engage in conversation, but how could it hurt to spend a short time in the company of a woman, albeit a whore. He looked again at Anabil le Polter. She was younger than he and wore her long black hair loose, framing her pale face and rouged lips. Seated directly in front of him, he could not help but notice her ample breasts, barely restrained by her russet shift, which, Simon imagined, was the effect she intended.

Anabil was speaking, but he was not listening, drawn in perhaps by her bosom.

"… and then he perished with the bloody flux not two winters ago, leaving me alone in the world."

"Your husband?" Simon asked, seemingly picking up the thread of her conversation.

"Aye, useless lump that he was." She reached a hand across the table. "Now, kind sir, how about that ale?" Anabil stood.

"I know Godfrey the innkeeper, who does owe me some jugs of his finest," she said, "so I shall order for the both of us." Her hips swayed suggestively as she shimmied her way towards the stacked oak barrels where the Innkeeper stood, returning soon with two jugs of the dark frothy liquid, placing both in front of Simon and sliding onto the bench beside him.

"You know my name, sir, but I know not yours."

Simon had no intention of revealing his identity, so he chose to ignore her question.

"So what brings you to our town, good sir?" He was reluctant to respond with the truth, so, between sips of ale, he suggested he was a pilgrim.

"Oh, a pilgrim, it it? We have so many pilgrims keen to make their devotion before the Shrine of the Martyr. I thought of taking the veil once."

Her observations continued, reminding Simon of the non-stop chatter of young de Berdesfold. He sipped his ale and found it no longer as bitter as before.

"You look like an important gentleman from the manner of your dress."

Anabil was seated beside him; indeed, she had moved her body closer to him and laid a hand upon his thigh, which he promptly removed.

"I am but a humble clerk of little importance."

"Nay, that I cannot believe. A man so well-attired. You must be a man of *some importance*." The hand reappeared on his thigh, gently inching higher and was again removed.

She continued to make conversation, but her words sounded distant, indistinct from the general hubbub of the inn. Simon's head swam; the ale must be more potent than he thought. He felt tired, his eyes heavy, and he had difficulty focusing. All was a blur. He placed a hand on the table to steady himself but lurched forward.

Anabil grabbed at him, pulling him back towards her as if the two were in a lover's embrace.

"Oh! That is very forward of you." The loudness of her voice alerted every customer. "Come you now, Master Lowys, have you had too much ale?" One hand snaked across his thigh while the other wrapped around his neck, drawing him further into the embrace. Simon's head was too befuddled to resist. Even in this state, he knew something Anabil had said was wrong, but his addled mind wouldn't let him focus on what it was.

Any casual observer in the Ragged Staff would see a man and a local whore engaged in a moment of passion, her hand raking his body in lust.

In truth, Anabil's raking hands were searching for Simon's purse. The draft of dwale she had slipped into his ale had taken effect and he was on the verge of losing consciousness. Already, his attempts at speech were coming out as a slow slur. His eyes closed and his head lolled to one side. She held him close; her hand closed on the metal-hardness of his purse, weighty with coin, she was delighted to note.

"Master Lowys! You must not be so forward." Her words were a mask as she half-turned him towards her, nimbly slipping her delicate fingers into Simon's pocket. She lifted his purse in one deft, experienced movement, scooping it into the hidden pocket in her russet shift. As she released him from her embrace, Simon slumped to the floor, upending the table and the half-finished clay jugs of ale, as he fell.

Alerted by the commotion, the bearded Innkeeper strode over to where Simon lay motionless on the floor. Two customers had come to his aid and were readying themselves to lift him up.

"Now, Anabil, what game do you play here?"

"No game, Godfrey. Our man here could not take the strength of your ale."

Godfrey, the Innkeeper, eyed her suspiciously, not trusting this whore. Two customers, the young man-boys, who had come to the stranger's aid, lifted him upright.

"These two fellows will take him outside to the horse trough," she suggested. "A good dunking in the water will sober him up."

Godfrey didn't argue but still mistrusted what Anabil had said and her motives.

An unconscious Simon, head slumped forward and supported on either side by the young men, was dragged roughly across the floor of the Ragged Staff, his boots scraping through the mushed rushes, leaving a toe trail on the floor behind him.

Anabil followed them out of the door, pleased with the easy coin she had earned by targeting the King's Man and delighted with herself for relieving him of his full purse before the man-boys, Kenric and Strep, had the opportunity.

Ж

____

Chapter Thirty-eight

*The Stables on Salipath beside the Abbey Gatehouse, St Albans,
June 1277.*

THE ANCIENT LANE OF SALIPATH sloped gently towards the
hamlet of St Michael's, a little over a mile away. At the
abbey end, John Ballard's stables, adjacent to the Ragged
Staff Inn, lay on land first leased from the monastery by Ballard's
grandfather early in the reign of old King John. Travellers towards
London, hiring one of his horses, could follow the mill lane south to
cross the River Ver at the Fishpool Dam to pick up the old Roman
road. Travellers always smelled John Ballard's stables before they
saw them. The warm, musty aroma of the ever-growing pile of dung
and the dusty, sweet smell of hay always permeated the air. Ballard
used only the more expensive hay, eschewing cheaper fluffy barley
straw. The ears of which could be prickly and cause skin irritation
and higher-priced oat straw, which horses enjoyed too much and
were inclined to eat.

Trade had been slack for some time and John had been glad to
rent a palfrey to a King's Man occasionally these past weeks. He
was expecting him again this day and had his apprentice Jakin make
ready the same sturdy mount he had hired previously. John,

meanwhile, was on the stable roof. The storm had damaged the thatch, opening holes through which the stormwater flowed freely. John Ballard was no thatcher but he could not afford to employ one, so he undertook the repairs himself.

From his position atop the roof, shrouded by dried reeds and willow fixings, Ballard looked down toward the Ragged Staff Inn and watched as two man-boys half-dragged and half-pulled the King's Man, Master Lowys, past the paddock towards the stables. John liked this Simon Lowys, not least because he paid coin in advance. Ballard's open paddock separated the stables from the Ragged Staff and high on his roof, he got a good view of the scene below. Neither of the young men had reached twenty summers and their nervous, furtive manner caught John's eye. Both were repeatedly peering behind them as if expecting trouble. Every action of these man-boys told John Ballard they were not friendly. And they had left the Ragged Staff in the company of Anabil le Polter, never a good sign, though she went the other way, towards the town.

To John Ballard, both men had the appearance of low lives and were shabbily dressed, with one showing a branding mark on his forehead. They seemed an ill-matched pair, one short and well-built and the other gaunt and lean. He lost sight of Simon Lowys as they entered the stables. John's apprentice, Jakin, was below and could deal with issuing the palfrey, but Master Lowys was surely in no fit state to ride. John had an uneasy feeling about the two men.

He had placed his ladder on the inside wall at the rear of the stables. He climbed down slowly and immediately saw Simon Lowys lying flat on the ground beside the stalls. The older of the suspicious men crouched low over Master Lowys as if checking that he lived. He could not see his apprentice, Jakin and John wondered where the second man was.

His answer came all too swiftly. The unseen man-boy stepped out of the shadows and struck John over the head with a small, heavy wooden club. John slumped to the floor. Jakin cowered beside the algae-covered water trough, watching, wide-eyed. He thought about tackling them men but recognised the futility of such an act.

The man who had struck his master barked a command at his colleague.

"Strep, tie the youth up."

The second man, who Jakin judged to be a few years older than himself because of the absence of a beard, approached him, carrying a hemp rope. He grabbed Jakin's wrists and bound them firmly.

Meanwhile, the first of the assailants bound Simon's wrists and feet before moving to the furthest stall, where Ballard kept his carts.

"Strep, give me help here." The oak-framed cart lay tight inside a narrow stall, its solid wood wheels inches from the sides. The second assailant slipped beneath the wagon and scrabbled to the rear. The two began pulling the cart from its stall. Had Jakin not been so scared at his predicament, he might have laughed at the action of the two. One was pushing, the other pulling the old heavy cart, but in opposite directions, serving merely to wedge it tight to the timber walls of the stall.

At length, they succeeded. The first assailant went to find a horse to hitch to the cart. The stables housed several horses of different ages, shapes and sizes, each in a stall of its own and Kenric realised he did not know what animal to choose. He came over to Jakin, tied up and seated beside the water trough.

"Which one?" he demanded.

Jakin used his head to indicate the third stall. Kenric went over, opened the lower door, grabbed a leather bridle hanging from the gatepost and put it onto a very old chestnut nag with many years of hard work on its shoulders.

He led the docile animal into the interior and placed it before the cart, hitching it to the staves. Meanwhile, Strep went to the prone body of Simon Lowys and tried to lift him but failed.

"Kenric," he called. "I cannot lift him alone."

Kenric left the old sumpter horse and came over. He took Simon's legs and Strep, the head end. Together, they manhandled the unconscious Simon onto the bed of the cart and threw sacking over him before at mounting the front. Strep flicked the reins and the old horse pulled out onto Salipath.

A cart leaving a stable, driven by two young men, was an everyday occurrence in the town. There was nothing to arouse suspicion.

It moved ponderously down Salipath towards St Michael's and then south toward the Roman Road and the hamlet of Colney.

They were long gone before John Ballard regained his senses; recalling what had happened took him even longer. He remembered being on the roof and struggling to focus. He saw Jakin trussed up hard against the stalls, a gag stuffed in his mouth and

John staggered over to untie him. His head throbbed and a swelling the size of an egg had already developed on the back of his head.

"What happened, lad?" he asked of Jakin.

Tears welled in the young boy's eyes. "Twas not my fault, Master John. I could do nought." He burst into tears of both inadequacy and anger.

John Ballard patted the boy's shoulder, not unkindly.

"Tis all right, lad. It was not your fault and there was nothing you could do."

"I was frightened, Master John.. Truly scared, I was."

John ruffled Jakin's hair. "Tis all right. Tis all right, lad." The words were soft and reassuring, although, deep down, John Ballard feared for the King's Man.

"Now Jakin, lad, you were expecting Master Lowys, the King's Man." The boy listened intently. "I did not see what happened, so do tell me what you saw."

Jakin took a deep gulp of air and the words raced from him. "I was expecting Master Lowys and he arrived with two men, though he did appear drunk."

John nodded. "Carry on, lad."

"They threw Master Lowys onto the floor and the stout man grabbed me and threw me into Galahad's stall. Then I heard you come down the ladder and he left me and I think he must have hit you too."

"Aye, you have the right of it, lad. Someone struck me hard on the head, as you saw."

"What do we do now, Master?"

"We have to tell the Seneschal and his constable."

"Why did the men take the King's Man, Master?"

"Who knows, lad? But as much as the abduction of Master Lowys is bad, I have lost a cart and a good sumpter horse. For we shall not see them again.?"

As John Ballard was lamenting his ill fortune, his cart had reached the village of St Michael's. The two man-boys drove the cart hard along the ancient Roman road south, juddering when the wheels hit a deep rut but keen to get to Colney before Sext. One of them, Strep, congratulated himself on a job well done. It was to be the first of two they had been given for that day. Seizing the King's Man was the easier of the tasks; the second, this evening, made him more apprehensive. Seated beside him, his companion, Kenric, had no qualms about killing. Strep did. He was a year younger and always did what Kenric said. But now, they had been instructed to kill a woman, which made him uneasy.

Ж

———————

Chapter Thirty-nine

Magpie Lane, St Albans, June 1277.

A S THE ABBEY BELL RANG summoning the brothers to Vespers. Isabella la Rus and Alia Parys slowly descended the Magna Vico, seemingly a mistress and her servant out late, perhaps visiting. They did not rush. There was little need for them to blend into the surroundings; two women walking on the street were unlikely to attract attention. Were they to stop and loiter, that would be another matter.

The Italian had arranged to meet them in Magpie Lane at Vespers on the Feast Day of St Vitus. Magpie Lane was a quiet, discreet location, surrounded by warehouses and run-down property.

Isabella and Alia left the security of the Magna Vico and turned into the cramped lane. Little of the sun's warming rays penetrated the winding alley at this hour. The heat of recent weeks had caked the disgusting underfoot detritus beneath their feet, so no longer did it claw and stick to their boots. They picked their way through the narrows, eyes scanning ahead, but there appeared to be no one about at this hour. The upper jetties of the shoddily built houses in Magpie Lane overhung them, casting dark shadows beneath. Every so often, they passed even narrower passages, barely the width of a person, down which lay the poorest dwellings.

Both women's senses were alert for the slightest sound beyond scurrying rodents.

Isabella raised her hand, signifying Alia to stop and then pointed to a shadowed recess ahead. Both women edged to the side furthest from the gap to give them a better sight of what lay ahead. They were perhaps three strides away when two figures emerged from the darkness. Both were shabbily dressed young men, one barely able to grow a beard. Together, they appeared comical, one short and stocky and the other stick thin. One carried a sword, the other a narrow, pointed dagger, the blades reflecting the little sunlight remaining at street level.

"She's not alone."

"I can see that," came the gruff reply.

"She is meant to be alone," said the second, obviously agitated at a plan unravelling before him.

With blades raised, both thugs stepped two paces towards the women. Isabella stood motionless as the short, stocky man placed the tip of his sword at her throat.

"A fine lady out on such a night and in such a dangerous part of the town." The voice was deep. He leered at her, his gaze fixed on her bosom.

"Strep. Hold firm with your blade." The second man, barely beyond a youth by the lack of facial hair, raised his dagger to cover both women.

"What are you doing?" The youth Strep appeared agitated. His companion ignored him.

"Now, my lady," said the gruff-voiced man, "what do we have here?" He reached a hand forward to grope Isabella's chest.

"Kenric! What are you doing? Just get on with it." His high pitch showed his anxiety.

"He told us what we must do."

"There's no reason not to enjoy ourselves first," the older man-boy leered. " 'Tis not every day two comely women present themselves before us, alone and defenceless. Why should we not have some fun?" As he spoke, his free hand groped roughly across Isabella's chest. He ogled at Isabella, pleasure etched across his face. It was a deadly mistake.

He didn't see the thin-bladed misericorde she pulled from her sleeve that sliced his chest and, in a blur, drove hard across his nose, the blood spurting hard, spraying his accomplice. Kenric, blinded by blood and screaming in agony, slumped onto the fetid earth.

The second man-boy, drenched in dark, sticky blood and still armed with his dagger, stood wide-eyed, shaking in fright. Alia drove her leather boot hard into his groin. The breath expelled from his body as he slumped onto his knees. Isabella whipped her thin blade across his cheek; blood poured, pooling dark on the ground as Strep howled in pain. When his beard hair eventually grew, a scar would always be visible. Beside him, Kenric's screams had become a long, low wail of pain and grief.

There was a brief look between the two women, a recognition to Alia that she had done well. The younger woman no longer recoiled at the sight of a dead body and had come to accept her mentor's unusual ways.

Sensing that the man slumped, writhing in pain before her, presented no danger, Isabella grabbed at the other, younger man's flowing locks, forcing his head backwards, her blade hovering close to the throbbing artery in his neck.

"Who sent you? Tell me now, or I will take out your eye." Isabella knew the answer full well but sought confirmation. "If you do not tell all, I will go lower, and you will have no reason ever again to visit a whore house."

Strep's screams intensified, either from pain or apprehension. Isabella laid the blade beneath one eye, drawing a rivulet of blood that trickled gently down one cheek.

"I will tell. I will tell." His words were a garbled scream, reflecting his fear of this woman.

She applied greater pressure to the blade. "Who sent you?"

Strep's breathing was laboured, and the fear was apparent in his tone. "Twas Giovanni. Giovanni sent us."

"And who is Giovanni?" She feigned ignorance.

"Giovanni di Bologna. He is a foreigner, a soldier…. or he *was* a soldier."

The Italian thought Isabella. "And what were you instructed to do this night?"

From beside them, a low wailing came now from Kenric's mouth.

"Please, Mistress, show us mercy for pity's sake, " Strep begged.

Isabella traced the sharp point of her misericorde from Strep's eye to his bloodied hose. She pressed hard and his frightened words tumbled out.

"Please, mistress, mercy, mercy. *I will tell. I will tell.*" He gulped in the air. "Giovanni sent Kenric here to finish you. He discovered you were not who he thought and twas Kenric who told me to come." That, Isabella, didn't believe one bit.

"He was to kill you here in the alley and make it appear like a robbery gone wrong. Tis all I know, mistress."

"And who does Giovanni work for?"

"I know not. Tis true, I truly know not."

The pressure from the tip of the misericorde on Strep's hose increased. Strep howled with fear once more. "*Mistress, I beg you, I cannot say.*" Isabella twisted the blade, cutting into the cloth and the soft flesh beneath. His scream pierced the evening like a pig being butchered in the meat market on Bothelingstock.

"Giovanni is powerful, Mistress, but his paymaster is more powerful still."

Isabella had the confirmation she needed, but she still wished Strep to identify him.

"His name?"

"Mistress, I cannot." Strep felt the blade push lower down his hose and onto his manhood.

Such was the intensity of Strep's scream that anyone abroad in the town at this hour would be sure that a beast was being slaughtered somewhere.

"Tis Bernardo, the Pope's man. He is behind it all." The words were forced out through grimaced teeth.

It was as Isabella suspected. "What more have you done for him?"

The pressure on his hose increased. "We took a maid, but she was the wrong one, so we were told to let her go. I did not know she was high-born."

Strep was scared for his life, but events were beginning to fall into place for Isabella. "What happens to the children you take?"

"Giovanni pays us to have other children lure them away and then we remove them to a barn at Windridge. Tis a tithe barn, the priests. He is part of it too; *was* part of it too," he corrected himself. "He was part of it, but he was killed, I know not who by."

"Giovanni killed him?" inquired Isabella, knowing that Simon Lowys had come north to investigate the death of a priest. Surely it was the same man?

"Aye mayhaps. He is skilled with a bow." Lying prone beside Strep, Kenric made cat-like mewling sounds as the pain from his deep wounds overwhelmed him.

Isabella lessened the blade's pressure on Strep's groin. "And then? The children?" she asked in a low, firm voice.

"I know not exactly. I do know they go by cart to Harwich and thence across the German sea, but I know not where they dock."

"How do you know they go to Harwich? Have you taken children there?

"Only the one time. Kenric asked me to go with him."

"Where is this barn where he keeps the children?"

"Twas an old woodcutter's barn that lies at Chiswell; it belongs to the church. There is a wood on the high ground called Bone Hill, above the track to Daneswick and Windridge. It lies inside." By now, the blood from Strep's cheek had slowed and his cheeks and forehead glistened with sweat. He had given over all he knew and now feared this mad woman would kill him.

"Is there a path to this barn?" inquired Isabella.

"Aye! ... Aye," he replied, seeking to be as helpful as possible, "a track goes through the wood up to and beyond."

Isabella released the pressure of her misericorde from his hose and Strep exhaled with relief.

"Mercy mistress, for the love of God, mercy."

"You are right to plead for your skin, though I afear your soul is already damned. You will live this day, but I hope your words were true, for you will not have another chance if you have been false."

"It is true, mistress. On the Virgin's eyes, all of it. I have not been false to you."

Isabella bent low to bring her face close to the kneeling Strep, her low whispering tone instilling a cold fear in him.

"As of now, you and your friend here are a caput lupinum. Do not try to tell Giovanni of this, or I will know of it, and I will find you."

Strep nodded his head quickly.

"We shall leave here and raise the Hue and Cry. We are but gentlewomen who witnessed a falling-out between two rifflers, and the one with the dagger did try to slay the other. See here; the weapon does lie on the earth in a pool of blood."

Strep looked down at his dagger on the ground, its blade sticky and glistening.

"You will not die by my hand this night," said Isabella, "but if you tarry, you will be taken and be swinging at the end of a rope by the time the sun sets on the morrow."

"But it was not I that cut him," whimpered Strep.

"Forsooth," said Isabella, wiping the thin blade of her misericorde on Strep's tunic. "Who would believe that two lost, defenceless women could have committed such a deed?"

Isabella and Alia turned and picked their way carefully through the detritus of Magpie Lane towards the Magna Vico.

Wondering how to help Kenric, a relieved, heavily sweating Strep, his breath fast, watched them leave. In a whimper, he asked aloud, "Who are you?" But his mind immediately provided him with an answer. She was the woman who would, henceforth, always haunt his dreams.

Ж

Chapter Forty

A Manor House somewhere beyond the town of St Albans, July 1277.

IGHTING HARD TO CALM his ragged breathing, Simon Lowys twisted on the linen-covered pallet to see what chamber this was. His head throbbed and his throat was parched. He remembered being in the town at the Ragged Staff and then….? He had awoken here, wherever '*here*' was.

He remembered a woman; he had supped ale with a woman, Anabil, a whore of the town. Anabil, had she got him drunk? There was something she had said, something that wasn't right, but it wouldn't come to him.

He tried to take in his surroundings to discover a weak point. A cloth tied tight about his eyes compromised his vision, with just a small area below the blindfold visible. His hands, bound in front of him with the hempen cord and tied to a bedpost, restricted how far he could stretch to one side. One foot was similarly tied to the foot of the pallet bed. The chamber appeared bare save for an old wooden coffer bound with black iron bands and a simple three-legged stool. Craning his neck from side to side, he could make out three stone walls covered in flaking limewash. That wasn't a good sign; it meant the chamber was used only infrequently. Not a peasant's home then, much more likely a dwelling of some status, perhaps abandoned. Shouting for help was unlikely to get any response.

A simple wooden crucifix hung askew on the wall furthest from him. The rushes on the floor had not been changed in many weeks, if not months and gave off an unpleasant, rancid aroma. He could not see a window, but a grey-white light filtered into the chamber from above, telling him there had to be one behind him. So, it wasn't nighttime, but he was unsure whether the flickering greyness was early dawn or twilight. Simon forced himself to think about the details of his prison. The window had ill-fitting shutters, allowing shafts of light to filter through them. Only having a single window in a chamber suggested that it faced east, for if its vista were westward, it would have more to maximise the daylight.

Simon shivered, or was it a tremble of fear? Chilling thoughts flooded his mind.

He clenched and unclenched his fingers, numbed by the cord binding his wrists, trying to stave off panic as best he could.

"Well, Simon Lowys," he said to himself. "Once more, you are caught and bound."

The realisation struck him as he said the words.

"Come you now, Master Lowys, have you had too much ale?" Anabil, the whore had said. She had used his name even though he had never given it to her. It had been no chance encounter with a whore; he had been the prey in someone's game. Now he lay here, caught, trussed and helpless.

Laying still on the pallet, he tried to listen for any sounds to help him identify where he was. There was the scurrying of mice among the rotting rushes and beyond, he could hear birdsong; did that mean it was the dawn hours? In the distance, there was a rhythmic tap, tap, tap sound and it took him some time to work out what it might be. At length, he was sure it was the sound of a mill with the noise of water striking and turning the wooden paddles.

As satisfied as he was at identifying the sound, he was no closer to knowing where he was. A stone house with several floors, an old manor perhaps with a mill close by; he could be anywhere and that caused his spirit to drop. No one knew he was here, he realised, which meant he had no prospect of rescue.

How long Simon lay alone with his thoughts and trying not to imagine the worst, he did not know. A gentle creaking of a floorboard broke the stillness. From beyond the heavy oak door, he caught the shuffle of light footsteps and the illumination from a candle lamp flickered underneath the door into the chamber. Simon craned his head back as far as he could, better to be able to see beneath the eye-covering. The old door groaned open. The cloth over his eyes restricted his vision, but he could make out a woman's lower body by tilting his head. What he could see of her clothing was that of a well-to-do lady with a fur-trimmed kermes cloak and mantle.

Although he couldn't fully see, Simon became aware of her approach. The warm, honey-like fragrance of amber and sandalwood grew stronger as she came closer. The woman balanced herself on the edge of the pallet bed. Simon could not tilt his head back far enough to see her face, but he felt soft, delicate fingers beside his eyes as she gently removed the cloth.

Simon blinked as his eyes became accustomed to the brightness of the chamber. He looked at her face. Her long dark hair was parted in the centre and styled in two long braids, coiled and brought back towards the crown of her head and topped with a mesh crespine. She was no maid, and he judged her about the same thirty summers as himself. Her skin was flawless with a light hue. She had piercing brown eyes set in a strong, alluring face, the face of the woman he recognised but did not know. The face of the woman from the market.

"Simon Lowys. Royal Nuncio." The words were softly spoken, precise and accented. Simon had been on crusade with the

King some years before and recognised the lilt of the southern Mediterranean in her voice.

"Mistress, you have the advantage of me. I really know you not and I afear there is a grave mistake here in my abduction."

Her pretty, full mouth gave way to a thin smile. "Nay, Master Lowys." She reached forward and lightly traced one of her delicate, ringed, fingers across the line of his lips. "There is no mistake here." Simon tensed.

"Who are you, Mistress? What do you want of me?" Simon's voice was almost shrill.

She stood and despite his predicament, Simon saw a woman poised and confident in her actions. Slowly, she removed her cloak, which she shook, carefully folded, and placed it on the wooden coffer on the far side of the chamber before again seating herself beside him on the pallet bed.

"Mistress! I must tell you that I hold the Royal Warrant. I have the authority of His Grace, the King."

The woman looked left and right, breaking into a peal of bright laughter.

"Now, Master Lowys, do you see how that does not frighten me?" Once again, she stroked one of her delicate, ringed fingers across his cheek toward his mouth. "Does the King's Warrant run here? Methinks, tis you who lie here bound and I who am free as the wind."

She stood and went to the coffer where she had laid her folded cloak; when she turned toward the bed, Simon saw the dancing sunlight reflected on a thin blade she held in one soft, elegant hand.

He shook in fear. "What is it you want of me?"

She sauntered toward him and laid a single finger on Simon's lips.

"Hush now, Master Lowys. Alas, I offer you my sorrow at having to bring you to such a place like this, in such a manner, but you needs forced my hand."

She waved her arm around. "You can be of great help to me by giving me answers to some questions that do trouble me." Her gentle, measured tone, which appeared so reasonable, only caused Simon greater alarm.

"But Mistress, I do not know you. I have done nothing to cause you offence. I… I.. know little that would be of help to you."

She brought the pointed stiletto up in front of the Nuncio's face. "Oh, but you see, Master Lowys, you do. Mayhaps you don't know it, but you do."

She traced the sharp blade down the contour of Simon's cheek, laying it against his lower lip. Simon froze in fear as her other hand affectionately stroked his hair.

Without warning, the sharp blade was withdrawn. Simon exhaled with relief as she lay the dagger reverently on the pallet bed, patting it affectionately as if it were a pet dog.

"Now, Master Lowys." She turned to look down; her brown eyes bored in on him. "All I seek is your assistance with some information."

Simon tensed, gripped by fear but still drinking in her heady aroma of amber and sandalwood. "Mistress, you have it wrong. I know not how I can help you."

"Oh, but you can." A delicate finger on her right hand gracefully traced across his lips. Simon wrenched his head away, only for her to grab his chin and force it back to face her.

"Do you not see I am asking you kindly, King's Man." Her words were soft and gentle, almost innocent. "But you must know, if you choose not to help me, I can persuade you by other means." Her gaze went to the stiletto lying on the bed beside him.

"You work for a great and terrible King. You are a man of influence whose role is to know things?"

She swept the blade upwards to Simon's neck. "Who is the woman you met in the town? The lady who masquerades as the Abbess de San Andreas de Anroyo?"

The tip of the knife lightly followed the contour of Simon's jaw, as softly and gently as a lover's caress.

Simon tensed. She repeated the question, applying greater pressure to the blade, now pushed hard against his throat. Simon felt a wet trickle run down his neck.

"You have met this woman in the town on several occasions. Who is she?"

"I meet with many women." It was a faint attempt at humour and wasn't appreciated. He felt a sharp pain under his ear.

"The woman you speak of, she is but a vintner's widow, Isabelle de Brun of Berkhamsted and St Albans." He used the identity Isabella had used a year before.

"Indeed? A Vintner's widow?" she sneered. "So pray, do tell me why she impersonated a foreign Abbess at the Lazar House off the north road these past weeks?"

As desperate as his situation was, Simon recognised that an element of the truth might help his story.

"A young maid had gone missing from this town, a niece of one of the Queen's ladies. It was the only way to gain entrance to the Lazar House." She thought for a time about his answer.

"And pray, Master Lowys, why would a humble vintner's widow seek the daughter of a royal Lady?" She pulled the blade away, took a small cloth from her mantle and tenderly dabbed away the blood on his neck.

Her fragrance grew stronger as she moved nearer to him; warm, deep and woody, he could not help but draw her subtle aroma. Her face was close to his, her deep, innocent brown eyes wide, locked on him.

"Tell me, King's Man, of all the convents, why would this same widow choose that house and that particular Abbess' name?"

Simon had a horrible feeling that this woman holding him prisoner already knew the answer and was toying with him.

"I know not why. Mayhaps, she had heard mention of such a name." His answer was hardly convincing. Did this woman believe him? He could not be sure. Either way, his situation had not improved. She had him seized and imprisoned and Simon thought she would hardly let him go free.

"This widow of the town, she is in the habit of impersonating a Sister of God?"

"Nay, how would I know this? But methinks twas the only way she could gain entrance to the Lazar House to find the maid."

"So, I ask again, why would a vintner's widow, not of London or the Court, seek the daughter of a royal Lady?"

He watched as she brought the blade to Simon's neck once more. Simon turned his face away.

"Nay, Master Lowys, I do not believe you." The woman used the blade to steer Simon's head back to face her. "You are a King's Man, a Nuncio to the Queen. You frequent the Royal Chancery," She spoke the 'Ch' as a 'shh' sound and her Iberian accent became more pronounced.

"What you say is true, but I can only tell you that I know this woman as Isabelle de Brun and she owns the Wheatsheaf tavern in St Albans."

She pulled her face away and sat back on the pallet. Simon's emotions were running high; not sure if this calm, alluring woman was about to kill him. He knew he needed to escape but saw no way out of his predicament. But what she asked next shocked him.

"Tell me, Master Lowys, what do you know of Benuic?" Simon hoped his eyes did not betray his alarm at mentioning the assassin's name in connection with Isabella, who had told him that Benuic was a woman.

His heart raced; his lips dried as it dawned on him who this woman must be.

"I er…. have heard that… that name at the Ch..Chancery; Benuic is an assassin, is he not?" His words were flustered.

"Is he? Is he now? And what do you know of this Benuic?" She was toying with him.

"I have no knowledge of him other than what I have heard. He is an assassin, available to him with the most coin, but more than that, I know not."

"For one in the employ of the King, you don't know a great deal, Master Lowys." She replied disdainfully. She again wiped away a trickle of sweat from his forehead.

In truth, he knew what Isabella had told him of Benuic and now he feared he was staring at the face of the assassin. He was not confident he could hold out and would have to reveal his knowledge if she tortured him. But in his mind, he found the thought of this enchanting woman being the notorious assassin and inflicting pain on him, impossible to reconcile. She broke the silence of his thought.

"Tell me truly, Master Lowys, for I hold no desire to hurt you; why is this widow masquerading as an Iberian Abbess?"

"I cannot say. In truth, I know not; mayhaps she is addled in the head," suggested Simon trying to sound convincing but knowing she would not believe him.

The pressure from the blade was released and Simon exhaled. But he quickly stilled his breath as she brought the tip close to hover over one eye.

"Nay, I do not believe you. Do you see how easy it would be for you to be sightless, Master Lowys? How useful would a blind man be to King Edward?" Simon watched nervously as the knife tip arced from one of his eyelids to the other.

She smiled, showing white teeth, the like of which he had never seen.

"So, we have a woman of the town who impersonates an Abbess and, mayhaps, an innkeeper's widow." She paused. "Does she impersonate ought else, a fox perhaps?"

Simon froze. The panic and fear of his situation had just risen dramatically. This could be no coincidence, as the woman mentioned a fox in connection with Isabella. Only a select few in the Chancery of King Edward knew that '*le Reynard*', the fox, was Isabella la Rus.

"Thank you, Master Lowys. I see the answer in your eyes. Now I know who I am dealing with. She is le Reynard, after all."

Despite his intention not to reveal anything further, Simon's eyes widened at the mention of the King's Intelligencer.

"You confirm this for me, Master Lowys." She laid a soft finger on his lips. "I so do not like it when I am lied to or misled." Her tone was soft, almost pleading. "You would not do that to me, King's Man?"

"*Nay, nay*, I have told you all I know," Simon replied, seeking to be brave in a desperate situation. She traced the blade from Simon's eyes up his forehead to his scalp, laying it against Simon's long, fair hair and gently stroking the Nuncio's locks. Without warning, she sliced away a clump, grasping it and bringing it close to her nose.

"*Meravellos*! I shall keep this as a remembrance of our meeting, Master Lowys."

Simon lay motionless as this unknown woman tenderly stroked his cheek. As desperate as his situation was, he did not recoil at her touch. As she brushed her delicate fingers along the contours of his face, her eyes wandered lower, taking in the form of his body.

Simon Lowys had been in desperate situations before, had been stalked by vicious killers and had faced death. Still, this mysterious, beautiful woman with flawless skin, a swan neck and a sultry gaze truly both intimidated and fascinated him. He didn't want to believe that she was the assassin Benuic.

"Mistress, who are you? Why have you brought me here? What are you going to do?" Simon pleaded. But all he received for his questions was a penetrating look from those piercing brown eyes. Simon tensed, his heart pounding.

"Shhh!" Her finger went to his lips to silence him. She leant toward him and gently brushed her lips on his forehead as tenderly as a lover.

At length, she pulled the blade away from his face, stood, walked to the coffer to retrieve her outer garment. She turned toward the pallet to look upon him almost affectionately, an action that scared the bound Royal Nuncio. She gazed at him for a moment and she smiled gently as if none of the previous minutes had occurred. Then, without further words, she lifted the latch on the door and this unknown woman was gone.

Simon's sense of relief was palpable, for he had feared for his sight. He doubted if she had believed him. Though laced with truth, his story was thin, and she must have recognised this. Simon was concerned about what this woman knew. She had appeared from nowhere and he had no idea who she was or what name she went by, other than that the King's Intelligencers hunting her called her Benuic.

What this woman knew troubled him, details someone beyond the Chancery shouldn't be privy to. She had connected Isabella to le Reynard, but did she really know the role Isabella performed for the King? Were this woman's questions about Isabella designed to confirm what she already knew, or were Isabella's secrets safe? His instinct was to get a message to Isabella to alert her, but he recognised the impossibility of that.

Still tied to the pallet, his predicament was not about to improve. He doubted the mysterious woman believed any of his denials about Isabella. She suspected Isabella was le Reynard and somehow his reaction had confirmed it. What pleased Simon was that she had not hurt him. She hadn't hurt him! He was alive. If she was indeed the assassin Benuic, then why wasn't he dead? She had every opportunity but chose not to inflict pain on him. Perhaps she was dallying, doing as she pleased, safe in the knowledge that Simon had no prospect of escape. In his heart, Simon knew this woman was the assassin and as such, why would she let him live? Perhaps all Simon had done was postpone his torture and pain for another day.

Ж

Chapter Forty-one

Bone Hill Wood, near the village of Daneswick, Hertfordshire, July 1277.

I AM MIGHTY IMPRESSED at your discovery. However, did you find such news?" asked Matilda Heacham, her fingers moving deftly at her embroidery.

"It matters not the how," replied Isabella la Rus softly, turning to meet the gaze of her protége, Alia. "What becomes vital is that we act quickly to discover if there are any children at this barn."

"But for surtees, armed men guard it?"

"Tis most unlikely that such a place is without guards, but we can both go there and have men-at-arms follow a distance behind, awaiting a signal to move in."

"What do we know of the location," inquired Matilda. It was a cheerful Alia Parys who responded.

"Tis a place called Chiswell, not far from the town. It sits on the crest of a low hill amid a wood that local people call Bone Hill. The barn stands in its centre. The nearest vill is Daneswick and there is a single track to and from the barn."

"How will we discover it if it is inside dense woodland?"

"Aye," Alia said, "Tis fairly wide, with waste on either side, but there are coppiced and pollarded branches which tells that it be managed at some point in the recent past."

"You have been there?" Matilda was surprised at Alia's knowledge.

"Of course. The track is the only route in and out of the woods. I spied the barn, which is much run down and was used by woodcutters to store wood for the church, but I could not get close enough to see if there were children inside."

"And guards?"

"I saw but two, an older man with a sword and a youth. Both sat with their backs to the door, dozing in the sun for all the time I espied them."

Alia turned to Isabella. "But even so, there may be more. Tis going to be mighty hard to approach by stealth."

Isabella smiled a smile both women had seen before and one that signified she had a plan.

"You have the right of it. It would be mighty hard to sneak up on the barn without noise, so they needs must see our approach and hear us long before that."

"But that would be madness!" said Mistress Heacham.

"Nay, not madness. Just two women foraging in the woods for fungus, wild herbs and roots. We do not sneak up on them; we take our time, let the guards hear and see us and conclude that two women could not possibly pose a threat."

The woodcutter's barn deep inside Bone Hill Wood was most likely built in the days of old King Richard and had seen better days. Its sun-bleached, gnarled oak planks were rough-hewn but still offered protection against wind and rain after so many years. Otul Fitzkeen sat propped up against the outer timbers, resting from the heat. His younger companion, Egenulf, had broken his rest to relieve himself in the wood.

The two men had been here for weeks, paid in cash to guard the barn and the children inside. The coin was good, much more than what they usually earned. Otul knew they were paid to stay silent and ask no questions. Both men were promised a bonus when the work was done. Occasionally, a cart would arrive and take a few of the children away to where, Otul didn't know. For now, he lazed in the sun, bored but content. Egenulf returned, wiping his hands on his hose before slumping beside his companion and belching.

From inside the barn came a whimpering, sobbing lament of a child. Otul thumped twice on a plank with his balled fist. "Be silent, or I'll take a rope to thee."

The child's lament stopped. Otul closed his eyes and tried to doze, but his fitful attempt at sleep was interrupted by a woman's singing coming from deep within the trees.

"Sumer is icumen in,
Loude sing cuckou!
Groweth seed and bloweth meed,
And springth the wode now.
Sing cuckou! Sumer is icumen in."

He struggled to his feet, his old bones stiff with ruhm. He aimed a kick at his young companion.

"Did you hear that? Find out what it is" he instructed Egenulf

The younger man rose slowly, apprehensive and a might scared. Beyond the barn, the woodland was dense and impenetrable to the naked eye.

"There be stories about those woods. Bugaboos and Spirits live there, my grandmother told me that."

"Nonsense," Otul pushed a reluctant Egenulf towards the trackway.

The eerie female voice continued its appealing song. Her voice rose and fell as a swift on the wind.

"Ewe bleteth after lamb,
Loweth after calve cow,
Merye sing cuckou! Cuckou."

"Nay, do you not hear? Tis true, these stories. Tis the maid's song. She lures you into the trees and you are taken into the world of the Hidden People. My grandmother did say that no good ever befalls him who hears the song of the Maid of the Woods."

"And springth the wode now.
Sing cuckou! Sing cuckou! Sumer is icumen in, icumen in."

A sharp slap across Egenulf's head made his eyes water.

"By God's teeth, get you into that wood and find out who is there. We don't want any prying strangers." He shoved the even-more reluctant Egenulf towards the track and the dark, denseness of the woodland.

The younger man whistled, seeking to overcome his apprehension. In a short time, although he kept to the trackway, either side of him was dense in dappled gloom.

Dark tree trunks and overhanging boughs seemed to close in on him. Although high above, the sun shone, it was cool here in this accursed wood. His senses were heightened. He took in the aromas of earthy fungus and rotting leaves. The singing had stopped, which only caused him to breathe more quickly.

"Loude sing cuckou!
"Groweth seed and bloweth meed,"

The radiant voice made him jump. The Song of the Maid; she was close by. It came from the Daneswick side, but he could not see her.

"And springth the wode now.
Sing cuckou! Sing cuckou! Sumer is icumen in."

Egenulf froze. The song now came from the the Chiswell side; a second Maid.

"Merye sing cuckou!"
Cuckou, cuckou. Sing cuckou! Sing cuckou! Sumer is icumen in."

He spun around, his heart pounding. The Song of the Maid assaulted him from all sides. Wide-eyed now, he was afraid even to blink; he wanted to run, but which way? The song did not stop and then he saw her. She wasn't there and then she was. He regarded the face of an angel framed by hair that was somewhere between light and dark, hanging loose down to her shoulders.

"Sing cuckou! Sing cuckou! Sumer is icumen in." Her voice matched her looks, the face of an angel. He stood transfixed until his world suddenly became one with the forest's darkness.

The unconscious body of Egenulf lay on the damp track, legs entangled with his scabbard. Any wanderer lost in the woods would have found the scene mismatched. The hulking figure of the youth slumped on the earth and the slight frame of the red-haired woman standing over him, club in one hand.

On reflection, Isabella thought she had struck him too hard. The youth carried a sword but had not drawn it, so she saw no reason to kill him. She pulled a ball of hemp from her scrip, bent low and bound his hand and feet before stuffing a rag into his mouth.

Alia joined her on the track. Both women had stopped singing.

"That worked well, Alia." Isabella beamed in pride, for the idea had come from her protégé.

"Aye, Mistress, if we wait a time, the other one will be greatly afeared." As if on cue, a call came from the top of the hill.

"Egenulf. Egenulf. Show yourself. Where have got to? The singing has stopped, now get you back here. Egenulf? Egenulf?"

Alia looked to Isabella and they nodded to each other in a silent accord.

"Loude sing cuckou!
Groweth seed and bloweth meed,
And springth the wode now.
Sing cuckou! Sing cuckou! Sumer is icumen in."

Outside the barn, Otul Fitzkeen was trembling. His eyes flitted left and right. Egenulf had been reluctant to enter the woods and hadn't returned. Now the damnable singing had resumed. Outul didn't believe the guff his younger companion had told him; he didn't believe in the Hidden People or the Maid of the Woods: at least, he thought he didn't. But the singing had resumed, not just one voice but two: sweet, melodic voices, singing in harmony.

Otul had been in battle. He had bled for his Lord, stood in line against the Welsh rebels years before and held firm. But this unseen threat, this Maid of the Woods from the world of the unseen, if indeed that was what it was, now scared him. Otul knew he ought to go into the woods to discover what was happening, but he shrank back, against the barn. His heart raced and his palms sweated. He stared at the woods, his eyes seeing nothing, but in his mind he saw moving shadows, dark, creeping shadows from the Spirit world, ready to leap out at him.

He realised that the singing had stopped. Why had it stopped? He called out for Egenulf, but no reply came back.

"Ewe bleteth after lamb,
Loweth after calve cow,
Merye sing cuckou!"

The song was closer now and almost upon him and only one voice. Again he froze as from behind him he heard….

"Bulloc sterteth, bucke verteth,
Merye sing cuckou!
Cuckou, cuckou."

His head swivelled from side to side, eyes raking the undergrowth.

"Show yourself," he screamed at the top of his voice, his words absorbed by the trees.

"I am not afeared of you." It was a lie. Still, the singing continued.

"Egenulf! Egenulf! For pity sake, where are you? Help me! Help me!" The words came out, half-sob and half-scream.

Otul's feet twitched. He looked down at his sword arm and saw his hand shaking.

An angry hiss broke his concentration as an arbalest quarrel thudded into the oak plank above one shoulder. His head jerked away from the thick bolt and Outul caught the fierce woosh of a second bolt, which embedded itself deep in the timber above his other shoulder. Pressed hard against the old barn, his breath was ragged, and he trembled with fear.

He screamed aloud. "Spare me, Maid. I mean, you no harm. I beg you spare me."

He waited, not knowing if another quarrel would finish him or if the Maid would show mercy. A silence hung over the barn; even the birdsong stopped. A twig snapped ahead of him beyond the first oaks and Outul saw the Maid of the Woods emerge from the dense undergrowth. She appeared with dappled sunlight framing her silhouette, her garment white like a shroud, her face ghostly pale, framed by long fair hair.

"Jesu, preserve me," he whimpered, as afraid as a deer running from the hunt. Outl began to rapidly recite the Ave Maria.

"*Ave Maria, gratia plena, Dominus tecum. Benedicta tu in ...*" A cold fear gripped his heart as the sharp pressure of a blade laid hard on his neck. He had heard nothing. He turned his gaze to one side to reveal a second Maid, nay a woman, one delicate hand holding a thin, sharp dagger against his throat and an arbalest slung over one shoulder.

Such a pretty, slight thing, Otul thought as he made to grab the blade. The rivulet of blood that spurted from his neck stopped him from continuing.

Otul's mind was conflicted. He was being held captive by a woman, one with piercing blue eyes and who was skilled in using a knife. The second, younger woman moved in to stand five paces away from him, arbalest primed. Even if he could leap at her, the arbalest quarrel would kill him before he got close.

"Up!" The older one commanded him, blade still dangerously close to his skin. Otul rose slowly, aware that the maid's arbalest was fully trained on him. The woman lowered the rondel from his neck. She forced first one arm and then the other behind his back and bound his wrists tight with a hempen cord. A push between his shoulders forced him to the earth face down. He quickly found his ankles bound, with the cord tied to his wrists so he resembled a trussed goat. She rolled him onto his side with her leather boot.

"Who pays you?" The rondel blade lightly brushed his face. His eyes blazed with fury.

"Alia, check the barn."

Keeping the arbalest trained on Otul, Alia moved the few paces towards the barn. She attempted to lift the wooden drawbar with one hand, but it proved too heavy.

"Mistress," she called out and passed the arbalest to Isabella. Alia heaved the drawbar upwards with both hands, letting it fall heavily to the ground in a billowing cloud of dust.

She opened the barn door into darkness. The heady, malodorous smell of its interior hit her immediately: a frowsty interior of unwashed bodies, vomit and farm animals.

Alia screwed up her face as the stench assaulted her nostrils. Amid the gloom, dust particles drifted in the few rays of sunlight that squeezed through the cracks in the timbers. And what was that sound, Alia wondered? Mournful, high-pitched wails and sobs emanated from the farthest corner. Alia looked around for a lantern but saw none. She followed the sound towards the eastern corner of the barn, where she saw a miserable huddle of young children and, ahead of them, a young maiden shakily waving a pointed blade at her.

Isabella la Rus, the King's Agent known as 'le Reynard', awaited the small party of King's Men-at-Arms who were to follow with carts to rescue the children believed to be inside the barn. She knew the Serjeant commanding the party, William atte Garstang, a wise, experienced veteran trusted by the King.

Inside the gloom of the woodcutter's barn, Alia Parys stood warily as the young maid, her hand shaking with fear, brandished a knife.

"Begone!" Her voice trembled as much as her hand. "Get you gone." Alia stood her ground. The maid before her was perhaps thirteen summers, not yet a woman but was, Alia guessed, placed here to look after the abducted children.

"Afear not," said Alia as confidently as she could. "I will not harm you."

The strained sunlight penetrating the interior of the barn flickered on the maid's wide eyes. The knife in her hand continued to jerk. Alia could make out a group of ragged children huddled in the corner behind the young girl, shaking, bound and gagged in this half-light.

"What is your name?" Alia held out an open palm towards the maid.

"Mabil," she replied in a soft, quivering, low voice. "I am Mabil."

"God give you good day, Mabil. I am Alia, Alia Parys. Let me help you. Please pass me the blade; and we may all leave here while the sun still shines."

Mabil looked at the older woman in front of her, hesitated and, at length, dropped the knife to the ground.

Alia let out a slow sigh of relief as she stepped forward to wrap an arm around the shaking Mabil.

"Tis alright, Mabil. We shall all get out of here." She called out for Isabella and together they began to give help to the children.

Alia had thought there were perhaps half a dozen children huddled together, pressed into the corner. As she and her mistress moved between them, removing the bonds and pulling cloth gags from mouths, Alia found two more of five or six summers, cowering beneath the older ones. Alia kept talking to the children, softly as her mother had once done to her, but most had a hollowed look from fear and lack of food and were unable or unwilling to trust her and respond.

"I am Alia. What is your name?" she said for the fourth or fifth time.

"Morcant," was the throaty response which caught Alia by surprise.

"Morcant, are you hurt?" She regarded the boy. He was about ten summers in age with hair that would be fair in colour were it not for the grime and mud caked into it. A blood scab lay above one eye with a trail of dried blood down his temple and cheek, a recent injury that had gone untreated.

"Mistress, this is Morcant." Isabella made her way over and greeted the lad.

"Morcant," she smiled at him. "My name is Isabella and this is Alia; we are here to help you." She passed the boy a skin of diluted ale for him to swig. The boy nodded understanding and drank fulsomely before handing the skin to Isabella, who indicated to pass it to the next child.

"Can you tell us of this place? How long have you been here?"

Morcant wiped a dirty sleeve across his mouth. "I know not, mistress. I know not how long I have been here…. more than two Sundays, I think."

How were you taken?

"I was in the market. It a day before the Feast of St John. I were seeking work carrying or cleaning to earn coin and I did see two young maids, well-clothed they were, standing at the cross gazing at me."

Isabella heard the advance guard long before she saw them. Two young soldiers, inexperienced in such circumstances, their sword sheaths bumping into the side shrubs, made their way along the track.

"There," said Rauffe, the younger of the two, pointing towards the barn. "See, a woman outside."

On seeing a man tied up like an animal lying on the earth, Rauffe and his colleague Walter warily approached the barn, swords drawn.

"What do you do here, Mistress? inquired Walter. Isabella did not respond.

He took a pace towards her. "Mistress, I asked what it is that brings you to this place?"

A sharp voice halted him. "That be none of your business, Walter," came a shout from the woods. "Get you inside the barn." Walter and Rauffe turned to see their serjeant, William atte Garstang, striding purposefully from the woods.

"Mistress." Both men were surprised that their serjeant greeted the woman and not them.

A chastened Walter and his colleague turned to join the remaining men-at-arms, following William atte Garstang into the barn.

Behind her, Alia heard the tramp of feet and the swoosh of swords drawn as William atte Garstang's men approached the corner where the children sat huddled together.

"Sheath your swords," the senior man barked. Alia was pushed to one side as one of his fellows and another stepped up to form a half-ring around the children.

"Serjeant," a woman's voice came from behind the men. "Will," a note of pleading in the tone. William atte Garstang turned to look at Isabella.

"These are but frightened children, Will, who have suffered greatly. The sight of your guards will only frighten them more. There is no danger within."

William nodded his agreement.

"Form a perimeter around the barn, swords at the ready," he barked and his men trooped out of the barn to follow his orders.

"How many?" Isabella enquired of Alia.

"Nine in all, though I found discarded garments, which suggests there have been more, Alia replied."

"We must get these foundlings to safety and get them fed. We have a cart outside with the guards."

"Where shall we take them? I afear the monks of the abbey may not be so welcoming of such a number."

"Aye, that may be true. But I was not thinking of placing the waifs in the care of brothers but sisters."

Alia gave her a quizzical look, but then she understood. "The nuns of the Lazar house. Tis an excellent idea."

"Aye," replied the older woman, "they have the space and the numbers to care for their bodies and souls and will give them and their Lazars a purpose."

Over the next hour, Isabella took charge. She instructed Will Garstang to have his men remove their jerkins and helmets, so as not to intimidate the waifs. One by one, the children were spoken with, given weak ale and some bread and taken to the cart where Alia soothed and reassured them.

Will had his men bring straw from the barn for the children to lie on during their journey to St Mary's. Despite being rescued, the children were apprehensive and nervous about the adults around them.

The journey to St Marys would take half an afternoon and Alia did her best to get the chrildren to sing, but most,, huddled against the cart's frame, alone in their thoughts, hollowed eyes staring vacantly, were oblivious to their surroundings.

Ж

Chapter Forty-two

The open fields of the Manor of Hanstead, south of St Albans, July 1277.

THE MIDSUMMER FULL MOON threw its bright bluish light wide across the Ver Valley this night, reflecting beautifully off the river in the distance and casting amazing shadows on the open fields on either side. Standing atop the crest of the ridge, Strep, the son of the widow Erith, could see far across the toward Hansted, whose population slept in preparation for the burial of the Corn Mother in the hour after dawn. The angry gash on his cheek still throbbed and wept.

None from Hansted bar Strep walked abroad this night. He, too, would be abed in his lodgings off New Lane were it not for a summons from Giovanni di Bologna. Strep had found Giovanni's message puzzling, for it would be far easier to meet in the town where no one would notice their presence. But the Legate's young messenger had been specific about the location. They were to meet in the strips atop the low ridge above Hanstead in the hour before Matins on the morn of Midsummer. Strep thought Giovanni was being cautious. If he wished to meet in secret, then there were far better places, but Giovanni was the man who paid him. So, Strep did as instructed and waited in the moonlit fields at the hour before Matins.

He saw the Legate's man approach, striding purposefully towards him, moon shadows of movement rising and falling on the recently harvested strips.

"Strep," the Italian pronounced the name in three syllables: *Str-epp-pe*. "How do you fare?" Pointing at the jagged red rent on Strep's cheek, that a stable lad had sewn crudely back together.

Strep winced at the reminder of the wound inflicted on him by a woman. "It heals, Master, thank you," Strep hesitated, fearing that Giovanni had not forgiven him for failing to kill the woman in Magpie Lane.

"The business with the woman, Master."

Giovanni held up his hand to silence Strep. "Say nothing more. Twas not your fault, Strep, though I do not understand how a mere woman can best two, near-grown men."

"Thank you, master."

"Now, Strep, the reason for us being here." Giovanni moved closer, placing an arm over Strep's shoulders. "The King's Man you brought from the stables; he is asking too many questions about our business with the children." Strep nodded his understanding. In truth, he did not fully grasp what was occurring with the children. He knew that waifs and orphans were lured off the streets of the town, drugged and held securely in a barn beside Chiswell and he and Kenric had taken a maid and released her only recently. But he was unsure about the full extent of what Giovanni was doing.

"Now, tis likely that this King's man will find his way to you."

"Me? How?" Strep was surprised. The King's man had been deep in his cups and could not possibly identify Strep or Kenric. Strep could not he see how he could be linked to such a person.

"The maid you and Kenric released, she may provide him with clues."

"But I know nought that could be of help, even if he could find me."

"*Si*, but I must be sure you let slip nothing. It would be best for you to go abroad." They walked slowly along a furrow at the crest of the ridge.

"Anything I can do for you, Master? Have I not always tried my best to serve you? But my mother....." He left the missive unsaid.

"*Si*, Strep, you have, but you must do one more thing for me."

With his arm still around Strep's shoulder, Giovanni pulled the young man close into him. Strep gasped. He had felt a pinprick in his chest but didn't immediately realise that he had been stabbed. Giovanni drove the baselard dagger deep into Strep's chest, twisting it hard to finish the young man off before pushing him away. Strep slumped face down in the furrow, his eyes wide in surprise, his life ebbing away.

Giovanni reached into his pocket and pulled out a clump of fair hair. He bent low to lift Strep's right hand and placed the hair into the palm, closing the fingers around it.

The yellow-grey hues of the midsummer dawn illuminated the body of Strep, the son of the widow Erith, who, in death, was performing one final task for his master, Giovanni di Bologna.

Ж

Chapter Forty-three

A Manor House somewhere beyond the town of St Albans, July 1277.

SIMON LOWYS WAS UNSURE how long he had lain there. He recalled watching the shadows of the sun's rays move across the room and at length, he must have fallen into a fitful sleep. He awakened to the sound of light footsteps and a familiar exotic aroma. Blinking, his eyes opened, and he saw a pretty maid approaching. It was not the woman he had seen earlier, although this young woman had the same olive hue to her skin but was quite a few years younger. She was dressed in a plain brown shift; her eyebrows were neatly plucked and her wide mouth framed white teeth. She leant over him, a heady aroma of bergamot and lavender, her body close. He went to ask who she was and what she was doing here, but she swiftly covered his mouth and nose with a cloth, muffling his words. His thoughts became muddled, and the words were lost in his gasping breath. The sleeping draught, *Il Sonno del Lazio* did its work and the Royal Nuncio fell unconscious.

In the first moments as he awoke later, Simon Lowys remembered the dusky figure of the pretty maid, the touch of her body and the aromatic fragrance that surrounded her. Then he recalled the wet cloth she had applied to his face and then.....? He could not remember what happened next. He now became aware of his surroundings. It was the same room, the same limewashed walls. He looked to one side and saw that the door was ajar; she had forgotten to lock it. There was something else; he looked down and saw his hands were unbound and no longer attached to the post of the pallet. He didn't recall the Moorish maiden cutting his bindings, but how else to explain it? His feet, which had been tied by rope to his hands, were now free of bonds. His thoughts had turned to the aroma of the maid, but his senses were overcome by another, altogether more noxious aroma of piss and animal dung. He peered over the side of the pallet bed. The fetid rushes were old and rotting but the smell was closer. He lifted an arm, put a sleeve to his nose and realised that the rank odour was coming from him. But this was not his sleeve; these were not his clothes. His own clothing had gone and instead, he wore the coarse wool garb of a common peasant, missing one sleeve, but with the addition of who-knows how much animal dung.

His hand went to his neck to feel the Paternoster cord Isabella had given him, which now, he always wore. He was relived to find it still there and he gave a silent prayer to the Holy Virgin. Simon sat up on the edge of the pallet bed and looked down towards his feet. Crude wooden clogs had replaced his finely tooled leather boots. The only personal item he retained was his belt and the baselard dagger–sheath strapped to it, but the deadly pointed blade was missing. Gone too was his scrip and his royal writ announcing him as a King's Man. John of Berwick would not be pleased with him losing that. Then he felt the wetness on his thigh. The harsh brown tunic was moist with dark, wet patches, not just the top of the legs but also on the arms. He went to wipe his fingers across the sticky wetness, only to realise that his hands were covered in the same gooey dampness. Even before he brought his hand to his nose, he knew from the metallic smell that it was blood. Simon's immediate reaction was to pat himself to see where he was wounded. Perhaps the mysterious woman had returned and stuck him with her dagger, but to his relief, he found no injuries. Much later, he realised he should have given it far more thought, but his joy at not being wounded overcame him.

Simon's head was clearing; the overpowering odour from his clothing may have had something to do with it. With the door left open, there was an opportunity to escape. His thoughts turned to the need to explore his surroundings, to discover where he was and who had taken him captive. But another, more prudent choice in his head told him of the folly of this. As useful as it would be to find out where he was and the mysterious woman, he had a chance to extricate himself from this desperate situation and he should take it.

Emerging into the morning light, he cast a glance back at his prison. It was a stone manor like so many others, but that gave him no clue to his whereabouts. Simon swiftly left the manor behind him, crouching low, he made his way through a wood heavy with hazel, oak and beech. The sun was rising into a blue, cloudless sky and he judged it to be near to Matins. After walking some distance, as the trees were thinning around him, Simon stood and listened. Beyond the birdsong, he could hear a rhythmic, dull sound of water striking the paddles of a mill: the sound he had first heard when incarcerated in the chamber. Find the mill and he would find a river that he could follow downstream to a larger settlement and discover where he was.

The trees gave way to a clearing of rough pasture where a few long-horned sheep grazed, oblivious to his presence. He spied the mill at the far edge, nestled in a dip in the low hill. Choosing to skirt around the mill Simon made for the river. He stopped on a bank about half a mile downstream, pulled off his rough clogs and gratefully stepped into the cold, clear water, halfway up his calve. He scooped a handful of the refreshing water to drink, looked at his bloodied hands and thought better of it. He thrust both hands back into the river and began to wash off the dried blood.

Ж

———

Chapter Forty-four

The open fields of the Manor of Hanstead, south of St Albans, July 1277.

HANSTEAD WAS NOT A prosperous village, but all agreed that this year's harvest had come very early and was the best for many a year. Old widow Alfgifu had cut the last ears of corn but a few days before and fashioned them into a doll the villagers called the '*Corn Mother.*' In the morning, when the first rays of the sun brushed the eastern horizon, Alediza, the daughter of Roger of the Plough, considered the prettiest maid in Hansted, would take the Corn Mother into the open fields and lay her in the soil, returning her spirit to the earth.

The procession assembled before dawn; most villagers were there. The children, deemed too young to be involved, remained asleep in their beds. Hanstead was a devout village, but the tradition of the Corn Mother survived, just in case. It was always the prettiest maiden who brought the Mother to the fields; the origins of the ritual were lost in the mists of time and no one thought about why it should be the prettiest maid who buried the Corn Mother.

The first hint of light flickered on the eastern horizon as the procession, with Alediza at its head, snaked its way out of the track that was Hanstead's main street. Moving slowly, they headed up the slope, seeking to arrive in the open strips as the sun's rays touched the soil. Still illuminated by the blue moonlight, the stubbled strips looked barren with the spring grains of barley and oats cut. All could see the approaching grey light of dawn and they hurried the last yards to the centre of the strips.

It was Alediza of the Plough who saw it first. The first rays fell onto the crest of the slope and her keen, young eyes took in the bundle straddled over the stubble. She slowed her pace and the procession backed up behind her.

Some of the more superstitious villagers crossed themselves, fearing the Devil's work.

"What be that? enquired Thorsten the Smith. Many eyes now peered towards the low ridge. Nothing moved; a bundle of rags, the size of a man, lay still, silhouetted against the rising sun.

Dearlaf, the Reeve, took charge and instructed Thorsten and two others to accompany him.

"All stay here until we discover what is afoot," he commanded as the four made their way slowly between the strips towards the bundle.

They approached apprehensively, wary that Satan may have been out this night. Dearlaf held out an arm to instruct the others to wait. He moved warily towards the bundle and then let out an audible gasp as he realised that it was no heap of rags but the corpse of a man. The body lay on its side atop a shallow ridge, its head facing away from him and dropped down into a furrow.

He gestured to the other three to approach and when they did, he pushed at the corpse with his boot and it rolled over to face him.

Now, the gasps came from the others.

"Tis Strep. Strep, the son of the widow Erith."

Dearlaf bent down to examine the body. Strep's eyes were wide open, a look of surprise on his young, unbearded face and his cote covered in dried blood. Thorsten's massive frame loomed over Dearlaf as he peered down at Strep's lifeless form.

"Well, there should be no concern about finding the cause of death," he said, pointing to the hilt of a baselard dagger sticking out of Strep's chest. "And see," said the blacksmith, pointing to a clump of fair hair gripped in Strep's lifeless fingers.

"The hair of the killer," opined Dearlaf. "Strep must have pulled it out trying to defend himself."

"Dearlaf." It was Tadg, the treewright, who spoke. "You needs must raise the Hue and Cry, for Strep's killer could still be close by."

The summer ceremony for Hanstead's Corn Mother was cut short, with Adeliza the Plough burying the doll in the earth where she stood. The women made their way home while the men rallied to Dearlaf's call for the Hue and Cry to be raised.

All agreed they had seen no strangers in the village, so Dearlaf split the men into three groups, one to go north, one east and the other towards the west in search of the perpetrator.

"Find him," shouted Dearlaf, "and avenge Strep, for his mother's sake."

The dawn had barely risen before the men of Hanstead began their hunt for a murderer.

Ж

―――――

Chapter Forty-five

To the west of the open fields of the Manor of Hanstead, July 1277.

THERE! DO SEE! That be him! There, hiding in the brook." The cry went up from the Ploughman's apprentice, part of the group that had struck east from the village. Others took up the call.

"We have him! Get him!" The young apprentices raced noisily toward the riverbank, splashing through the shallows to grab hold of their prey.

As Simon Lowys rubbed his hands together in the cool water, the dried blood fell away, forming a crimson pool in the brook where he stood. He heard shouts from behind him and glanced over his shoulder to see a group of men approaching, some running ahead and older ones waddling more slowly behind. Many hands grabbed at his dirty tunic, their combined weight forcing him beneath the shallow water. Simon thrashed about, unable to breathe. His hair was yanked upwards out of the water and he gasped for air. He was on his knees, his arms pinned behind his back.

"Unhand me now!" Simon screamed at the young churls, who must have mistaken him for someone else in their japes. The sound of new splashing in the water beyond the youths drew Simon's attention and he saw the approach of a bull of a man with shovels for hands.

"I hold the King's…" The man's hands balled into fists, connected with Simon's temple and the Nuncio's world again fell into darkness.

Another older man arrived.

"Thorsten, why in God's name did ye do that?" His words tumbled out in a breathless hurry. "You could have killed him. We needs him alive to stand trial."

The massive frame of the blacksmith glared at Wilfred, the new arrival.

"That was for Strep, he was my friend." Thorsten angrily aimed one of his big clogs at the belly of the unconscious Simon, lying face-up in the shallow water. "The way he stuck Strep like a pig, hanging will be too good for him."

"But how do we get him back to the village, lamented Wilfred, fearing he may have to help carry the unconscious man back home.

Thorsten pointed at one of the apprentices. "Go and fetch the handcart." The youth responded instantly, leaping onto the bank and sprinting back towards Hanstead.

The sun was full risen when Thorsten's apprentice returned with the handcart. Simon had been dragged onto the riverbank and the men grabbed Simon's arms and the limp body was dumped unceremoniously onto the back of the cart. Thorsten removed the leather thong he used as a belt and tied Simon's hands together behind his back. The apprentices pushed and pulled the cart a half mile back to Hansted.

Dearlaf the Reeve was waiting for them when they arrived, concern on his face.

"He is not dead, is he?"

"Nay," Thorsten snorted, "he just sleeps. Tis but a gentle slap I gives him. He'll be right to dance the gallows jig, right enough."

Tadg the treewright tugged at Dearlaf's sleeve.

"Do see," he said, pointing at Simon's belt. "He has a sheath, but no dagger in it."

"Aye," said the Reeve, "and we have a body with a dagger through the heart."

"And it was a thin blade that did for Strep," Tadg added, "and that sheath does hold a thin dagger." His words came out triumphantly as if it were the clinching piece of evidence.

"Aye, we have our man," the Reeve agreed. "He is covered in Strep's blood and his was the murder weapon."

"And he was apprehended running from the Hue and Cry," added Tadg.

"And trying to wash off the blood," added another.

"Aye, you have the right of it. Tis all the evidence we needs," Dearlaf stroked his prominent chin. "I don't see any need to worry the King's Justices. The man's guilt is as clear as the nose on your face. He will hang."

The Reeve turned to the blacksmith. "Can you hold him secure in your wood store?"

The smith pondered the question, his face contorting in thought. "Aye, tis solid enough and if I ties him to the big spar, he will be going nowhere."

A wizened old man, Walter the Wright had listened to all that was said and now added his piece. "Dearlaf, should we not send now for the Sheriff?"

"Aye, that we should, but the Sheriff died these months past and his deputy was taken last autumn. There be no Sheriff, Walter," pronounced Dearlaf.

Dearlaf turned to the Blacksmith. "Hold him secure, Thorsten and we shall send word to the Lord, summon a jury and we shall try him on the morrow."

Ж

____

Chapter Forty-six

The Manor of Hanstead, Hertfordshire, July 1277.

CONSCIOUSNESS ONLY SLOWLY returned to Simon Lowys, aware that his head hurt, though why he could not recall. Where was he? It was dark, with just a few thin beads of light penetrating through the cracks of the timber walls around him. Only then did he realise his hands had been lashed to a stout beam. Once again, he was a prisoner, though he had no idea why.

His thinking was hazy. He had been tied to a bed in an unknown house. And…… the first woman. He recalled an exotic scent, an aroma of amber and sandalwood. And he had found himself untied and free. His hair. She had cut some of his hair when she threatened him. And his clothes. Another woman, younger and not English, had come and….and what? He had awoken to find his clothes gone and substituted for the rags of a peasant. Simon struggled to remember. There was something about the clothes. What was it? He was finding it difficult to breathe through his nose, whether it was broken or perhaps blocked with blood. He remembered a man with huge hands approaching and punching him and after that, nothing.

Blood! The clothes he was wearing had been covered in blood, but not his own. And he had found a stream to wash the blood from his hands. And then some men approached and a big man had punched him. Now he was here, once again, wherever here was.

He took in his surroundings; dawn was long since past, for there was more light now. Wherever he was, smelled damp. He could see logs, likely drying out, perhaps it was a wood store. His hands were bound to a large wooden spar that held up the ceiling. There was also an acrid smell emanating from close by, the smell of a forge, he thought. All this was very good, but it didn't tell him where he was, why he was tied up here and more importantly, how he would regain his freedom.

Early morning sun filtered through the cracks in the timber as the rough-hewn door opened and three men entered.

"He is awakened," said one who carried a pail of water, presumably to throw over Simon if he had not regained consciousness.

The taller man, standing in the middle, spoke next. "I am Dearlaf, the Reeve of Hanstead, what name do you go by, stranger?"

Simon ignored his question. "Hanstead? That is the name of this manor? Where is this place and why am I tied up so?"

"*Why am I tied up so?*" mimicked Tadg the treewright.

Dearlaf snorted. "You knows well enough why. You will be brought before the court at noon, charged with murder and you will dance the gallows jig at dawn a day hence."

"Murder?" Simon was incredulous. "What murder? I am Simon Lowys, in the service of Her Grace the Queen. You have no right to hold me."

Dearlaf turned to the third man, who Simon recognised as the bull of a man who had hit him. "Do you see, Thorsten, how they do dress at the royal court these days? Tis the height of fashion to don the garb of a lowly churl and cover yourself in another man's blood."

"I am Simon Lowys, a King's Man."

"Of course you are. King Edward is scraping the barrel for King's Men then. So, you will show me your royal writ then?"

His scrip. Whoever had taken him and held him in the manor house had taken his scrip and inside was his royal writ that would prove his identity.

"I do not have my writ, twas taken from me."

"Do you have your dagger?" inquired the Reeve. "Tis a special sort, is it not?"

Simon looked own at his belt. His dagger was not there. Then he recalled that when he made his escape from the manor house, his sheath had been empty.

"Nay. I do not. It, too was taken from me."

There was an air of triumph in Dearlaf's voice. Tadg the treewright tugged at the Reeve's sleeve and pointed to Simon's scalp where a clump of his fair hair was missing.

"Aye, Tadg, you have the right of it, as if we need more evidence." Dearlaf took a step towards Simon.

"How do you explain having Strep's blood on your clothes and when the Hue and Cry took you, you were seeking to hide in a stream and wash the blood from your hands."

"*Nay, tis not true.* You must send word to the Chancery, to John of Berwick. He will vouch for me."

Dearlaf chuckled. "Your tricks and smooth lies will not buy you time and deny you the rope, stranger. Strep, the man you murdered, was from here and people will want justice."

"You have this wrong. You have to listen to me. I have committed no murder. I am a King's Man. I hold a royal writ."

They were not listening; his pleas were in vain. Dearlaf spat on the earth before the three left the wood store. They had ignored all he said. He slumped back, seeking to bring relief to his aching arms, sore from being pulled and tied up. He tried to think clearly and make sense of the events of the past day. One thing he knew was that he had to get word to the Chancery and have John of Berwick intervene to save him. But how?

ж

Chapter Forty-seven

The Manor of Hanstead, July 1277.

WRISTS BOUND IN FRONT OF HIM, flanked by two men holding swords, Simon Lowys was pulled by Thorsten, the blacksmith, along the snaking path leading from the wood store to the church. Inside, the nave of St Botolph's church was packed with villagers whose unfriendly eyes bored in on Simon. Throughout the night, he had been confident that this misunderstanding, for that was what it was, would be recognised and that his status as a Royal Nuncio of the Queen would be established. Now, he appreciated how Daniel had felt walking into the lion's den.

The smith had told him that the court would convene at the hour of Terce. The nave of St Botolph's held that pungent, musty smell of damp, rotting rushes on the earth floor, familiar to most churches. The interior was chilly despite the sunlight that pierced through holes in the thatch, illuminating the solid elm pillars that supported the roof.

Simon saw no friendly faces assembled before him. These people were here not for justice but for vengeance. Simon had not been unduly concerned overnight. Yes, that he was accused of murder shocked him and he was angered that they had refused to acknowledge his identity as a King's Man. But such a murder trial would be before the King's Justices in Eyre, one of three who shared the Christian name, Walter - de Helyn, Hopton and Wimborne. All three knew him and would recognise him immediately, resulting in the charges being dismissed.

But upon being dragged into the centre of the nave, Simon's spirits sunk. This was no royal court of Eyre but a lowly Manorial Court, which had no jurisdiction to try a murder case. And then Simon's eyes fell on the far end of the nave and saw the man presiding over the court. A face he knew and who knew him. Giovanni di Bologna.

He began to shout and struggle, pulling towards the front of the nave. "Giovanni di Bologna, I am Simon Lowys, Nuncio to my Lady the Queen; you know me. I am Simon Lowys, King's Man."

Di Bologna was impassive. "Silence him," he instructed, gesturing as if swatting away a fly.

"No! I am…." But Simon's words were stifled by a stinking rag stuffed into his mouth. Only then did the reality of his situation become apparent. Someone had gone to great lengths to make it appear that Simon had committed murder and now he would go on trial and face the prospect of the rope.

He tried to spit out the gag, but it proved impossible.

"Restrain the accused," commanded di Bologna and a rope was slipped around Simon's neck and jerked each time he tried to move.

"Record that the accused needed to be restrained for the good order of the court," he commanded his clerk, who carefully scribed the instruction.

Giovanni di Bologna took his seat at the head of the nave; a large wooden chair sat on a raised dais and draped with furs. He cleared his throat and addressed the assembled men of Halstead, who waited expectantly.

"His Excellency, our Papal Legate Bernardo Ravennate, would in ordinary circumstances be seated here before you as the

new Lord of this manor. But given the," he coughed lightly, "….
delicacies of this case, being a murder involving the shedding of
blood, he felt it was not right for a man so close to God to be
involved. He has sent me, his Steward, in his stead. The Lord of the
Manor of Hanstead holds the Right of Gallows, Pillory and Tumbril,
so this court has the legal right to try this man."

There was a murmur among the assembled men of the village.
The only man present with any knowledge of the law in the nave
was gagged and restrained. Simon alone knew that this court had no
standing, no jurisdiction to try the case and no authority to
pronounce sentence. But that mattered for naught. The Right of
Gallows, Pillory and Tumbril was an ancient custom but had been
superseded by the King's Justices in Eyre. Wild-eyed, Simon pulled
at his bounds and did his best to spit out the gag, but to no avail; he
was powerless and unable to stop this charade.

"Has the jury been sworn in?" It was a desultory question from
the Legate's man, seeking to move events on.

"They have your…." The Reeve Dearlaf struggled with what
to call di Bologna, resorting to 'My Lord,' even though he did not
merit such a designation.

To one side of the nave stood fourteen men, all local of the
parish, the sworn jurymen who would determine Simon's fate. The
Nuncio looked on their faces and saw stern, resolute eyes.

Di Bologna gave an imperceptible nod of his head and the
Reeve commenced the proceedings.

"Twas, the Feast of the Noble Virgin, St Marina, but two days
since. The whole village was partaking of the ceremony of the Corn
Mother. The dawn sun was close risen and all were climbing to the
top of the slope when we saw a body lying in the open strips."

"Who first saw the body?" inquired di Bologna.

"Twas Adeliza, the daughter of Roger the Ploughman, who
first laid eyes on the body from a distance", Dearlaf spoke with
confident authority.

"Is she present?"

"Aye," replied the Reeve, pushing the maid forward, who nervously confirmed her sighting of the body.

"Who else?" di Bologna asked in a bored tone.

Huddled in the nave, more than a dozen hands went up.

"Some of us approached the body and saw it was Strep, the son of the widow, Erith. He was dead with a dagger through his heart."

"You saw the dagger?"

"Aye, my……" Dearlaf remained confused as how to address di Bologna. "Aye, we all saw the dagger in his chest."

"Can you produce the dagger?" Di Bologna seemed more interested now.

The Reeve delved into his scrip and pulled out a thin baselard dagger and showed it to di Bologna.

"Are there others here present who can identify this as the murder weapon?" Four men stepped forward, regarded the weapon and swore that this was the same that they had seen in Strep's chest.

"So," di Bologna spoke thoughtfully, "we have established that this is indeed the murder weapon and," he turned to the jury, "you must establish its value for the deodand." The dagger was handed to the jury foreman, who examined it and passed it to his fellow jurors.

He addressed the Reeve. "Can we establish who owns this weapon?"

"Aye," Dearlaf was almost gleeful. "We can. This thin dagger fits exactly this sheath." He rummaged in his scrip and pulled out Simon's baselard sheath, showing it to di Bologna.

"When we caught him, the accused was wearing this sheath and there be no dagger in it."

"Indeed?" said di Bologna. "And who is there who will verify this?"

Tadg, Thorsten the smith and two others came forward and testified that this was so.

Dearlaf continued. "Upon discovering the body, I raised the Hue and Cry and divided up the men of the village to search for the perpetrator. We, that is myself and others, went east and discovered the accused, hiding in the river."

"Who discovered the accused?"

A young apprentice stepped forward. "That was me. I saw him hiding down beneath the riverbank and washing the blood from his hands." He mimicked, crouching down to hide. As shocked as he was with the fabrication unfolding before his eyes, as a man of law, Simon could not help but note the apparent contradiction in the apprentice's evidence.

"And who else saw the accused hiding from the Hue and Cry?" asked di Bologna, inviting those men who had been present to agree that Simon had been hiding from his pursuers.

Half a dozen hands went up.

"Do any of you men have aught to add to this?"

One, Peter the Ostler, a bean of a man, spoke up. "We did not see him and then we did when he raised his head above the riverbank. I also saw him trying to wash the blood off his hands." There was a murmur of agreement at this.

"My …. Lord," Dearlaf was reluctant to use the word but knew no other way to address di Bologna. "There is more." He reached into his scrip and pulled out a clump of fair hair. "This," he held up the hair high for all to see, "was found in Strep's hand. He must have pulled it from the head of his attacker." Dearlaf pointed at Simon. "Do you all see how the accused has fair locks and is missing just such hair on his head."

A murmur ran through the assembled villagers.

Dearlaf was triumphant, and some men around him patted him on the back.

Di Bologna cleared his throat. "Does anyone speak for the accused?" Simon gazed at the assembled men; all he saw was hatred in their eyes. No one stepped forward. As a man of law, he knew the procedure. An accused person was not permitted to speak on their own behalf. Others had to do that to testify to his good character. But no one in Halstead knew him other than di Bologna, who was pretending not to. The realisation dawned on him; Simon now knew why. Di Bologna wanted him dead. Simon had got too close to the truth in his investigation. If di Bologna could achieve this legally, there would be no come-back for him or his master, the Papal Legate. The truth would come out eventually, of course, but di Bologna would claim that, dressed in peasant rags, he had not recognised the Royal Nuncio.

It had all been a skilfully concocted plot; he recognised that now. The death of the priest and the abduction of the children both led back to di Bologna's door, of that he was sure. And now Simon was being silenced. In the nave, men shuffled uneasily; all eyes were fixed on him.

"So, there is no one to speak for the stranger."

"He goes by Simon," came a voice from the assembled men.

"No one here present speaks for Simon, the stranger?" Di Bologna turned to his clerk. "Do note that down," he commanded.

Although he was a man of law and had never previously been involved in a murder trial, only in coroner's courts, the unfairness of not permitting the accused to speak on their own behalf struck him for the first time.

Di Bologna imperiously turned to the jury, standing to one side of the nave.

"Members of the jury, you have heard the evidence presented. Will you now deliberate? You are to judge the accused on the charge of murder and to establish the value of the murder weapon for the deodand.

The fourteen men gathered into a huddle; muffled voices whispering throughout the church made it impossible for their words to be heard.

At length, one man broke from their ranks. "We have reached a decision, My Lord."

"Is it one on which you are all agreed?

"Aye, tis. We find the accused, Simon the stranger, guilty of the murder of Strep, son of Erith."

"And the deodand?" asked di Bologna.

"Tis a fine foreign weapon which we judge to be worth two shillings."

Di Bologna gave a long sniff. "There we have it." As the presiding judge, he should have looked the accused directly in the eyes, but di Bologna avoided Simon's gaze. Simon continued to push at the gag in his mouth and the men either side of him, gripped harder in their restraint.

"Simon the stranger, it is the verdict of this court that you have been found guilty of the murder of Strep, son of Erith. It is the judgement of this court that you shall be hanged by the neck the day following the feast of St. Secunda, two days hence."

Simon slumped into the arms of his restrainers upon hearing this. They were going to hang him. He was going to die. He was an innocent man, a Royal Nuncio and man-of-law. He had tried to tell them, but no one believed him, and, in the case of Giovanni di Bologna, the man wanted him dead.

The law was meant to protect the innocent, and Simon Lowys was an innocent man condemned to death. He was bundled from the nave and the crowd, now emboldened with the guilty verdict, became hostile. Some lashed out at him with their fists and heavy globules of spittle landed on his face. He was dragged the length of the village, with the men restraining him doing little to stop the assaults from the villagers.

As far as these men were concerned, the guilty man had been found and tried and would hang in two days. This was their contribution to the village's revenge for the death of one of their own.

Once again, Simon Lowys found himself a prisoner, wrists bound and tied to the enormous oak spar that supported the roof of the wood store. The cord length was longer this time, allowing him to lie down on the earth, albeit with his hands elevated.

The two shovels that were the hands of Thorsten the Smith, tied the knot binding Simon's wrists with surprising agility. He tugged on the strong, thick cord, lashing it around the huge oak spar in the centre of the store. A malevolent leer crossed his face as he pulled hard to secure the binding.

"Twill keep you good and safe, now. Can't have you escaping."

"I must see a priest," demanded Simon. "If you intend to kill me, at least let me be shriven."

Thorsten spat on the earth. "We has no priest. We have to send to another village to find one and mayhaps, he won't get here in time." Thorsten gave a manic laugh. "Twould be rightly poor if he gets here and finds you dangling at the end of a rope."

The Smith tugged hard on the cord one final time to ensure its security and headed for the door.

"A priest?" Simon begged. The smith turned and, with perhaps some compassion, said, "I will ask for you."

Sleep would not come. Simon Lowys lay on the bare earth, arms stretched up and bound above him. He watched the dawn rise and heard the village cockerels crow their morning welcome and the local dog's bark. In time, the sounds of village life permeated the wood store. The smith's apprentice entered sometime after dawn, his gaze not meeting Simon's while he collected logs for the forge. When Simon closed his eyes, the recurring thought in his head was that this was a pointless way to lose his life. And that the man responsible, Giovanni di Bologna, would get away with it.

He heard the latch of the wood store rattle and the door open. The huge shadow blocking the light in the doorway had to be the Smith, but with him was a smaller man. The sunlight flooding in made it difficult for Simon to focus.

"I am here to shrive you, my son." The voice was soft, calming and gentle, just what a condemned man might need. Yet, Simon thought, it was a voice he knew.

Thorsten the Smith remained in the background, beside the door, while the priest approached the beaten, bloodied and bedraggled figure lying on the earth.

The priest knelt beside the man and made the Signum Christi. Coming from the bright sunlight into the gloomy store, the prisoner was at first a blur of darkness on the floor. But when he could focus more clearly, the priest made out the condemned man's features.

"Master Lowys!" he exclaimed in astonishment. "Tis you Master Lowys. I was told I was to shrive a condemned man, a common murderer and a stranger to these parts." Sire Peter's lower lip quivered. "But how is it you find yourself here?"

"You know this man, priest?" inquired Thorsten the Smith suspiciously, stepping deeper into his wood store.

Sire Peter half-turned to look at the Smith. "Of course, I know this man. He is Simon Lowys, a King's Man and Royal Nuncio to her grace, the Queen."

Thorsten the Smith's face froze, his mouth slowly forming into the shape of an O. It took some moments before he answered.

"This man killed one of our villagers and has been tried by the Manor Court and found guilty of murder."

"I told you who I was, that I was a King's Man, but you people were in too much of a hurry to hang someone for the crime," replied Simon.

"I can tell the Reeve, Dearlaf, but the sentence has been passed. He is to hang on the morrow," Thorsten told Sire Peter.

"The Manorial Court has no jurisdiction over murder," said Simon angrily. "As a man-of-law, I should know."

"Good Master Smith, pray go to see your Reeve and explain to him the identity of this man. I can vouch for who he is and that he is no common murderer."

Thorsten thought hard and eventually agreed to go to see Dearlaf the Reeve. When he had left, Simon gripped the priest's arm.

"There is a plot afoot here, Sire Peter. Someone seeks to have me killed and is using the law to make it appear legal. I did not kill any man, though it was done with my weapon and hair was cut from my head and placed in the dead man's hand." Simon went on to explain his abduction, being held prisoner in a manor house, the mysterious woman who had threatened him and how he had been rendered unconscious and his clothing substituted.

He gripped the priest's arm. "I know my story sounds hard to believe, but tis true; I do swear so before the Blessed Virgin."

The kindly priest, in turn, squeezed Simon's arm. "I know you Master Lowys and if you do say it is truth, I believe you."

Simon sensed a slim opportunity to save himself. "Sire Peter, I do not have any belief that establishing my identity will change the decision to hang me. The Lord's representative, who sat in judgement, Giovanni di Bologna, knew who I was but ordered me gagged. Some in the village and I suspect the Reeve, are in league with di Bologna and will carry out the sentence on the morrow."

"What can I do to help? I afear not a great deal."

A thought struck Simon. "I know not where this village is, but as it is you who has been called, does that mean we are close to St Michael's?"

"Nay, not truly close, about five miles hence."

"I need to get word to John of Berwick at the Royal Chancery."

"I can leave for Westminster after my morning mass."

"Nay, that would not be swift enough. You, or someone you trust completely, must take this request to the house of Mistress Matilda Heacham in Sopwellstrete in St Albans. Tis the fourth house before the gates south to London, close beside the town ditch."

"A woman?" He sounded sceptical. "And this woman can help you more than I?"

"Aye! She will get a message urgently to the Royal Chancery, far faster than yourself. And Sire Peter…." The Nuncio regarded the priest. "Pray that we are in time to save my neck.

Ж

Chapter Forty-eight

The Gallows Tree, Hanstead, July 1277.

THE ANCIENT GALLOWS OAK of Hanstead stood in the centre of the village around a small green used for village meetings; the grass was grazed short by sheep. Its thick, gnarled, twisted boughs snaked outwards and upwards. All in Hanstead had known the oak their whole lives, just as their fathers and grandfathers had done. Six men holding hands could not circle its girth. The youth of the village were up with the dawn, awaiting the theatre of the day. Hanstead's Gallows Tree had not seen a hanging for more than two years and the young boys were full of excited anticipation. A strong, hempen rope had been thrown over its strongest bough with Gilbert Forester's cart and tethered oxen waiting beneath, casually crewing the short stalks of grass.

A steady trickle of villagers made their way towards the tree. Young boy's made grotesque expressions with their face, mimicking what they imagined to be the death throes of a condemned man. The womenfolk stood at the rear and to one side of the ever-growing crowd. There was no silent reverence among the villagers; most had come to see retribution for one of their own. Strep, the son of the widow Erith, had not, in fact, been well-liked and had fled the village for sanctuary in the town two years past. He had spent a year and a day in St Albans and had thus gained his freedom. Most of the younger men in Hanstead remembered Strep as a bully and had little remorse at his demise. But he was, nevertheless, one of their own and the stranger would die this day as payment for what he had done.

They came for Simon in the hour after dawn. Hands bound behind him; he was led the hundred paces from the wood store to the Gallows Oak. Flanked by two burley villagers who steered him forward, he was pushed through the jeering crowd to the waiting cart. His attendants bundled him onto the deck of the cart and dragged him to standing, all the time holding him at the elbow lest he fall. There was no priest present, Sire Peter having shriven him.

Thorsten had passed on Sire Peter's confirmation of Simon's identity to Dearlaf, but the Reeve was not prepared to accept the priest's word. "Just another man of God seeking to save a soul from the gallows," he had said. And so, Simon had languished in the wood store to await his fate.

Standing on the cart, Simon went to speak, to proclaim his innocence, but a rough slap across his face prevented him.

"Get on with it," Dearlaf shouted to the executioner. Gilbert Forester lifted the noose and placed it on Simon's neck, drawing the knot tight, before moving to the front of the cart.

With the rope drawn tight against his throat, Simon strained to speak, to cry out to stop this travesty, but all that came was a throaty croak.

Dearlaf the Reeve dropped his arm and Gilbert Forester ushered his oxen gently forward. The two attendants released Simon, and he wobbled before his feet were dragged off the end of the cart, and his weight under the rope dropped downwards.

His world slowed down almost to a stop. Through bulging eyes, he could see the faces staring at him, see the hate, horror, terror and, in the eyes of some of the women, sympathy. The catcalls became a continuous cacophony of noise. Thoughts collided in his head. He saw the face of Amy, his dead wife and their stillborn son, who never took a breath, so he was denied baptism and a name by the Holy Church. The malevolent, screaming visage of Maud Blount replaced the image of his dead son, the hate and fury of Alice le Blunde and then the blue eyes and flowing red locks of Isabella la Rus appeared, one by one in his head, followed by the flaxen locks of Alia Parys.

Simon's throat tightened; he jerked on the rope, struggling for breath, legs thrashing, eyes wide in panic. He bit his tongue but could not taste the metallic tang of his blood. He was choking, mouth wide, gasping for any air that might come and oblivious to the raucous noise and the surrounding crowd when darkness finally overwhelmed him.

Ж

Chapter Forty-nine

The Manor of Hanstead, July 1277.

THE ONLY SYMPATHY for Simon Lowy's plight came from a few of the younger women of Hanstead who had known Strep, son of Erith, of old and felt he had got what he deserved. The young boys of the village, enthralled at the man's struggle against the rope, jeered and threw stones at his legs. There was real hatred from many of the men who stood close together in a circle around the gallows tree, despite most having had no time for Strep.

Simon choked and thrashed at the end of the rope, his tongue grotesquely protruding from his mouth as the noise of the crowd intensified in his ears. Thorsten the Smith, who had not been jeering, was the first to hear the cries coming from beyond the crowd. A cloud of dust approached from the southern horizon, floating in the breeze as it got closer toward Hanstead.

A woman leant out of a horse-drawn litter, peering through the dust toward the village in the distance. Ahead of her were mounted men-at-arms, their royal livery of three lions passant guardant billowing, mounts snorting as they rode hard in the summer breeze.

Isabella la Rus shouted up to the driver to push hard towards the village and he flicked his whip to drive the horses faster.

Ahead, she could make out the track that led into the village and a large oak tree at its centre. It took such a long time to make the final furlongs to Hanstead. The royal men-at-arms arrived at the village green first and alarm raced across Isabella's face as she watched them move toward a figure dangling from the bough of the large oak.

Her face tightened and her breath quickened. She had saved his life before, three times, he would say, but he wasn't privy to the other occasions when she had been his guardian. Frustration coursed through her, and a ripple of fury as she fought to hold back her rising emotions. She lifted her arm and angrily brushed away a tear. The body ahead of her hung limp on the gallows rope. She was too late.

———————

"*You there*! Desist. Stop now. I command you." Thorsten turned away from the execution and saw a party of horsemen riding fiercely at the head of the dust storm toward the gallows tree. At their head was an imposing figure on a large bay destrier, roaring something Thorsten could not make out.

"Stop. I command you in the name of His Grace the King," boomed the voice as it got closer.

Hearing the command and the sound of hoofbeats, many of the villagers turned, puzzled at this new development. The crowd parted instinctively to allow the riders through.

A dozen men, their mounts sweating white with exertion, drew to an abrupt halt. Dearlaf, the Reeve knew horses and could see that the animals had been hard ridden; the stallions were tucked, wild-eyed, snorting, with froth dripping from their mouths, their flanks white with sweat. At their head was a man with a tight, pursed mouth, beak-like nose and stern eyes. His rich, red cloak swirled as he brought his mount to a stop, issuing a sharp command.

Ahead, the violent jerking of Simon Lowys had lessened as death crept up on him.

"By my order, this stops now." Even as he was uttering the words, a mounted Man-at-Arms drew his sword, rode up beside Simon Lowys' limp body, and sliced through the hanging rope with a swinging arc. Simon Lowys slumped to the ground beneath the Gallows Oak, falling like a sack of miller's grain.

Dearlaf stepped up to confront the rider who had stopped the execution.

"By what authority do you do this? This man is a murderer, tried and duly convicted by a jury."

The cold, hard eyes of John of Berwick fell upon the Reeve.

"I possess every authority to stop this charade. As you do see." Berwick pointed to the mounted men, all wearing the three golden lions' passant guardant, the livery of King Edward of England.

Berwick fixed Dearlaf with an icy stare. "This man, as you, Master Reeve, do well know, is an agent of the King. He told you so, did he not?"

The Reeve shuffled nervously, saying nothing, standing beside Berwick's Bay destrier, shifting his feet uneasily from side to side. Berwick continued, "I would know from you who arranged this trial outside the purview of the King's Justice in Eyre."

One of the Household men called for water for the horses while some of his companions dismounted to form a perimeter around the fallen King's Man, gradually pushing the crowd further and further back.

Dearlaf didn't reply, shifting his gaze to stare uneasily at the ground. "Take him," Berwick pointed, addressing his instruction to no-one in particular, but the Household guards beside him swiftly dismounted to flank the Reeve and place him into their custody.

Two others, a wizened serjeant and a younger man, both wearing the royal livery, moved to the prone body of Simon Lowys, lying face down under the bough of the gallows tree, where he fell, the noose still tight around his neck.

The Guard serjeant was Simon's friend, the twenty-year veteran Nate Brynkhill. He bent down to examine Simon and loosened the noose pulled tight against Simon's throat. He placed a finger on his neck to check if blood still coursed through the body.

Still full of pent-up energy, John of Berwick's stallion snapped and bit at those in the crowd who had been too tardy in retreating. Without a care, Berwick advanced his skittish destrier toward the gallows tree and loomed tall over the Guard serjeant, the question unsaid. Nate Brynkhill half-turned to look up at the King's Intelligencer and slowly shook his head.

Chapter Fifty

The Manor House of the Papal Legate Bernardo Ravennate,
Westwick, August 1277.

MY LORD BERWICK, I assure you that I am most distressed by this news. Tis, …*tragico*," he paused. Standing beside the Papal Legate, Giovanni di Bologna whispered in Bernardo's ear.

"*Si Giovanni*, a tragedy, that is the word, yes?"

"*Si Excellency*." Di Bologna now addressed John of Berwick, his southern accent emphasising the final syllable of each word. "We received news from Hanstead that the execution had been carried out and only later did we learn that the felon was a King's Man."

Berwick was determined to converse with the Legate rather than his Steward.

"As you say, Your Eminence, it is tragic, but your man, Giovanni here, presided over the trial."

"Indeed, he did. As a man so close to God, I cannot be associated with the death of peasants, which is the usual result in such cases. So, Giovanni acted for me."

John of Berwick turned to face the Steward. "You had met with Simon Lowys, the King's Man, had you not?"

Giovanni di Bologna's face was impassive and self-assured. "You are right, I believe; His Excellency here did introduce him when he first came to this house."

"Yet you did not recognise him, standing but a few paces from you in the nave of the church, even when he called out to you, identifying himself. "

Giovanni di Bologna gave a half-laugh. "Tis true. I meet so very many people in my role for His Eminence. You cannot remember all." He half-shrugged apologetically and paused as if thinking about what his next lie should be.

"I saw before me a peasant in rags and twas noisy in the nave. I heard no-one call out to me and I am sure that the scribe who kept the record also did not hear this."

"How convenient. Yet you ordered him gagged."

Giovanni shrugged again. "To speed the proceedings, My Lord, nothing more."

Berwick scoffed at this. "So, you do tell me you did not recognise a King's Man who had stood beside you but weeks before?"

"Indeed, My Lord, I did not. Can you tell me that you notice the faces of the low-born?" Berwick could feel the bile rise in his throat, angered by the mendacity of this man. He could tell di Bologna was lying but could not prove it.

"My Lord Berwick," Bernardo Ravennate's intervention was obsequious. " Tis a terrible thing when an innocent man is hanged. All we can do is proffer our apologies for this mishap. I will, of course, meet the expense of Master Lowy's funeral. And a generous payment to his widow, perhaps?"

Berwick nodded. "That is kindly, Your Excellency, though Master Lowys was a widower." Berwick twirled the signet ring on his right hand. "I find his death most irregular and, I might add, deeply suspicious."

The faces of the Legate and his steward were masks of feigned innocence.

"My Lord," Ravennate emphasized the word. "My Steward and I are as saddened by these events as you are, but what is done is done. All I can do now is make *ricompensa*, how do you say in English, recompense? I am a man of God; I could not have anything to do with such a thing."

John of Berwick inhaled, clearing his throat. Ravennate may not have been implicated directly, but Berwick was sure that di Bologna, had arranged everything.

Berwick made his obeisance to the Legate, who, in turn, offered the Signum Crucis and blessing. A young boy of a dozen years, with the features of an angel, escorted him from the chamber through the labyrinth of wood-panelled corridors to the main door.

Berwick's horse awaited him with the half-dozen Household Men-at-Arms who had escorted him. As he left, he was sure that eyes were watching him from the upstairs window.

He now accepted what le Reynard had told him, that the Papal Legate was not to be trusted and that the Steward, Giovanni, was far more than a personal man-servant or steward. Le Reynard -Isabella - believed that Giovanni was more of a soldier, acting as the Legate's enforcer. John of Berwick had arrived at the same conclusion.

Both the Legate and his man knew that Lowys was dead. If di Bologna truly believed that the man he sentenced to death was a peasant, why was it necessary to send news that the execution had succeeded? Berwick noted that Ravennate had not enquired about the lost maid, almost as if he and his henchman knew that she had been found.

As he and his guards rode away from Westwick, south towards the Roman road to London, Berwick recalled an image of the body of Simon Lowys slumped on the ground beneath the Gallows Tree at Hanstead. Berwick had raced north once de Berdesfold had presented himself at the Chancery with news that Lowys would hang. En route, they had linked up with the litter carrying le Reynard to Hanstead. They had ridden onwards, pushing the horses hard in the hope that they could get there in time to prevent tragedy.

Ж

Chapter Fifty-one

The old mill in the village of Bricket, July 1277.

H E FLOATED IN A TUNNEL of darkness; the merest flicker of light danced in the far distance. There was no pain and why would there be? This was the path to Heaven. All he had to do was to follow the light to eternal paradise. He heard an angel gently call out his name, beckoning him to accompany her to join the Heavenly Host in God's kingdom.

"Master Lowys! Master Lowys!" This whispering angel was most formal in its salutation.

The light grew stronger as he gently glided towards it. His senses were overwhelmed with the fragrance of heaven; amber, sandalwood and lavender.

"Master Lowys, Master Lowys," He felt the soft touch of the angel lightly stroking his cheek. "Wake up. Master Lowys, wake up."

Light rippled on the darkness of his eyelids. Simon spluttered and gasped for air.

A cawing sound emanated from his throat as his eyes flickered, blinked and looked upon Alia Parys' smiling face.

He was lying cradled in her lap. "Master Lowys, you are back with us," she said joyfully, wiping his face with a damp rag and tenderly brushing his cheek.

Simon's head jerked violently as he recalled standing on the back of a hay cart, hands bound, with a death rope placed around his neck. He remembered the choking, gasping for lungfuls of air and the terrible darkness that had engulfed him.

He made to say something to Alia, but intense pain in his neck prevented any words from coming out. He found his hands were no longer tied and placed one against his throat, trying to relieve the pain. In this manner, he could speak in a short, croaked voice.

A throaty "how?" was all that came out.

"Tis a miracle, really," she replied. "They had placed the rope over your neck and pulled the cart free, so you were on the end of the rope struggling for your life-breath when John of Berwick did arrive with a company of Royal guards." Her words came out in a relieved rush.

"Mistress Isabella and I were in a litter and we were afeared that you were lost to us. We both shed tears for you as we watched My Lord Berwick walk his mount through the crowd, then Nate, the serjeant, dismounted and rushed to your side. He put his hand to your neck and turned and shook his head. I admit, Master Lowys, both the Mistress and I howled in anguish, for we afeared you were dead. But, do you see, twas all a ploy by My Lord Berwick."

Alia wiped the relieving wet cloth gently across Simon's forehead.

"My Lord Berwick had asked Nate if you were dead. So all around believed that you were." Tears returned to Alia's eyes as her thoughts returned to the awful events of the dawn hours.

"Oh Master Lowys, twas awful, truly awful."

———

John of Berwick pushed his destrier through the crowd toward the gallows tree and loomed tall over the Guard serjeant, the question unsaid. Nate Brynkhill cradled Simon in his crooked arm and half-turned to look up at the King's Intelligencer, slowly shaking his head. All in the silent crowd took that action as a sign that the killer of Strep was dead. The King's Intelligencer brought his feisty destrier to a halt beside the serjeant.

His gaze bored in on the Master Serjeant. The question in his eyes going unsaid but, nonetheless, understood.

"Nay, my Lord," replied Nate Brynkhill in a whisper, "he lives, just." Nate deftly loosened the gallows knot that was pulled hard against Simon's neck. "Had we tarried, he would be dead, My Lord. I will get him to the mill at Bricket, two miles yonder and seek a physician."

"Do but make your actions as if he is dead. These people around us will soon spread that message." Nate Brynkhill didn't know what his Lord Berwick was planning, but knew it was not his position to ask.

"And do tell the physician not to let him die, I needs must speak with Lowys as soon as possible."

Having watched justice being done, the crowd of villagers began to drift away. Only a few children remained, fascinated at witnessing their first hanging.

Royal Guards commandeered Gilbert Forester's cart and hoisted the body of Simon Lowys onto its deck, throwing a woollen cloth over it. Nate climbed up front and flicked the reins to drive the old horse towards the lane leading to the village of Bricket.

"And the Mistress and I followed the cart, still believing that you were dead. Once we were beyond the village, Nate stopped the cart and transferred you to our litter. That was when we first realised that you lived. I said I would tend to your wounds until the physician arrived."

Simon listened intently to Alia as she related the rest of the tale of his rescue, resisting any urge to speak, for his throat was terribly sore and swollen.

He squeezed Alia's arm to signify his thanks, seeking to spare the pain of speaking. Fatigue swept over him and he struggled to stay awake, flitting in and out of sleep.

"Do stay awake, Master Lowys." Alia's voice was soft and reassuring as she cradled his head, taking care not to touch his swollen neck. Closing his eyes brought little relief from the pain that seared through his throat.

"How fares he?" an older female voice inquired. Simon painfully turned to look upon Isabella la Rus. He lifted his arm and reached out to her in recognition.

"He is still with us, Mistress, though I afear his neck is badly injured." Isabella took Simon's hand, briefly but tenderly.

"Do you see the bother you do get yourself into when I am not there to watch over you?" she said. It was a gentle attempt at humour, but Isabella recognised how close Simon Lowys had come to death.

"He lives, Alia, we could not have hoped for better, and we must thank God for that. But we must find out why such a thing was done to him. This Italian wanted Master Lowys silenced and went to much trouble to ensure he was. He cannot discover the truth, Alia, so it falls to us."

She pushed a soft lock of her red hair back under her wimple and the King's agent, known as le Reynard, left for an audience with John of Berwick.

$$Ж$$

Chapter Fifty-two

The King's Highway south toward the village of Windridge, August 1277.

A FTER MANY WEEKS, Jasliena van Leuven had been surprised to receive the message from Giovanni, the Legate's Man. The youth who had brought the sealed parchment stressed the urgency of its contents. Giovanni sought a remote meeting with Benuic where they would not be seen together. Given what they had done to the King's Man, she thought it prudent. Caution always drove Jasliena's actions; it was a necessary trait in her world. She remained suspicious of Giovanni. She, Giovanni and possibly the Legate knew what they had done to Simon Lowys, and Jasliena was no naive maid; if it were her, she would seek to cover her trail by eliminating Giovanni.

With those thoughts in her mind, she found herself edging her palfrey along a track off the King's Highway south toward Windridge. The track was wide enough for a cart, though the dense bracken undergrowth encroached on its edges, despite Royal ordinances to have such shrubbery cut well back to deter wolf's heads. Little of the heavy rain of recent days had penetrated the verdant canopy of the trees, so the track remained rutted and dusty, making it impossible to progress at more than a walking pace.

The air became noticeably cooler as she rode deeper into woodland; the earthy scents of damp woodland mingled with the fragrance of greenery. The village lay atop a low hill and soon, she hoped, the trees on either side would give way to the sight of habitation and beyond it, the manor house. An exodus of birds upwards from the trees startled her, and her ears picked up the probable cause. From deep within the heavy undergrowth came growls, grunts and the occasional scream, the sound of the King of the Forest, a wild boar.

A mischief of magpies chattered high up in the canopy of the trees and on either side of the track, she could hear the scurrying of small animals, startled by the noise and smell of her mount. The rutted way climbed gently up to a crest, where an ancient, gnarled wooden barn was nestled, its timbers bleached white: the agreed, remote meeting place.

If she were being watched, which she fully expected, they would see a youth arriving. Jasliena had dressed as a groom, donning a cap to cover her long black hair. The male attire made riding easier, for a young man on horseback attracted far less attention than a woman. Although dressing as a man was a mortal sin in the eyes of the church, Jasliena van Leuven cared not a bit.

She was right in anticipating that there would be eyes upon her. A man was observing from a hidden mossy gully hewn out over centuries by a brook trickling through the roots of an ancient oak tree. He was at home in the woodland, for he was a wolf's head, a man who would receive no mercy from the law if apprehended. Anyone could take him dead or alive for a guaranteed cash reward, so Ivo Shaldeforde hid in the shadows; the woodland was his friend.

Shaldeforde's reputation also brought him work. '*The Italian*', as Ivo called Giovanni, had heard of Ivo and had sought him out for this day. In truth, all Ivo knew was that they were to seize a woman and kill her; the Italian had never said who she was. Perhaps a secret rendezvous with a noble lady gone wrong or the abduction of a rival's wife to force a concession? Ivo neither knew nor cared as he maintained his vigil from afar, blending into the gully beneath the old oak.

Ivo had not come alone; he had his trusted lieutenant John Pyecart accompany him. They had arrived hours earlier to fulfil the instructions from the Italian - kill the woman and ensure her body was never found. While John kept lookout, Ivo had gone far into the woods. He dug a hole deep enough to accept a body, not as deep as a churchyard grave but not so shallow as to attract predatory animals. When he was done, he found the water-carved gully and settled down to wait and watch. John Pyecart hid himself on the opposite side, about one hundred paces down the gentle slope.

The sounds emanating from deep inside the woods did not frighten the wolf's head; he was at one with the forest. That was the sound of a crow, that, the song of a Blackcap. A murmuration of starlings left the tops of the trees, making an ever-changing pattern as they soared skywards, seeking a new landing spot. Far to the east, perhaps a mile hence, Ivo picked out the screams of hunger of a wild boar. Trees rustled and bushes moved as the small animals of the forest sought the safety of shelter. A family of magpies flew from the trees, spooked by something approaching.

Below Ivo, John Pyecart watched keenly as a single rider picked their way up the gentle slope towards the village. A lone rider with no guard; this would be an easy shilling to earn, he thought. Once the rider was beyond him, Pyecart clasped his hands together, pressed his thumbs against his lips, curled his lips over his lower teeth and blew hard. From above, Ivo heard Pyecart's owl call; the signal that someone approached.

As the rider drew near, Ivo made out a youth rather than a woman, with a cap pulled down tight over his head and wearing peasant garb. Maybe's this was another; the woman was yet to appear. Approaching the old barn, the youth began to cast furtive eyes all around as if expecting someone.

Ivo stared hard at the youth. His face was not pale as Ivo would have expected, but it had an olive hue, that of a foreigner. Then, he removed his cap and long, black hair tumbled out. A leering smile broke on his lips. This youth was a woman in disguise. The woman shook out her long hair before pushing it back into the cap, pulling it down tight against her head.

Jasliena van Leuven anticipated trouble. Furtively, her eyes scanned the dense undergrowth ahead, seeking movement. If Giovanni wished her dead, he would not wait until she was upon Westwick, for there would be too many villagers to see her arrive. If it were to happen, it would be here and soon.

She noticed a subtle movement behind a gnarled oak thirty paces to the west, a brown flash against some moss. She reached inside her sleeve and rested her hand on the polished handle of a long stiletto. Ahead of her, the hawthorn bushes rustled as a dishevelled peasant wielding a long dagger pushed his way through the undergrowth to appear beside the track. It was as she expected, not Giovanni, but one of his hired thugs. A malicious grin appeared on his face as he stepped towards her and grabbed the reins, jerking the palfrey's head upwards. He brought two fingers to his mouth and made a long whistle.

Another man, garbed in rags and holding a sword, appeared from behind. Just the two, then, thought Jasliena. The first man, clearly the leader, motioned for her to dismount. She kept her left sleeve slightly raised as she did so, to prevent her stiletto from falling.

The second man silently took the reins and led the palfrey towards the undergrowth. Stepping behind Jasliena, the leader pressed the point of his dagger into her back and forced her to follow. They had gone no more than a dozen paces into the woodland when a succession of blood-curdling screams and growls broke the stillness of the interior. The birds abandoned the trees, alerted to the noise of a predator on the forest floor beneath.

Behind Jasliena, Ivo Shaldeforde didn't break his stride; he was well used to the noises of a wild boar and wasn't surprised to find one in this area of oak, ash and hazel, a perfect place to hunt boar. Jasliena van Leuven had also heard the cries of the beast, but no shiver of fear ran through her; she sensed an opportunity.

The two wolf's heads and their prisoner pushed deeper and deeper into the woodland where mighty oaks and beech crowded close together and the air held a dampness of rotting vegetation. Ivo cast his eyes around, seeking the trees he had used as his landmark.

"Stop here," he commanded to John Pyecart.

In the dappled light, Jasliena took in the surroundings. They were in a small clearing between stands of trees, fallen, moss-covered boughs and bracken. John laid down his weapon, loosely hitched the palfrey to a bush, picked up his sword and took a few steps away from Jasliena.

She spied the fresh hole in the forest floor with the recently dug earth piled up beside it and felt the point of Ivo's dagger in her back guiding her towards the hurriedly dug grave.

Ivo Shaldeforde experienced the searing pain before the piercing howl left his mouth. He gazed down at his bloodied thigh, a gaping slash from which blood poured as Jasliena's stiletto then slashed across his wrist, with the sword falling to the earth. John Pyecart had spun around at Ivo's scream, wide-eyed at the scene unfolding. He instinctively advanced toward her, brandishing his blade. It was a mistake. Jasliena's throwing knife thudded into his chest. He dropped to his knees, gasping for breath and thinking that his life could not end here, in a God-forsaken forest. In the distance, the snorts and grunts of the angry wild boar permeated the air, closer now having picked up the scent of fresh blood. Jasliena van Leuven walked the few paces to the prone body of the outlaw Pyecart. Vacant eyes set in a pale face stared up at her as she pulled her throwing knife from his chest, bringing him closer to his Day of Judgement.

Behind her, Ivo Shaldeforde writhed on the ground, a deep gash in his upper thigh and his wrist, his lifeblood staining the forest floor. As she kicked his sword into the undergrowth, the screams and snorts of the boar grew ever closer. She had not intended to kill whoever Giovanni sent, but circumstance had forced her hand. She considered finishing the remaining outlaw but allowed him to take his chance with nature. The growls and screeching were getting closer, so that may not be much of a chance unless he could hobble to a safe place.

The undergrowth fifty or so paces to the east rustled and stirred as the small animals of the woodland floor sought safety from the approaching predator. Jasliena grabbed her palfrey's reins, mounted and carefully picked her way back to the track. When she found it, she turned away from Windridge, heading back toward St Albans. Giovanni had sought to eliminate Benuic, the assassin; now, she would exact revenge upon the Legate's Man.

Ivo Shaldeforde gritted his teeth, fighting the pain which throbbed through his body as he dragged himself along the forest floor. He heard the warning signs behind him, the high-pitched screams and growls of the king of the woods. As a wolf's head, Ivo was at one with the forest and was well aware of the dangers posed by aggressive male boars. He knew that they had an uncanny sense of smell and that the scent of his blood seeping from his wounds had been picked up already. Ivo was seeking the safety of height, but his wound precluded climbing a tree. A dozen paces ahead, a low-hanging bough of a once mighty oak jutted out like a pointing arm. It was not tall, perhaps the height of a child, but was broad and would afford him some protection from the rampant boar. Through the pain, he scrabbled toward the limb of the oak and safety, his stiffening, wounded leg hindering his progress. A panicked sweat glistened on his face; he was in a race against death and he knew he was losing.

Ivo Shaldeforde was tantalisingly close to the oak bough as the snarling growl behind him grew louder. Summoning all his strength, he reached to grasp the bough but was tossed sideways like a rag doll flung to the floor, gasping for breath and writhing in agony. He couldn't know it, but the wild boar's tusk had punctured his lung. Breath would not come as the creature, driven wild by the scent of Ivo's blood, dropped its head and charged again. Its teeth ripped deep into his torso, crushing bone and flesh, feasting on the soft organs inside. Pain disappeared as Ivo Shaldeforde truly became one with the forest.

Ж

___

Chapter Fifty-three

A wharf at the Scheldt Quays, Antwerp, August 1277.

FOUR BURLY MEN GRUNTED and heaved at their heavy oars, fighting the swell to pull '*The Vrouve van der Zee*' from the harbour's edge to her mooring at the Scheldt Quays. Her ungainly approach to the wharf belied her name of '*The Lady of the Sea*'. Tied to the wherry by a single hemp line, its lone mast was without its square sail, as onboard, crewmen shouted instructions to the rowers to bring the Vrouve about and decrease their oar speed.

'*The Vrouve van der Zee*'s destination was the' mooring place known locally as the Bierwerf. Close beside the harbour houses built against the city walls, it was a flurry of activity. Located hard against the walls was '*Tsertogen*,' just one of many inns dotted around the Scheldt Quays. The open window in the rear of the inn gave a fine view of ships coming and going from the river wharf.

Leyn Reinaert stopped moving wooden kegs to watch '*The Vrouve van der Zee*' pull alongside the wooden pier before the crew tied ropes to stout oak beams to hold her in position. He had owned '*Tsertogen*' for almost seven years. A burly bull of a man, Reinaert had been Man-at-Arms for the Count of Flanders in a former life.

He had fought the heathens under the burning sun of Outremer. His immense strength and intimidating presence made him the perfect owner of a dock-side inn. He pulled an empty barrel toward him and, skilfully with feet and hands, rolled it outside and around to the front of '*Tsertogen*'. Reinaert planned his work for the hours before noon to always keep '*The Vrouve van der Zee*' in sight. He had expected her to dock this morning, having left Harwich two days since.

The heady aroma of fish, rope and excrement melded into one that assaulted the senses of newcomers, but Leyn was immune to the stench. He loitered at the front, busying himself with sweeping up and rearranging the barrels that served as tables. His patient observance brought its reward when two guards appeared on the narrow plank that led from the ship to the wharf. Their eyes scanned along the harbour, seeking threats and danger; when none was forthcoming, they signalled to another, who appeared with four scared children, bound by the hand, overwhelmed by their situation.

Leyn Reinaert did his best to appear not to notice, going about his daily business. But he took in what was happening. A cart, drawn by two oxen, pulled up alongside '*The Vrouve van der Zee*' and the four children were bundled onto the back with two of the guards accompanying them. In but a short time, the cart moved off. Leyn Reinaert could not follow it, for that was not part of his instructions. As well as being a former Man-at-Arms and innkeeper of '*Tsertogen*', Leyn Reinaert served John of Berwick and King Edward of England, whom he had first met years before when on crusade. He was a small part of this operation. He did not know the significance of the children and he imagined John of Berwick would have someone else follow the oxcart to its destination. But Leyn had one further act to complete before he received payment.

Rain fell that evening and the inn became quiet. A stranger in his middle years entered and found a table in a recessed corner close to the door. Leyn approached, greeting him in Flemish.

"*Welkom.*"

"Do you have English ale?" inquired the stranger.

"*Nee*, not English but the finest Flemish ale," came the response.

Leyn laid four clay jugs on the rough-hewn table before the stranger, one for each child he had seen. The man inclined his head and gave an imperceptible nod of acknowledgement.

"Nay, just me," he replied before sliding a gold coin across the table, which Leyn deftly swept up before anyone could see. With a bow to the stranger, he removed three jugs and carried them to his barrels. When he turned, the jug of ale remained on the oak table, but the stranger was gone.

Ж

____

Chapter Fifty-four

Eyewoodlane, St Albans, August 1277.

EYEWOODLANE LAY SOUTH of the Abbey of the Martyr, at the foot of the muddy hill beside the Holywell Stream and next to the thick woodland that gave the lane its name. It was beyond the city ditch but was an area of growing importance and popular with the town's wealthier merchants. Its wide roadway was, as yet, uncobbled and a cluster of modest but neat cottages lay set back from the lane. Fifty paces along was a two-storey house, built some ten years before by a successful spice merchant, Gilbert de Shethesere, for his wife, Amice. Three years ago, Gilbert had fallen through a trapdoor beside his shop in the Magna Vico, pulling down a barrel of ginger on top of him. He lingered in agony from his crushed limbs for many days before succumbing to death. It left Amice a widow and in control of a thriving spice business.

Amice de Shethesere had not remarried despite the many suitors in the Guild in London and widower spice merchants from other towns who pursued her, not for her looks or shapely figure, but to control her wealth. And she faced pressure too from the church, who wanted her to take the veil. She was more than halfway through her third decade of life and enjoyed the freedom and privileges widowhood brought her. Amice didn't think of herself as comely but plain.

One man was different. He made her laugh and happy, flirted with her and made her think of a future rather than dwell in the past. She had known him for just a short time, formal friends at first who quickly became lovers; if he ever found out, her priest, Sire James, would disapprove and condemn her for committing the sin of fornication. But Amice did not care; she was happy. Giovanni, her Italian lover, made her happy.

On this summer morning, Amice had been giddy with excitement to receive a message from Giovanni. A young boy of barely ten years hand-delivered it to her house a few hours after dawn. A litter would arrive for her at Sext to bring her to the manor of Westwick for their secret assignation.

Amice closed her eyes and thoughts of Giovanni entered her head. She had never known a man like him. Certainly not Gilbert, her late husband, who had always been unadventurous. Not any of the older, wizened men of the Spice Merchants Guild whose only thought was to get their grasping hands on her business. No, Giovanni di Bologna was kind and tender. She trembled as she recalled his touch, gently stroking her body as they lay together. Amice lifted a hand, remembering the time she traced his battle scars with her fingers and how he had not recoiled but taken her in his arms and passionately kissed her.

Amice spent the morning hours making herself ready for the liaison. The bell for Sext was tolling as the two-horse litter arrived outside her house in Eyewoodlane. The litter was an elaborate covered box, resplendent in red and green, with a horse front and back. A cloth cover over open windows prevented Amice from seeing out but kept the dust and dirt from the roads getting in.

The litter rocked to and fro, mirroring the gait of the walking horses as it headed for the Roman road and the route to Westwick. Inside , Amice accustomed herself to the gentle side-sway and a slight smile of naughtiness came to her lips. She was travelling to an appointment with the man she had fallen in love with and just the two of them knew the secret.

In that, Amice was partly correct. Two people did know of this secret assignation, but the other was not Giovanni di Bologna. From a distance, hidden by the trees that gave the lane its name, Isabella la Rus watched the ponderous gait of the litter as it manoeuvred out of Eyewoodlane toward Watling Street. The widow would be out of her house for many hours and Isabella could begin to lay the next part of her plan.

It was Isabella who had sent the instructions about the secret meeting to Amice de Shethesere. She had also arranged the litter, all to vacate Amice's residence. Giovanni, too, had received a message; one inviting him to Amice's house on Eyewoodlane. That had also come from Isabella. There was a slight chance that the two might cross on the road, but Giovanni travelled by horse and his fastest route was to cut through the old Roman town. Amice's litter would have to follow the King's Highway south before turning west to Westwick. Isabella was playing a hazardous game of chess, moving the pieces around the board to achieve her ultimate goal.

Giovanni di Bologna was dangerous and needed to be stopped, but his position within the household of the Papal Legate afforded him protection from King Edward's law. Isabella had wrestled with her conscience, but Giovanni's hiring of thugs to kill her made up her mind; she would stop Giovanni and his wretched child abduction trade. He was a man beyond the jurisdiction of the King's Courts, protected by his affinity to the Papal Legate. So, if that meant his death, then so be it.

But Isabella la Rus was not a cold-blooded assassin. She had taken lives in her role as an Intelligencer to the King only when her own or another life was threatened, such as the slaying of the witch Maud Blount the previous year to save the life of Simon Lowys. Isabella had conceived this plan to lure Giovanni to his lover's house, but it would not be by her hand if he died. She would allow

God to decide, although chance would be heavily skewed against the Italian.

Isabella held a wicker basket over her arm to blend in with the women of the town. Inside the basket was a hemp sack in which slept a red viper. Days since, she had gone to the docks in London, where she met with a thoroughly disreputable trader, Adam Dragfoot, to buy the creature. For a price, he sourced items for the city's criminal fraternity. Adam Dragfoot didn't blink an eye at serving a woman or the request that he find her a venomous asp. Isabella knew that the price demanded -ten pounds - was robbery, but she paid up. In under two weeks, Isabella received a message that the goods were ready for collection.

Adam Dragfoot had procured an African Morsus, a three-foot-long viper reddish-brown in colour with dark bands on its head. Isabella knew that in Latin, Morsus meant '*death bite*'. This was just the serpent she sought. All she needed now was Amice de Shethesere's warming stone to make the plan succeed.

The rusted iron hinges of the stout rear gate to Amice's garden groaned as Giovanni di Bologna pushed against it. He had visited Amice in Eyewoodlane twice before and entered through the small garden at the back each time. He left his horse with his young groom, sheltered in the trees of the woods behind the lane. Its discreet location suited him, being away from the town, secluded and beyond prying eyes. He moved across the neat vegetable garden, past the well-weeded rows of half-picked onions, cabbage and a pear tree laden with soon-to-be ripe fruit. The solid oak door into the kitchen was unlocked, just as he expected.

Amice's kitchen was spotless; the stone flagstones were well-scrubbed and pots were arranged on shelves with everything in its place. A small fire danced in the hearth, over which a cauldron of pottage bubbled gently. Beside it, a flat warming stone still gave off its radiant heat and prompted Giovanni to think that Amice was so thoughtful, taking the trouble to warm her bed for him. His gaze fell on the large rectangular table in the middle of the room, where clay cups sat beside a jug of ale, a plate of cut sheep's milk cheese and a small fresh loaf of maslin bread. A small scrap of parchment lay propped against the jug of ale, the sort lettered people used to write messages to others.

Taking a piece of the cheese and stuffing it into his mouth, Giovanni picked up the parchment, read it and grinned.

"Dearest Giovanni, pray you eat and then wait for me in my chamber."

Without sitting, Giovanni poured himself a cup of ale, drank it in one gulp and poured another. Ignoring the bread, he scooped up more of the cheese and, with the cup of ale in his other hand, made his way to the steep steps that led up to Amice's first-floor bedchamber.

Giovanni had been with many women over the years and in many nations and he had not always been gentle and kind to them. He had a momentary pang of regret at his past behaviour before his thoughts turned to Amice.

She hadn't been distant and aloof to his attentions and if he thought about it, he had tried hard to impress her. Well, it had worked, hadn't it? An afternoon in bed with a beautiful woman would take his mind off the problems that seemed to be closing in on him.

He had been in Amice's bedchamber before and mused about how womanly it was. Fresh rushes, sprinkled with herbs, lay on the wooden floor, giving the room its fragrant aroma of lavender and beeswax, making it a lady's chamber. It was well-proportioned, with a south-facing double window paned with glass, a sure sign of wealth. A large bed dominated one side. An intricately carved pillar at each corner held a cornice supporting the heavy curtains that would be drawn closed in cold weather.

Giovanni sat on the edge of the bed, kicked off his boots and pulled off his cote and hose. The anticipation of the pleasure that lay ahead aroused him. He allowed his imagination to think of Amice without her garments. She was not tall but had an alluring beauty that likely grew with the years. His thoughts went to her small pale face and its delicate features, her thin, inviting lips and her lingering gaze upon him. She had deep grey-brown eyes that might see deep into his soul. He closed his eyes and envisioned her comely body entwined with his. He anticipated her loosening her white-laced gorget headdress that framed her face and he smiled at how her brown hair would tumble down her back. He imagined how, in the coming hours, he would run his fingers through that soft hair as they embraced in tender passion.

Giovanni stood up, threw back the coverings and rolled himself into her bed. The bed had the same familiar, fragrant aroma of lavender. He felt the warmth beneath his feet, where Amice had placed a warming stone to heat the bed for him and he mentally thanked her. Was his heart truly racing at the anticipation of holding her in his arms and seeing her naked? I am acting like a skittish, virgin youth, he mused, recalling his first time with a whore in some unknown town in Liguria. Days before, they had been in a dogged fight. It was a hot day, he recalled. The dark-haired whore had lain with all the older men in his company and when they had satisfied their lust, they had pushed him forward for his first time. He didn't even know her name, but he remembered her pox-marked face and how….

Giovanni screamed as a searing pain shot through his leg.

"*Che cazzo*?" The pain coursed through him before he could finish his expletive.

His right leg throbbed as if bitten by a rodent. Seething, he threw back the blankets and swung his legs out of the bed; watery blood seeped from two puncture wounds in his right calf. He pushed a hand under the blanket to discover what had wounded him and immediately regretted it. He screamed in pain as again he was bitten.

"What devilry is this?" he asked himself aloud, throwing back the blankets even further. His eyes widened and his mind raced at what he saw nestled on the sheets.

A bead of sweat ran down his forehead. Giovanni had stood in the vanguard of battle and knew the fear of death. He felt that fear now.

A coiled serpent lay not the length of an arm away from him, its head raised, hissing in anger at being disturbed, its gaze fixed upon him.

He backed away from the bed, his hands shaking but never taking his eyes off the serpent. His legs buckled and he half-tumbled onto the rushes. His leg throbbed and he chanced a look at the wound; around the puncture marks, the leg had reddened and begun to swell. When he succeeded in standing, he looked toward the bed and recoiled: the serpent had disappeared.

Giovanni di Bologna, who had fought and bore the wounds of war, shivered; trickles of sweat rolled down his face, his hands trembled and he felt chilled despite the summer sun.

He needed to think. The serpent was still at large in the chamber. Where? He had to get out and down the stairs to safety. He backed toward the door, fixing his eyes on the rushes beneath his feet for any movement. He reached behind him, carefully lifting the latch before easing out of Amice's bedchamber.

He scrambled down the steps to the kitchen, grasped the table and gulped in lungfuls of air. His breathing was ragged; he released one hand from its grip on the table and stared down at it. His fingers shook and his arm twitched. He tried desperately to stop the shaking and gripped the edge of the table again, but to no avail; his arm and hand were beyond his command.

His sight had blurred and the shelving on the far side of the kitchen where Amice stored her pots swam in front of him. He closed his eyes to stop the sensation, but dark blotches danced across his vision. He flopped onto a stool beside the table.

Reaching for the jug of ale, his trembling hand knocked over a clay cup. He grabbed the jug in both shaking hands and took a long draught before dropping it onto the floor with a loud crash. His breath became more laboured and his eyes rolled, a sensation he knew from combat when wounded and losing blood came before fainting.

Giovanni grimaced, his teeth grinding to fight off the stinging pain that swept over him. Knuckles white, he clenched his fists, seeking, above all else, to stay conscious.

His breathing now came shorter, laboured and guttural. He attempted to reach down to his leg to examine the wound again, but his jerking arm would not obey his thoughts. Beads of cold sweat trickled profusely down his forehead and into his eyes. The room shimmered and tumbled around him. In panic, he tried to focus his thoughts, but to no avail. Fighting the pain and between strained breaths, he tried to make sense of what had happened.

How did a serpent get into the bed? He groaned again as pain seared through his leg, like a sword slicing through flesh. White light washed over his eyes and his arm jerked uncontrollably. Think! Try to think, he commanded himself, even though the very act was becoming increasingly difficult.

Swaying, he was losing the fight to stay awake as the room spun. Giovanni sensed someone else here with him. In his agony, he smelled a familiar fragrance of rosemary and bergamot. Through grimaced teeth, he screamed, "Help me. By God's mercy ......help me." The last words came as a high-pitched wail.

His head slumped to the table. His vision danced between white and black, making it hard to focus, but from the aroma, he was sure a woman stood close beside him. Giovanni strained every sinew in an attempt to speak. His throat was tight and his mouth could not form the words he sought. When the wheezy, guttural words came, they were pushed out through clenched teeth between laboured breaths.

"Amice, Aiutami. Aiutami." He had slipped into courtly Italian, imploring her. Why was she not helping him? Between the needles of pain stabbing his whole body now, the thought raced through his mind. It was clear that he was in agony and suffering desperately.

"Help me, Amice," he screamed in confusion, but no words came out. A twitching arm reached out pleadingly toward her but fell away, no longer under his command.

The agony of a thousand cuts sliced his skin. The hardened veteran in him fought desperately not to surrender to the pain, but at length, he gave a blood-curdling howl as the wave of torment became too much to bear, his breathing shallow as his body succumbed to the unconsciousness that was the harbinger of death.

$$\text{Ж}$$

Chapter Fifty-five

Eyewoodlane St Albans, August 1277.

ISABELLA LA RUS LOOKED impassively at Giovanni slumped across the table like one deep in his cups in a local alehouse. He had implored her to help him, but she waited behind him, immune to his suffering.

Standing by the dying Giovanni, Isabella's attention turned to the death-snake. She could not be sure where it was and had brought two cages laced with dead mice to attract the serpent. Very soon, royal Men-at-Arms would arrive and they would capture the creature. More royal guards were in position to delay Amice de Shethesere's return from Westwick.

Thus far, all of Isabella's plans have worked out as she had hoped. She had compassion for Amice's situation and did not want the widow to return to her home to find her lover dead in her kitchen. That, too, would be dealt with by the royal Men-at-Arms. Giovanni di Bologna would disappear. The King's agents in Ghent were on to the Italian's partner and a Nuncio had been dispatched to Viterbo to inform the Papal authorities of the Legate's possible involvement in child abduction.

Isabella stared down at the now lifeless body of the Legate's henchman, awaiting the imminent arrival of the King's men. The kitchen had suffered little disturbance and the guards would locate and deal with the serpent. She drew in a deep breath and blinked, her eyes stinging as her nose picked up an acrid, nauseous smell that lodged in the back of her throat. Her gaze immediately went to the fire; barely smouldering, just a few logs crackled and burned brightly; it was not out of control. Turning, Isabella froze. Whiteish-grey smoke seeped into the kitchen from the rear of the house, billowing and rising like a ghostly apparition. Sensing the danger, Isabella raced toward the back door, seeking escape, but the heat pushed her back. Amice de Shethesere's house was ablaze.

Ж

Chapter Fifty-six

Eyewoodlane, St Albans, August 1277.

FROM BEHIND THE BROAD ancient oaks, in the lane opposite Amice de Shethesere's burning townhouse, Jasliena van Leuven watched, her smile a chilling reflection of the chaos she had unleashed. Her target had always been Giovanni di Bologna and discovering the location of his mistress's house had been relatively straightforward. Giovanni was not well-liked in the Legate's household at Westwick and a few silver coins had loosened the servant's tongues. The Legate's old carter had proved the most useful, having previously brought Amice home from Westwick. Only by chance did Jasliena discover that Giovanni would be here today. Giovanni's sweet young groom, Alaric, had been unable to resist her charms and had been as easy to manipulate as Adam of Brazbourne had been. Alaric had informed her that the Italian would be visiting Amice's house this day. But one in Jasliena's profession had to be adaptable and able to improvise, so she was prepared.

Jasliena had no regrets. Giovanni had brought her fury upon himself by seeking her death in the forest. He would believe that the wolf's heads had succeeded. But she did not wish to incur the wrath of the Hue and Cry by killing the Italian in public. Amice's house provided her with an excellent opportunity to stage an accident.

From afar, she had observed Amice leaving and, later, Giovanni entering the house through the rear. What she had not expected was the later arrival of another woman. At first, Jasliena believed it was Amice returning but quickly realised that this woman was younger than the one she had seen leave earlier. There was something about this woman: the way she carried herself and her demeanour as if she was constantly aware of the danger around her. When she spied the lock of red hair falling from beneath her wimple, it confirmed for Jasliena that this must be le Reynard, the King's agent she had sought, who had been identified by Simon Lowys. That caused a sense of inward satisfaction. She had not set out to eliminate le Reynard, but this was a heaven-sent opportunity to remove her and the Italian in one go.

The sap of the green oak beams of Amice de Shethesere's house had evaporated in the ten years since its construction. The long, hot summer had dried out the exterior wattle and daub infill in the walls, making the whole structure tinder dry. The flames fascinated Jasliena, clawing their way through the walls, fuelled by the straw at the heart of the daub infill, charring the mighty beams that supported the roof. The blaze erupted with a suddenness that made Jasliena gasp. One moment, the house stood untouched; the next, flames engulfed it with a deafening roar. The speed of the inferno was mesmerizing, blue tongues of fire ripping through the front wall in an instant, exposing the charred, smouldering ribs of the structure. The reed thatch on the roof was soon overwhelmed in a wave of white heat, condemning the house to its fate.

It had been but a short while since she had set the blaze. In her wicker basket, she had secreted faggots and dry straw for kindling, which she laid before each door. Both erupted in flames with the first spark from her fire steel and soon billowing plumes of a white-blue inferno engulfed Amice's home.

Isabella la Rus gasped in acrid air, her heart racing as she fought hard to hold down the panic coursing through her veins. The roar of the flames competed with the groaning of the rafters as they twisted and cracked in the intense heat. She had no route out of the burning house; flames leapt high from both doors, generating an intense heat that drove back her attempts to exit. Isabella felt the walls shudder as the floor timbers of Amice's chamber groaned and cracked and, with a screeching roar, gave way, causing the floor to fail, crashing down in one corner. Isabella was assailed by burning reeds falling from the conflagration that had once been the roof. Even in her despair, she mused at the futility of the situation she now found herself in. The wall in front of her, facing onto Eyewoodlane, bulged as the pressure of the collapsing upper storey pressed down on it before the ever-blackening limewash exploded into the room.

One shard of red-hot lath and daub struck Isabella a glancing blow on the temple, throwing her to the ground and, looking up from the floor, she wondered if in death she imagined seeing an axe cutting a swathe in the wall where the limewashed interior had been.

Jasliena's contentment with her work turned quickly to anger when a detachment of royal Men at Arms arrived and immediately began to attack the lower walls of Amice's house with their bardiche's. Her fury grew as the broad-bladed axes cut through the wattle and daub, creating an opening wide enough for someone to get through. At first, rushing air caused a flame to shoot out, but immediately, it died down; two liveried guards raced inside and emerged, dragging the woman to safety. As annoyed as she was at '*le Reynard's*' escape, Jasliena had to wait; she could not risk Giovanni also escaping the flames. However, as she hid behind the oak, Giovanni did not emerge, nor did any royal guards enter to rescue him. Had he got out, she was prepared to finish him with her arbalest and risk the wrath of the Hue-and-Cry. She imagined that, in the commotion, she would be able to affect her escape. That escape awaited her in the woods behind Amice's house, where Giovanni's young groom, Alaric, awaited him.

The billowing plume of smoke danced on the breeze high above the dense thicket of trees at the rear of Amice's house. Alaric, the groom, could smell the acrid fumes long before he caught sight of the smoke cloud drifting in the blue sky above him. He awaited his master's return, knowing not to leave his position and incur the disapproval of Giovanni di Bologna. So, he waited and soon, his patience was rewarded with the appearance of Jasliena, the mysterious Saracen woman who had befriended him despite the difference in their ages. He expected her, having said he would be here alone this day while his master visited the widow.

Alaric was mesmerised by her sinuous movement, her small steps gliding along the track towards him. She no longer wore the clothes of a fine lady but dressed more modestly and could even be taken as a woman of the town. She was unlike the young maids he knew, womanly, with flawless olive skin and a sensual mouth, but above all else, she knew how to listen. She stood before him, offering an elegant bow of her head. Jasliena tenderly stroked his cheek with the back of her hand before embracing him. Alaric inhaled her heady, honeyed fragrance of amber and sandalwood, closing his eyes and resting his head gently on her shoulder as he tightened his embrace of this beautiful woman. It was an embrace of death. Alaric did not see and hardly felt, the thin, sharp blade that penetrated between his ribs and into his heart, killing him before his body touched the ground.

Jasliena wiped the misericorde clean using the hem of Alaric's jerkin before secreting it in her cote. She regarded his lifeless body, eyes still wide open in surprise. There was no regret; he was a sweet boy but could not live, as he could identify her and place her here at the scene of the fire.

The snap of a twig close by broke her moment of reflection as she observed the red and gold livery of the royal Men-at-Arms moving towards her. As yet, the thicket of alder and beech shielded her from their view, but the moment she moved, they would see her. Giovanni's stallion and his groom's palfrey stood tied close by, contentedly munching on sparse tufts of grass. She had her escape planned, she always did and that involved her own palfrey, which was tied up further along the lane and now beyond her reach.

The royal guards would find Alaric's body and, by law, had to raise the Hue and Cry. That gave Jasliena just minutes to make her escape and the presence of the guards now forced her to head north away from them. Jasliena van Leuven always sought to control the risks she took, but at this moment, Giovanni's stallion betrayed her.

The bay destrier picked up the scent of blood pooling on the ground beside Alaric's lifeless body and, spooked by the stench of death; he snorted loudly. The sound carried across the stillness of the thicket like a ringing bell. Jasliena was almost upon the animal when its panicked snorting and squeals alerted Nate Brynkhill and his detachment of royal Men-at-Arms. The horse was partly hidden and the guards caught a fleeting sight of Jasliena moving toward it. They were intrigued but not alarmed at what they saw, for there was no reason to suspect the figure ahead of them. A few paces more and they would see the body of Alaric lying in a pool of blood on the ground. Jasliena had just an instant to act. Standing on a log, she ripped the reins from their tether, hoisting herself inelegantly, man-like, into the saddle before kicking her heels into the destrier's flank and riding hard toward the soldiers.

The war horse scattered the royal Men-at-Arms, who jumped to safety to avoid its crushing hooves. Jasliena spurred the mount down the track toward Eyewoodlane, where she would head northwest toward St Michael's village and safety.

Standing in front of the charred bones of Amice de Shethesere's house, a much-relieved Isabella la Rus gulped in lungful's of clean air. A kindly neighbour had brought her a jug of ale with which she rinsed away the foul, acrid taste in her mouth. She looked up, alerted by a flock of pigeons abandoning the safety of the tree-canopy to take to the air as one. A destrier thundered toward the road, its rider cutting a tiny figure against the bulk of the warhorse. It pulled to an abrupt halt no more than ten paces from Isabella, the rider looking left and right as if uncertain where to go.

Despite her recent ordeal, Isabella was momentarily intrigued by this incongruous event: A warhorse and, seemingly, an ill-suited horseman. Her gaze fixed on the rider; it was a woman. In but an instant, Isabella knew who it was. Her long dark hair, braided and coiled, the polished olive hue of her face, the wide mouth and piercing brown eyes, it was the woman Simon Lowys had described: the woman who had him abducted and who was responsible for his hanging.

Isabella's face tensed, her gaze hardened and narrowed as anger coursed through her. That was the moment the rider noticed the lone figure of the King's agent standing beside the burned shell of the house. From where she stood, Isabella could see the woman's eyes widen in surprise and recognition. The two women, Royal Intelligencer and assassin locked their gaze on each other. Jasliena's wide mouth curled into a snarl, and furrows of hate ridged her flawless skin. Her eyes glowed with fury.

Jasliena yanked the reins hard to her left, kicking her heels into the destrier's flanks and charged at the Royal Intelligencer. It was what Isabella had been expecting and her eyes never left the beast's hooves as it came at her. She threw herself to the side to avoid being trampled, rolling to a standing position to face the assassin. Jasliena pulled up and half-turned; her face was no longer smooth and flawless; her jaw was tense, her lips tight, rage etched deep across her visage.

Their eyes locked again, assassin and Intelligencer, each regarding the other and calculating their next move. Where Jasliena van Leuven's face showed anger, the Royal Agent's face was a study of calm and composure. Perhaps a dozen paces separated them; Isabella kept her gaze firmly on the assassin, aware that she had nothing with which she could defend herself.

"You! Stop!" The guttural command came from the serjeant of the guard, Nate Brynkhill, emerging from the woods with his men beside him.

Without warning, Jasliena wheeled the huge bay destrier around, its front legs rearing high, its teeth bared. The assassin, Benuic, pulled her hood over her head and drove the beast into a gallop, heading down Eyewoodlane west toward the ancient Roman town and the hamlet of St Michael's beyond.

A crowd had gathered, fascinated by the commotion. Isabella regarded the faces, wide-eyed with excitement, drawn to watch the flames consume a neighbour's house, gladdened that it had not been theirs. She had come face-to-face with the assassin, the perpetrator of the attack on Her Grace, the Queen, a year before. A thin smile came to her lips, a smile of contentment. She had set out to track down those who had aided the assassin's escape from England, but today, she had looked deep into the eyes of Benuic.

To the west, at that exact moment, no contentment showed on the face of Jasliena van Leuven. She had driven her mount hard through the old Roman ruins and had reached the comparative safety of the house in St Michael's. As she rode, she knew she had miscalculated. She had left a witness alive, one who could identify her, which was a mistake. She pushed that thought from her mind. What was of immediate concern was making good her escape. The King's Men would anticipate that she would seek passage to the continent from a southern port, Harwich, Dover or Rye. So, she would head north to cross the German Sea from Bishop's Lynn or Dunwich. Time was on her side; she would leave the unfinished business behind her and deal with '*le Reynard*' another time.

Ж

Chapter Fifty-seven

The village of Windridge, Hertfordshire, September 1277.

THE OPEN FIELDS AROUND Windridge wore the effects of the long, dry summer as the first hues of autumn crept in. As far as the horizon, little greenery poked now through the shabby sea of brown. The winter-sown barley was recently cut and the stubble stood out like jagged rocks in a sea of dark earth. Even the newly planted winter vegetable crops suffered in the heat.

A little before the bell rang for the sixth hour, Simon Lowys rode his bay palfrey into Windridge. Stopping at the entrance to the village, seeking to hail the blacksmith he had encountered on his previous visit, he reached down for his wineskin, put it to his lips and took a long draught. A youth appeared from the rear of the smithy.

"Can I help thee, Meister?" came his wary greeting.

"I seek the smith I met on my last visit. I am Simon Lowys, Nuncio to Her Grace the Queen."

The youth's expression changed from one of suspicion to wonderment.

"God give you good day, Queen's Man. Master Smith is not here; he was taken into the King's army to fight the Welsh."

"Indeed," replied Simon, in understanding. Many skilled men, smiths, carpenters, wheelwrights, ostlers, grooms and more had received summons for the King's army in their campaign against the rebel Llywelyn ap Gruffyd.

Simon gave the lad a cursory thanks before moving off into the heart of the village. It was many months since he was last here, a time of his life he wished greatly to forget.

Windridge looked much as it did when he first came to investigate the death of the priest. Smoke drifted through thatch from fires that were necessary, even in the warmest of summers. Dogs barked to herald his arrival as he rode his horse slowly along the dry, rutted track that served as the village's main thoroughfare. Simon tapped his heels on the palfrey's belly to move ahead, and she trotted on, passing the Church of St Mary Magdalene and the cottage of the Reeve, Henry de Bray, scattering scratching chickens as he went. He would pay a courtesy visit to the Reeve once his business was complete.

In but a short time, he was through the main part of the village and at its western, poorer end. At the run-down cottage of Bortwyn the Labourer, he pulled up his palfrey, dismounted and tied her to the branches of a straggly hawthorn bush. Simon approached the door and was certain more of the wattle-and-daub filling had fallen from its walls since he was last here.

He rapped loudly on the oak door and Bortwyn's wife, Hild, opened it. Her face turned from rosy pink to ashen as she recognised her visitor.

"My… My husband is at work in the fields," she flustered.

"Tis not Bortwyn I seek, Mistress. May I come inside?"

She made a frightened obeisance and opened the door wider to allow him in. The small, single room was as gloomy as before. As when he had previously been here, the young maid cowered in a corner, intimidated by his presence. If it were possible, she looked even thinner than before with her hollowed-out cheeks and deep, vacant eyes.

Hild offered Simon the stool to sit, but he declined.

"Mistress, I needs must have more words with you about the death of the priest."

Before him, Hild trembled, even though the small chamber was warm.

"My husband has told you all he knows, King's Man."

"Indeed! That is yet to be established," said Simon. "But, Mistress, have you told me all you know."

She could not bring herself to look at him.

"Mistress."

"I have and cannot help you further," she snapped.

"Nay, I think not." He fixed her with his gaze. "You reproached Sire Roger for having words with little Marjorie here. Did you not tell me he called her wicked and sinful."

Hild's head drooped. "Aye, he did."

"I asked before, what had the maid done for Sire Roger to accuse her of wickedness?"

"She did nought. Nought wrong, I tell you. Twas him who was wicked."

"Indeed? And what did the priest do that was wicked, Mistress? What did he do to induce you to have such words."

Hild turned her face away from Simon, tears in her eyes. "I cannot say," she sobbed back.

"Mistress! Look at me."

She turned, tears snaking down her ashen cheeks.

Simon sought to soften his tone. "Mistress, tis said by others hereabouts that Sire Roger favoured young maids and did ungodly things with them." Hild's face stiffened, lips trembling.

"Is that the reason you spoke harsh words with him?"

Hild's face contorted with rage, reaching out to draw her daughter close. "Ungodly! Ungodly! He was no man of God." She pulled Marjorie close to her, the slip of a girl blending into the mother's garments.

"She is but ten summers in age and he violated her. He raped her and blamed her for his wickedness." Her words tumbled out in a mixture of tears and rage.

"Mistress," Simon said softly, "Pray, sit yourself down." He gestured to Hild, who sat on the three-pronged stool, Marjorie on her lap.

"I have made enquiries and your husband, Bortwyn, was born in this village. Is that correct?"

"Aye, he was," came Hild's sobbed reply, suspicious of the direction of the question.

"Has he worked in Windridge all his years?"

"He has, all the years we are married."

"And before that?" Alarm flickered in her eyes.

"He worked as a labourer," she paused, "Save for a time, a year mayhaps, when the old Lord of the Manor took him as a soldier to Wales to fight for the old King."

It was as Simon had thought. "This Lord, he took Bortwyn with him, why so?"

Even in the dim light of the cottage, Simon could see a trembling Hild grasping where this questioning was going.

"Mayhaps, because he was young, big and strong?" she suggested.

"Nay, Mistress, I think not." He took a pace towards her. "I think Bortwyn was taken to Wales with his Lord because of his skill with a bow."

"Nay, tis not so." The tears streamed down her cheeks.

"Mistress, it would be but a simple task for me to find out."

"Bortwyn is a good man."

"Mistress, did Bortwyn know what Sire Roger had done to your daughter?"

Hild's lower lip quivered. "He has always provided for us, even in the hardest of times."

"That was not what I asked. Did Bortwyn know what the priest had done?"

Hild hugged her daughter tight. "I told him." Her words were barely a whisper. "Bortwyn was worried about Marjorie and said he would take her to Sire Roger to see if he could cure her timidness. That was when I told him."

"And when was this?"

"A day before the priest was slain." Hild looked up from her stool, fright showing in her narrowed, red eyes.

"After I told him, he went out. He keeps his bow in a hiding place in the chicken coop. None knew his arrows, for he fletched new ones he used when he went poaching. He did not tell me what he was about, but the next day, when I heard the news that the priest was dead, I knew what Bortwyn had done." Her confession came out in half-sobs, her breath heavy and fractured.

"He will hang, will he not?" she sobbed. "He is a good man; he does not deserve to die." She burst into uncontrollable tears. "'Tis my words that have condemned him," she whimpered.

As he stood before the crying Hild, the King's Man felt a pang of guilt. He had come to Windridge to solve the murder of the priest. Now, having solved it, Simon felt no satisfaction. For a long time, he believed Giovanni di Bologna was the murderer and Hild was correct; her account condemned Bortwyn the Labourer to the gallows, even though, as his wife, she could not give evidence against him at the trial.

Against Hild's wailing tears, Simon Lowys felt deep remorse. Of all people, he knew the fate that awaited Bortwyn at the end of a gallows rope. The circumstances of his death would make pariahs of Hild and their child. With no man to provide for them, they would be forced from their home and the village and few would choose to take a murderer's widow as his wife. She and her daughter would be evicted from their cottage and, come winter, Hild and Marjorie would likely freeze and starve and the fault would be his.

Ж

Chapter Fifty-eight

The Royal Chancery at Westminster, September 1277.

THE DAYS OF SUMMER HAD passed as Michaelmas fast approached, nights becoming noticeably cooler as the sunlight hours shortened. Still suffering nightly torment in his dreams, Simon Lowys had only been back at his lodgings in Tothillstrete for a few days, having recovered in the Abbey Infirmarium. As much as he appreciated the care given to him by the monks and their lay Brothers, it was Mistress Heacham's daily salves of thyme, poppies, belladonna and honey that proved most effective in healing his scarred neck.

Before he returned to his role as Nuncio and Man-of-Law, he made the journey back to Windridge to fulfil the task given to him in the spring. Lying in his cot recuperating had given him plenty of time to reflect on the slaying of Sire Roger and who was responsible.

Early that morn, a rooster crowed far in the distance, heralding the dawn as young Robert de Berdesfold had again come to his lodgings with an instruction to attend on John of Berwick.

As he had done many times before, Simon Lowys navigated his way through the labyrinth of corridors to arrive at the chamber where John of Berwick worked, perhaps appreciating the heady

295

scent of wax and lavender far more than he might have done some months before.

The small, horn-covered windows were open to allow the river breeze into the room. Simon gave a low rap at the open door and the Royal Intelligencer, John of Berwick, bade him entry without looking up from his desk. To one side sat his scrivener, Raynold Dodderell, head down and busy crafting a new document on his writing slope, his quill moving sleekly over the parchment, only stopping occasionally to wipe the tip and dip it into the inkhorn.

Simon Lowys stood before the King's Senior Intelligencer, his scrip over one shoulder and holding a rolled-up parchment in one hand. Berwick finished reading the document in front of him and pushed it to one side of his desk before looking up. An expression almost of sympathy came across his face.

He gestured towards Simon's face. " Ahh, Master Lowys. I must say that you look so much better than when I last saw you. How fares your neck; you have recovered, I trust?"

Involuntarily, Simon reached a hand up to the thin cloth he always now wrapped around his neck to hide the red, ugly wheal left by the hanging.

"It has healed well, My Lord." In truth, it hadn't and still gave him pain, but Berwick, never one for small talk, didn't wish to know that.

"Good, good." It was the nearest to solace Simon would get from the man.

Berwick's lips pursed as if he tasted a bitter brew. "You found the maid for Her Grace. I had meant to thank you for that."

"Aye, my Lord. Though it was not I who located her, but Mistress la Rus and Mistress Parys, who also found the stolen children. In truth, the Lady Jeanne's high-born status was not known to her abductors, for they took her in error. So, once they knew of this, they did set her free and she found her way to a church and the priest there made contact with the Abbey. I suspect that it was I who alerted di Bologna to their error when I visited the Legate. Tis all written up here."

He held out a parchment and Berwick took it from him, placing it in front of him before unfurling and laying it flat.

"I know much of what occurred from others, you understand, but I wished for your view, Master Lowys," Berwick said. He quickly scanned the parchment, head moving, reminding Simon of a bird of prey pecking at its food.

John of Berwick lifted his gaze and fixed the royal nuncio with a cold stare. "So, you set off to find a lost maid and discover child abduction is widespread in the town."

"Not just in St Albans, my Lord; it extended to London, Oxford and perhaps beyond. And the man behind it was the Legate's man, Giovanni di Bologna".

"You have scant reason to like the Italian," suggested Berwick.

"Aye. As I think on what happened, I see that it was di Bologna who plotted my death, though I truly know not why."

"You got too close to his abductions and he feared you knew more than you did. But we have moved to shut down his business of abducting children and transporting them to Flanders and beyond." Berwick cleared his throat. "However, I can assure you that he is dead."

"I did hear that he no longer lived," said Simon, "but none could tell me the circumstances of his death. Did he die by your hand, My Lord?"

Berwick bristled.

"Nay, Master Lowys, he did not," Berwick said emphatically. "Twas '*le Reynard*', who told me that di Bologna died in a tragic fire in a house beyond the Abbey town. I have all the details here." He picked up another parchment but didn't offer it to Simon.

"We do not have the satisfaction of di Bologna standing before a King's Justice in Eyre, but that was always an unlikely outcome."

Simon had always known that, but somehow, the death of di Bologna by accident left him with an empty feeling.

"My Lord," Simon enquired. "What of the Papal Legate, Bernardo Ravennate?"

Berwick's beady eyes narrowed. "What of him?"

"Giovanni di Bologna was the henchman to Ravennate. It is inconceivable that the Legate was not privy to such an operation, if not the man behind it all."

Berwick pursed his lips again. "His Eminence has denied any knowledge of this sordid affair. He says his man, di Bologna, did all without him knowing aught about it."

"Nay! That cannot be, My Lord." A dumbfounded Simon couldn't understand how the Legate could be allowed to get away with his part in the child abduction and murder.

"But he must have known what was happening. He and di Bologna were very close."

"Master Lowys, you are a Man-of-Law. What jurisdiction do the King's Courts have over an emissary from the Pope?"

Simon knew Berwick was correct, of course. Such a man was not accountable to English Law. Even if there were evidence against him, he would not be tried, even in an English Ecclesiastical Court. Bernardo Ravennate was a Papal Legate, the personal representative of the Pope and held a rank greater than Cardinal. He was accountable only to the Holy Father and God himself.

"So, Ravennate will go free and unpunished," suggested Simon.

Berwick shook his head. "Nay! You are aware that the Pope is dead?"

"Aye," replied Simon, "I was told Pope John died but days after the Feast of the Ascension, this May past."

"Ravennate has already left England for Viterbo," announced Berwick. "As a Papal Legate, he has the right to be part of the Holy Conclave. We have done all we can to inform the Papal Magistratus of his crimes and it will be for them to decide. But, Ravennate can never escape the Final Judgement and his clerical status will not stop him from burning in the fires of Hell."

Simon thought that was the most eloquent he had ever heard John of Berwick.

And then, in an instant, Berwick became business-like once more.

"And the business of the priest at Windridge? Twas, you recall, the reason you were going north in the first place."

"Aye, My Lord." Simon ran his tongue over his lips, thinking, seeking to craft his words. "I have visited Windridge, twice and spoken with many of its villagers, including the Reeve. Few had good words for the priest, for he alienated many in the community."

"How so?" Berwick peered hard at Lowys.

"When I went north, you charged me with investigating two matters, the maid's disappearance and the slaying of the priest. But, as events turned out, both were linked."

"Linked, you say?"

"Aye! Sire Roger, the priest, knew di Bologna and had been seen together by villagers more than once. And, the priest was known among the women-folk of Windridge to….umm," Simon tightened his lips, seeking the right phrase.

"Known to…?" Berwick's penetrating stare fixed on him.

"Known to…. break his holy vows by molesting young maids."

"God's blood!" John of Berwick's mouth hung loose, his eyebrows raised. "So, many in the village would wish him dead?"

"Probably every wife with a child, but not so the men, for surely the womenfolk did not tell."

"Aye, or the priest would have been dead long since," Berwick agreed.

"And we can rule out the women of Windridge, for the priest was slain with a longbow and no woman could ever draw such a weight."

"Hmmm! So, you are no further in discovering the killer?" Berwick sounded annoyed.

"Nay, My Lord. I know the identity of the man who slew Sire Roger." Simon's face tensed; his lips dry. "The evidence places Giovanni di Bologna in the village meeting the priest."

"di Bologna? Do you have proof?"

"I do not have a confession. Nor will anything come out in legal proceedings."

John of Berwick held up a hand, his bony fingers resembling the talons of a bird of prey.

"If you have no confession, then how can you be so sure di Bologna slew the priest."

"Not proof, but compelling evidence from villagers connecting the priest to di Bologna- one who abused maids - and the other who abducted them."

John of Berwick gave a harumph of dissatisfaction, the flesh around his mouth contorting as he thought this through.

"Then we shall agree that the rogue, di Bologna, slew the priest for his involvement in the taking of the young maids."

"Aye My Lord." Inwardly, Simon was pleased that he hadn't actually had to lie to John of Berwick. The evidence could suggest that it was Giovanni di Bologna. The Italian was a skilled hunter with a bow and may have been the man the cunning woman saw at the priest's house. Standing before a sobbing Hild in that gloomy room in the pitiful labourer's cottage in Windridge, he had decided to allow a murderer to go free. He had not done it for Bortwyn the Labourer but for the future of his wife and child. Still, it was a decision that sat heavily on his heart.

"Now, Master Lowys," Berwick fixed him intently. "As you are truly recovered, your services are needed in Paris."

Ж

Chapter Fifty-nine

The Royal Chancery, Westminster September 1277.

PARIS?" SURPRISE REGISTERED on Simon's face.
"The Palais des Rois, the court of Philippe of France, your skills as a Man-of-Law will be required."
Simon's head tilted quizzically. It was not unusual for him to be dispatched abroad and he had a courtier's fluency in French. Still, he had not expected to be sent overseas so soon after his recovery. In truth, he had hoped to find Isabella. He had not seen her since the morning of his hanging. She had not visited in the months of his recovery, which pained him. His hand went to his neck, touching the Paternoster beads he wore, which Isabella had given him in Mistress Heacham's garden months before. He recalled their parting in Mistress Heacham's garden the day following the thunderstorm, the tenderness she had shown him as she placed her hand on his arm, looked up at his face and the thrill that coursed through his body. Now, John of Berwick was sending him to Paris; for how long, he did not know. He would be further away from Isabella in both time and distance.

"We have a delegation attending the court of King Philippe at the Palais des Rois," Berwick continued, though Simon's thoughts were far away. "Are you familiar with Milon de Bazoches, the Bishop of Soissons?"

Simon shook his head.

"de Bazoches' sympathies lie with His Grace, King Edward and one among our delegation, the Lady Clemence d'Lisle, is to receive certain documents from de Bazoches. I need not impress upon you that we do not wish these parchments to fall into the hands of King Philippe's people."

"I understand, My Lord. But what is my role?"

"You are to authenticate these documents when the Lady Clemence receives them and be seen to bring these dispatches back here to the Chancery." Berwick passed three rolled documents to Simon.

Berwick's face broke into a thin-lipped smile and he gave a mild chuckle. "You will travel as an Epicière, not from London, for the French merchants would know their counterparts. No, you will pose as a trader from Norwich, visiting shrines on pilgrimage, though one prepared to trade if the opportunity arises. You will have a pack-pony loaded with pepper, mace, cinnamon and even some sugar."

"My Lord? I do not understand."

"Come now, Master Lowys; despite your guise, King Philippe's Intelligencers will know full well who you work for. Tis surtees that you or your baggage will be searched, with or without your knowledge ….."

"….and they will find and copy these dispatches," Simon held up the rolled parchments Berwick had given him.

"Aye. And the Lady Clemence will bring the true documents to me."

"I understand, my Lord." Simon appreciated the danger to himself from Berwick's plan. *King Philippe's Intelligencers may view him as a spy. I will be lucky to see England again,* he thought to himself.

"Oh yes and you will take de Berdesfold with you as your manservant."

That remark did not prompt the disdain it once had, for Simon was growing fond of the lad and his ways.

"Dodderell!" Berwick's reedy tone broke Simon's thoughts. At Berwick's command, his senior clerk rose and passed a collection of small, unrolled parchments to Simon Lowys.

"Your writ to obtain horses en route, here in England, Ponthieu and from our people in the French capital." Raymond Dodderell's clipped and shrill voice seemed well-suited to his small, bony frame.

"A writ to secure food and supplies. A letter of introduction for the Abbots of the houses where you will stay. Another with your bona fide as a Serjeant-at-Law to her Grace the Queen and....." Dodderel paused, rummaged in a drawer and brought up a large leather purse. "And coin for the journey, five pounds in silver pennies, should you need it."

Simon held out his hand to accept the heavy leather purse.

"I fully expect to receive most of that coin back upon the successful conclusion of your business," interjected John of Berwick.

Simon gave a knowing smile and accepted the purse and the parchments, placing them in his scrip.

"The English delegation is at the Abbaye de Maubuisson, on the Roman highway, from Rouen toward the capital."

"Master Lowys," Raymond Dodderell spoke. "On the morrow, at cock-crow, your escort will be ready when you present yourself here. You will have three Men-at-Arms to provide close protection, there and back."

"Thank you, Master Dodderell," replied Simon. He knew the road to the abbey and throwing his scrip onto his shoulder, he made to leave. Berwick's head was already buried in a new parchment, his thoughts elsewhere.

"God give you good speed, Master Lowys," said Berwick without looking up. Simon smiled, knowing that despite the crusty exterior, the words of King's Intelligencer were said with genuine warmth.

304

Ж

____

Chapter Sixty

Abbaye de Maubuisson, northwest of Paris, September 1277.

FOLLOWING THE KING'S HIGHWAY south to the coast should have taken Simon Lowy's party less than two days, but the dryness of the summer left the track rutted and dangerous, and they could not push their mounts as fast as he had hoped. So it was that he arrived at Folkstone at mid-morn on the third day. Fortunately, the crossing of the Narrow Sea was calm and uneventful. They landed at Montreuil in Ponthieu a day later. Montreuil had several advantages, being a personal possession of Queen Eleanor and lying on the Roman road south to King Philippe's capital.

The journey to Paris consumed the better part of four days, with stops mainly at roadside inns and a single night at the Abbaye Saint-Germer-de-Fly, east of Rouen. Along the way, Simon discovered he had developed a greater patience for de Berdesfold's incessant inquiries and chatter.

It was the day before Michaelmas, the Feast of St Simon and St Jude, when they finally arrived, dusty and weary, at the gates to Abbaye de Maubuisson, the Cistercian house founded decades before by King Philippe's grandmother, Blanche. The Abbey was situated on the Oise, a tributary of the Seine, joining it before the mighty river bent westwards towards the high ground of the Vexin. It lay a day's ride northwest of the Île de la Cité, away from the odours and disease of Paris.

Around its centre were buildings housing Cistercian nuns. No men were allowed inside, bar their priest. Simon and his party would stay within the complex in a guesthouse close to the south wall. The autumn sun caught on the honeyed stone, giving it the appearance of centuries even though it was not years old. The guesthouse was like many manor houses he had visited in England, built for comfort rather than defence. A wide channel surrounded it on three sides, fed by a fast-flowing stream, a barrier between the nuns and the secular world of the guesthouse. Unusually for a convent, guards patrolled the gate area, which led to an inner courtyard. They were no youngsters, all having the appearance of seasoned campaigners. One scanned Simon's letter of introduction. He was unlikely to be lettered and would view the seal for authenticity.

The abbey was a place of calmness and serenity and belied its name, which came from '*Maudit buisson*', 'the cursed bush' because the area had once been the preserve of wolf's heads and robbers.

A two-horse litter, adorned in bright colours, stood outside the entrance to the guesthouse, attended by three young grooms. Simon, de Berdesfold and his three Men-at-Arms dismounted. Before they departed Westminster, Simon was pleased to see Nate Brynkill placed in charge of the detachment, the veteran sergeant he had first met while en route to Outremer seven years before. Gone were the bright red and gold royal liveries of three lions' passant guardant. The Men-at-Arms appeared a motley crew, with mismatched, worn jerkins and hose, suggestive of a less-than-prosperous merchant who could not afford the very best protection.

As they dismounted, young boys stepped forward to take the reins and another offered them a skin of wine, from which all drank copiously to quench their thirst. Simon instructed the boys to leave the horse containing the spices, for he would unpack it himself later.

A kitchen block connected by a tiled covered way to a central hall lay on the far side of the courtyard. On its eastern corner lay a large stone-built chapel, accessed from inside the nun's *dortoir.*

A tall, well-dressed man of middle years approached.

"You hail from England?"

"Aye," came the reply, " I am Simon of Norwich, an Epicière on pilgrimage."

"Hale to thee, Master Simon, tis good to have another Englishman here. Too many damn Frenchmen, if you ask me. I am Nicholas de Malham, Steward of the Household of the pilgrim, the Lady Clemence d'Lisle. I bid you welcome." He made a low, respectful bow.

He spoke courtly French with a slight accent of someone who hailed from the north of England.

"Is she here, the Lady," inquired Simon, but before he could get a response, a lay brother appeared and showed the newcomers to their modest dormitory, informing them that there would be ale available in the Hall beside the guesthouse.

Stepping through a heavy oak doorway, they entered a well-appointed antechamber. Fresh rushes, sprinkled with herbs, crunched beneath their feet. Polished wooden crucks complemented the bright, white limewash on the walls, gleaming in the sunshine that streamed through the windows' glass panes, another sign that this was a wealthy house. Tiny dust particles danced in the beams, catching the eye. The room smelled pleasantly of wax and crushed lavender. The nuns of Maubuisson clearly cared about how visitors perceived their abbey.

The refreshments were a welcome relief after the dust of the journey. De Malham joined Simon, making small talk and enquiring about his plans.

"I seek to visit some of the Holy Shrines of France," said Simon. At Westminster, it was decided that a pilgrimage would provide a compelling cover story. The *'Via Turonensis,' south to*

Angouleme, was the main pilgrim route south from northern France and the Low Countries.

"The Lady Clemence also makes a pilgrimage toward the shrine of St Basil in Bruges. Mayhaps you and your group should join with us, for there is safety in numbers."

De Malham does not know who I am or my purpose here, thought Simon, wondering how and when he would meet with the Lady Clemence. He thought perhaps he should ask de Malham again but did not wish to appear too keen.

"Indeed, that would be most accommodating, tis a long time since I was in Bruges,"

"Are you trading in spices as you travel," inquired the Steward, his eyes narrowing with interest.

"Aye," responded Simon, keeping up the pretence. "I have loaded some choice ones onto my pack horse with a view to bartering should my coin not be accepted."

"Do you say! And what have you brought with you?" The Steward took a step closer, his voice tinged with excitement.

"Mace, cinnamon, pepper and some sugar."

"You have sugar?" De Malham's eyes widened further, his gaze fixed on Simon. "I have heard of sugar but have never seen any. Is it true it is as sweet as honey? Can you show me? Mayhaps I could purchase some for the Lady Clemence." He reached for his pouch, the clink of coins sounding within.

"My pack pony is at the stables; come now and I can show you."

With a sense of ease, the two men slipped from the Great Hall, their footsteps echoing on the almost-empty cobbled courtyard as they made for the stable block. Simon's pack pony, its coat covered in sweat, munched contentedly on a bag of oats, the leather scrips still securely tied to its saddle.

Simon patted the horse's flank and the scrips seemed to rustle with promise. His hands moved with practised ease to untie the scrips. De Malham stood watchfully beside him before moving in close.

"Master Lowys," he whispered, his voice barely audible over the pony's contented crunching. "Be aware, we have an audience. Our every word could be overheard."

Simon's hands faltered, surprise flickering across his face. "I thought you unaware of my true identity," he murmured, matching de Malham's hushed tones.

"I, too, have my orders," came the cryptic response.

"And the Lady Clemence?" enquired Simon.

"She is in counsel with the Bishop. She will join us at table before Vespers."

With a flourish, Simon drew a darkish-brown lump, roughly the size of a man's hand, from the leather depths of the saddle scrip. "A marvel, Master Simon!" de Malham's voice boomed out, starkly contrasting their furtive whispers, performing for unseen eyes. "The Lady Clemence would dearly prize such a treasure. What is your asking price?"

Their faux conversation continued as they admired the sugar block, before turning back towards the guesthouse, their steps measured and unhurried. Inside the hall, men gathered around a new arrival. De Malham leaned into Simon and whispered, "That is Milon de Bazoches, the Bishop of Soissons, said to be the holiest man in France."

Simon regarded the clergyman, a willowy individual of about his own age. His thin, tight features gave him the appearance of a magpie, his monk's habit worn and aged.

"They do say he wears a shirt woven of goat hair next to his skin and scourges his flesh nightly with a flail." Simon's gaze drifted back to the bishop, who looked the picture of robust health for a man so mortifying his flesh.

There were more people now, the chamber full of the hum of conversation, a tapestry of Burgundian, French, Brabant and Fleming. Pilgrims, clergy, merchants and soldiers moved in small clusters, their faces aglow in the candlelight. How many among them, Simon wondered, were Intelligencers playing a double game like him, their true loyalties hidden behind masks of piety?

A lone bell tolled, summoning guests and pilgrims to the final meal of the day. With its imposing elm doors, the refectory lay across the courtyard, hard beside the Great Hall. As Simon entered, Nicholas de Malham fell into step beside him.

"Do you see there," he said, pointing to a slightly built woman, her back to him, in conversation with a small ferret-like clergyman. "That is the Lady Clemence d'Lisle and the snake she is talking to is Abbot Languet de Gergy, who is for King Philippe, what my Lord of Berwick is to His Grace, King Edward.

"Then why is the lady conversing with him?" whispered Simon.

De Malham chuckled, "Because she has no choice. De Gergy is suspicious of everyone; he wonders why she is here at this time. He believes all women are the daughters of Eve, tainted sinners. Likeways, at some point, he will interrogate you, as you are new here. He will be affable and polite but beware de Gergy; he may wear the robes of a monk, but he is a creature of Satan."

The woman had broken off her conversation and glided across the room toward de Malham She wore a fashionable, white-laced gorget headdress and a deep green gown, a colour Simon had seen many Ladies wearing at the English Royal Court. Nicholas de Malham made his obeisance as Simon stood, perplexed, mouth agape.

"My Lady," said de Malham, "this is an English Master Epicière, Simon of Norwich. Master Simon, this is the Lady Clemence d'Lisle."

Simon gazed at the small pale face standing just a few feet away. Deep, penetrating blue eyes looked back at him; a lock of soft red hair had escaped from under her headdress to lie across a perfect cheek.

Her eyes twinkled as she inclined her head, smiling demurely.

"God give you good day, Simon of Norwich," said Isabella la Rus.

Isabella la Rus, Simon Lowys, Matilda Heacham and Alia Parys will return in the third volume of the St Albans Medieval Mysteries, 'The Cursed Coins.'

Preview: The Cursed Coins.

A St Albans Medieval Mystery, Book 3

Prologue: Eywood St Albans December 1276

GOD HAD THROWN A white blanket across the Ver Valley this December morning. It wasn't the hardest of frosts, just enough to make the glistening crust of the soil hard and crunchy underfoot for the lone man shuffling along the furrows close to Eywood. His bent form silhouetted in the early morning's blue stillness; his faded cote wrapped tightly about his body; the coif pulled tight down around his ears. As he exhaled, his breath made a light, bright mist in front of him. Age made walking difficult these days, not that he knew how old he was. He recalled his father telling him of the death of old King John, which had been many years before. He paused, straightened and twisted to ease his aching back. Leaning hard on his wood fork, which served as his walking stick this morning, he moved off again.

Alongside him, his faithful hound, Tymon, sniffed and pawed the solid earth, picking up scents of the night creatures that had passed this way. The old man's few strips lay just below Eywood, where the River Ver snaked its path south towards the old Roman road and the vill of Park. They lay in a rectangle, bordered on one side by the dense beech wood and a jealously guarded pasture where the abbey grazed their sheep. These strips were Abbot Roger de Norton's demesne, but only the poorest of villeins farmed here. Every year, the bare rectangle of land attracted the cold autumn air, frequently causing a mist to hang eerily above the ground. In winter, the frost lingered, making the soil difficult to work. Today was one such day.

Nonetheless, Hamo atte Gate left his tiny cottage early to pick what remained of his turnips before the worst of the winter frosts penetrated the crop. For as long as he had farmed here, he had lifted his turnips after the first frost, believing it made them taste that much sweeter. The low winter sun cast little warmth at this early hour after Terce. Hamo squinted, gazing across to the Abbey pasture and the sheep huddled together against the chill of the morning.

He stopped; a gust of chill breeze whipped across the valley and brought thoughts of his wife, Maud, taken by the bloody flux twenty summers past. "Wrap your bones against the Devil's wind," she had always told him. His gaze fell on the treeline at the far side of the valley, towards the small vill of Park, where Maud and her family had lived before their betrothal. Fond memories swept across him, bringing a thin smile to his lips as he remembered a better time, long ago. He nuzzled Tymon's head, the loyal hound twisting to lick the back of his hand.

Hamo was alone with his thoughts as he picked his way carefully across the barren, icy ridges and furrows, using his pitchfork for balance. His rough wooden clogs made little impression on the frozen earth beneath his feet. Ahead, on his weed-free strips, the bright green leafy tops of his turnips sparkled in the morning frost. Hamo was always diligent in his weeding, even if those villeins whose strips bordered his were not.

His turnip crop was not bountiful, but it would store well over the winter months and make an acceptable pottage that would stave off hunger until the spring.

The pitchfork, its handle smooth from years of Hamo's grip, felt like an extension of his own arm. He'd crafted it long ago from a gnarled oak branch, shaping it with care to perfectly suit his needs. It supported his weight as he carefully picked his way through his strips, the frozen dew, glistened on the green tops of his turnips.

With a practised eye, Hamo surveyed his crop. His calloused hand brushed over the leaves, feeling their damp coolness. Satisfied, he swung the wicker basket off his back and set it in the furrow beside him. Then, with a grunt of familiar effort, he plunged the pitchfork into the earth.

The tines bit deep into the soil with a satisfying crunch. Hamo could feel the root's resistance as if it clung to the warm earth with a will of its own. He heaved, his back and arms straining against the weight. Slowly, the turnip began to yield, the soil crumbling as it was dragged into the morning light.

He lifted the turnip free with a heave, its white bulb glistening with earthy moisture and placed it gently in his basket, anticipating the hearty stew it would make. As he worked, a rustling in the next row caught his attention. Tymon, his faithful old hound, was scratching furiously at the icy soil. Hamo could see the dog's nose twitching; his ears perked up in excitement.

"Tymon," Hamo called out. Tymon looked up, his tail wagging furiously. The thumb-sized mark on the top of his head stood out in the cold air. The King's mark, his father had called it, was found only on special hounds and Tymon was one. Hamo thought the hound was fascinated with this patch of ground, likely the scent of a fox. He continued to methodically lift his crop, occasionally stretching out to ease the ache of his old bones.

Halfway through lifting the white-fleshed bulbs, Hamo sat down on the furrow to refresh himself with a swig of ale from a clay jug. Despite the pain of age that came with such work, he was pleased with what he had achieved. At first, he hadn't noticed what Tymon had uncovered, but as he surveyed the upturned earth, something glinted in the thin morning sun. Hamo's eyes widened as his heart quickened, with the realisation that it was a coin.

His first instinct was to look over each shoulder, to check he was alone. Why did I do that, he thought? He knew that, given the hour and the weather, it was unlikely anyone else would be abroad.

Hamo slowly reached for the shining metal. He snatched it, drawing his hand close to his chest. A clod of earth covered its lower half and he felt the coldness of the soil through his rough wool mitt. He stared at his hand and scratched the caked earth feverishly. As it fell away, his breath shortened, his throat went dry and his mouth opened and closed in surprise. It was as wide as his thumb and shone brightly. He had never seen anything more than a silver penny in all his years, but he was sure now that he was looking at a gold coin.

Tymon's attention had moved on, spying a coney and chasing after it. Once more, Hamo atte the Gate made furtive glances over his shoulders to confirm he was alone. A gold coin, and it was his; he had found it on his strips. He stood up, beaming. His foot pushed lazily at the upturned, frozen soil where the coin had lain and he exposed a scar of red. He bent down, ignoring the ache in the small of his back and prodded at the cold earth. The red scar fell away, clinging to a lump of the icy soil, revealing itself as the neck of a clay pot. He scrabbled with his near-numb fingers, working feverishly to expose its contents.

"By the Blessed Virgin." Hamo, breathed, his voice barely audible. His mouth hung open, his eyes wide with a wonder that bordered on disbelief. He could not take his gaze from the red shards of broken pot and gleaming gold coins strewn amongst his unpicked turnips, each glint promising a future he'd never imagined.

Historical Note

The Guilt of the Penitent is a work of fiction. The main characters, Isabella la Rus, Simon Lowys and John of Berwick, are real people, with the latter two employed by the Queen of England, Eleanor of Castile, in her Royal Household. The storyline of the novel is fiction.

One of the significant issues facing the world today is human trafficking. While the illicit trade in children during the medieval period has a paucity of documentation, a thirteenth-century chronicler named Henry of Livonia does refer to northern European trafficking networks around the Baltic. Starting in the early thirteenth century, Italian merchants established a lucrative trade route supplying the Eastern Mediterranean with slaves from the Caucasus region of the Black Sea and Eurasian steppes via the Bosporus. Although the medieval church prohibited the enslavement of Christians, it turned a blind eye to Christian slavers trading with the Muslim world. What little documentation survives shows that abducted children commanded a high price. Although laws were in place to ban the trading of fellow Christians, there was little that authorities could do to stop such commerce, even if they had wanted to prevent it. The abducted children of the medieval age left no documentary trail for historians to follow. Their lives were stolen from them, making them shadows of history.

Michael Long
Apsley, Hertfordshire

October 2024